THE KING IN YELLOW
and Other Horror Stories

ROBERT W. CHAMBERS

Selected, with an Introduction, by
E. F. Bleiler

DOVER PUBLICATIONS, INC.
Mineola, New York

Copyright

Bibliographical Note

The King in Yellow and Other Horror Stories is a selection of the supernatural fiction of Robert W. Chambers, first published by Dover Publications, Inc. in 1970, and republished in 2004. The stories were selected by Everett F. Bleiler, who also wrote the Introduction especially for the Dover edition. The specific source of the text of each story in this collection is as follows:

"The Yellow Sign," "The Repairer of Reputations," "In the Court of the Dragon," "The Mask," "The Demoiselle d'Ys," and the poem entitled "Cassilda's Song" are reprinted from *The King in Yellow,* as first published by F. Tennyson Neely, New York, in 1895.

"The Maker of Moons" and "A Pleasant Evening" are reprinted from *The Maker of Moons,* as first published by G. P. Putnam's Sons, New York, in 1896.

"The Messenger," "The Key to Grief," and the untitled verse beginning "Little gray messenger . . ." are reprinted from *The Mystery of Choice,* as first published by D. Appleton & Company, New York, in 1897.

"The Harbor-Master," "In Quest of the Dingue," "Is the Ux Extinct?" and the untitled verse beginning "Where the slanting forest eaves . . ." are reprinted from *In Search of the Unknown,* as originally published by Harper and Brothers Publishers, New York, in 1904.

Library of Congress Cataloging-in-Publication Data

Chambers, Robert W. (Robert William), 1865-1933.
   The king in yellow and other horror stories / Robert W. Chambers ; selected, with an introduction by E.F. Bleiler.
      p. cm.
   Contents: The yellow sign — The repairer of reputations — The Demoiselle d'Ys — The mask — In the Court of the Dragon — The maker of moons — A pleasant evening — The messenger — The key to grief — The harbor-master — In quest of the dingue — Is the ux extinct?
   ISBN 0-486-43750-7 (pbk.)
      1. Horror tales, American. I. Bleiler, Everett Franklin. II. Title.

PS1282.B55 2004
813'.52—dc22

2004047827

Manufactured in the United States of America
Dover Publications, Inc., 31 East 2nd Street, Mineola, N.Y. 11501

Contents

Introduction to the Dover Edition

DURING the last decade or so of the nineteenth century, some forgotten impulse drove several unexpected persons into brief association with supernatural fiction. The architect Ralph Adams Cram wrote a collection of ghost stories entitled *Black Spirits and White* (1895). The historical novelist F. Marion Crawford wrote *The Upper Berth* (1894). The social worker Charlotte Perkins Gilman mixed psychology and supernatural adumbrations in *The Yellow Wallpaper* (1899). Two authors of somewhat saccharine children's books, Mrs. Nesbit and Mrs. Molesworth, wrote respectively *Grim Tales* (1893) and *Uncanny Tales* (1896). And Robert William Chambers—"the shopgirl Sheherezade," "the barker of the New York society side show"— wrote *The King in Yellow* (1895), one of the most important books in the literature of supernatural horror.

The King in Yellow is a major work in supernatural fiction by anyone's standard. But its authorship is a puzzlement, for it is very different from everything else that its author wrote. It is the one jarring note in an otherwise consistent life and writing personality.

One of the most popular novelists of the early twentieth century, Robert W. Chambers (1865–1933) had originally hoped to become an artist. He was one of the first students at the New York Art Students League, where Charles Dana Gibson was his fellow student and close friend. Chambers then went to Paris to study art at the École des Beaux Arts and the Académie Julien. On his return to New York, according to literary folklore, he and Gibson went together to the offices of *Life* and submitted cartoons. Chambers's was accepted, while Gibson's was rejected. Perhaps this anecdote is not true, but in any case Chambers's illustrations were published before Gibson's.

Just why Chambers decided to abandon art, or what steps led him into writing are not known, beyond the bare statement by one of his friends that storytelling came easy to him. He discovered to his surprise that if he wrote down his impressions of life in student Paris, they could be sold. In this vague way began one of the financially most successful literary careers of the day.

Chambers wrote steadily for some forty years, during which time he wrote more than seventy novels, much verse, many short stories, articles, and two stage and opera books which were performed. It is impossible to give precise figures on his output, since he often reworked material and resold it; in any case no one has cared enough about his work to trace it all. After an early period of experimentation he seems to have followed literary market trends carefully, and showed himself very sensitive in determining what his readers wanted. While his novels never reachĕd official best-seller status (100,000 or more), they always sold well, in many instances, too, with magazine publication.

Chambers's fiction can be classified fairly easily. Many of his novels were historical. There was a series about the American Revolution, of which the best-remembered book is *Cardigan*. Four novels centered in the Franco-Prussian War, the best-known being *The Red Republic*. Others took place in the American Civil War. Perhaps most popular, however, were his society novels, which in a certain way were problem novels. Aimed at the shopgirl market and deliberately written on a trivial level, they were framed around such questions as social mésalliances, marriage and divorce, hereditary alcoholism in the upper crust, the morality of posing "in the altogether" for artists, and similar topics in the pre-Titanic social world of New York. These include *The Fighting Chance*, *The Danger Mark*, *The Younger Set*, and *The Firing Line*. He also touched briefly, with less financial success, the modern pastorale, the detective story, and other forms.

In addition to filling pages of magazines that might otherwise have been filled with even worse fiction, and occupying the reading time of several million Americans, Chambers influenced American cultural history in several small ways. He was one of the earliest exponents of the nature mysticism of the Northern Forest, a theme that was later worked out with more thoroughness in the popular work of Gene Stratton Porter. He also assisted in the creation of the Gibson Girl, or as she was then sometimes called, the Chambers Girl. Just as Gibson created her visually, Chambers provided her with a verbal individuality.

Today almost all Chambers's work is forgotten. It is doubtful if his novels are even read for period nostalgia. Indeed, their fate has taken a paradoxical turn. They were once so common and in so little demand that used-book stores discarded them or consigned them to the ten-cent bin. As a result they are now sometimes more difficult to find than many books that were once scarcer.

This rejection of Chambers is as it should be, for he wrote very consciously for his present, and wrote to the level where he could make the most money. He had no illusions about the quality or permanency of his writing, and candidly admitted that he was more interested in collecting antique furniture and restoring his ancestral home in the Appalachians than in literary reputation. His novels are bad from the point of view of craftsmanship: the American historical novels read like parodies of Stanley Weyman, the French novels are hysterical, and the society novels are simply incredible. In a certain sense, too, most of his work is immoral in implanting or reinforcing vulgar attitudes. A contemporary attack on the grounds of immorality was made by John Curtis Underwood: "The prince of wholesale and cheap illusion . . . the highest current prices for literary lies and extravagant frivolity based on false social distinctions . . . he reminds us irresistibly of Kipling's Tomlinson, for whose soul after death not even Satan himself could find room or use."

Yet if all this verbiage is washed away, all six or seven million words of it, something of Robert W. Chambers remains that is still worthwhile. This is *The King in Yellow* and certain other early pieces that he wrote before commercialization set in. Perhaps he still had a youthful exuberance that was later overwhelmed by cynicism. Perhaps there was a thoughtfulness that was later brushed aside by the need for improvisation. Perhaps there was a feeling of work-conscience, a desire to produce the best, that somehow vanished later. Or, perhaps, there may have been outside assistance.

II

The King in Yellow appeared in 1895 as a rather attractive little book bound in light green cloth, with a salamander (or butterfly) printed on its cover. It was a member of Neely's Prismatic Library, a series of popular novels and short story collections, mostly by unknowns. In addition to several Parisian sketches, reprinted from an earlier publication, it contained five stories which have been included in this collection: "The Yellow Sign," "The Repairer of Reputations," "The Mask," "The Court of the Dragon," and "The Demoiselle d'Ys."

Ambrose Bierce stands behind much of this book, with his "Inhabitant of Carcosa" furnishing a mythology within which Chambers worked. But there are also obvious differences between Bierce's work and Chambers's. The stories of *The King in Yellow* lack Bierce's tortuous craftsmanship and narrative complexity; they are more conventional in pattern. They have recognizable heroes and heroines, and what happens has a beginning, a middle, and an end. Gone, too, is Bierce's icy, macabre irony. Instead there are undercurrents of direct terror and (probably in compensation) oversweetness.

Chambers also wrote from an aesthetic of the supernatural that was quite different from Bierce's. For Bierce the supernatural had meaning of a sort, not in the literal terms of his stories, but in their psychological equivalents. The ideas within his stories were for him ideas of power that had motivated or wrecked much of his life. For Chambers, on the other hand, there is no evidence that the horrors he wrote about were personal in any profound way. With Bierce there is usually a question of psychological interpretation: how much of what is happening is taking place in the darknesses of the psyche and how much is objective? Or, is there anything really objective? For Chambers the imprecision is metaphysical rather than psychological, a matter of evil rather than of evil men. There are suggestions of other worlds of experience where there may really be a King in Yellow, where the Yellow Sign may exist. Like *The Mysterious Card* by Cleveland Moffett, *The King in Yellow* sets up a deliberate barrier to comprehension and solution.

The stories in this book have been very important in the developmental history of American fantastic literature. All the major writers in the emergence period of the pulp story seem to have known the book. Its influence spread almost universally, even when it was out of print. Motives were lifted from it, story lines imitated and rechanneled, and, most of all, the new concepts of metaphysical-physical horror were taken over by a host of writers who were tired of stock ghosts, weary of occult phenomena, and unconcerned with mysticism or psychological probing. Indeed, one might even single out *The King in Yellow* as the most important book in American supernatural fiction between Poe and the moderns.

After *The King in Yellow* Chambers gradually drifted away from supernatural fiction, with only occasional stories in periodicals or collections. On the whole these show a decline from *The King in Yellow*, but an occasional story is still worth examining. For this collection I have selected what I consider the best of this material.

"The Maker of Moons," from the book of the same title first published in 1896, has long been one of Chambers's best-liked stories. In its blending of the Oriental menace, the Secret Service, black magic, adventure and love it anticipates a popular form of the 1920's, which Sax Rohmer practiced skillfully. To my mind, however, it is an unsuccessful venture into a subgenre, both undeveloped and too long, naive and sentimental. Still, it has exciting pictorial moments —as was often the case with Chambers's work—and the image of the Maker at work is likely to remain in the reader's memory long after the rest of the story has been forgotten. In the same collection appeared "A Pleasant Evening," a somewhat individual development of a common theme in fantastic fiction: the revenant who announces his own death. It is unusual in Chambers's work in having an occasional naturalistic touch.

"The Messenger," which is reprinted from *The Mystery of Choice* (1897), is one of a series of stories set in the Breton countryside that Chambers seems to have loved. It is a material-horror story, possibly a little unsubtle, but it does have the characteristics of a nightmare with its disruptions of the time dimension, interlocked identities, and repetitive fate, which are all novel touches for the period. "The Key to Grief," from the same collection of stories, is basically a restatement of Bierce's "An Occurrence at Owl Creek Bridge," but

xii E. F. BLEILER

sentimentalized, without Bierce's precision or hardness of prose. Also in *The Mystery of Choice*, but not reprinted here, is "The Purple Emperor," a rather interesting detective story with slight touches of the supernatural.

A persistent trend in Chambers's work was an attempt to achieve the "light touch." He tried to create a story that would be bright, cheerful, flippant, elegant, sophisticated and slightly cynical. In this he usually failed. Sometimes he resorted to the light manner in the wrong place, as in "The Maker of Moons," and became garrulous and diffuse. In one extended area, however, he was successful. This was a collection of biological science-fiction stories published under the title *In Search of the Unknown* (1904). Their hero, an Edwardian Archie Goodwin, is a little coy at times, but on the whole these biological fantasies are among the most successful science-fiction humor.

Three stories have been reprinted from *In Search of the Unknown:* "The Harbor-Master," "In Quest of the Dingue," and "Is the Ux Extinct?" I have supplied titles, since they are presented as chapters in a novel, a device the original publishers used to increase sales of the book. All three stories carry obvious reminiscences of H. G. Wells and A. C. Doyle. It should be pointed out that Chambers's more scientifically minded contemporaries were more aware of the Prince of Monaco's (historical) interest in biology than modern readers are likely to be, and that the third story probably had humorous extensions that are now partly lost. The original collection contains three other stories in a similar vein which are not quite as successful.

The four books from which the stories in this collection were taken were not Chambers's only attempts at fantasy. Approximately another dozen books fall into the same category, although in several the fantastic element is slight and secondary. *The Tracer of Lost Persons* (1906) introduced Mr. Keene, the private detective. Mr. Keene, who used to be called Bayard Keene on the radio back in the 1930's, was still alive on television not too many years ago. His original adventures were a peculiarly sentimental detective form—which Bernard Capes handled better—in which occasional elements of the supernatural entered. *The Tree of Heaven* (1907) is a series of slight stories vaguely connected with the symbolism of an Oriental carpet. It is not worth reading. *Police!!!* (1915) continues the adventures of the young zoologist of *In Search of the Unknown*, in search of biological marvels and beautiful women. The individual stories are sometimes more fantastic than those of the earlier book, but are carelessly written and lack spontaneity and conviction. *The Talkers* (1923) is an occult novel, more distressing and unpleasant than terrifying. Much the most important of these secondary books is *The Slayer of Souls* (1920), a novel set in the same milieu as "The Maker of Moons," which was a preparatory version of it: the Yellow Peril, German-Bolshevik plots, black magic from Central Asia, secret agents and romance. In it Chambers achieved a seacoast of Bohemia feat by bringing China into geographical contact with the devil-worshiping Yezidees of Kurdistan. *The Slayer of Souls* has its faults, but it is a real thriller with many memorable scenes.

III

AT this moment it seems probable that Robert W. Chambers is going to end as a magnetic pattern in the memory tank of some bibliographic machine of the late twentieth century. The generation that once read his work is mostly gone, and in another decade or two Chambers will have been completely outlived except as a possible topic in social research. Yet there is one exception to this judgment: as long as there are readers of supernatural fiction, *The King in Yellow* will survive.

E. F. BLEILER

New York, 1969

THE KING IN YELLOW
and Other Horror Stories

The
Yellow Sign

Along the shore the cloud waves break,
The twin suns sink behind the lake,
The shadows lengthen
                    In Carcosa.

Strange is the night where black stars rise,
And strange moons circle through the skies,
But stranger still is
                    Lost Carcosa.

Songs that the Hyades shall sing,
Where flap the tatters of the King,
Must die unheard in
                    Dim Carcosa.

Song of my soul, my voice is dead,
Die thou, unsung, as tears unshed
Shall dry and die in
                    Lost Carcosa.

Cassilda's Song in *The King in Yellow*.
                    Act i. Scene 2.

I. BEING THE CONTENTS OF AN UNSIGNED LETTER SENT TO THE AUTHOR

THERE are so many things which are impossible to explain! Why should certain chords in music make me think of the brown and golden tints of autumn foliage? Why should the Mass of Sainte Cécile send my thoughts wandering among caverns whose walls blaze with ragged masses of virgin silver? What was it in the roar and turmoil of Broadway at six o'clock that flashed before my eyes the picture of a still Breton forest where sunlight filtered through spring foliage and Silvia bent, half curiously, half tenderly, over a small green lizard, murmuring: "To think that this also is a little ward of God!"

When I first saw the watchman his back was toward me. I looked at him indifferently until he went into the church. I paid no more attention to him than I had to any other man who lounged through Washington Square that morning, and when I shut my window and turned back into my studio I had forgotten him. Late in the afternoon, the day being warm, I raised the window again and leaned out to get a sniff of air. A man was standing in the courtyard of the church, and I noticed him again with as little interest as I had that morning. I looked across the square to where the fountain was playing and then, with my mind filled with vague impressions of trees, asphalt drives, and the moving groups of nursemaids and holiday-makers, I started to walk back to my easel. As I turned, my listless glance included the man below in the churchyard. His face was toward me now, and with a perfectly involuntary movement I bent to see it. At the same moment he raised his head and looked at me. Instantly I thought of a coffin-worm. Whatever it was about the man that repelled me I did not know, but the impression of a plump white grave-worm was so intense and nauseating that I must have shown it in my expression, for he turned his puffy face away with a movement which made me think of a disturbed grub in a chestnut.

I went back to my easel and motioned the model to resume her pose. After working awhile I was satisfied that I was spoiling what I had done as rapidly as possible, and I took up a palette knife and scraped the color out again. The flesh tones were sallow and unhealthy, and I did not understand how I could have painted such sickly color into a study which before that had glowed with healthy tones.

I looked at Tessie. She had not changed, and the clear flush of health dyed her neck and cheeks as I frowned.

"Is it something I've done?" she said.

"No,—I've made a mess of this arm, and for the life of me I can't see how I came to paint such mud as that into the canvas," I replied.

"Don't I pose well?" she insisted.

"Of course, perfectly."

"Then it's not my fault?"

"No. It's my own."

"I'm very sorry," she said.

I told her she could rest while I applied rag and turpentine to the plague spot on my canvas, and she went off to smoke a cigarette and look over the illustrations in the *Courier Français*.

I did not know whether it was something in the turpentine or a defect in the canvas, but the more I scrubbed the more that gangrene seemed to spread. I worked like a beaver to get it out, and yet the disease appeared to creep from limb to limb of the study before me. Alarmed I strove to arrest it, but now the color on the breast changed and the whole figure seemed to absorb the infection as a sponge soaks up water. Vigorously I plied palette knife, turpentine, and scraper, thinking all the time what a séance I should hold with Duval who had sold me the canvas; but soon I noticed that it was not the canvas which was defective nor yet the colors of Edward. "It must be the turpentine," I thought angrily, "or else my eyes have become so blurred and confused by the afternoon light that I can't see straight." I called Tessie, the model. She came and leaned over my chair blowing rings of smoke into the air.

"What *have* you been doing to it?" she exclaimed.

"Nothing," I growled, "it must be this turpentine!"

"What a horrible color it is now," she continued. "Do you think my flesh resembles green cheese?"

"No, I don't," I said angrily, "did you ever know me to paint like that before?"

"No, indeed!"

"Well, then!"

"It must be the turpentine, or something," she admitted.

She slipped on a Japanese robe and walked to the window. I scraped and rubbed until I was tired and finally picked up my brushes and hurled them through the canvas with a forcible expression, the tone alone of which reached Tessie's ears.

Nevertheless she promptly began: "That's it! Swear and act silly and ruin your brushes! You have been three weeks on that study, and now look! What's the good of ripping the canvas? What creatures artists are!"

I felt about as much ashamed as I usually did after such an outbreak, and I turned the ruined canvas to the wall. Tessie helped me clean my brushes, and then danced away to dress. From the screen she regaled me with bits of advice concerning whole or partial loss of temper, until, thinking, perhaps, I had been tormented sufficiently, she came out to implore me to button her waist where she could not reach it on the shoulder.

"Everything went wrong from the time you came back from the window and talked about that horrid-looking man you saw in the churchyard," she announced.

"Yes, he probably bewitched the picture," I said, yawning. I looked at my watch.

"It's after six, I know," said Tessie, adjusting her hat before the mirror.

"Yes," I replied, "I didn't mean to keep you so long." I leaned out of the window but recoiled with disgust, for the young man with the pasty face stood below in the churchyard. Tessie saw my gesture of disapproval and leaned from the window.

"Is that the man you don't like?" she whispered.

I nodded.

"I can't see his face, but he does look fat and soft. Someway or other," she continued, turning to look at me, "he reminds me of a dream,—an awful dream I once had. Or," she mused, looking down at her shapely shoes, "was it a dream after all?"

"How should I know?" I smiled.

Tessie smiled in reply.

"You were in it," she said, "so perhaps you might know something about it."

"Tessie! Tessie!" I protested, "don't you dare flatter by saying you dream about me!"

"But I did," she insisted; "shall I tell you about it?"

"Go ahead," I replied, lighting a cigarette.

Tessie leaned back on the open window-sill and began very seriously.

"One night last winter I was lying in bed thinking about nothing at all in particular. I had been posing for you and I was tired out, yet it seemed impossible for me to sleep. I heard the bells in the city ring ten, eleven, and midnight. I must have fallen asleep about midnight because I don't remember hearing the bells after that. It seemed to me that I had scarcely closed my eyes when I dreamed that something impelled me to go to the window. I rose, and raising the sash, leaned out. Twenty-fifth Street was deserted as far as I could see. I began to be afraid; everything outside seemed so—so black and uncomfortable. Then the sound of wheels in the distance came to my ears, and it seemed to me as though that was what I must wait for. Very slowly the wheels approached, and, finally, I could make out a vehicle moving along the street. It came nearer and nearer, and when it passed beneath my window I saw it was a hearse. Then, as I trembled with fear, the driver turned and looked straight at me. When I awoke I was standing by the open window shivering with cold, but the black-plumed hearse and the driver were gone. I dreamed this dream again in March last, and again awoke beside the open window. Last night the dream came again. You remember how it was raining; when I awoke, standing at the open window, my night-dress was soaked."

"But where did I come into the dream?" I asked.

"You—you were in the coffin; but you were not dead."

"In the coffin?"

"Yes."

"How did you know? Could you see me?"

"No; I only knew you were there."

"Had you been eating Welsh rarebits, or lobster salad?" I began laughing, but the girl interrupted me with a frightened cry.

"Hello! What's up?" I said, as she shrank into the embrasure by the window.

"The—the man below in the churchyard;—he drove the hearse."

"Nonsense," I said, but Tessie's eyes were wide with terror. I went to the window and looked out. The man was gone. "Come, Tessie," I urged, "don't be foolish. You have posed too long; you are nervous."

"Do you think I could forget that face?" she murmured. "Three times I saw the hearse pass below my window, and every time the driver turned and looked up at me. Oh, his face was so white and —and soft? It looked dead—it looked as if it had been dead a long time."

I induced the girl to sit down and swallow a glass of Marsala. Then I sat down beside her, and tried to give her some advice.

"Look here, Tessie," I said, "you go to the country for a week or two, and you'll have no more dreams about hearses. You pose all day, and when night comes your nerves are upset. You can't keep this up. Then again, instead of going to bed when your day's work is done, you run off to picnics at Sulzer's Park, or go to the Eldorado or Coney Island, and when you come down here next morning you are fagged out. There was no real hearse. That was a soft-shell crab dream."

She smiled faintly.

"What about the man in the churchyard?"

"Oh, he's only an ordinary unhealthy, everyday creature."

"As true as my name is Tessie Reardon, I swear to you, Mr. Scott, that the face of the man below in the churchyard is the face of the man who drove the hearse!"

"What of it?" I said. "It's an honest trade."

"Then you think I *did* see the hearse?"

"Oh," I said, diplomatically, "if you really did, it might not be unlikely that the man below drove it. There is nothing in that."

Tessie rose, unrolled her scented handkerchief, and taking a bit of gum from a knot in the hem, placed it in her mouth. Then drawing on her gloves she offered me her hand, with a frank, "Good-night, Mr. Scott," and walked out.

II

THE next morning, Thomas, the bellboy, brought me the *Herald* and a bit of news. The church next door had been sold. I thanked Heaven for it, not that being a Catholic I had any repugnance for the congregation next door, but because my nerves were shattered by a blatant exhorter, whose every word echoed through the aisle of the church as if it had been my own rooms, and who insisted on his r's with a nasal persistence which revolted my every instinct. Then, too, there was a fiend in human shape, an organist, who reeled off some of the grand old hymns with an interpretation of his own, and I longed for the blood of a creature who could play the doxology with an amendment of minor chords which one hears only in a quartet of very young undergraduates. I believe the minister was a good man, but when he bellowed: "And the Lorrrrd said unto Moses, the Lorrrd is a man of war; the Lorrrd is his name. My wrath shall wax hot and I will kill you with the sworrrd!'' I wondered how many centuries of purgatory it would take to atone for such a sin.

"Who bought the property?" I asked Thomas.

"Nobody that I knows, sir. They do say the gent wot owns this 'ere 'Amilton flats was lookin' at it. 'E might be a bildin' more studios.''

I walked to the window. The young man with the unhealthy face stood by the churchyard gate, and at the mere sight of him the same overwhelming repugnance took possession of me.

"By the way, Thomas," I said, "who is that fellow down there?"

Thomas sniffed. "That there worm, sir? 'E's night-watchman of the church, sir. 'E maikes me tired a-sittin' out all night on them steps and lookin' at you insultin' like. I'd a punched 'is 'ed, sir—beg pardon, sir—"

"Go on, Thomas."

"One night a comin' 'ome with 'Arry, the other English boy, I sees 'im a sittin' there on them steps. We 'ad Molly and Jen with us, sir, the two girls on the tray service, an' 'e looks so insultin' at us that I up and sez: 'Wat you looking hat, you fat slug?'—beg pardon, sir, but that's 'ow I sez, sir. Then 'e don't say nothin' and I sez: 'Come out and I'll punch that puddin' 'ed.' Then I hopens the gate an' goes in, but 'e don't say nothin', only looks insultin' like. Then I 'its 'im one, but, ugh! 'is 'ed was that cold and mushy it ud sicken you to touch 'im.''

"What did he do then?" I asked, curiously.

"'Im? Nawthin'.''

"And you, Thomas?"

The young fellow flushed with embarrassment and smiled uneasily.

"Mr. Scott, sir, I ain't no coward an' I can't make it out at all why I run. I was in the 5th Lawncers, sir, bugler at Tel-el-Kebir, an' was shot by the wells.''

"You don't mean to say you ran away?"

"Yes, sir; I run.''

"Why?"

"That's just what I want to know, sir. I grabbed Molly an' run, an' the rest was as frightened as I.''

"But what were they frightened at?"

Thomas refused to answer for a while, but now my curiosity was aroused about the repulsive young man below and I pressed him. Three years' sojourn in America had not only modified Thomas' cockney dialect but had given him the American's fear of ridicule.

"You won't believe me, Mr. Scott, sir?"

"Yes, I will."

"You will lawf at me, sir?"

"Nonsense!"

He hesitated. "Well, sir, it's God's truth that when I 'it 'im 'e grabbed me wrists, sir, and when I twisted 'is soft, mushy fist one of 'is fingers come off in me 'and."

The utter loathing and horror of Thomas' face must have been reflected in my own for he added:

"It's orful, an' now when I see 'im I just go away. 'E maikes me hill."

When Thomas had gone I went to the window. The man stood beside the church-railing with both hands on the gate, but I hastily retreated to my easel again, sickened and horrified, for I saw that the middle finger of his right hand was missing.

At nine o'clock Tessie appeared and vanished behind the screen with a merry "Good-morning, Mr. Scott." When she had reappeared and taken her pose upon the model-stand I started a new canvas much to her delight. She remained silent as long as I was on the drawing, but as soon as the scrape of the charcoal ceased and I took up my fixative she began to chatter.

"Oh, I had such a lovely time last night. We went to Tony Pastor's."

"Who are 'we'?" I demanded.

"Oh, Maggie, you know, Mr. Whyte's model, and Pinkie McCormick—we call her Pinkie because she's got that beautiful red hair you artists like so much—and Lizzie Burke."

I sent a shower of spray from the fixative over the canvas, and said: "Well, go on."

"We saw Kelly and Baby Barnes the skirt-dancer and—and all the rest. I made a mash."

"Then you have gone back on me, Tessie?"

She laughed and shook her head.

"He's Lizzie Burke's brother, Ed. He's a perfect gen'l'man."

I felt constrained to give her some parental advice concerning mashing, which she took with a bright smile.

"Oh, I can take care of a strange mash," she said, examining her chewing gum, "but Ed is different. Lizzie is my best friend."

Then she related how Ed had come back from the stocking mill in Lowell, Massachusetts, to find her and Lizzie grown up, and what an accomplished young man he was, and how he thought nothing of squandering half a dollar for ice-cream and oysters to celebrate his entry as clerk into the woollen department of Macy's. Before she finished I began to paint, and she resumed the pose, smiling and chattering like a sparrow. By noon I had the study fairly well rubbed in and Tessie came to look at it.

"That's better," she said.

I thought so too, and ate my lunch with a satisfied feeling that all was going well. Tessie spread her lunch on a drawing table opposite me and we drank our claret from the same bottle and lighted our cigarettes from the same match. I was very much attached to Tessie. I had watched her shoot up into a slender but exquisitely formed woman from a frail, awkward child. She had posed for me during the last three years, and among all my models she was my favorite. It would have troubled me very much indeed had she become "tough" or "fly," as the phrase goes, but I never noticed any deterioration of her manner, and felt at heart that she was all right. She and I never discussed morals at all, and I had no intention of doing so, partly because I had none myself, and partly because I knew she would do what she liked in spite of me. Still I did hope she would steer clear of complications, because I wished her well, and then also I had a selfish desire to retain the best model I had. I knew that mashing, as she termed it, had no significance with girls like Tessie, and that such things in America did not resemble in the least the same things in Paris. Yet, having lived with my eyes open, I also knew that somebody would take Tessie away some day, in one manner or another, and though I professed to myself that marriage was nonsense, I sincerely hoped that, in this case, there would be a priest at the end of the vista. I am a Catholic. When I listen to high mass, when I sign myself, I feel that everything, including myself, is more cheerful, and when I confess, it does me good. A man who lives as much alone as I do, must confess to somebody. Then, again,

Sylvia was Catholic, and it was reason enough for me. But I was speaking of Tessie, which is very different. Tessie also was Catholic and much more devout than I, so, taking it all in all, I had little fear for my pretty model until she should fall in love. But *then* I knew that fate alone would decide her future for her, and I prayed inwardly that fate would keep her away from men like me and throw into her path nothing but Ed Burkes and Jimmy McCormicks, bless her sweet face!

Tessie sat blowing rings of smoke up to the ceiling and tinkling the ice in her tumbler.

"Do you know, Kid, that I also had a dream last night?" I observed. I sometimes called her "the Kid."

"Not about that man," she laughed.

"Exactly. A dream similar to yours, only much worse."

It was foolish and thoughtless of me to say this, but you know how little tact the average painter has.

"I must have fallen asleep about 10 o'clock," I continued, "and after awhile I dreamt that I awoke. So plainly did I hear the midnight bells, the wind in the tree-branches, and the whistle of steamers from the bay, that even now I can scarcely believe I was not awake. I seemed to be lying in a box which had a glass cover. Dimly I saw the street lamps as I passed, for I must tell you, Tessie, the box in which I reclined appeared to lie in a cushioned wagon which jolted me over a stony pavement. After a while I became impatient and tried to move but the box was too narrow. My hands were crossed on my breast so I could not raise them to help myself. I listened and then tried to call. My voice was gone. I could hear the trample of the horses attached to the wagon and even the breathing of the driver. Then another sound broke upon my ears like the raising of a window sash. I managed to turn my head a little, and found I could look, not only through the glass cover of my box, but also through the glass panes in the side of the covered vehicle. I saw houses, empty and silent, with neither light nor life about any of them excepting one. In that house a window was open on the first floor and a figure all in white stood looking down into the street. It was you."

Tessie had turned her face away from me and leaned on the table with her elbow.

"I could see your face," I resumed, "and it seemed to me to be very sorrowful. Then we passed on and turned into a narrow black lane. Presently the horses stopped. I waited and waited, closing my eyes with fear and impatience, but all was silent as the grave. After what seemed to me hours, I began to feel uncomfortable. A sense that somebody was close to me made me unclose my eyes. Then I saw the white face of the hearse-driver looking at me through the coffin-lid—"

A sob from Tessie interrupted me. She was trembling like a leaf. I saw I had made an ass of myself and attempted to repair the damage.

"Why, Tess," I said, "I only told you this to show you what influence your story might have on another person's dreams. You don't suppose I really lay in a coffin, do you? What are you trembling for? Don't you see that your dream and my unreasonable dislike for that inoffensive watchman of the church simply set my brain working as soon as I fell asleep?"

She laid her head between her arms and sobbed as if her heart would break. What a precious triple donkey I had made of myself! But I was about to break my record. I went over and put my arm about her.

"Tessie dear, forgive me," I said; "I had no business to frighten you with such nonsense. You are too sensible a girl, too good a Catholic to believe in dreams."

Her hand tightened on mine and her head fell back upon my shoulder, but she still trembled and I petted her and comforted her.

"Come, Tess, open your eyes and smile."

Her eyes opened with a slow languid movement and met mine, but their expression was so queer that I hastened to reassure her again.

"It's all humbug, Tessie, you surely are not afraid that any harm will come to you because of that."

"No," she said, but her scarlet lips quivered.

"Then what's the matter? Are you afraid?"

"Yes. Not for myself."

"For me, then?" I demanded gayly.

"For you," she murmured in a voice almost inaudible, "I—I care for you."

At first I started to laugh, but when I understood her, a shock passed through me and I sat like one turned to stone. This was the crowning bit of idiocy I had committed. During the moment which elapsed between her reply and my answer I thought of a thousand responses to that innocent confession. I could pass it by with a laugh, I could misunderstand her and reassure her as to my health, I could simply point out that it was impossible she could love me. But my reply was quicker than my thoughts, and I might think and think now when it was too late, for I had kissed her on the mouth.

That evening I took my usual walk in Washington Park, pondering over the occurrences of the day. I was thoroughly committed. There was no back out now, and I stared the future straight in the face. I was not good, not even scrupulous, but I had no idea of deceiving either myself or Tessie. The one passion of my life lay buried in the sunlit forests of Brittany. Was it buried forever? Hope cried "No!" For three years I had been listening to the voice of Hope, and for three years I had waited for a footstep on my threshold. Had Sylvia forgotten? "No!" cried Hope.

I said that I was not good. That is true, but still I was not exactly a comic opera villain. I had led an easy-going reckless life, taking what invited me of pleasure, deploring and sometimes bitterly regretting consequences. In one thing alone, except my painting, was I serious, and that was something which lay hidden if not lost in the Breton forests.

It was too late now for me to regret what had occurred during the day. Whatever it had been, pity, a sudden tenderness for sorrow, or the more brutal instinct of gratified vanity, it was all the same now, and unless I wished to bruise an innocent heart my path lay marked before me. The fire and strength, the depth of passion of a love which I had never even suspected, with all my imagined experience in the world, left me no alternative but to respond or send her away. Whether because I am so cowardly about giving pain to others, or whether it was that I have little of the gloomy Puritan in me, I do not know, but I shrank from disclaiming responsibility for that thoughtless kiss, and in fact had no time to do so before the gates of her heart opened and the flood poured forth. Others who habitually do their duty and find a sullen satisfaction in making themselves and everybody else unhappy, might have withstood it. I did not. I dared not.

After the storm had abated I did tell her that she might better have loved Ed Burke and worn a plain gold ring, but she would not hear of it, and I thought perhaps that as long as she had decided to love somebody she could not marry, it had better be me. I, at least, could treat her with an intelligent affection, and whenever she became tired of her infatuation she could go none the worse for it. For I was decided on that point although I knew how hard it would be. I remembered the usual termination of Platonic liaisons and thought how disgusted I had been whenever I heard of one. I knew I was undertaking a great deal for so unscrupulous a man as I was, and I dreaded the future, but never for one moment did I doubt that she was safe with me. Had it been anybody but Tessie I should not have bothered my head about scruples. For it did not occur to me to sacrifice Tessie as I would have sacrificed a woman of the world. I looked the future squarely in the face and saw the several probable endings to the affair. She would either tire of the whole thing, or become so unhappy that I should have either to marry her or go away. If I married her we would be unhappy. I with a wife unsuited to me, and she with a husband unsuitable for any woman. For my past life could scarcely entitle me to marry. If I went away she might either fall ill, recover, and marry some Eddie Burke, or she might recklessly or deliberately go and do something foolish. On the other hand if she tired of me, then her whole life would be before her with beautiful vistas of Eddie Burkes and marriage rings and twins and Harlem flats and Heaven knows what. As I strolled along through the trees by the Washington Arch, I decided that she should find a substantial friend in me anyway and the future could take care of itself. Then I went into the house and put on my evening dress for the little faintly perfumed note on my dresser said, "Have a cab at the stage door at eleven," and the note was signed "Edith Carmichel, Metropolitan Theater, June 19th, 189—."

I took supper that night, or rather we took supper, Miss Carmichel and I, at Solari's and the dawn was just beginning to gild the cross on the Memorial Church as I entered Washington Square after leaving Edith at the Brunswick. There was not a soul in the park as I passed among the trees and took the walk which leads from the Garibaldi statue to the Hamilton Apartment House, but as I passed the churchyard I saw a figure sitting on the stone steps. In spite of myself a chill crept over me at the sight of the white puffy face, and I hastened to pass. Then he said something which might have been addressed to me or might merely have been a mutter to himself, but a sudden furious anger flamed up within me that such a creature should address me. For an instant I felt like wheeling about and smashing my stick over his head, but I walked on, and entering the Hamilton went to my apartment. For some time I tossed about the bed trying to get the sound of his voice out of my ears, but could not. It filled my head, that muttering sound, like thick oily smoke from a fat-rendering vat or an odor of noisome decay. And as I lay and tossed about, the voice in my ears seemed more distinct, and I began to understand the words he had muttered. They came to me slowly as if I had forgotten them, and at last I could make some sense out of the sounds. It was this:

"Have you found the Yellow Sign?"
"Have you found the Yellow Sign?"
"Have you found the Yellow Sign?"

I was furious. What did he mean by that? Then with a curse upon him and his I rolled over and went to sleep, but when I awoke later I looked pale and haggard, for I had dreamed the dream of the night before and it troubled me more than I cared to think.

I dressed and went down into my studio. Tessie sat by the window, but as I came in she rose and put both arms around my neck for an innocent kiss. She looked so sweet and dainty that I kissed her again and then sat down before the easel.

"Hello! Where's the study I began yesterday?" I asked.

Tessie looked conscious, but did not answer. I began to hunt among the piles of canvases, saying, "Hurry up, Tess, and get ready; we must take advantage of the morning light."

When at last I gave up the search among the other canvases and turned to look around the room for the missing study I noticed Tessie standing by the screen with her clothes still on.

"What's the matter," I asked, "don't you feel well?"

"Yes."

"Then hurry."

"Do you want me to pose as—as I have always posed?"

Then I understood. Here was a new complication. I had lost, of course, the best nude model I had ever seen. I looked at Tessie. Her face was scarlet. Alas! Alas! We had eaten of the tree of knowledge, and Eden and native innocence were dreams of the past—I mean for her.

I suppose she noticed the disappointment on my face, for she said: "I will pose if you wish. The study is behind the screen here where I put it."

"No," I said, "we will begin something new;" and I went into my wardrobe and picked out a Moorish costume which fairly blazed with tinsel. It was a genuine costume, and Tessie retired to the screen with it enchanted. When she came forth again I was astonished. Her long black hair was bound above her forehead with a circlet of turquoises, and the ends curled about her glittering girdle. Her feet were encased in the embroidered pointed slippers and the skirt of her costume, curiously wrought with arabesques in silver, fell to her ankles. The deep metallic blue vest embroidered with silver and the short Mauresque jacket spangled and sewn with turquoises became her wonderfully. She came up to me and held up her face smiling. I slipped my hand into my pocket and drawing out a gold chain with a cross attached, dropped it over her head.

"It's yours, Tessie."

"Mine?" she faltered.

"Yours. Now go and pose." Then with a radiant smile she ran behind the screen and presently reappeared with a little box on which was written my name.

"I had intended to give it to you when I went home to-night," she said, "but I can't wait now."

I opened the box. On the pink cotton inside lay a clasp of black onyx, on which was inlaid a curious symbol or letter in gold. It was neither Arabic nor Chinese, nor as I found afterwards did it belong to any human script.

"It's all I had to give you for a keepsake," she said, timidly.

I was annoyed, but I told her how much I should prize it, and promised to wear it always. She fastened it on my coat beneath the lapel.

"How foolish, Tess, to go and buy me such a beautiful thing as this," I said.

"I did not buy it," she laughed.

"Where did you get it?"

Then she told me how she had found it one day while coming from the Aquarium in the Battery, how she had advertised it and watched the papers, but at last gave up all hopes of finding the owner.

"That was last winter," she said, "the very day I had the first horrid dream about the hearse."

I remembered my dream of the previous night but said nothing, and presently my charcoal was flying over a new canvas, and Tessie stood motionless on the model-stand.

III

THE day following was a disastrous one for me. While moving a framed canvas from one easel to another my foot slipped on the polished floor and I fell heavily on both wrists. They were so badly sprained that it was useless to attempt to hold a brush, and I was obliged to wander about the studio, glaring at unfinished drawings and sketches until despair seized me and I sat down to smoke and twiddle my thumbs with rage. The rain blew against the windows and rattled on the roof of the church, driving me into a nervous fit with its interminable patter. Tessie sat sewing by the window, and every now and then raised her head and looked at me with such innocent compassion that I began to feel ashamed of my irritation and looked about for something to occupy me. I had read all the papers and all the books in the library, but for the sake of something to do I went to the bookcases and shoved them open with my elbow. I knew every volume by its color and examined them all, passing slowly around the library and whistling to keep up my spirits. I was turning to go into the dining-room when my eye fell upon a book bound in yellow, standing in a corner of the top shelf of the last bookcase. I did not remember it and from the floor could not decipher the pale lettering on the back, so I went to the smoking-room and called Tessie. She came in from the studio and climbed up to reach the book.

"What is it?" I asked.

"'The King in Yellow.'"

I was dumfounded. Who had placed it there? How came it in my rooms? I had long ago decided that I should never open that book, and nothing on earth could have persuaded me to buy it. Fearful lest curiosity might tempt me to open it, I had never even looked at it in book-stores. If I ever had had any curiosity to read it, the awful tragedy of young Castaigne, whom I knew, prevented me from exploring its wicked pages. I had always refused to listen to any description of it, and indeed, nobody ever ventured to discuss the second part aloud, so I had absolutely no knowledge of what those leaves might reveal. I stared at the poisonous yellow binding as I would at a snake.

"Don't touch it, Tessie," I said; "come down."

Of course my admonition was enough to arouse her curiosity, and before I could prevent it she took the book and, laughing, danced away into the studio with it. I called to her but she slipped away with a tormenting smile at my helpless hands, and I followed her with some impatience.

"Tessie!" I cried, entering the library, "listen, I am serious. Put that book away. I do not wish you to open it!" The library was empty. I went into both drawing-rooms, then into the bedrooms, laundry, kitchen, and finally returned to the library and began a systematic search. She had hidden herself so well that it was half an hour later when I discovered her crouching white and silent by the latticed window in the store-room above. At the first glance I saw she had been punished for her foolishness. "The King in Yellow" lay at her feet, but the book was open at the second part. I looked at Tessie and saw it was too late. She had opened "The King in Yellow." Then I took her by the hand and led her into the studio. She seemed dazed, and when I told her to lie down on the sofa she obeyed me without a word. After a while she closed her eyes and her breathing became regular and deep, but I could not determine whether or not she slept. For a long while I sat silently beside her, but she neither stirred nor spoke, and at last I rose and entering the unused store-room took the yellow book in my least injured hand. It seemed heavy as lead, but I carried it into the studio again, and sitting down on the rug beside the sofa, opened it and read it through from beginning to end.

When, faint with the excess of my emotions, I dropped the volume and leaned wearily back against the sofa, Tessie opened her eyes and looked at me.

We had been speaking for some time in a dull monotonous strain before I realized that we were discussing "The King in Yellow." Oh the sin of writing such words,—words which are clear as crystal, limpid and musical as bubbling springs, words which sparkle and glow like the poisoned diamonds of the Medicis! Oh the wickedness, the hopeless damnation of a soul who could fascinate and paralyze human creatures with such words,—words understood by the ignorant and wise alike, words which are more precious than jewels, more soothing than Heavenly music, more awful than death itself.

We talked on, unmindful of the gathering shadows, and she was begging me to throw away the clasp of black onyx quaintly inlaid with what we now knew to be the Yellow Sign. I never shall know why I refused, though even at this hour, here in my bedroom as I write this confession, I should be glad to know *what* it was that prevented me from tearing the Yellow Sign from my breast and casting it into the fire. I am sure I wished to do so, but Tessie pleaded with me in vain. Night fell and the hours dragged on, but still we murmured to each other of the King and the Pallid Mask, and midnight sounded from the misty spires in the fog-wrapped city. We spoke of Hastur and of Cassilda, while outside the fog rolled against the blank window-panes as the cloud waves roll and break on the shores of Hali.

The house was very silent now and not a sound from the misty streets broke the silence. Tessie lay among the cushions, her face a gray blot in the gloom, but her hands were clasped in mine and I knew that she knew and read my thoughts as I read hers, for we had understood the mystery of the Hyades and the Phantom of Truth was laid. Then as we answered each other, swiftly, silently, thought on thought, the shadows stirred in the gloom about us, and far in the distant streets we heard a sound. Nearer and nearer it came, the dull crunching of wheels, nearer and yet nearer, and now, outside before the door it ceased, and I dragged myself to the window and saw a black-plumed hearse. The gate below opened and shut, and I crept shaking to my door and bolted it, but I knew no bolts, no locks, could keep that creature out who was coming for the Yellow Sign. And now I heard him moving very softly along the hall. Now he was at the door, and the bolts rotted at his touch. Now he had entered. With eyes starting from my head I peered into the darkness, but when he came into the room I did not see him. It was only when I felt him envelop me in his cold soft grasp that I cried out and struggled with deadly fury, but my hands were useless and he tore the onyx clasp from my coat and struck me full in the face. Then, as I fell, I heard Tessie's soft cry and her spirit fled to God, and even while falling I longed to follow her, for I knew that the King in Yellow had opened his tattered mantle and there was only Christ to cry to now.

I could tell more, but I cannot see what help it will be to the world. As for me I am past human help or hope. As I lie here, writing, careless even whether or not I die before I finish, I can see the doctor gathering up his powders and phials with a vague gesture to the good priest beside me, which I understand.

They will be very curious to know the tragedy—they of the outside world who write books and print millions of newspapers, but I shall write no more, and the father confessor will seal my last words with the seal of sanctity when his holy office is done. They of the outside world may send their creatures into wrecked homes and death-smitten firesides, and their newspapers will batten on blood and tears, but with me their spies must halt before the confessional. They know that Tessie is dead and that I am dying. They know how the people in the house, aroused by an infernal scream, rushed into my room and found one living and two dead, but they do not know what I shall tell them now; they do not know that the doctor said as he pointed to a horrible decomposed heap on the floor—the livid corpse of the watchman from the church: "I have no theory, no explanation. That man must have been dead for months!"

I think I am dying. I wish the priest would—

The Repairer of Reputations

Ne raillons pas les fous; leur folie dure
plus longtemps que la nôtre . . . Voilà
toute la differénce.

I

TOWARD the end of the year 1920 the Government of the United
States had practically completed the programme, adopted during
the last months of President Winthrop's administration. The country
was apparently tranquil. Everybody knows how the Tariff and Labor
questions were settled. The war with Germany, incident on that
country's seizure of the Samoan Islands, had left no visible scars upon
the republic, and the temporary occupation of Norfolk by the
invading army had been forgotten in the joy over repeated naval
victories and the subsequent ridiculous plight of General Von
Gartenlaube's forces in the State of New Jersey. The Cuban and
Hawaiian investments had paid one hundred per cent. and the
territory of Samoa was well worth its cost as a coaling station. The
country was in a superb state of defence. Every coast city had been
well supplied with land fortifications; the army under the parental
eye of the General Staff, organized according to the Prussian system,
had been increased to 300,000 men with a territorial reserve of a
million; and six magnificent squadrons of cruisers and battle-ships
patrolled the six stations of the navigable seas, leaving a steam

reserve amply fitted to control home waters. The gentlemen from the West had at last been constrained to acknowledge that a college for the training of diplomats was as necessary as law schools are for the training of barristers. Consequently we were no longer represented abroad by incompetent patriots. The nation was prosperous. Chicago, for a moment paralyzed after a second great fire, had risen from its ruins, white and imperial, and more beautiful than the white city which had been built for its plaything in 1893. Everywhere good architecture was replacing bad and even in New York, a sudden craving for decency had swept away a great portion of the existing horrors. Streets had been widened, properly paved and lighted, trees had been planted, squares laid out, elevated structures demolished and underground roads built to replace them. The new government buildings and barracks were fine bits of architecture, and the long system of stone quays which completely surrounded the island had been turned into parks which proved a godsend to the population. The subsidizing of the state theatre and state opera brought its own reward. The United States National Academy of Design was much like European institutions of the same kind. Nobody envied the Secretary of Fine Arts, either his cabinet position or his portfolio. The Secretary of Forestry and Game Preservation had a much easier time, thanks to the new system of National Mounted Police. We had profited well by the latest treaties with France and England; the exclusion of foreign-born Jews as a measure of national self-preservation, the settlement of the new independent negro state of Suanee, the checking of immigration, the new laws concerning naturalization, and the gradual centralization of power in the executive all contributed to national calm and prosperity. When the Government solved the Indian problem and squadrons of Indian cavalry scouts in native costume were substituted for the pitiable organizations tacked on to the tail of skeletonized regiments by a former Secretary of War, the nation drew a long sigh of relief. When, after the colossal Congress of Religions, bigotry and intolerance were laid in their graves and kindness and charity began to draw warring sects together, many thought the millennium had arrived, at least in the new world, which after all is a world by itself.

But self-preservation is the first law, and the United States had to look on in helpless sorrow as Germany, Italy, Spain and Belgium writhed in the throes of Anarchy, while Russia, watching from the Caucasus, stooped and bound them one by one.

In the city of New York the summer of 1899 was signalized by the dismantling of the Elevated Railroads. The summer of 1900 will live in the memories of New York people for many a cycle; the Dodge Statue was removed in that year. In the following winter began that agitation for the repeal of the laws prohibiting suicide which bore its final fruit in the month of April, 1920, when the first Government Lethal Chamber was opened on Washington Square.

I had walked down that day from Dr. Archer's house on Madison Avenue, where I had been as a mere formality. Ever since that fall from my horse, four years before, I had been troubled at times with pains in the back of my head and neck, but now for months they had been absent, and the doctor sent me away that day saying there was nothing more to be cured in me. It was hardly worth his fee to be told that; I knew it myself. Still I did not grudge him the money. What I minded was the mistake which he made at first. When they picked me up from the pavement where I lay unconscious, and some-body had mercifully sent a bullet through my horse's head, I was carried to Doctor Archer, and he, pronouncing my brain affected, placed me in his private asylum where I was obliged to endure treat-ment for insanity. At last he decided that I was well, and I, knowing that my mind had always been as sound as his, if not sounder, "paid my tuition" as he jokingly called it, and left. I told him, smiling, that I would get even with him for his mistake, and he laughed heartily, and asked me to call once in a while. I did so, hoping for a chance to even up accounts, but he gave me none, and I told him I would wait.

The fall from my horse had fortunately left no evil results; on the contrary it had changed my whole character for the better. From a lazy young man about town, I had become active, energetic, tem-perate, and above all—oh, above all else—ambitious. There was only one thing which troubled me, I laughed at my own uneasiness, and yet it troubled me.

During my convalescence I had bought and read for the first time, "The King in Yellow." I remember after finishing the first act that it occurred to me that I had better stop. I started up and flung the book into the fire-place; the volume struck the barred grate and fell open on the hearth in the fire-light. If I had not caught a glimpse of the opening words in the second act I should never have finished it, but as I stooped to pick it up, my eyes became riveted to the open page, and with a cry of terror, or perhaps it was of joy so poignant that I suffered in every nerve, I snatched the thing out of the coals and crept shaking to my bedroom, where I read it and reread it, and wept and laughed and trembled with a horror which at times assails me yet. This is the thing that troubles me, for I cannot forget Carcosa where black stars hang in the heavens; where the shadows of men's thoughts lengthen in the afternoon, when the twin suns sink into the Lake of Hali; and my mind will bear forever the memory of the Pallid Mask. I pray God will curse the writer, as the writer has cursed the world with this beautiful, stupendous creation, terrible in its simplicity, irresistible in its truth—a world which now trembles before the King in Yellow. When the French Government seized the translated copies which had just arrived in Paris, London, of course, became eager to read it. It is well known how the book spread like an infectious disease, from city to city, from continent to continent, barred out here, confiscated there, denounced by press and pulpit, censured even by the most advanced of literary anarchists. No definite principles had been violated in those wicked pages, no doctrine promulgated, no convictions outraged. It could not be judged by any known standard, yet, although it was acknowledged that the supreme note of art had been struck in "The King in Yellow," all felt that human nature could not bear the strain, nor thrive on words in which the essence of purest poison lurked. The very banality and innocence of the first act only allowed the blow to fall afterward with more awful effect.

It was, I remember, the 13th day of April, 1920, that the first Government Lethal Chamber was established on the south side of Washington Square, between Wooster Street and South Fifth Avenue. The block which had formerly consisted of a lot of shabby old buildings, used as cafés and restaurants for foreigners, had been acquired by the Government in the winter of 1898. The French and Italian cafés and restaurants were torn down; the whole block was enclosed by a gilded iron railing, and converted into a lovely garden with lawns, flowers and fountains. In the centre of the garden stood a small, white building, severely classical in architecture, and surrounded by thickets of flowers. Six Ionic columns supported the roof, and the single door was of bronze. A splendid marble group of "The Fates" stood before the door, the work of a young American sculptor, Boris Yvain, who had died in Paris when only twenty-three years old.

The inauguration ceremonies were in progress as I crossed University Place and entered the square. I threaded my way through the silent throng of spectators, but was stopped at Fourth Street by a cordon of police. A regiment of United States lancers were drawn up in a hollow square around the Lethal Chamber. On a raised tribune facing Washington Park stood the Governor of New York, and behind him were grouped the Mayor of New York and Brooklyn, the Inspector-General of Police, the Commandant of the state troops, Colonel Livingston, military aid to the President of the United States, General Blount, commanding at Governor's Island, Major-General Hamilton, commanding the garrison of New York and Brooklyn, Admiral Buffby of the fleet in the North River, Surgeon General Lanceford, the staff of the National Free Hospital, Senators Wyse and Franklin of New York, and the Commissioner of Public Works. The tribune was surrounded by a squadron of hussars of the National Guard.

The Governor was finishing his reply to the short speech of the Surgeon-General. I heard him say: "The laws prohibiting suicide and providing punishment for any attempt at self-destruction have been repealed. The Government has seen fit to acknowledge the right of man to end an existence which may have become intolerable to him, through physical suffering or mental despair. It is believed that the community will be benefited by the removal of such people from their midst. Since the passage of this law, the number of suicides in the United States has not increased. Now that the Government has determined to establish a Lethal Chamber in every city, town and village in the country, it remains to be seen whether or not that class of human creatures from whose desponding ranks new victims of self-destruction fall daily will accept the relief thus provided." He paused, and turned to the white Lethal Chamber. The silence in the street was absolute. "There a painless death awaits him who can no longer bear the sorrows of this life. If death is welcome let him seek it there." Then quickly turning to the military aid of the President's household, he said, "I declare the Lethal

Chamber open," and again facing the vast crowd he cried in a clear voice: "Citizens of New York and of the United States of America, through me the Government declares the Lethal Chamber to be open."

The solemn hush was broken by a sharp cry of command, the squadron of hussars filed after the Governor's carriage, the lancers wheeled and formed along Fifth Avenue to wait for the commandant of the garrison, and the mounted police followed them. I left the crowd to gape and stare at the white marble Death Chamber, and, crossing South Fifth Avenue, walked along the western side of that thoroughfare to Bleecker Street. Then I turned to the right and stopped before a dingy shop which bore the sign,

HAWBERK, ARMORER.

I glanced into the doorway and saw Hawberk busy in his little shop at the end of the hall. He looked up at the same moment, and catching sight of me cried in his deep, hearty voice, "Come in, Mr. Castaigne!" Constance, his daughter, rose to meet me as I crossed the threshold, and held out her pretty hand, but I saw the blush of disappointment on her cheeks, and knew that it was another Castaigne she had expected, my Cousin Louis. I smiled at her confusion and complimented her on the banner which she was embroidering from a colored plate. Old Hawberk sat riveting the worn greaves of some ancient suit of armor, and the ting! ting! ting! of his little hammer sounded pleasantly in the quaint shop. Presently he dropped his hammer, and fussed about for a moment with a tiny wrench. The soft clash of the mail sent a thrill of pleasure through me. I loved to hear the music of steel brushing against steel, the mellow shock of the mallet on thigh pieces, and the jingle of chain armor. That was the only reason I went to see Hawberk. He had never interested me personally, nor did Constance, except for the fact of her being in love with Louis. This did occupy my attention, and sometimes even kept me awake at night. But I knew in my heart that all would come right, and that I should arrange their future as I expected to arrange that of my kind doctor, John Archer. However, I should never have troubled myself about visiting them just then, had it not been, as I say, that the music of the tinkling hammer had for me this strong fascination. I would sit for hours, listening and listening, and when a stray sunbeam struck the inlaid steel, the sensation it gave me was almost too keen to endure. My eyes would become fixed, dilating with a pleasure that stretched every nerve almost to breaking, until some movement of the old armorer cut off the ray of sunlight, then, still thrilling secretly, I leaned back and listened again to the sound of the polishing rag, swish! swish! rubbing rust from the rivets.

Constance worked with the embroidery over her knees, now and then pausing to examine more closely the pattern in the colored plate from the Metropolitan Museum.

"Who is this for?" I asked.

Hawberk explained, that in addition to the treasures of armor in the Metropolitan Museum of which he had been appointed armorer, he also had charge of several collections belonging to rich amateurs. This was the missing greave of a famous suit which a client of his had traced to a little shop in Paris on the Quai d'Orsay. He, Hawberk, had negotiated for and secured the greave, and now the suit was complete. He laid down his hammer and read me the history of the suit, traced since 1450 from owner to owner until it was acquired by Thomas Stainbridge. When his superb collection was sold, this client of Hawberk's bought the suit, and since then the search for the missing greave had been pushed until it was, almost by accident, located in Paris.

"Did you continue the search so persistently without any certainty of the greave being still in existence?" I demanded.

"Of course," he replied coolly.

Then for the first time I took a personal interest in Hawberk.

"It was worth something to you," I ventured.

"No," he replied, laughing, "my pleasure in finding it was my reward."

"Have you no ambition to be rich?" I asked smiling.

"My one ambition is to be the best armorer in the world," he answered gravely.

Constance asked me if I had seen the ceremonies at the Lethal Chamber. She herself had noticed cavalry passing up Broadway that morning, and had wished to see the inauguration, but her father wanted the banner finished, and she had stayed at his request.

"Did you see your cousin, Mr. Castaigne, there?" she asked, with the slightest tremor of her soft eyelashes.

"No," I replied carelessly. "Louis' regiment is manœuvreing out in Westchester County." I rose and picked up my hat and cane.

"Are you going upstairs to see the lunatic again?" laughed old Hawberk. If Hawberk knew how I loathe that word "lunatic," he would never use it in my presence. It rouses certain feelings within me which I do not care to explain. However, I answered him quietly:

"I think I shall drop in and see Mr. Wilde for a moment or two."

"Poor fellow," said Constance, with a shake of her head, "it must be hard to live alone year after year, poor, crippled and almost demented. It is very good of you, Mr. Castaigne, to visit him as often as you do."

"I think he is vicious," observed Hawberk, beginning again with his hammer. I listened to the golden tinkle on the greave plates; when he had finished I replied:

"No, he is not vicious, nor is he in the least demented. His mind is a wonder chamber, from which he can extract treasures that you and I would give years of our lives to acquire."

Hawberk laughed.

I continued a little impatiently: "He knows history as no one else could know it. Nothing, however trivial, escapes his search, and his memory is so absolute, so precise in details, that were it known in New York that such a man existed, the people could not honor him enough."

"Nonsense," muttered Hawberk, searching on the floor for a fallen rivet.

"Is it nonsense," I asked, managing to suppress what I felt, "is it nonsense when he says that the tassets and cuissards of the enamelled suit of armor commonly known as the 'Prince's Emblazoned' can be found among a mass of rusty theatrical properties, broken stoves and ragpicker's refuse in a garret in Pell Street?"

Hawberk's hammer fell to the ground, but he picked it up and asked, with a great deal of calm, how I knew that the tassets and left cuissard were missing from the "Prince's Emblazoned."

"I did not know until Mr. Wilde mentioned it to me the other day. He said they were in the garret of 998 Pell Street."

"Nonsense," he cried, but I noticed his hand trembling under his leathern apron.

"Is this nonsense too?" I asked pleasantly, "is it nonsense when Mr. Wilde continually speaks of you as the Marquis of Avonshire and of Miss Constance—"

I did not finish, for Constance had started to her feet with terror written on every feature. Hawberk looked at me and slowly smoothed his leathern apron. "That is impossible," he observed, "Mr. Wilde may know a great many things—"

"About armor, for instance, and the 'Prince's Emblazoned,'" I interposed, smiling.

"Yes," he continued, slowly, "about armor also—may be—but he is wrong in regard to the Marquis of Avonshire, who, as you know, killed his wife's traducer years ago, and went to Australia where he did not long survive his wife."

"Mr. Wilde is wrong," murmured Constance. Her lips were blanched but her voice was sweet and calm.

"Let us agree, if you please, that in this one circumstance Mr. Wilde is wrong," I said.

II

I CLIMBED the three dilapidated flights of stairs, which I had so often climbed before, and knocked at a small door at the end of the corridor. Mr. Wilde opened the door and I walked in.

When he had double-locked the door and pushed a heavy chest against it, he came and sat down beside me, peering up into my face with his little light-colored eyes. Half a dozen new scratches covered his nose and cheeks, and the silver wires which supported his artificial ears had become displaced. I thought I had never seen him so hideously fascinating. He had no ears. The artificial ones, which now stood out at an angle from the fine wire, were his one weakness. They were made of wax and painted a shell pink, but the rest of his face was yellow. He might better have revelled in the luxury of some artificial fingers for his left hand, which was absolutely fingerless, but it seemed to cause him no inconvenience, and he was satisfied with his wax ears. He was very small, scarcely higher than a child of ten, but his arms were magnificently developed, and his thighs as thick as any athlete's. Still, the most remarkable thing about Mr. Wilde was that a man of his marvellous intelligence and knowledge should have such a head. It was flat and pointed, like the heads of many of those unfortunates whom people imprison in asylums for the weak-minded. Many called him insane but I knew him to be as sane as I was.

I do not deny that he was eccentric; the mania he had for keeping that cat and teasing her until she flew at his face like a demon, was certainly eccentric. I never could understand why he kept the creature, nor what pleasure he found in shutting himself up in his room with the surly, vicious beast. I remember once, glancing up from the manuscript I was studying by the light of some tallow dips, and seeing Mr. Wilde squatting motionless on his high chair, his eyes fairly blazing with excitement, while the cat, which had risen from her place before the stove, came creeping across the floor right at him. Before I could move she flattened her belly to the ground, crouched, trembled, and sprang into his face. Howling and foaming they rolled over and over on the floor, scratching and clawing, until the cat screamed and fled under the cabinet, and Mr. Wilde turned over on his back, his limbs contracting and curling up like the legs of a dying spider. He *was* eccentric.

Mr. Wilde had climbed into his high chair, and, after studying my face, picked up a dog's-eared ledger and opened it.

"Henry B. Matthews," he read, "book-keeper with Whysot Whysot and Company, dealers in church ornaments. Called April 3d. Reputation damaged on the race-track. Known as a welcher. Reputation to be repaired by August 1st. Retainer Five Dollars." He turned the page and ran his fingerless knuckles down the closely-written columns.

"P. Greene Dusenberry, Minister of the Gospel, Fairbeach, New Jersey. Reputation damaged in the Bowery. To be repaired as soon as possible. Retainer $100."

He coughed and added, "Called, April 6th."

"Then you are not in need of money, Mr. Wilde," I inquired.

"Listen," he coughed again.

"Mrs. C. Hamilton Chester, of Chester Park, New York City. Called April 7th. Reputation damaged at Dieppe, France. To be repaired by October 1st. Retainer $500.

"Note.—C. Hamilton Chester, Captain U.S.S. 'Avalanche,' ordered home from South Sea Squadron October 1st."

"Well," I said, "the profession of a Repairer of Reputations is lucrative."

His colorless eyes sought mine. "I only wanted to demonstrate that I was correct. You said it was impossible to succeed as a Repairer of Reputations; that even if I did succeed in certain cases it would cost me more than I would gain by it. To-day I have five hundred men in my employ, who are poorly paid, but who pursue the work with an enthusiasm which possibly may be born of fear. These men enter every shade and grade of society; some even are pillars of the most exclusive social temples; others are the prop and pride of the financial world; still others, hold undisputed sway among the 'Fancy and the Talent.' I choose them at my leisure from those who reply to my advertisements. It is easy enough, they are all cowards. I could treble the number in twenty days if I wished. So you see, those who have in their keeping the reputations of their fellow-citizens, *I* have in my pay."

"They may turn on you," I suggested.

He rubbed his thumb over his cropped ears, and adjusted the wax substitutes. "I think not," he murmured thoughtfully, "I seldom have to apply the whip, and then only once. Besides they like their wages."

"How do you apply the whip?" I demanded.

His face for a moment was awful to look upon. His eyes dwindled to a pair of green sparks.

"I invite them to come and have a little chat with me," he said in a soft voice.

A knock at the door interrupted him, and his face resumed its amiable expression.

"Who is it?" he inquired.

"Mr. Steylette," was the answer.

"Come to-morrow," replied Mr. Wilde.

"Impossible," began the other, but was silenced by a sort of bark from Mr. Wilde.

"Come to-morrow," he repeated.

We heard somebody move away from the door and turn the corner by the stairway.

"Who is that?" I asked.

"Arnold Steylette, Owner and Editor in Chief of the great New York daily."

He drummed on the ledger with his fingerless hand adding: "I pay him very badly, but he thinks it a good bargain."

"Arnold Steylette!" I repeated amazed.

"Yes," said Mr. Wilde with a self-satisfied cough.

The cat, which had entered the room as he spoke, hesitated, looked up at him and snarled. He climbed down from the chair and squatting on the floor, took the creature into his arms and caressed her. The cat ceased snarling and presently began a loud purring which seemed to increase in timbre as he stroked her.

"Where are the notes?" I asked. He pointed to the table, and for the hundreth time I picked up the bundle of manuscript entitled "THE IMPERIAL DYNASTY OF AMERICA."

One by one I studied the well-worn pages, worn only by my own handling, and although I knew all by heart, from the beginning, "When from Carcosa, the Hyades, Hastur, and Aldebaran," to "Castaigne, Louis de Calvados, born December 19th, 1877," I read it with an eager rapt attention, pausing to repeat parts of it aloud, and dwelling especially on "Hildred de Calvados, only son of Hildred Castaigne and Edythe Landes Castaigne, first in succession," etc., etc.

When I finished, Mr. Wilde nodded and coughed.

"Speaking of your legitimate ambition," he said, "how do Constance and Louis get along?"

"She loves him," I replied simply.

The cat on his knee suddenly turned and struck at his eyes, and he flung her off and climbed on to the chair opposite me.

"And Doctor Archer! But that's a matter you can settle any time you wish," he added.

"Yes," I replied, "Doctor Archer can wait, but it is time I saw my cousin Louis."

"It is time," he repeated. Then he took another ledger from the table and ran over the leaves rapidly.

"We are now in communication with ten thousand men," he muttered. "We can count on one hundred thousand within the first twenty-eight hours, and in forty-eight hours the state will rise *en masse*. The country follows the state, and the portion that will not,

I mean California and the Northwest, might better never have been inhabited. I shall not send them the Yellow Sign."

The blood rushed to my head, but I only answered, "A new broom sweeps clean."

"The ambition of Cæsar and of Napoleon pales before that which could not rest until it had seized the minds of men and controlled even their unborn thoughts," said Mr. Wilde.

"You are speaking of the King in Yellow," I groaned with a shudder.

"He is a king whom Emperors have served."

"I am content to serve him," I replied.

Mr. Wilde sat rubbing his ears with his crippled hand. "Perhaps Constance does not love him," he suggested.

I started to reply, but a sudden burst of military music from the street below drowned my voice. The twentieth dragoon regiment, formerly in garrison at Mount St. Vincent, was returning from the manœuvres in Westchester County, to its new barracks on East Washington Square. It was my cousin's regiment. They were a fine lot of fellows, in their pale-blue, tight-fitting jackets, jaunty busbys and white riding breeches with the double yellow stripe, into which their limbs seemed molded. Every other squadron was armed with lances, from the metal points of which fluttered yellow and white pennons. The band passed, playing the regimental march, then came the colonel and staff, the horses crowding and trampling, while their heads bobbed in unison, and the pennons fluttered from their lance points. The troopers, who rode with the beautiful English seat, looked brown as berries from their bloodless campaign among the farms of Westchester, and the music of their sabres against the stirrups, and the jingle of spurs and carbines was delightful to me. I saw Louis riding with his squadron. He was as handsome an officer as I have ever seen. Mr. Wilde, who had mounted a chair by the window, saw him too, but said nothing. Louis turned and looked straight at Hawberk's shop as he passed, and I could see the flush on his brown cheeks. I think Constance must have been at the window. When the last troopers had clattered by, and the last pennons vanished into South 5th Avenue, Mr. Wilde clambered out of his chair and dragged the chest away from the door.

"Yes," he said, "it is time that you saw your cousin Louis."

He unlocked the door and I picked up my hat and stick and stepped into the corridor. The stairs were dark. Groping about, I set my foot on something soft, which snarled and spit, and I aimed a murderous blow at the cat, but my cane shivered to splinters against the balustrade, and the beast scurried back into Mr. Wilde's room.

Passing Hawberk's door again I saw him still at work on the armor, but I did not stop, and stepping out into Bleecker Street, I followed it to Wooster, skirted the grounds of the Lethal Chamber, and crossing Washington Park went straight to my rooms in the Benedick. Here I lunched comfortably, read the *Herald* and the *Meteor*, and finally went to the steel safe in my bedroom and set the time combination. The three and three-quarter minutes which it is necessary to wait, while the time lock is opening, are to me golden moments. From the instant I set the combination to the moment when I grasp the knobs and swing back the solid steel doors, I live in an ecstasy of expectation. Those moments must be like moments passed in Paradise. I know what I am to find at the end of the time limit. I know what the massive safe holds secure for me, for me alone, and the exquisite pleasure of waiting is hardly enhanced when the safe opens and I lift, from its velvet crown, a diadem of purest gold, blazing with diamonds. I do this every day, and yet the joy of waiting and at last touching again the diadem, only seems to increase as the days pass. It is a diadem fit for a King among kings, an Emperor among emperors. The King in Yellow might scorn it, but it shall be worn by his royal servant.

I held it in my arms until the alarm on the safe rang harshly, and then tenderly, proudly, I replaced it and shut the steel doors. I walked slowly back into my study, which faces Washington Square, and leaned on the window-sill. The afternoon sun poured into my windows, and a gentle breeze stirred the branches of the elms and maples in the park, now covered with buds and tender foliage. A flock of pigeons circled about the tower of the Memorial Church; sometimes alighting on the purple tiled roof, sometimes wheeling downward to the lotos fountain in front of the marble arch. The gardeners were busy with the flower beds around the fountain, and the freshly-turned earth smelled sweet and spicy. A lawn mower, drawn by a fat white horse, clinked across the green sward, and watering carts poured showers of spray over the asphalt drives. Around the statue of Peter Stuyvesant, which in 1897 had replaced the monstrosity supposed to represent Garibaldi, children played in the spring sunshine, and nurse girls wheeled elaborate baby-carriages with a reckless disregard for the pasty-faced occupants, which could probably be explained by the presence of half a dozen trim dragoon troopers languidly lolling on the benches. Through the trees, the Washington Memorial Arch glistened like silver in the sunshine, and beyond, on the eastern extremity of the square the gray stone barracks of the dragoons, and the white granite artillery stables were alive with color and motion.

I looked at the Lethal Chamber on the corner of the square opposite. A few curious people still lingered about the gilded iron railing, but inside the grounds the paths were deserted. I watched the fountains ripple and sparkle; the sparrows had already found this new bathing nook, and the basins were crowded with the dusty-feathered little things. Two or three white peacocks picked their way across the lawns, and a drab-colored pigeon sat so motionless on the arm of one of the Fates, that it seemed to be a part of the sculptured stone.

As I was turning carelessly away, a slight commotion in the group of curious loiterers around the gates attracted my attention. A young man had entered, and was advancing with nervous strides along the gravel path which leads to the bronze doors of the Lethal Chamber. He paused a moment before the Fates, and as he raised his head to those three mysterious faces, the pigeon rose from its sculptured perch, circled about for a few moments and flew to the east. The young man pressed his hands to his face, and then with an undefinable gesture sprang up the marble steps, the bronze doors closed behind him, and half an hour later the loiterers slouched away, and the frightened pigeon returned to its perch in the arms of Fate.

I put on my hat and went out into the park for a little walk before dinner. As I crossed the central driveway a group of officers passed, and one of them called out, "Hello, Hildred," and came back to shake hands with me. It was my Cousin Louis, who stood smiling and tapping his spurred heels with his riding-whip.

"Just back from Westchester," he said; "been doing the bucolic; milk and curds, you know, dairy-maids in sunbonnets, who say 'haeow' and 'I don't think' when you tell them they are pretty. I'm nearly dead for a square meal at Delmonico's. What's the news?"

"There is none," I replied pleasantly. "I saw your regiment coming in this morning."

"Did you? I didn't see you. Where were you?"

"In Mr. Wilde's window."

"Oh, hell!" he began impatiently, "that man is stark mad! I don't understand why you—"

He saw how annoyed I felt by this outburst, and begged my pardon.

"Really, old chap," he said, "I don't mean to run down a man you like, but for the life of me I can't see what the deuce you find in common with Mr. Wilde. He's not well-bred, to put it generously; he's hideously deformed; his head is the head of a criminally insane person. You know yourself he's been in an asylum—"

"So have I," I interrupted calmly.

Louis looked startled and confused for a moment, but recovered and slapped me heartily on the shoulder.

"You were completely cured," he began, but I stopped him again.

"I suppose you mean that I was simply acknowledged never to have been insane."

"Of course that—that's what I meant," he laughed.

I disliked his laugh because I knew it was forced, but I nodded gaily and asked him where he was going. Louis looked after his brother officers who had now almost reached Broadway.

"We had intended to sample a Brunswick cocktail, but to tell you the truth I was anxious for an excuse to go and see Hawberk instead. Come along, I'll make you my excuse."

We found old Hawberk, neatly attired in a fresh spring suit, standing at the door of his shop and sniffing the air.

"I had just decided to take Constance for a little stroll before dinner," he replied to the impetuous volley of questions from Louis. "We thought of walking on the park terrace along the North River."

At that moment Constance appeared and grew pale and rosy by turns as Louis bent over her small gloved fingers. I tried to excuse myself, alleging an engagement up-town, but Louis and Constance would not listen, and I saw I was expected to remain and engage old Hawberk's attention. After all it would be just as well if I kept my eye on Louis, I thought, and when they hailed a Spring Street horsecar, I got in after them and took my seat beside the armorer.

The beautiful line of parks and granite terraces overlooking the wharves along the North River, which were built in 1910 and finished in the autumn of 1917, had become one of the most popular promenades in the metropolis. They extended from the battery to 190th Street, overlooking the noble river and affording a fine view of the Jersey shore and the Highlands opposite. Cafés and restaurants were scattered here and there among the trees, and twice a week military bands from the garrison played in the kiosques on the parapets.

We sat down in the sunshine on the bench at the foot of the equestrian statue of General Sheridan. Constance tipped her sunshade to shield her eyes, and she and Louis began a murmuring conversation which was impossible to catch. Old Hawberk, leaning on his ivory-headed cane, lighted an excellent cigar, the mate to which I politely refused, and smiled at vacancy. The sun hung low above the Staten Island woods, and the bay was dyed with golden hues reflected from the sun-warmed sails of the shipping in the harbor.

Brigs, schooners, yachts, clumsy ferry-boats, their decks swarming with people, railroad transports carrying lines of brown, blue and white freight cars, stately sound steamers, *declassé* tramp steamers, coasters, dredgers, scows, and everywhere pervading the entire bay impudent little tugs puffing and whistling officiously;—these were the crafts which churned the sunlit waters as far as the eye could reach. In calm contrast to the hurry of sailing vessel and steamer a silent fleet of white warships lay motionless in midstream.

Constance's merry laugh aroused me from my reverie.

"What *are* you staring at?" she inquired.

"Nothing—the fleet," I smiled.

Then Louis told us what the vessels were, pointing out each by its relative position to the old Red Fort on Governor's Island.

"That little cigar-shaped thing is a torpedo boat," he explained; "there are four more lying close together. They are the 'Tarpon,' the 'Falcon,' the 'Sea Fox' and the 'Octopus.' The gun-boats just above are the 'Princeton,' the 'Champlain,' the 'Still Water' and the 'Erie.' Next to them lie the cruisers 'Farragut' and 'Los Angeles,' and above them the battle-ships 'California' and 'Dakota,' and the

'Washington' which is the flag-ship. Those two squatty-looking chunks of metal which are anchored there off Castle William are the double-turreted monitors 'Terrible' and 'Magnificent'; behind them lies the ram, 'Osceola.'"

Constance looked at him with deep approval in her beautiful eyes. "What loads of things you know for a soldier," she said, and we all joined in the laugh which followed.

Presently Louis rose with a nod to us and offered his arm to Constance, and they strolled away along the river wall. Hawberk watched them for a moment and then turned to me.

"Mr. Wilde was right," he said. "I have found the missing tassets and left cuissard of the 'Prince's Emblazoned,' in a vile old junk garret in Pell Street."

"998?" I inquired, with a smile.

"Yes."

"Mr. Wilde is a very intelligent man," I observed.

"I want to give him the credit of this most important discovery," continued Hawberk. "And I intend it shall be known that he is entitled to the fame of it."

"He won't thank you for that," I answered sharply; "please say nothing about it."

"Do you know what it is worth?" said Hawberk.

"No, fifty dollars, perhaps."

"It is valued at five hundred, but the owner of the 'Prince's Emblazoned' will give two thousand dollars to the person who completes his suit; that reward also belongs to Mr. Wilde."

"He doesn't want it! He refuses it!" I answered angrily. "What do you know about Mr. Wilde? He doesn't need the money. He is rich—or will be—richer than any living man except myself. What will we care for money then—what will we care, he and I, when—when—"

"When what?" demanded Hawberk, astonished.

"You will see," I replied, on my guard again.

He looked at me narrowly, much as Doctor Archer used to, and I knew he thought I was mentally unsound. Perhaps it was fortunate for him that he did not use the word lunatic just then.

"No," I replied to his unspoken thought, "I am not mentally weak; my mind is as healthy as Mr. Wilde's. I do not care to explain

just yet what I have on hand, but it is an investment which will
pay more than mere gold, silver and precious stones. It will secure
the happiness and prosperity of a continent—yes, a hemisphere!"

"Oh," said Hawberk.

"And eventually," I continued more quietly, "it will secure the
happiness of the whole world."

"And incidentally your own happiness and prosperity as well as
Mr. Wilde's?"

"Exactly," I smiled. But I could have throttled him for taking
that tone.

He looked at me in silence for a while and then said very gently,
"Why don't you give up your books and studies, Mr. Castaigne, and
take a tramp among the mountains somewhere or other? You used
to be fond of fishing. Take a cast or two at the trout in the Rangelys."

"I don't care for fishing any more," I answered, without a shade
of annoyance in my voice.

"You used to be fond of everything," he continued; "athletics,
yachting, shooting, riding—"

"I have never cared to ride since my fall," I said quietly.

"Ah, yes, your fall," he repeated, looking away from me.

I thought this nonsense had gone far enough, so I turned the
conversation back to Mr. Wilde; but he was scanning my face again
in a manner highly offensive to me.

"Mr. Wilde," he repeated, "do you know what he did this afternoon? He came downstairs and nailed a sign over the hall door
next to mine; it read:

MR. WILDE,
REPAIRER OF REPUTATIONS,
3d Bell.

Do you know what a Repairer of Reputations can be?"

"I do," I replied, suppressing the rage within.

"Oh," he said again.

Louis and Constance came strolling by and stopped to ask if we
would join them. Hawberk looked at his watch. At the same moment
a puff of smoke shot from the casemates of Castle William, and the
boom of the sunset gun rolled across the water and was re-echoed
from the Highlands opposite. The flag came running down from the

flag-pole, the bugles sounded on the white decks of the warships, and the first electric light sparkled out from the Jersey shore.

As I turned into the city with Hawberk I heard Constance murmur something to Louis which I did not understand; but Louis whispered "My darling," in reply; and again, walking ahead with Hawberk through the square I heard a murmur of "sweetheart," and "my own Constance," and I knew the time had nearly arrived when I should speak of important matters with my Cousin Louis.

III

ONE morning early in May I stood before the steel safe in my bed-room, trying on the golden jewelled crown. The diamonds flashed fire as I turned to the mirror, and the heavy beaten gold burned like a halo about my head. I remembered Camilla's agonized scream and the awful words echoing through the dim streets of Carcosa. They were the last lines in the first act, and I dared not think of what followed—dared not, even in the spring sunshine, there in my own room, surrounded with familiar objects, reassured by the bustle from the street and the voices of the servants in the hallway outside. For those poisoned words had dropped slowly into my heart, as death-sweat drops upon a bed-sheet and is absorbed. Trembling, I put the diadem from my head and wiped my forehead, but I thought of Hastur and of my own rightful ambition, and I remembered Mr. Wilde as I had last left him, his face all torn and bloody from the claws of that devil's creature, and what he said—ah, what he said! The alarm bell in the safe began to whirr harshly, and I knew my time was up; but I would not heed it, and replacing the flashing circlet upon my head I turned defiantly to the mirror. I stood for a long time absorbed in the changing expression of my own eyes. The mirror reflected a face which was like my own, but whiter, and so thin that I hardly recognized it. And all the time I kept repeating between my clenched teeth, "The day has come! the day has come!" while the alarm in the safe whirred and clamored, and the diamonds sparkled and flamed above my brow. I heard a door open but did not heed it. It was only when I saw two faces in the mirror;—it was only when another face rose over my shoulder, and two other eyes met mine. I wheeled like a flash and seized a long knife from my dressing-table, and my cousin sprang back very pale, crying: "Hildred! for God's sake!" then as my hand fell, he said: "It is I, Louis, don't you know me?" I stood silent. I could not have spoken for my life. He walked up to me and took the knife from my hand.

"What is all this?" he inquired, in a gentle voice. "Are you ill?"

"No," I replied. But I doubt if he heard me.

"Come, come, old fellow," he cried, "take off that brass crown and toddle into the study. Are you going to a masquerade? What's all this theatrical tinsel anyway?"

I was glad he thought the crown was made of brass and paste, yet I didn't like him any the better for thinking so. I let him take it from my hand, knowing it was best to humor him. He tossed the splendid diadem in the air, and catching it, turned to me smiling.

"It's dear at fifty cents," he said. "What's it for?"

I did not answer, but took the circlet from his hands, and placing it in the safe shut the massive steel door. The alarm ceased its infernal din at once. He watched me curiously, but did not seem to notice the sudden ceasing of the alarm. He did, however, speak of the safe as a biscuit box. Fearing lest he might examine the combination I led the way into my study. Louis threw himself on the sofa and flicked at flies with his eternal riding-whip. He wore his fatigue uniform with the braided jacket and jaunty cap, and I noticed that his riding-boots were all splashed with red mud.

"Where have you been?" I inquired.

"Jumping mud creeks in Jersey," he said. "I haven't had time to change yet; I was rather in a hurry to see you. Haven't you got a glass of something? I'm dead tired; been in the saddle twenty-four hours."

I gave him some brandy from my medicinal store, which he drank with a grimace.

"Damned bad stuff," he observed. "I'll give you an address where they sell brandy that is brandy."

"It's good enough for my needs," I said indifferently. "I use it to rub my chest with." He stared and flicked at another fly.

"See here, old fellow," he began, "I've got something to suggest to you. It's four years now that you've shut yourself up here like an owl, never going anywhere, never taking any healthy exercise, never doing a damn thing but poring over those books up there on the mantelpiece."

He glanced along the row of shelves. "Napoleon, Napoleon, Napoleon!" he read. "For heaven sake, have you nothing but Napoleons there?"

"I wish they were bound in gold," I said. "But wait, yes, there is another book, *The King in Yellow*." I looked him steadily in the eye. "Have you never read it?" I asked.

"I? No, thank God! I don't want to be driven crazy."

I saw he regretted his speech as soon as he had uttered it. There is only one word which I loathe more than I do lunatic and that word is crazy. But I controlled myself and asked him why he thought "The King in Yellow" dangerous.

"Oh, I don't know," he said, hastily. "I only remember the excitement it created and the denunciations from pulpit and press. I believe the author shot himself after bringing forth this monstrosity, didn't he?"

"I understand he is still alive," I answered.

"That's probably true," he muttered; "bullets couldn't kill a fiend like that."

"It is a book of great truths," I said.

"Yes," he replied, "of 'truths' which send men frantic and blast their lives. I don't care if the thing is, as they say, the very supreme essence of art. It's a crime to have written it, and I for one shall never open its pages."

"Is that what you have come to tell me?" I asked.

"No," he said, "I came to tell you that I am going to be married."

I believe for a moment my heart ceased to beat, but I kept my eyes on his face.

"Yes," he continued, smiling happily, "married to the sweetest girl on earth."

"Constance Hawberk," I said mechanically.

"How did you know?" he cried, astonished. "I didn't know it myself until that evening last April, when we strolled down to the embankment before dinner."

"When is it to be?" I asked.

"It was to have been next September, but an hour ago a dispatch came ordering our regiment to the Presidio, San Francisco. We leave at noon to-morrow. To-morrow," he repeated. "Just think, Hildred, to-morrow I shall be the happiest fellow that ever drew breath in this jolly world, for Constance will go with me."

I offered him my hand in congratulation, and he seized and shook it like the good-natured fool he was—or pretended to be.

"I am going to get my squadron as a wedding present," he rattled on. "Captain and Mrs. Louis Castaigne, eh, Hildred?"

Then he told me where it was to be and who were to be there, and made me promise to come and be best man. I set my teeth and listened to his boyish chatter without showing what I felt, but—

I was getting to the limit of my endurance, and when he jumped up, and, switching his spurs till they jingled, said he must go, I did not detain him.

"There's one thing I want to ask of you," I said quietly.

"Out with it, it's promised," he laughed.

"I want you to meet me for a quarter of an hour's talk to-night."

"Of course, if you wish," he said, somewhat puzzled. "Where?"

"Anywhere, in the park there."

"What time, Hildred?"

"Midnight."

"What in the name of—" he began, but checked himself and laughingly assented. I watched him go down the stairs and hurry away, his sabre banging at every stride. He turned into Bleecker Street, and I knew he was going to see Constance. I gave him ten minutes to disappear and then followed in his footsteps, taking with me the jewelled crown and the silken robe embroidered with the Yellow Sign. When I turned into Bleecker Street, and entered the doorway which bore the sign,

Mr. Wilde,

Repairer of Reputations.

3d Bell,

I saw old Hawberk moving about in his shop and imagined I heard Constance's voice in the parlor; but I avoided them both and hurried up the trembling stairways to Mr. Wilde's apartment. I knocked, and entered without ceremony. Mr. Wilde lay groaning on the floor, his face covered with blood, his clothes torn to shreds. Drops of blood were scattered about over the carpet, which had also been ripped and frayed in the evidently recent struggle.

"It's that cursed cat," he said, ceasing his groans, and turning his colorless eyes to me; "she attacked me while I was asleep. I believe she will kill me yet."

This was too much, so I went into the kitchen and seizing a hatchet from the pantry, started to find the infernal beast and settle her then and there. My search was fruitless, and after a while I gave it up and came back to find Mr. Wilde squatting on his high chair by the table. He had washed his face and changed his clothes. The great furrows which the cat's claws had ploughed up in his face he had filled with collodion, and a rag hid the wound in his throat. I told him I should kill the cat when I came across her, but he only shook his head and turned to the open ledger before him. He read name after name of the people who had come to him in regard to their reputation, and the sums he had amassed were startling.

"I put on the screws now and then," he explained.

"One day or other some of these people will assassinate you," I insisted.

"Do you think so?" he said, rubbing his mutilated ears.

It was useless to argue with him, so I took down the manuscript entitled Imperial Dynasty of America, for the last time I should ever take it down in Mr. Wilde's study. I read it through, thrilling and trembling with pleasure. When I had finished Mr. Wilde took the manuscript and, turning to the dark passage which leads from his study to his bed-chamber, called out in a loud voice, "Vance." Then for the first time, I noticed a man crouching there in the shadow. How I had overlooked him during my search for the cat, I cannot imagine.

"Vance, come in," cried Mr. Wilde.

The figure rose and crept toward us, and I shall never forget the face that he raised to mine, as the light from the window illuminated it.

"Vance, this is Mr. Castaigne," said Mr. Wilde. Before he had finished speaking, the man threw himself on the ground before the table, crying and gasping, "Oh, God! Oh, my God! Help me! Forgive me—Oh, Mr. Castaigne, keep that man away. You cannot, you cannot mean it! You are different—save me! I am broken down —I was in a madhouse and now—when all was coming right—when

I had forgotten the King—the King in Yellow and—but I shall go mad again—I shall go mad—"

His voice died into a choking rattle, for Mr. Wilde had leapt on him and his right hand encircled the man's throat. When Vance fell in a heap on the floor, Mr. Wilde clambered nimbly into his chair again, and rubbing his mangled ears with the stump of his hand, turned to me and asked me for the ledger. I reached it down from the shelf and he opened it. After a moment's searching among the beautifully written pages, he coughed complacently, and pointed to the name Vance.

"'Vance," he read aloud, "Osgood Oswald Vance." At the sound of his voice, the man on the floor raised his head and turned a convulsed face to Mr. Wilde. His eyes were injected with blood, his lips tumefied. "Called April 28th," continued Mr. Wilde. "Occupation, cashier in the Seaforth National Bank; has served a term of forgery at Sing Sing, from whence he was transferred to the Asylum for the Criminal Insane. Pardoned by the Governor of New York, and discharged from the Asylum, January 19, 1918. Reputation damaged at Sheepshead Bay. Rumors that he lives beyond his income. Reputation to be repaired at once. Retainer $1,500.

"Note—Has embezzled sums amounting to $30,000 since March 20th, 1919, excellent family, and secured present position through uncle's influence. Father President of Seaforth Bank."

I looked at the man on the floor.

"Get up, Vance," said Mr. Wilde in a gentle voice. Vance rose as if hypnotized. "He will do as we suggest now," observed Mr. Wilde, and opening the manuscript, he read the entire history of the Imperial Dynasty of America. Then in a kind and soothing murmur he ran over the important points with Vance, who stood like one stunned. His eyes were so blank and vacant that I imagined he had become half-witted, and remarked it to Mr. Wilde who replied that it was of no consequence anyway. Very patiently we pointed out to Vance what his share in the affair would be, and he seemed to understand after a while. Mr. Wilde explained the manuscript, using several volumes on Heraldry, to substantiate the result of his researches. He mentioned the establishment of the Dynasty in Carcosa, the lakes which connected Hastur, Aldebaron and the mystery of the Hyades. He spoke of Cassilda and Camilla, and sounded the cloudy depths of Demhe, and the Lake of Hali. "The scalloped tatters of the King in Yellow must hide Yhtill forever," he muttered, but I do not believe Vance heard him. Then by degrees he led Vance along the ramifications of the Imperial family, to Uoht and Thale, from Naotalba and Phantom of Truth, to Aldones, and then tossing aside his manuscript and notes, he began the wonderful story of the Last King. Fascinated and thrilled I watched him. He threw up his head, his long arms were stretched out in a magnificent gesture of pride and power, and his eyes blazed deep in their sockets like two emeralds. Vance listened stupefied. As for me, when at last Mr. Wilde had finished, and pointing to me, cried, "The cousin of the King!" my head swam with excitement.

Controlling myself with a superhuman effort, I explained to Vance why I alone was worthy of the crown and why my cousin must be exiled or die. I made him understand that my cousin must never marry, even after renouncing all his claims, and how that least of all he should marry the daughter of the Marquis of Avonshire and bring England into the question. I showed him a list of thousands of names which Mr. Wilde had drawn up; every man whose name was there had received the Yellow Sign which no living human being dared disregard. The city, the state, the whole land, were ready to rise and tremble before the Pallid Mask.

The time had come, the people should know the son of Hastur, and the whole world bow to the Black Stars which hang in the sky over Carcosa.

Vance leaned on the table, his head buried in his hands. Mr. Wilde drew a rough sketch on the margin of yesterday's *Herald* with a bit of lead pencil. It was a plan of Hawberk's rooms. Then he wrote out the order and affixed the seal, and shaking like a palsied man I signed my first writ of execution with my name Hildred-Rex.

Mr. Wilde clambered to the floor and unlocking the cabinet, took a long square box from the first shelf. This he brought to the table and opened. A new knife lay in the tissue paper inside and I picked it up and handed it to Vance, along with the order and the plan of Hawberk's apartment. Then Mr. Wilde told Vance he could go; and he went, shambling like an outcast of the slums.

I sat for a while watching the daylight fade behind the square tower of the Judson Memorial Church, and finally, gathering up the manuscript and notes, took my hat and started for the door.

Mr. Wilde watched me in silence. When I had stepped into the hall I looked back. Mr. Wilde's small eyes were still fixed on me. Behind him, the shadows gathered in the fading light. Then I closed the door behind me and went out into the darkening streets.

I had eaten nothing since breakfast, but I was not hungry. A wretched half-starved creature, who stood looking across the street at the Lethal Chamber, noticed me and came up to tell me a tale of misery. I gave him money, I don't know why, and he went away without thanking me. An hour later another outcast approached and whined his story. I had a blank bit of paper in my pocket, on which was traced the Yellow Sign and I handed it to him. He looked at it stupidly for a moment, and then with an uncertain glance at me, folded it with what seemed to me exaggerated care and placed it in his bosom.

The electric lights were sparkling among the trees, and the new moon shone in the sky above the Lethal Chamber. It was tiresome waiting in the square; I wandered from the Marble Arch to the artillery stables, and back again to the lotos fountain. The flowers and grass exhaled a fragrance which troubled me. The jet of the fountain played in the moonlight, and the musical splash of falling drops reminded me of the tinkle of chained mail in Hawberk's shop. But it was not so fascinating, and the dull sparkle of the moonlight on the water brought no such sensations of exquisite pleasure, as when the sunshine played over the polished steel of a corselet on Hawberk's knee. I watched the bats darting and turning above the water plants in the fountain basin, but their rapid, jerky flight set my nerves on edge, and I went away again to walk aimlessly to and fro among the trees.

The artillery stables were dark, but in the cavalry barracks the officer's windows were brilliantly lighted, and the sallyport was constantly filled with troopers in fatigue, carrying straw and harness and baskets filled with tin dishes.

Twice the mounted sentry at the gates was changed, while I wandered up and down the asphalt walk. I looked at my watch. It was nearly time. The lights in the barracks went out one by one, the barred gate was closed, and every minute or two an officer passed in through the side wicket, leaving a rattle of accoutrements and a jingle of spurs on the night air. The square had become very silent. The last homeless loiterer had been driven away by the gray-coated park policeman, the car tracks along Wooster Street were deserted, and the only sound which broke the stillness was the stamping of the sentry's horse and the ring of his sabre against the saddle pommel. In the barracks, the officer's quarters were still lighted, and military servants passed and repassed before the bay windows. Twelve o'clock sounded from the new spire of St. Francis Xavier, and at the last stroke of the sad-toned bell a figure passed through the wicket beside the portcullis, returned the salute of the sentry, and crossing the street entered the square and advanced toward the Benedick apartment house.

"Louis," I called.

The man pivoted on his spurred heels and came straight toward me.

"Is that you, Hildred?"

"Yes, you are on time."

I took his offered hand, and we strolled toward the Lethal Chamber.

He rattled on about his wedding and the graces of Constance, and their future prospects, calling my attention to his captain's shoulder-straps, and the triple gold arabesque on his sleeve and fatigue cap. I believe I listened as much to the music of his spurs and sabre as I did to his boyish babble, and at last we stood under the elms on the Fourth Street corner of the square opposite the Lethal Chamber. Then he laughed and asked me what I wanted with him. I motioned him to a seat on a bench under the electric light, and sat down beside him. He looked at me curiously, with that same searching glance which I hate and fear so in doctors. I felt the insult of his look, but he did not know it, and I carefully concealed my feelings.

"Well, old chap," he enquired, "what can I do for you?"

I drew from my pocket the manuscript and notes of the Imperial Dynasty of America, and looking him in the eye said:

"I will tell you. On your word as a soldier, promise me to read this manuscript from beginning to end, without asking me a question. Promise me to read these notes in the same way, and promise me to listen to what I have to tell later."

"I promise, if you wish it," he said pleasantly, "Give me the paper, Hildred."

He began to read, raising his eyebrows with a puzzled whimsical air, which made me tremble with suppressed anger. As he advanced, his eyebrows contracted, and his lips seemed to form the word, "rubbish."

Then he looked slightly bored, but apparently for my sake read, with an attempt at interest, which presently ceased to be an effort. He started when in the closely written pages he came to his own name, and when he came to mine he lowered the paper, and looked sharply at me for a moment. But he kept his word, and resumed his reading, and I let the half-formed question die on his lips unanswered. When he came to the end and read the signature of Mr. Wilde, he folded the paper carefully and returned it to me. I handed him the notes, and he settled back, pushing his fatigue cap up to his forehead, with a boyish gesture, which I remembered so well in school. I watched his face as he read, and when he finished I took the notes with the manuscript, and placed them in my pocket. Then I unfolded a scroll marked with the Yellow Sign. He saw the sign, but he did not seem to recognize it, and I called his attention to it somewhat sharply.

"Well," he said, "I see it. What is it?"

"It is the Yellow Sign," I said, angrily.

"Oh, that's it, is it?" said Louis, in that flattering voice, which Doctor Archer used to employ with me, and would probably have employed again, had I not settled his affair for him.

I kept my rage down and answered as steadily as possible, "Listen, you have engaged your word?"

"I am listening, old chap," he replied soothingly.

I began to speak very calmly.

"Dr. Archer, having by some means become possessed of the secret of the Imperial Succession, attempted to deprive me of my right, alleging that because of a fall from my horse four years ago, I had become mentally deficient. He presumed to place me under restraint in his own house in hopes of either driving me insane or poisoning me. I have not forgotten it. I visited him last night and the interview was final."

Louis turned quite pale, but did not move. I resumed triumphantly, "There are yet three people to be interviewed in the

interests of Mr. Wilde and myself. They are my cousin Louis,
Mr. Hawberk, and his daughter Constance."

Louis sprang to his feet and I arose also, and flung the paper
marked with the Yellow Sign to the ground.

"Oh, I don't need that to tell you what I have to say," I cried with
a laugh of triumph. "You must renounce the crown to me, do you
hear, to *me*."

Louis looked at me with a startled air, but recovering himself said
kindly, "Of course I renounce the—what is it I must renounce?"

"The crown," I said angrily.

"Of course," he answered, "I renounce it. Come, old chap, I'll
walk back to your rooms with you."

"Don't try any of your doctor's tricks on me," I cried, trembling
with fury. "Don't act as if you think I am insane."

"What nonsense," he replied. "Come, it's getting late, Hildred."

"No," I shouted, "you must listen. You cannot marry, I forbid
it. Do you hear? I forbid it. You shall renounce the crown, and in
reward I grant you exile, but if you refuse you shall die."

He tried to calm me but I was roused at last, and drawing my
long knife barred his way.

Then I told him how they would find Dr. Archer in the cellar
with his throat open, and I laughed in his face when I thought of
Vance and his knife, and the order signed by me.

"Ah, you are the King," I cried, "but I shall be King. Who are
you to keep me from Empire over all the habitable earth. I was born
the cousin of a king, but I shall be King!"

Louis stood white and rigid before me. Suddenly a man came
running up Fourth Street, entered the gate of the Lethal Temple,
traversed the path to the bronze doors at full speed, and plunged
into the death chamber with the cry of one demented, and I laughed
until I wept tears, for I had recognized Vance, and knew that
Hawberk and his daughter were no longer in my way.

"Go," I cried to Louis, "you have ceased to be a menace. You
will never marry Constance now, and if you marry any one else in
your exile, I will visit you as I did my doctor last night. Mr. Wilde
takes charge of you to-morrow." Then I turned and darted into
South Fifth Avenue, and with a cry of terror Louis dropped his belt
and sabre and followed me like the wind. I heard him close behind

me at the corner of Bleecker Street, and I dashed into the doorway under Hawberk's sign. He cried, "Halt, or I fire!" but when he saw that I flew up the stairs leaving Hawberk's shop below, he left me, and I heard him hammering and shouting at their door as though it were possible to arouse the dead.

Mr. Wilde's door was open, and I entered crying, "It is done, it is done! Let the nations rise and look upon their King!" but I could not find Mr. Wilde, so I went to the cabinet and took the splendid diadem from its case. Then I drew on the white silk robe, embroidered with the yellow sign, and placed the crown upon my head. At last I was King, King by my right in Hastur, King because I knew the mystery of the Hyades, and my mind had sounded the depths of the Lake of Hali. I was King! The first gray pencillings of dawn would raise a tempest which would shake two hemispheres. Then as I stood, my every nerve pitched to the highest tension, faint with the joy and splendor of my thought, without, in the dark passage, a man groaned.

I seized the tallow dip and sprang to the door. The cat passed me like a demon, and the tallow dip went out, but my long knife flew swifter than she, and I heard her screech, and I knew that my knife had found her. For a moment I listened to her tumbling and thumping about in the darkness, and then when her frenzy ceased, I lighted a lamp and raised it over my head. Mr. Wilde lay on the floor with his throat torn open. At first I thought he was dead, but as I looked, a green sparkle came into his sunken eyes, his mutilated hand trembled, and then a spasm stretched his mouth from ear to ear. For a moment my terror and despair gave place to hope, but as I bent over him his eyeballs rolled clean around in his head, and he died. Then while I stood, transfixed with rage and despair, seeing my crown, my empire, every hope and every ambition, my very life, lying prostrate there with the dead master, *they* came, seized me from behind, and bound me until my veins stood out like cords, and my voice failed with the paroxysms of my frenzied screams. But I still raged, bleeding and infuriated among them, and more than one policeman felt my sharp teeth. Then when I could no longer move they came nearer; I saw old Hawberk, and behind him my cousin Louis' ghastly face, and farther away, in the corner, a woman, Constance, weeping softly.

"Ah! I see it now!" I shrieked. "You have seized the throne and the empire. Woe! woe to you who are crowned with the crown of the King in Yellow!"

[EDITOR'S NOTE.—Mr. Castaigne died yesterday in the Asylum for Criminal Insane.]

The Demoiselle d'Ys

Mais je croy que je
Suis descendu on puiz
Tenebreux onquel disoit
Heraclytus estre Verité cachée.

There be three things which are too
wonderful for me, yea, four which I
know not:
The way of an eagle in the air; the
way of a serpent upon a rock; the way
of a ship in the midst of the sea; and
the way of a man with a maid.

I

THE utter desolation of the scene began to have its effect; I sat down
to face the situation and, if possible, recall to mind some landmark
which might aid me in extricating myself from my present position.
If I could only find the ocean again all would be clear, for I knew
one could see the island of Groix from the cliffs.

I laid down my gun, and kneeling behind a rock lighted a pipe.
Then I looked at my watch. It was nearly four o'clock. I might have
wandered far from Kerselec since daybreak.

Standing the day before on the cliffs below Kerselec with Goulven,
looking out over the sombre moors among which I had now lost my
way, these downs had appeared to me level as a meadow, stretching
to the horizon, and although I knew how deceptive is distance, I
could not realize that what from Kerselec seemed to be mere grassy
hollows were great valleys covered with gorse and heather, and what
looked like scattered boulders were in reality enormous cliffs of
granite.

"It's a bad place for a stranger," old Goulven had said; "you'd better take a guide;" and I had replied, "I shall not lose myself." Now I knew that I had lost myself, as I sat there smoking, with the sea-wind blowing in my face. On every side stretched the moorland, covered with flowering gorse and heath and granite boulders. There was not a tree in sight, much less a house. After a while, I picked up the gun, and turning my back on the sun tramped on again.

There was little use in following any of the brawling streams which every now and then crossed my path, for, instead of flowing into the sea, they ran inland to reedy pools in the hollows of the moors. I had followed several, but they all led me to swamps or silent little ponds from which the snipe rose peeping and wheeled away in an ecstasy of fright. I began to feel fatigued, and the gun galled my shoulder in spite of the double pads. The sun sank lower and lower, shining level across yellow gorse and the moorland pools.

As I walked my own gigantic shadow led me on, seeming to lengthen at every step. The gorse scraped against my leggings, crackled beneath my feet, showering the brown earth with blossoms, and the brake bowed and billowed along my path. From tufts or heath rabbits scurried away through the bracken, and among the swamp grass I heard the wild duck's drowsy quack. Once a fox stole across my path, and again, as I stooped to drink at a hurrying rill, a heron flapped heavily from the reeds beside me. I turned to look at the sun. It seemed to touch the edges of the plain. When at last I decided that it was useless to go on, and that I must make up my mind to spend at least one night on the moors, I threw myself down thoroughly fagged out. The evening sunlight slanted warm across my body, but the sea-winds began to rise, and I felt a chill strike through me from my wet shooting-boots. High overhead gulls were wheeling and tossing like bits of white paper; from some distant marsh a solitary curlew called. Little by little the sun sank into the plain, and the zenith flushed with the after-glow. I watched the sky change from palest gold to pink and then to smouldering fire. Clouds of midges danced above me, and high in the calm air a bat dipped and soared. My eyelids began to droop. Then as I shook off the drowsiness a sudden crash among the bracken roused me. I raised my eyes. A great bird hung quivering in the air above my face. For an instant I stared, incapable of motion; then something leaped past me in the ferns and the bird rose, wheeled, and pitched headlong into the brake.

I was on my feet in an instant peering through the gorse. There came the sound of a struggle from a bunch of heather close by, and then all was quiet. I stepped forward, my gun poised, but when I came to the heather the gun fell under my arm again, and I stood motionless in silent astonishment. A dead hare lay on the ground, and on the hare stood a magnificent falcon, one talon buried in the creature's neck, the other planted firmly on its limp flank. But what astonished me, was not the mere sight of a falcon sitting upon its prey. I had seen that more than once. It was that the falcon was fitted with a sort of leash about both talons, and from the leash hung a round bit of metal like a sleigh-bell. The bird turned its fierce yellow eyes on me, and then stooped and struck its curved beak into the quarry. At the same instant hurried steps sounded among the heather, and a girl sprang into the covert in front. Without a glance at me she walked up to the falcon, and passing her gloved hand under its breast, raised it from the quarry. Then she deftly slipped a small hood over the bird's head, and holding it out on her gauntlet, stooped and picked up the hare.

She passed a cord about the animal's legs and fastened the end of the thong to her girdle. Then she started to retrace her steps through the covert. As she passed me I raised my cap and she acknowledged my presence with a scarcely perceptible inclination. I had been so astonished, so lost in admiration of the scene before my eyes, that it had not occurred to me that here was my salvation. But as she moved away I recollected that unless I wanted to sleep on a windy moor that night I had better recover my speech without delay. At my first word she hesitated, and as I stepped before her I thought a look of fear came into her beautiful eyes. But as I humbly explained my unpleasant plight, her face flushed and she looked at me in wonder.

"Surely you did not come from Kerselec!" she repeated.

Her sweet voice had no trace of the Breton accent nor of any accent which I knew, and yet there was something in it I seemed to have heard before, something quaint and indefinable, like the theme of an old song.

I explained that I was an American, unacquainted with Finistère, shooting there for my own amusement.

"An American," she repeated in the same quaint musical tones. "I have never before seen an American."

For a moment she stood silent, then looking at me she said: "if you should walk all night you could not reach Kerselec now, even if you had a guide."

This was pleasant news.

"But," I began, "if I could only find a peasant's hut where I might get something to eat, and shelter."

The falcon on her wrist fluttered and shook its head. The girl smoothed its glossy back and glanced at me.

"Look around," she said gently. "Can you see the end of these moors? Look, north, south, east, west. Can you see anything but moorland and bracken?"

"No," I said.

"The moor is wild and desolate. It is easy to enter, but sometimes they who enter never leave it. There are no peasants' huts here."

"Well," I said, "if you will tell me in which direction Kerselec lies, to-morrow it will take me no longer to go back than it has to come."

She looked at me again with an expression almost like pity.

"Ah," she said, "to come is easy and takes hours; to go is different —and may take centuries."

I stared at her in amazement but decided that I had misunderstood her. Then before I had time to speak she drew a whistle from her belt and sounded it.

"Sit down and rest," she said to me; "you have come a long distance and are tired."

She gathered up her pleated skirts and motioning me to follow picked her dainty way through the gorse to a flat rock among the ferns.

"They will be here directly," she said, and taking a seat at one end of the rock invited me to sit down on the other edge. The after glow was beginning to fade in the sky and a single star twinkled faintly through the rosy haze. A long wavering triangle of water-fowl drifted southward over our heads and from the swamps around plover were calling.

"They are very beautiful—these moors," she said quietly.

"Beautiful, but cruel to strangers," I answered.

"Beautiful and cruel," she repeated dreamily, "beautiful and cruel."

"Like a woman," I said stupidly.

"Oh," she cried with a little catch in her breath and looked at me. Her dark eyes met mine and I thought she seemed angry or frightened.

"Like a woman," she repeated under her breath, "how cruel to say so!" Then after a pause, as though speaking aloud to herself, "how cruel for him to say that."

I don't know what sort of an apology I offered for my inane, though harmless speech, but I know that she seemed so troubled about it that I began to think I had said something very dreadful without knowing it, and remembered with horror the pitfalls and snares which the French language tends for foreigners. While I was trying to imagine what I might have said, a sound of voices came across the moor and the girl rose to her feet.

"No," she said, with a trace of a smile on her pale face, "I will not accept your apologies, Monsieur, but I must prove you wrong and that shall be my revenge. Look. Here come Hastur and Raoul."

Two men loomed up in the twilight. One had a sack across his shoulders and the other carried a hoop before him as a waiter carries a tray. The hoop was fastened with straps to his shoulders and around the edge of the circlet sat three hooded falcons fitted with tinkling bells. The girl stepped up to the falconer, and with a quick turn of her wrist transferred her falcon to the hoop where it quickly sidled off and nestled among its mates who shook their hooded heads and ruffled their feathers till the belled jesses tinkled again. The other man stepped forward and bowing respectfully took up the hare and dropped it into the game-sack.

"These are my piqueurs," said the girl turning to me with a gentle dignity. "Raoul is a good fauconnier and I shall some day make him grand veneur. Hastur is incomparable."

The two silent men saluted me respectfully.

"Did I not tell you, Monsieur, that I should prove you wrong?" she continued. "This then is my revenge, that you do me the courtesy of accepting food and shelter at my own house."

Before I could answer she spoke to the falconers who started instantly across the heath, and with a gracious gesture to me she followed. I don't know whether I made her understand how profoundly grateful I felt, but she seemed pleased to listen, as we walked over the dewy heather.

"Are you not very tired?" she asked.

I had clean forgotten my fatigue in her presence and I told her so.

"Don't you think your gallantry is a little old-fashioned," she said; and when I looked confused and humbled, she added quietly, "oh, I like it, I like everything old-fashioned, and it is delightful to hear you say such pretty things."

The moorland around us was very still now under its ghostly sheet of mist. The plover had ceased their calling; the crickets and all the little creatures of the fields were silent as we passed, yet it seemed to me as if I could hear them beginning again far behind us. Well in advance the two tall falconers strode across the heather and the faint jingling of the hawks' bells came to our ears in distant murmuring chimes.

Suddenly a splendid hound dashed out of the mist in front, followed by another and another until half a dozen or more were bounding and leaping around the girl beside me. She caressed and quieted them with her gloved hand, speaking to them in quaint terms which I remembered to have seen in old French manuscripts.

Then the falcons on the circlet borne by the falconer ahead began to beat their wings and scream, and from somewhere out of sight the notes of a hunting-horn floated across the moor. The hounds sprang away before us and vanished in the twilight, the falcons flapped and squealed upon their perch and the girl taking up the song of the horn began to hum. Clear and mellow her voice sounded in the night air

> Chasseur, chasseur, chassez encore,
> Quittez Rosette et Jeanneton,
> Tonton, tonton, tontaine, tonton,
> Ou, pour, rabattre, dès l'aurore,
> Que les Amours soient de planton,
> Tonton, tontaine, tonton.

As I listened to her lovely voice a gray mass which rapidly grew more distinct loomed up in front, and the horn rang out joyously through the tumult of the hounds and falcons. A torch glimmered at a gate, a light streamed through an opening door, and we stepped upon a wooden bridge which trembled under our feet and rose creaking and straining behind us as we passed over the moat and into a small stone court, walled on every side. From an open doorway a man came and bending in salutation presented a cup to the girl beside me. She took the cup and touched it with her lips, then lowering it turned to me and said in a low voice, "I bid you welcome."

At that moment one of the falconers came with another cup, but before handing it to me, presented it to the girl, who tasted it. The falconer made a gesture to receive it, but she hesitated a moment and then stepping forward offered me the cup with her own hands. I felt this to be an act of extraordinary graciousness, but hardly knew what was expected of me, and did not raise it to my lips at once. The girl flushed crimson. I saw that I must act quickly.

"Mademoiselle," I faltered, "a stranger whom you have saved from dangers he may never realize, empties this cup to the gentlest and loveliest hostess of France."

"In His name," she murmured crossing herself as I drained the cup. Then stepping into the doorway she turned to me with a pretty gesture and taking my hand in hers, led me into the house, saying again and again: "You are very welcome, indeed you are welcome to the Château d'Ys."

II

I AWOKE next morning with the music of the horn in my ears, and leaping out of the ancient bed, went to a curtained window where the sunlight filtered through little deep-set panes. The horn ceased as I looked into the court below.

A man who might have been brother to the two falconers of the night before stood in the midst of a pack of hounds. A curved horn was strapped over his back, and in his hand he held a long-lashed whip. The dogs whined and yelped, dancing around him in anticipation; there was the stamp of horses too in the walled yard.

"Mount!" cried a voice in Breton, and with a clatter of hoofs the two falconers, with falcons upon their wrists, rode into the courtyard among the hounds. Then I heard another voice which sent the blood throbbing through my heart: "Piriou Louis, hunt the hounds well and spare neither spur nor whip. Thou Raoul and thou Gaston, see that the *epervier* does not prove himself *niais*, and if it be best in your judgment, *faites courtoisie a l'oiseau. Jardiner un oiseau* like the *mué* there on Hastur's wrist is not difficult, but thou, Raoul, mayest not find it so simple to govern that *hagard.* Twice last week he foamed *au vif* and lost the *beccade* although he is used to the *leurre.* The bird acts like a stupid *branchier. Paître un hagard n'est pas si facile.*"

Was I dreaming? The old language of falconry which I had read in yellow manuscripts—the old forgotten French of the middle ages was sounding in my ears while the hounds bayed and the hawk's bells tinkled accompaniment to the stamping horses. She spoke again in the sweet forgotten language:

"If you would rather attach the *longe* and leave thy *hagard au bloc,* Raoul, I shall say nothing; for it were a pity to spoil so fair a day's sport with an ill-trained *sors. Essimer abaisser,*—it is possibly the best way. *Ça lui donnera des reins.* I was perhaps hasty with the bird. It takes time to pass *à la filière* and the exercises *d'escap.*"

Then the falconer Raoul bowed in his stirrups and replied: "If it be the pleasure of Mademoiselle, I shall keep the hawk."

"It is my wish," she answered. "Falconry I know, but you have yet to give me many a lesson in *Autourserie,* my poor Raoul. Sieur Piriou Louis, mount!"

The huntsman sprang into an archway and in an instant returned, mounted upon a strong black horse, followed by a piqueur also mounted.

"Ah!" she cried joyously, "speed Glemarec René! speed! speed all! Sound thy horn Sieur Piriou!"

The silvery music of the hunting-horn filled the courtyard, the hounds sprang through the gateway and galloping hoof-beats plunged out of the paved court; loud on the drawbridge, suddenly muffled, then lost in the heather and bracken of the moors. Distant and more distant sounded the horn, until it became so faint that the sudden carol of a soaring lark drowned it in my ears. I heard the voice below responding to some call from within the house.

"I do not regret the chase, I will go another time. Courtesy to the stranger, Pelagie, remember!"

And a feeble voice came quavering from within the house, "*Courtoisie.*"

I stripped, and rubbed myself from head to foot in the huge earthen basin of icy water which stood upon the stone floor at the foot of my bed. Then I looked about for my clothes. They were gone, but on a settle near the door lay a heap of garments which I inspected with astonishment. As my clothes had vanished I was compelled to attire myself in the costume which had evidently been placed there for me to wear while my own clothes dried. Everything was there, cap, shoes, and hunting doublet of silvery gray homespun; but the close-fitting costume and seamless shoes belonged to another century, and I remembered the strange costumes of the three falconers in the courtyard. I was sure that it was not the modern dress of any portion of France or Brittany; but not until I was dressed and stood before a mirror between the windows did I realize that I was clothed much more like a young huntsman of the middle ages than like a Breton of that day. I hesitated and picked up the cap. Should I go down and present myself in that strange guise? There seemed to be no help for it, my own clothes were gone and there was no bell in the ancient chamber to call a servant, so I contented myself with removing a short hawk's feather from the cap, and opening the door went downstairs.

By the fireplace in the large room at the foot of the stairs an old Breton woman sat spinning with a distaff. She looked up at me when I appeared, and, smiling frankly, wished me health in the Breton language, to which I laughingly replied in French. At the same moment my hostess appeared and returned my salutation with a grace and dignity that sent a thrill to my heart. Her lovely head with its dark curly hair was crowned with a head-dress which set all doubts as to the epoch of my own costume at rest. Her slender figure was exquisitely set off in the homespun hunting-gown edged with silver, and on her gauntlet-covered wrist she bore one of her petted hawks. With perfect simplicity she took my hand and led me into the garden in the court, and seating herself before a table invited me very sweetly to sit beside her. Then she asked me in her soft quaint accent how I had passed the night and whether I was very much inconvenienced by wearing the clothes which old Pelagie had put there for me while I slept. I looked at my own clothes and shoes, drying in the sun by the garden-wall, and hated them. What horrors they were compared with the graceful costume which I now wore! I told her this laughing, but she agreed with me very seriously.

"We will throw them away," she said in a quiet voice. In my

astonishment I attempted to explain that I not only could not think of accepting clothes from anybody, although for all I knew it might be the custom of hospitality in that part of the country, but that I should cut an impossible figure if I returned to France clothed as I was then.

She laughed and tossed her pretty head, saying something in old French which I did not understand, and then Pelagie trotted out with a tray on which stood two bowls of milk, a loaf of white bread, fruit, a platter of honeycomb, and a flagon of deep red wine. "You see I have not yet broken my fast because I wished you to eat with me. But I am very hungry," she smiled.

"I would rather die than forget one word of what you have said!" I blurted out while my cheeks burned, "She will think me mad," I added to myself, but she turned to me with sparkling eyes.

"Ah!" she murmured. "Then Monsieur knows all that there is of chivalry—"

She crossed herself and broke bread—I sat and watched her white hands, not daring to raise my eyes to hers.

"Will you not eat," she asked; "why do you look so troubled?"

Ah, why? I knew it now. I knew I would give my life to touch with my lips those rosy palms—I understood now that from the moment when I looked into her dark eyes there on the moor last night I had loved her. My great and sudden passion held me speechless.

"Are you ill at ease?" she asked again.

Then like a man who pronounces his own doom I answered in a low voice: "Yes, I am ill at ease for love of you." And as she did not stir nor answer, the same power moved my lips in spite of me and I said, "I, who am unworthy of the lightest of your thoughts, I who abuse hospitality and repay your gentle courtesy with bold presumption, I love you."

She leaned her head upon her hands, and answered softly, "I love you. Your words are very dear to me. I love you."

"Then I shall win you."

"Win me," she replied.

But all the time I had been sitting silent, my face turned toward her. She also silent, her sweet face resting on her upturned palm, sat facing me, and as her eyes looked into mine, I knew that neither she nor I had spoken human speech; but I knew that her soul had answered mine, and I drew myself up feeling youth and joyous love coursing through every vein. She, with a bright color in her lovely face, seemed as one awakened from a dream, and her eyes sought mine with a questioning glance which made me tremble with delight. We broke our fast, speaking of ourselves. I told her my name and she told me hers, the Demoiselle Jeanne d'Ys.

She spoke of her father and mother's death, and how the nineteen of her years had been passed in the little fortified farm alone with her nurse Pelagie, Glemarec René the piqueur, and the four falconers, Raoul, Gaston, Hastur, and the Sieur Piriou Louis, who had served her father. She had never been outside the moorland—never even had seen a human soul before, except the falconers and Pelagie. She did not know how she had heard of Kerselec; perhaps the falconers had spoken of it. She knew the legends of Loup Garou and Jeanne la Flamme from her nurse Pelagie. She embroidered and spun flax. Her hawks and hounds were her only distraction. When she had met me there on the moor she had been so frightened that she almost dropped at the sound of my voice. She had, it was true, seen ships at sea from the cliffs, but as far as the eye could reach the moors over which she galloped were destitute of any sign of human life. There was a legend which old Pelagie told, how anybody once lost in the unexplored moorland might never return, because the moors were enchanted. She did not know whether it was true; she never had thought about it until she met me. She did not know whether the falconers had even been outside or whether they could go if they would. The books in the house which Pelagie the nurse had taught her to read were hundreds of years old.

All this she told me with a sweet seriousness seldom seen in any one but children. My own name she found easy to pronounce and insisted, because my first name was Philip, I must have French blood in me. She did not seem curious to learn anything about the outside world, and I thought perhaps she considered it had forfeited her interest and respect from the stories of her nurse.

We were still sitting at the table and she was throwing grapes to the small field birds which came fearlessly to our very feet.

I began to speak in a vague way of going, but she would not hear of it, and before I knew it I had promised to stay a week and hunt with hawk and hound in their company. I also obtained permission to come again from Kerselec and visit her after my return.

"Why," she said innocently, "I do not know what I should do if you never came back;" and I, knowing that I had no right to awaken her with the sudden shock which the avowal of my own love would bring to her, sat silent, hardly daring to breathe.

"You will come very often?" she asked.

"Very often," I said.

"Every day?"

"Every day."

"Oh," she sighed, "I am very happy—come and see my hawks."

She rose and took my hand again with a childish innocence of possession, and we walked through the garden and fruit trees to a grassy lawn which was bordered by a brook. Over the lawn were scattered fifteen or twenty stumps of trees—partially imbedded in the grass—and upon all of these except two sat falcons. They were attached to the stumps by thongs which were in turn fastened with steel rivets to their legs just above the talons. A little stream of pure spring water flowed in a winding course within easy distance of each perch.

The birds set up a clamor when the girl appeared, but she went from one to another caressing some, taking others for an instant upon her wrist, or stooping to adjust their jesses.

"Are they not pretty?" she said. "See, here is a falcon-gentil. We call it 'ignoble,' because it takes the quarry in direct chase. This is a blue falcon. In falconry we call it 'noble' because it rises over the quarry, and wheeling, drops upon it from above. This white bird is a gerfalcon from the north. It is also 'noble!' Here is a merlin, and this tiercelet is a falcon-heroner."

I asked her how she had learned the old language of falconry. She did not remember, but thought her father must have taught it to her when she was very young.

Then she led me away and showed me the young falcons still in the nest. "They are termed *niais* in falconry," she explained. "A *branchier* is the young bird which is just able to leave the nest and hop from branch to branch. A young bird which has not yet moulted is called a *sors*, and a *mué* is a hawk which has moulted in captivity. When we catch a wild falcon which has changed its plumage we term it a *hagard*. Raoul first taught me to dress a falcon. Shall I teach you how it is done?"

She seated herself on the bank of the stream among the falcons and I threw myself at her feet to listen.

Then the Demoiselle d'Ys held up one rosy-tipped finger and began very gravely,

"First one must catch the falcon."

"I am caught," I answered.

She laughed very prettily and told me my *dressage* would perhaps be difficult as I was noble.

"I am already tamed," I replied; "jessed and belled."

She laughed, delighted. "Oh, my brave falcon; then you will return at my call?"

"I am yours," I answered gravely.

She sat silent for a moment. Then the color heightened in her cheeks and she held up her finger again saying, "Listen; I wish to speak of falconry—"

"I listen, Countess Jeanne d'Ys."

But again she fell into the reverie, and her eyes seemed fixed on something beyond the summer clouds.

"Philip," she said at last.

"Jeanne," I whispered.

"That is all,—that is what I wished," she sighed,—"Philip and Jeanne."

She held her hand toward me and I touched it with my lips.

"Win me," she said, but this time it was the body and soul which spoke in unison.

After a while she began again: "Let us speak of falconry."

"Begin," I replied; "we have caught the falcon."

Then Jeanne d'Ys took my hand in both of hers and told me how with infinite patience the young falcon was taught to perch upon the wrist, how little by little it became used to the belled jesses and the *chaperon à cornette*.

"They must first have a good appetite," she said; "then little by little I reduce their nourishment which in falconry we call *pât*. When after many nights passed *au bloc* as these birds are now, I prevail upon the *hagard* to stay quietly on the wrist, then the bird is ready to be taught to come for its food. I fix the *pât* to the end of a thong or *leurre,* and teach the bird to come to me as soon as I begin to whirl the cord in circles about my head. At first I drop the *pât* when the falcon comes, and he eats the food on the ground. After a little he will learn to seize the *leurre* in motion as I whirl it around my head, or drag it over the ground. After this it is easy to teach the falcon to strike at game, always remembering to '*faire courtoisie á l'oiseau,*' that is, to allow the bird to taste the quarry."

A squeal from one of the falcons interrupted her, and she arose to adjust the *longe* which had become whipped about the *bloc,* but the bird still flapped its wings and screamed.

"What *is* the matter?" she said; "Philip, can you see?"

I looked around and at first saw nothing to cause the commotion which was now heightened by the screams and flapping of all the birds. Then my eye fell upon the flat rock beside the stream from which the girl had risen. A gray serpent was moving slowly across the surface of the bowlder, and the eyes in its flat triangular head sparkled like jet.

"A couleuvre," she said quietly.

"It is harmless, is it not?" I asked.

She pointed to the black V-shaped figure on the neck.

"It is certain death," she said; "it is a viper."

We watched the reptile moving slowly over the smooth rock to where the sunlight fell in a broad warm patch.

I started forward to examine it, but she clung to my arm crying, "Don't, Philip, I am afraid."

"For me?"

"For you, Philip,—I love you."

Then I took her in my arms and kissed her on the lips, but all I could say was: "Jeanne, Jeanne, Jeanne." And as she lay trembling on my breast, something struck my foot in the grass below, but I did not heed it. Then again something struck my ankle, and a sharp pain shot through me. I looked into the sweet face of Jeanne d'Ys and kissed her, and with all my strength lifted her in my arms and flung her from me. Then bending, I tore the viper from my ankle and set my heel upon its head. I remember feeling weak and numb, —I remember falling to the ground. Through my slowly glazing eyes I saw Jeanne's white face bending close to mine, and when the light in my eyes went out I still felt her arms about my neck, and her soft cheek against my drawn lips.

When I opened my eyes, I looked around in terror. Jeanne was gone. I saw the stream and the flat rock; I saw the crushed viper in the grass beside me, but the hawks and *blocs* had disappeared, I sprang to my feet. The garden, the fruit trees, the drawbridge and the walled court were gone. I stared stupidly at a heap of crumbling ruins, ivy-covered and gray, through which great trees had pushed their way. I crept forward, dragging my numbed foot, and as I moved, a falcon sailed from the tree-tops among the ruins, and soaring, mounting in narrowing circles, faded and vanished in the clouds above.

"Jeanne, Jeanne," I cried, but my voice died on my lips, and I fell on my knees among the weeds. And as God willed it, I, not knowing, had fallen kneeling before a crumbling shrine carved in stone for our Mother of Sorrows. I saw the sad face of the Virgin wrought in the cold stone. I saw the cross and thorns at her feet, and beneath it I read:

"Pray for the soul of the
Demoiselle Jeanne d'Ys,
who died
in her youth for love of
Philip, a Stranger.
A. D. 1573."

But upon the icy slab lay a woman's glove still warm and fragrant.

The Mask

CAMILLA: You, sir, should unmask.
STRANGER: Indeed?
CASSILDA: Indeed it's time. We all
  have laid aside disguise but you.
STRANGER: I wear no mask.
CAMILLA: (Terrified, aside to Cassilda.)
  No mask? No mask?
Act I. Scene 2.

I

ALTHOUGH I knew nothing of chemistry, I listened fascinated. He picked up an Easter lily which Geneviève had brought that morning from Notre Dame and dropped it into the basin. Instantly the liquid lost its crystalline clearness. For a second the lily was enveloped in a milk-white foam, which disappeared, leaving the fluid opalescent. Changing tints of orange and crimson played over the surface, and then what seemed to be a ray of pure sunlight struck through from the bottom where the lily was resting. At the same instant he plunged his hand into the basin and drew out the flower. "There is no danger," he explained, "if you choose the right moment. That golden ray is the signal."

He held the lily toward me and I took it in my hand. It had turned to stone, to the purest marble.

"You see," he said, "it is without a flaw. What sculptor could reproduce it?"

The marble was white as snow, but in its depths the veins of the lily were tinged with palest azure, and a faint flush lingered deep in its heart.

"Don't ask me the reason of that," he smiled, noticing my wonder. "I have no idea why the veins and heart are tinted, but they always are. Yesterday I tried one of Geneviève's gold fish,—there it is."

The fish looked as if sculptured in marble. But if you held it to the light the stone was beautifully veined with a faint blue, and from somewhere within came a rosy light like the tint which slumbers in an opal. I looked into the basin. Once more it seemed filled with clearest crystal.

"If I should touch it now?" I demanded.

"I don't know," he replied, "but you had better not try."

"There is one thing I'm curious about," I said, "and that is where the ray of sunlight came from."

"It looked like a sunbeam true enough," he said. "I don't know, it always comes when I immerse any living thing. Perhaps," he continued smiling, "perhaps it is the vital spark of the creature escaping to the source from whence it came."

I saw he was mocking and threatened him with a mahl-stick, but he only laughed and changed the subject.

"Stay to lunch. Geneviève will be here directly."

"I saw her going to early mass," I said, "and she looked as fresh and sweet as that lily—before you destroyed it."

"Do you think I destroyed it?" said Boris gravely.

"Destroyed, preserved, how can we tell?"

We sat in the corner of a studio near his unfinished group of "The Fates." He leaned back on the sofa, twirling a sculptor's chisel and squinting at his work.

"By the way," he said, "I have finished pointing up that old academic Ariadne and I suppose it will have to go to the Salon. It's all I have ready this year, but after the success the 'Madonna' brought me, I feel ashamed to send a thing like that."

The "Madonna," an exquisite marble for which Geneviève had sat, had been the sensation of last year's Salon. I looked at the Ariadne. It was a magnificent piece of technical work, but I agreed with Boris that the world would expect something better of him than that. Still it was impossible now to think of finishing in time for the Salon, that splendid terrible group half shrouded in the marble behind me. "The Fates" would have to wait.

We were proud of Boris Yvain. We claimed him and he claimed us on the strength of his having been born in America, although his father was French and his mother was a Russian. Every one in the Beaux Arts called him Boris. And yet there were only two of us whom he addressed in the same familiar way; Jack Scott and myself.

Perhaps my being in love with Geneviève had something to do with his affection for me. Not that it had ever been acknowledged between us. But after all was settled, and she had told me with tears in her eyes that it was Boris whom she loved, I went over to his house and congratulated him. The perfect cordiality of that interview did not deceive either of us, I always believed, although to one at least it was a great comfort. I do not think he and Geneviève ever spoke of the matter together, but Boris knew.

Geneviève was lovely. The Madonna-like purity of her face might have been inspired by the Sanctus in Gounod's Mass. But I was always glad when she changed that mood for what we called her "April Manœuvres." She was often as variable as an April day. In the morning grave, dignified and sweet, at noon laughing, capricious, at evening whatever one least expected. I preferred her so rather than in that Madonna-like tranquillity which stirred the depths of my heart. I was dreaming of Geneviève when he spoke again.

"What do you think of my discovery, Alec?"

"I think it wonderful."

"I shall make no use of it, you know, beyond satisfying my own curiosity so far as may be and the secret will die with me."

"It would be rather a blow to sculpture, would it not? We painters lose more than we ever gain by photography."

Boris nodded, playing with the edge of the chisel.

"This new vicious discovery would corrupt the world of art. No, I shall never confide the secret to any one," he said slowly.

It would be hard to find any one less informed about such phenomena than myself; but of course I had heard of mineral springs so saturated with silica that the leaves and twigs which fell into them were turned to stone after a time. I dimly comprehended the process, how the silica replaced the vegetable matter, atom by atom, and the result was a duplicate of the object in stone. This I confess had never interested me greatly, and as for the ancient fossils thus produced, they disgusted me. Boris, it appeared, feeling curiosity instead of repugnance, had investigated the subject, and had accidentally stumbled on a solution which, attacking the immersed object with a ferocity unheard of, in a second did the work of years. This was all I could make out of the strange story he had just been telling me. He spoke again after a long silence.

"I am almost frightened when I think what I have found. Scientists would go mad over the discovery. It was so simple too; it discovered itself. When I think of that formula, and that new element precipitated in metallic scales—"

"What new element?"

"Oh, I haven't thought of naming it, and I don't believe I ever shall. There are enough precious metals now in the world to cut throats over."

I pricked up my ears. "Have you struck gold, Boris?"

"No, better;—but see here, Alec!" he laughed, starting up. "You and I have all we need in this world. Ah! how sinister and covetous you look already!" I laughed too, and told him I was devoured by the desire for gold, and we had better talk of something else; so when Geneviève came in shortly after, we had turned our backs on alchemy.

Geneviève was dressed in silvery gray from head to foot. The light glinted along the soft curves of her fair hair as she turned her cheek to Boris; then she saw me and returned my greeting. She had never before failed to blow me a kiss from the tips of her white fingers, and I promptly complained of the omission. She smiled and held out her hand which dropped almost before it had touched mine; then she said, looking at Boris,

"You must ask Alec to stay for luncheon." This also was something new. She had always asked me herself until to-day.

"I did," said Boris shortly.

"And you said yes, I hope," she turned to me with a charming conventional smile. I might have been an acquaintance of the day before yesterday. I made her a low bow. "J'avais bien l'honneur, madame," but refusing to take up our usual bantering tone she murmured a hospitable commonplace and disappeared. Boris and I looked at one another.

"I had better go home, don't you think?" I asked.

"Hanged if I know!" he replied frankly.

While we were discussing the advisability of my departure Geneviève reappeared in the doorway without her bonnet. She was wonderfully beautiful, but her color was too deep and her lovely eyes were too bright. She came straight up to me and took my arm.

"Luncheon is ready. Was I cross, Alec? I thought I had a headache but I haven't. Come here, Boris"; and she slipped her other arm through his. "Alec knows that after you there is no one in the world whom I like as well as I like him, so if he sometimes feels snubbed it won't hurt him."

"A la bonheur!" I cried, "who says there are no thunderstorms in April?"

"Are you ready?" chanted Boris. "Aye ready," and arm in arm we raced into the dining-room scandalizing the servants. After all we were not so much to blame; Geneviève was eighteen, Boris was twenty-three and I not quite twenty-one.

II

Some work that I was doing about this time on the decorations for Geneviève's boudoir kept me constantly at the quaint little hotel in the rue Sainte-Cécile. Boris and I in those days labored hard but as we pleased, which was fitfully, and we all three, with Jack Scott, idled a great deal together.

One quiet afternoon I had been wandering alone over the house examining curios, prying into odd corners, bringing out sweetmeats and cigars from strange hiding-places, and at last I stopped in the bathing-room. Boris all over clay stood there washing his hands.

The room was built of rose-colored marble excepting the floor which was tessellated in rose and gray. In the centre was a square pool sunken below the surface of the floor; steps led down into it, sculptured pillars supported a frescoed ceiling. A delicious marble Cupid appeared to have just alighted on his pedestal at the upper end of the room. The whole interior was Boris' work and mine. Boris, in his working clothes of white canvas, scraped the traces of clay and red modelling wax from his handsome hands, and coquetted over his shoulder with the Cupid.

"I see you," he insisted, "don't try to look the other way and pretend not to see me. You know who made you, little humbug!"

It was always my rôle to interpret Cupid's sentiments in these conversations, and when my turn came I responded in such a manner, that Boris seized my arm and dragged me toward the pool, declaring he would duck me. Next instant he dropped my arm and turned pale. "Good God!" he said, "I forgot the pool is full of the solution!"

I shivered a little, and drily advised him to remember better where he had stored the precious liquid.

"In Heaven's name why do you keep a small lake of that grewsome stuff here of all places!" I asked.

"I want to experiment on something large," he replied.

"On me, for instance!"

"Ah! that came too close for jesting; but I do want to watch the action of that solution on a more highly organized living body; there is that big white rabbit," he said, following me into the studio.

Jack Scott, wearing a paint-stained jacket, came wandering in, appropriated all the Oriental sweetmeats he could lay his hands on, looted the cigarette case, and finally he and Boris disappeared together to visit the Luxembourg gallery, where a new silver bronze by Rodin and a landscape of Monet's were claiming the exclusive attention of artistic France. I went back to the studio, and resumed my work. It was a Renaissance screen, which Boris wanted me to paint for Geneviève's boudoir. But the small boy who was unwillingly dawdling through a series of poses for it, to-day refused all bribes to be good. He never rested an instant in the same position, and inside of five minutes, I had as many different outlines of the little beggar.

"Are you posing, or are you executing a song and dance, my friend?" I inquired.

"Whichever monsieur pleases," he replied with an angelic smile.

Of course I dismissed him for the day, and of course I paid him for the full time, that being the way we spoil our models.

After the young imp had gone, I made a few perfunctory daubs at my work, but was so thoroughly out of humor, that it took me the rest of the afternoon to undo the damage I had done, so at last I scraped my pallette, stuck my brushes in a bowl of black soap, and strolled into the smoking-room. I really believe that, excepting Geneviève's apartments, no room in the house was so free from the perfume of tobacco as this one. It was a queer chaos of odds and ends hung with threadbare tapestry. A sweet-toned old spinet in good repair stood by the window. There were stands of weapons, some old and dull, others bright and modern, festoons of Indian and Turkish armor over the mantel, two or three good pictures, and a pipe-rack. It was here that we used to come for new sensations in smoking. I doubt if any type of pipe ever existed which was not represented in that rack. When we had selected one, we immediately carried it somewhere else and smoked it; for the place was, on the whole, more gloomy and less inviting than any in the house. But this afternoon, the twilight was very soothing, the rugs and skins on the floor looked brown and soft and drowsy; the big couch was piled with cushions, I found my pipe and curled up there for an unaccustomed smoke in the smoking-room. I had chosen one with a long flexible stem, and lighting it fell to dreaming. After a while it went out, but I did not stir. I dreamed on and presently fell asleep.

I awoke to the saddest music I had ever heard. The room was quite dark, I had no idea what time it was. A ray of moonlight silvered one edge of the old spinet, and the polished wood seemed to exhale the sounds as perfume floats above a box of sandal wood. Some one rose in the darkness, and came away weeping quietly, and I was fool enough to cry out "Geneviève!"

She dropped at my voice, and I had time to curse myself while I made a light and tried to raise her from the floor. She shrank away with a murmur of pain. She was very quiet, and asked for Boris. I carried her to the divan, and went to look for him, but he was not in the house, and the servants were gone to bed. Perplexed and anxious, I hurried back to Geneviève. She lay where I had left her, looking very white.

"I can't find Boris nor any of the servants," I said.

"I know," she answered faintly, "Boris has gone to Ept with Mr. Scott. I did not remember when I sent you for him just now."

"But he can't get back in that case before to-morrow afternoon, and—are you hurt? Did I frighten you into falling? What an awful fool I am, but I was only half awake."

"Boris thought you had gone home before dinner. Do please excuse us for letting you stay here all this time."

"I have had a long nap," I laughed, "so sound that I did not know whether I was still asleep or not when I found myself staring at a figure that was moving toward me, and called out your name. Have you been trying the old spinet? You must have played very softly."

I would tell a thousand more lies worse than that one to see the look of relief that came into her face. She smiled adorably and said in her natural voice: "Alec, I tripped on that wolf's head, and I think my ankle is sprained. Please call Marie and then go home."

I did as she bade me and left her there when the maid came in.

III

At noon next day when I called, I found Boris walking restlessly about his studio.

"Geneviève is asleep just now," he told me, "the sprain is nothing, but why should she have such a high fever? The doctor can't account for it; or else he will not," he muttered.

"Geneviève has a fever?" I asked.

"I should say so, and has actually been a little light-headed at intervals all night. The idea, gay little Geneviève, without a care in the world,—and she keeps saying her heart's broken, and she wants to die."

My own heart stood still.

Boris leaned against the door of his studio, looking down, his hands in his pockets, his kind, keen eyes clouded, a new line of trouble drawn "over the mouth's good mark, that made the smile." The maid had orders to summon him the instant Geneviève opened her eyes. We waited and waited, and Boris growing restless wandered about fussing with modelling wax and red clay. Suddenly he started for the next room. "Come and see my rose-colored bath full of death," he cried.

"Is it death?" I asked to humor his mood.

"You are not prepared to call it life, I suppose," he answered. As he spoke he plucked a solitary gold fish squirming and twisting out of its globe. "We'll send this one after the other—wherever that is," he said. There was feverish excitement in his voice. A dull weight of fever lay on my limbs and on my brain as I followed him to the fair crystal pool with its pink-tinted sides; and he dropped the creature in. Falling, its scales flashed with a hot orange gleam in its angry twistings and contortions; the moment it struck the liquid it became rigid and sank heavily to the bottom. Then came the milky foam, the splendid hues radiating on the surface and then the shaft of pure serene light broke through from seemingly infinite depths. Boris plunged in his hand and drew out an exquisite marble thing, blue-veined, rose-tinted and glistening with opalescent drops.

"Child's play," he muttered, and looked wearily, longingly at me, as if I could answer such questions. But Jack Scott came in and entered into the "game" as he called it with ardor. Nothing would do but to try the experiment on the white rabbit then and there. I was willing that Boris should find distraction from his cares, but I hated to see the life go out of a warm, living creature and I declined to be present. Picking up a book at random I sat down in the studio to read. Alas, I had found "The King in Yellow." After a few moments which seemed ages, I was putting it away with a nervous shudder, when Boris and Jack came in bringing their marble rabbit. At the same time the bell rang above and a cry came from the sick room. Boris was gone like a flash, and the next moment he called "Jack, run for the doctor; bring him back with you. Alec, come here."

I went and stood at her door. A frightened maid came out in haste and ran away to fetch some remedy. Geneviève, sitting bolt upright, with crimson cheeks and glittering eyes, babbled incessantly and resisted Boris' gentle restraint. He called me to help. At my first touch she sighed and sank back, closing her eyes, and then— then—as we still bent above her, she opened them again, looked straight into Boris' face, poor fever-crazed girl, and told her secret. At that same instant, our three lives turned into new channels; the bond that had held us so long together snapped forever and a new bond was forged in its place, for she had spoken my name, and as the fever tortured her, her heart poured out its load of hidden sorrow. Amazed and dumb I bowed my head, while my face burned like a live coal, and the blood surged in my ears, stupefying me with its clamor. Incapable of movement, incapable of speech, I listened to her feverish words in an agony of shame and sorrow. I could not silence her, I could not look at Boris. Then I felt an arm upon my shoulder, and Boris turned a bloodless face to mine.

"It is not your fault, Alec, don't grieve so if she loves you—" but he could not finish; and as the doctor stepped swiftly into the room saying—"Ah, the fever!" I seized Jack Scott and hurried him to the street saying, "Boris would rather be alone." We crossed the street to our own apartments and that night, seeing I was going to be ill too, he went for the doctor again. The last thing I recollect with any distinctness was hearing Jack say, "For Heaven's sake, doctor, what ails him, to wear a face like that?" and I thought of "The King in Yellow" and the Pallid Mask.

I was very ill, for the strain of two years which I had endured since that fatal May morning when Geneviève murmured, "I love you, but I think I love Boris best" told on me at last. I had never imagined that it could become more than I could endure. Outwardly tranquil, I had deceived myself. Although the inward battle raged night after night, and I, lying alone in my room, cursed myself for rebellious thoughts unloyal to Boris and unworthy of Geneviève, the morning always brought relief, and I returned to Geneviève and to my dear Boris with a heart washed clean by the tempests of the night.

Never in word or deed or thought while with them, had I betrayed my sorrow even to myself.

The mask of self-deception was no longer a mask for me, it was a part of me. Night lifted it, laying bare the stifled truth below; but there was no one to see except myself, and when day broke the mask fell back again of its own accord. These thoughts passed through my troubled mind as I lay sick, but they were hopelessly entangled with visions of white creatures, heavy as stone, crawling about in Boris' basin,—of the wolf's head on the rug, foaming and snapping at Geneviève, who lay smiling beside it. I thought, too, of The King in Yellow wrapt in the fantastic colors of his tattered mantle, and that bitter cry of Cassilda, "Not upon us, oh King, not upon us!" Feverishly I struggled to put it from me, but I saw the lake of Hali, thin and blank, without a ripple or wind to stir it, and I saw the towers of Carcosa behind the moon. Aldebaran, The Hyades,

Alar, Hastur, glided through the cloud rifts which fluttered and flapped as they passed like scolloped tatters of The King in Yellow. Among all these, one sane thought persisted. It never wavered, no matter what else was going on in my disordered mind, that my chief reason for existing, was to meet some requirement of Boris and Geneviève. What this obligation was, its nature was never clear; sometimes it seemed to be protection, sometimes support through a great crisis. Whatever it seemed to be for the time, its weight rested only on me, and I was never so ill or so weak that I did not respond with my whole soul. There were always crowds of faces about me, mostly strange, but a few I recognized, Boris among them. Afterward they told me that this could not have been, but I know that once at least he bent over me. It was only a touch, a faint echo of his voice, then the clouds settled back on my senses, and I lost him, but he *did* stand there and bend over me *once* at least.

At last, one morning I awoke to find the sunlight falling across my bed, and Jack Scott reading beside me. I had not strength enough to speak aloud, neither could I think, much less remember, but I could smile feebly, as Jack's eye met mine, and when he jumped up and asked eagerly if I wanted anything, I could whisper, "Yes, Boris." Jack moved to the head of my bed, and leaned down to arrange my pillow: I did not see his face, but he answered heartily, "You must wait Alec, you are too weak to see even Boris."

I waited and I grew strong; in a few days I was able to see whom I would, but meanwhile I had thought and remembered. From the moment when all the past grew clear again in my mind, I never doubted what I should do when the time came, and I felt sure that Boris would have resolved upon the same course so far as he was concerned; as for what pertained to me alone, I knew he would see that also as I did. I no longer asked for any one. I never inquired why no message came from them; why during the week I lay there, waiting and growing stronger, I never heard their name spoken. Preoccupied with my own searchings for the right way, and with my feeble but determined fight against despair, I simply acquiesced in Jack's reticence, taking for granted that he was afraid to speak of them, lest I should turn unruly and insist on seeing them. Meanwhile I said over and over to myself, how it would be when life began again for us all. We would take up our relations exactly as they were before Geneviève fell ill. Boris and I would look into each other's eyes and there would be neither rancor nor cowardice nor mistrust in that glance. I would be with them again for a little while in the dear intimacy of their home, and then, without pretext or explanation, I would disappear from their lives forever. Boris would know, Geneviève—the only comfort was that she would never know. It seemed, as I thought it over, that I had found the meaning of that sense of obligation which had persisted all through my delirium, and the only possible answer to it. So, when I was quite ready, I beckoned Jack to me one day, and said,

"Jack, I want Boris at once; and take my dearest greeting to Geneviève. . . ."

When at last he made me understand that they were both dead, I fell into such a wild rage as to throw all my little convalescent strength to atoms. I raved and cursed myself into a relapse, from which I crawled forth some weeks afterward a boy of twenty-one who believed that his youth was gone forever. I seemed to be past the capability of further suffering, and one day when Jack handed me a letter and the keys to Boris' house, I took them without a tremor and asked him to tell me all. It was cruel of me to ask him, but there was no help for it, and he leaned wearily on his thin hands, to reopen the wound which could never entirely heal. He began very quietly.

"Alec, unless you have a clue that I know nothing about, you will not be able to explain any more than I, what has happened. I suspect that you would rather not hear these details, but you must learn them, else I would spare them the relation. God knows I wish I could be spared the telling. I shall use few words.

"That day when I left you in the doctor's care and came back to Boris, I found him working on the 'Fates.' Geneviève, he said, was sleeping under the influence of drugs. She had been quite out of her mind, he said. He kept on working, not talking any more, and I watched him. Before long, I saw that the third figure of the group —the one looking straight ahead, out over the world—bore his face; not as you ever saw it, but as it looked then and to the end. This is one thing for which I should like to find an explanation, but I never shall.

"Well, he worked and I watched him in silence, and we went on that way until nearly midnight. Then we heard a door open and shut sharply, and a swift rush in the next room. Boris sprang through the doorway and I followed; but we were too late. She lay at the bottom of the pool, her hands across her breast. Then Boris shot himself through the heart." Jack stopped speaking, drops of sweat stood under his eyes, and his thin cheeks twitched. "I carried Boris to his room. Then I went back and let that hellish fluid out of the pool, and turning on all the water, washed the marble clean of every drop. When at length I dared descend the steps, I found her lying there as white as snow. At last, when I had decided what was best to do, I went into the laboratory, and first emptied the solution in the basin into the waste-pipe; then I poured the contents of every jar and bottle after it. There was wood in the fire-place, so I built a fire, and breaking the locks of Boris' cabinet I burnt every paper, note-book and letter that I found there. With a mallet from the studio I smashed to pieces all the empty bottles, then loading them into a coal scuttle, I carried them to the cellar and threw them over the red-hot bed of the furnace. Six times I made the journey, and at last, not a vestige remained of anything which might again aid in seeking for the formula which Boris had found. Then at last I dared call the doctor. He is a good man, and together we struggled to keep it from the public. Without him I never could have succeeded. At last we got the servants paid and sent away into the country, where old Rosier keeps them quiet with stories of Boris' and Geneviève's travels in distant lands, from whence they will not return for years. We buried Boris in the little cemetery of Sèvres. The doctor is a good creature and knows when to pity a man who can bear no more. He gave his certificate of heart disease and asked no questions of me."

Then lifting his head from his hands, he said, "Open the letter, Alec; it is for us both."

I tore it open. It was Boris' will dated a year before. He left everything to Geneviève, and in case of her dying childless, I was to take control of the house in the Rue Sainte-Cécile, and Jack Scott, the management at Ept. On our deaths the property reverted to his mother's family in Russia, with the exception of the sculptured marbles executed by himself. These he left to me.

The page blurred under our eyes, and Jack got up and walked to the window. Presently he returned and sat down again. I dreaded to hear what he was going to say, but he spoke with the same simplicity and gentleness.

"Geneviève lies before the Madonna in the marble room. The Madonna bends tenderly above her, and Geneviève smiles back into that calm face that never would have been except for her."

His voice broke, but he grasped my hand, saying, "Courage, Alec." Next morning he left for Ept to fulfil his trust.

IV

THE same evening I took the keys and went into the house I had known so well. Everything was in order, but the silence was terrible. Though I went twice to the door of the marble room, I could not force myself to enter. It was beyond my strength. I went into the smoking-room and sat down before the spinet. A small lace handkerchief lay on the keys, and I turned away, choking. It was plain I could not stay, so I locked every door, every window, and the three front and back gates, and went away. Next morning Alcide packed my valise, and leaving him in charge of my apartments I took the Orient express for Constantinople. During the two years that I wandered through the East, at first, in our letters, we never mentioned Geneviève and Boris, but gradually their names crept in. I recollect particularly a passage in one of Jack's letters replying to one of mine.

"What you tell me of seeing Boris bending over you while you lay ill, and feeling his touch on your face, and hearing his voice of course troubles me. This that you describe must have happened a fortnight after he died. I say to myself that you were dreaming, that it was part of your delirium, but the explanation does not satisfy me, nor would it you."

Toward the end of the second year a letter came from Jack to me in India so unlike any thing that I had ever known of him that I decided to return at once to Paris. He wrote, "I am well and sell all my pictures as artists do, who have no need of money. I have not a care of my own, but I am more restless than if I had. I am unable to shake off a strange anxiety about you. It is not apprehension, it is rather a breathless expectancy, of what God knows. I can only say it is wearing me out. Nights I dream always of you and Boris.

I can never recall anything afterward, but I wake in the morning with my heart beating, and all day the excitement increases until I fall asleep at night to recall the same experience. I am quite exhausted by it, and have determined to break up this morbid condition. I must see you. Shall I go to Bombay or will you come to Paris?"

I telegraphed him to expect me by the next steamer.

When we met I thought he had changed very little; I, he insisted, looked in splendid health. It was good to hear his voice again, and as we sat and chatted about what life still held for us, we felt that it was pleasant to be alive in the bright spring weather.

We stayed in Paris together a week, and then I went for a week to Ept with him, but first of all we went to the cemetery at Sèvres, where Boris lay.

"Shall we place the 'Fates' in the little grove above him?" Jack asked, and I answered,

"I think only the 'Madonna' should watch over Boris' grave."

But Jack was none the better for my home-coming. The dreams of which he could not retain even the least definite outline continued, and he said that at times the sense of breathless expectancy was suffocating.

"You see I do you harm and not good," I said. "Try a change without me." So he started alone for a ramble among the Channel Islands and I went back to Paris. I had not yet entered Boris' house, now mine, since my return, but I knew it must be done. It had been kept in order by Jack; there were servants there, so I gave up my own apartment and went there to live. Instead of the agitation I had feared, I found myself able to paint there tranquilly. I visited all the rooms—all but one. I could not bring myself to enter the marble room where Geneviève lay, and yet I felt the longing growing daily to look upon her face, to kneel beside her.

One April afternoon, I lay dreaming in the smoking-room, just as I had lain two years before, and mechanically I looked among the tawny Eastern rugs for the wolf-skin. At last I distinguished the pointed ears and flat cruel head, and I thought of my dream where I saw Geneviève lying beside it. The helmets still hung against the threadbare tapestry, among them the old Spanish morion which I remembered Geneviève had once put on when we were amusing ourselves with the ancient bits of mail. I turned my eyes to the spinet;

every yellow key seemed eloquent of her caressing hand, and I rose, drawn by the strength of my life's passion to the sealed door of the marble room. The heavy doors swung inward under my trembling hands. Sunlight poured through the window, tipping with gold the wings of Cupid, and lingered like a nimbus over the brows of the Madonna. Her tender face bent in compassion over a marble form so exquisitely pure that I knelt and signed myself. Geneviève lay in the shadow under the Madonna, and yet, through her white arms, I saw the pale azure vein, and beneath her softly clasped hands the folds of her dress were tinged with rose, as if from some faint warm light within her breast.

Bending with a breaking heart I touched the marble drapery with my lips, then crept back into the silent house.

A maid came and brought me a letter, and I sat down in the little conservatory to read it; but as I was about to break the seal, seeing the girl lingering, I asked her what she wanted.

She stammered something about a white rabbit that had been caught in the house and asked what should be done with it. I told her to let it loose in the walled garden behind the house and opened my letter. It was from Jack, but so incoherent that I thought he must have lost his reason. It was nothing but a series of prayers to me not to leave the house until he could get back; he could not tell me why, there were the dreams, he said—he could explain nothing, but he was sure that I must not leave the house in the Rue Sainte-Cécile.

As I finished reading I raised my eyes and saw the same maid-servant standing in the doorway holding a glass dish in which two gold fish were swimming: "Put them back into the tank and tell me what you mean by interrupting me," I said.

With a half suppressed whimper she emptied water and fish into an aquarium at the end of the conservatory, and turning to me asked my permission to leave my service. She said people were playing tricks on her, evidently with a design of getting her into trouble; the marble rabbit had been stolen and a live one had been brought into the house; the two beautiful marble fish were gone and she had just found those common live things flopping on the dining-room floor. I reassured her and sent her away saying I would look about myself. I went into the studio; there was nothing there but my canvasses and some casts, except the marble of the Easter Lily. I saw it on a table across the room. Then I strode angrily over to it. But the flower I lifted from the table was fresh and fragile and filled the air with perfume.

Then suddenly I comprehended and sprang through the hall-way to the marble room. The doors flew open, the sunlight streamed into my face and through it, in a heavenly glory, the Madonna smiled, as Geneviève lifted her flushed face from her marble couch, and opened her sleepy eyes.

In the Court
of the Dragon

Oh Thou who burn'st in heart for those who burn
In Hell, whose fires thyself shall feed in turn;
How long be crying, "Mercy on them, God!"
Why, who art thou to teach and He to learn?

In the Church of St. Barnabé vespers were over; the clergy left the altar; the little choir-boys flocked across the chancel and settled in the stalls. A Suisse in rich uniform marched down the south aisle, sounding his staff at every fourth step on the stone pavement; behind him came that eloquent preacher and good man, Monseigneur C—.

My chair was near the chancel rail. I now turned toward the west end of the church. The other people between the altar and the pulpit turned too. There was a little scraping and rustling while the congregation seated itself again; the preacher mounted the pulpit stairs, and the organ voluntary ceased.

I had always found the organ-playing at St. Barnabé highly interesting. Learned and scientific, it was too much for my small knowledge, but expressing a vivid if cold intelligence. Moreover, it possessed the French quality of taste. Taste reigned supreme, self-controlled, dignified and reticent.

To-day, however, from the first chord I had felt a change for the worse, a sinister change. During vespers it had been chiefly the chancel organ which supported the beautiful choir, but now and again, quite wantonly as it seemed, from the west gallery where the great organ stands, a heavy hand had struck across the church, at the serene peace of those clear voices. It was something more than harsh and dissonant, and it betrayed no lack of skill. As it recurred again and again, it set me thinking of what my architect's books say about the custom in early times to consecrate the choir as soon as it was built, and that the nave, being finished sometimes half a century later, often did not get any blessing at all: I wondered idly if that had been the case as St. Barnabé, and whether something not usually supposed to be at home in a Christian church, might have entered undetected, and taken possession of the west gallery. I had read of such things happening too, but not in works on architecture.

Then I remembered that St. Barnabé was not much more than a hundred years old, and smiled at the incongruous association of mediæval superstitions with that cheerful little piece of eighteenth century rococo.

But now vespers were over, and there should have followed a few quiet chords, fit to accompany meditation, while we waited for the sermon. Instead of that, the discord at the lower end of the church broke out with the departure of the clergy, as if now nothing could control it.

I belong to those children of an older and simpler generation, who do not love to seek for psychological subtleties in art; and I have ever refused to find in music anything more than melody and harmony, but I felt that in the labyrinth of sounds now issuing from that instrument there was something being hunted. Up and down the pedals chased him, while the manuals blared approval. Poor devil! whoever he was, there seemed small hope of escape!

My nervous annoyance changed to anger. Who was doing this? How dare he play like that in the midst of divine service? I glanced at the people near me: not one appeared to be in the least disturbed. The placid brows of the kneeling nuns, still turned toward the altar, lost none of their devout abstraction, under the pale shadow of their white head-dress. The fashionable lady beside me was looking expectantly at Monseigneur C—. For all her face betrayed, the organ might have been singing an Ave Maria.

But now, at last, the preacher had made the sign of the cross, and commanded silence. I turned to him gladly. Thus far I had not found the rest I had counted on, when I entered St. Barnabé that afternoon.

I was worn out by three nights of physical suffering and mental trouble: the last had been the worst, and it was an exhausted body, and a mind benumbed and yet acutely sensitive, which I had brought to my favorite church for healing. For I had been reading "The King in Yellow."

"The sun ariseth; they gather themselves together and lay them down in their dens." Monseigneur C— delivered his text in a calm voice, glancing quietly over the congregation. My eyes turned, I knew not why, toward the lower end of the church. The organist was coming from behind his pipes, and passing along the gallery on his way out, I saw him disappear by a small door that leads to some stairs which descend directly to the street. He was a slender man, and his face was as white as his coat was black. "Good riddance!" I thought, "with your wicked music! I hope your assistant will play the closing voluntary."

With a feeling of relief, with a deep, calm feeling of relief, I turned back to the mild face in the pulpit, and settled myself to listen. Here at last, was the ease of mind I longed for.

"My children," said the preacher, "one truth the human soul finds hardest of all to learn; that it has nothing to fear. It can never be made to see that nothing can really harm it."

"Curious doctrine!" I thought, "for a Catholic priest. Let us see how he will reconcile that with the Fathers."

"Nothing can really harm the soul," he went on, in his coolest, clearest tones, "because—"

But I never heard the rest; my eye left his face, I knew not for what reason, and sought the lower end of the church. The same man was coming out from behind the organ, and was passing along the gallery *the same way*. But there had not been time for him to return, and if he had returned, I must have seen him. I felt a faint chill, and my heart sank; and yet, his going and coming were no affair of mine. I looked at him: I could not look away from his black figure and his white face. When he was exactly opposite to me, he turned and sent across the church, straight into my eyes, a look of hate, intense and deadly: I have never seen any other like it; would to God I might never see it again! Then he disappeared by the same door through which I had watched him depart less than sixty seconds before.

I sat and tried to collect my thoughts. My first sensation was like that of a very young child badly hurt, when it catches its breath before crying out.

To suddenly find myself the object of such hatred was exquisitely painful: and this man was an utter stranger. Why should he hate me so? Me, whom he had never seen before? For the moment all other sensation was merged in this one pang: even fear was subordinate to grief, and for that moment I never doubted; but in the next I began to reason, and a sense of the incongruous came to my aid.

As I have said, St. Barnabé is a modern church. It is small and well lighted; one sees all over it almost at a glance. The organ gallery gets a strong white light from a row of long windows in the clerestory, which have not even colored glass.

The pulpit being in the middle of the church, it followed that, when I was turned toward it, whatever moved at the west end could not fail to attract my eye. When the organist passed it was no wonder that I saw him: I had simply miscalculated the interval between his first and his second passing. He had come in that last time by the other side-door. As for the look which had so upset me, there had been no such thing, and I was a nervous fool.

I looked about. This was a likely place to harbor supernatural horrors! That clear-cut, reasonable face of Monseigneur C—, his collected manner, and easy, graceful gestures, were they not just a little discouraging to the notion of a gruesome mystery? I glanced above his head, and almost laughed. That flyaway lady, supporting one corner of the pulpit canopy, which looked like a fringed damask table-cloth in a high wind, at the first attempt of a basilisk to pose up there in the organ loft, she would point her gold trumpet at him, and puff him out of existence! I laughed to myself over this conceit, which, at the time, I thought very amusing, and sat and chaffed myself and everything else, from the old harpy outside the railing, who had made me pay ten centimes for my chair, before she would let me in (she was more like a basilisk, I told myself, than was my organist with the anæmic complexion): from that grim old dame, to, yes, alas! to Monseigneur C—, himself. For all devoutness had fled. I had never yet done such a thing in my life, but now I felt a desire to mock.

As for the sermon, I could not hear a word of it, for the jingle in my ears of

> The skirts of St. Paul has reached,
> Having preached us those six Lent lectures,
> More unctuous than ever he preached:

keeping time to the most fantastic and irreverent thoughts.

It was no use to sit there any longer: I must get out of doors and shake myself free from this hateful mood. I knew the rudeness I was committing, but still I rose and left the church.

A spring sun was shining on the rue St. Honoré, as I ran down the church steps. On one corner stood a barrow full of yellow jonquils, pale violets from the Riviera, dark Russian violets, and white Roman hyacinths in a golden cloud of mimosa. The street was full of Sunday pleasure seekers. I swung my cane and laughed with the rest. Some one overtook and passed me. He never turned, but there was the same deadly malignity in his white profile that there had been in his eyes. I watched him as long as I could see him. His lithe back expressed the same menace; every step that carried him away from me seemed to bear him on some errand connected with my destruction.

I was creeping along, my feet almost refusing to move. There began to dawn in me a sense of responsibility for something long forgotten. It began to seem as if I deserved that which he threatened: it reached a long way back—a long, long way back. It had lain dormant all these years: it was there though, and presently it would rise and confront me. But I would try to escape; and I stumbled as best I could into the rue de Rivoli, across the Place de la Concorde and on to the Quai. I looked with sick eyes upon the sun, shining through the white foam of the fountain, pouring over the backs of the dusky bronze river-gods, on the far-away Arc, a structure of amethyst mist, on the countless vistas of gray stems and bare branches faintly green. Then I saw him again coming down one of the chestnut alleys of the Cours la Reine.

I left the river side, plunged blindly across to the Champs Elysées and turned toward the Arc. The setting sun was sending its rays along the green sward of the Rond-point: in the full glow he sat on a bench, children and young mothers all about him. He was nothing but a Sunday lounger, like the others, like myself. I said the words almost aloud, and all the while I gazed on the malignant hatred of his face. But he was not looking at me. I crept past and dragged my leaden feet up the Avenue. I knew that every time I met him brought him nearer to the accomplishment of his purpose and my fate. And still I tried to save myself.

The last rays of sunset were pouring through the great Arc. I passed under it, and met him face to face. I had left him far down the Champs Elysées, and yet he came in with a stream of people who were returning from the Bois de Boulogne. He came so close that he brushed me. His slender frame felt like iron inside its loose black covering. He showed no signs of haste, nor of fatigue, nor of any human feeling. His whole being expressed but one thing: the will, and the power to work me evil.

In anguish I watched him, where he went down the broad crowded Avenue, that was all flashing with wheels and the trappings of horses, and the helmets of the Garde Republicaine.

He was soon lost to sight; then I turned and fled. Into the Bois, and far out beyond it—I know not where I went, but after a long while as it seemed to me, night had fallen, and I found myself sitting at a table before a small café. I had wandered back into the Bois. It was hours now since I had seen him. Physical fatigue, and mental suffering had left me no more power to think or feel. I was tired, so tired! I longed to hide away in my own den. I resolved to go home. But that was a long way off.

I live in the Court of the Dragon, a narrow passage that leads from the rue de Rennes to the rue du Dragon.

It is an "Impasse;" traversable only for foot passengers. Over the entrance on the rue de Rennes is a balcony, supported by an iron dragon. Within the court tall old houses rise on either side, and close the ends that give on the two streets. Huge gates, swung back during the day into the walls of the deep archways, close this court, after midnight, and one must enter then by ringing at certain small doors on the side. The sunken pavement collects unsavory pools. Steep stairways pitch down to doors that open on the court. The ground floors are occupied by shops of second-hand dealers, and by iron workers. All day long the place rings with the clink of hammers, and the clang of metal bars.

Unsavory as it is below, there is cheerfulness, and comfort, and hard, honest work above.

Five flights up are the ateliers of architects and painters, and the hiding-places of middle-aged students like myself who want to live alone. When I first came here to live I was young, and not alone.

I had to walk awhile before any conveyance appeared, but at last, when I had almost reached the Arc de Triomphe again, an empty cab came along and I took it.

From the Arc to the rue de Rennes is a drive of more than half an hour, especially when one is conveyed by a tired cab horse that has been at the mercy of Sunday fête makers.

There had been time before I passed under the Dragon's wings, to meet my enemy over and over again, but I never saw him once, and now refuge was close at hand.

Before the wide gateway a small mob of children were playing. Our concierge and his wife walked about among them with their black poodle, keeping order; some couples were waltzing on the side-walk. I returned their greetings and hurried in.

All the inhabitants of the court had trooped out into the street. The place was quite deserted, lighted by a few lanterns hung high up, in which the gas burned dimly.

My apartment was at the top of the house, half way down the court, reached by a staircase that descended almost into the street, with only a bit of passage-way intervening. I set my foot on the threshold of the open door, the friendly, old ruinous stairs rose before me, leading up to rest and shelter. Looking back over my right shoulder, I saw *him*, ten paces off. He must have entered the court with me.

He was coming straight on, neither slowly, nor swiftly, but straight on to me. And now he was looking at me. For the first time since our eyes encountered across the church they met now again, and I knew that the time had come.

Retreating backward, down the court, I faced him. I meant to escape by the entrance on the rue du Dragon. His eyes told me that I never should escape.

It seemed ages while we were going, I retreating, he advancing, down the court in perfect silence; but at last I felt the shadow of the archway, and the next step brought me within it. I had meant to turn here and spring through into the street. But the shadow was not that of an archway; it was that of a vault. The great doors on the rue du Dragon were closed. I felt this by the blackness which surrounded me, and at the same instant I read it in his face. How his face gleamed in the darkness, drawing swiftly nearer! The deep vaults, the huge closed doors, their cold iron clamps were all on his side. The thing which he had threatened had arrived: it gathered and bore down on me from the fathomless shadows; the point from which it would strike was his infernal eyes. Hopeless I set my back against the barred doors and defied him.

There was a scraping of chairs on the stone floor, and a rustling as the congregation rose. I could hear the Suisse's staff in the south aisle, preceding Monseigneur C— to the sacristy.

The kneeling nuns, roused from their devout abstraction, made their reverence and went away. The fashionable lady, my neighbor, rose also, with graceful reserve. As she departed her glance just flitted over my face in disapproval.

Half dead, or so it seemed to me, yet intensely alive to every trifle, I sat among the leisurely moving crowd, then rose too and went toward the door.

I had slept through the sermon. Had I slept through the sermon? I looked up and saw him passing along the gallery to his place. Only his side I saw; the thin bent arm in its black covering looked like one of those devilish, nameless instruments which lie in the disused torture chambers of mediæval castles.

But I had escaped him, though his eyes had said I should not. *Had* I escaped him? That which gave him the power over me came back out of oblivion, where I had hoped to keep it. For I knew him now. Death and the awful abode of lost souls, whither my weakness long ago had sent him—they had changed him for every other eye, but not for mine. I had recognized him almost from the first; I had never doubted what he was come to do; and now I knew that while my body sat safe in the cheerful little church, he had been hunting my soul in the Court of the Dragon.

I crept to the door; the organ broke out overhead with a blare. A dazzling light filled the church, blotting the altar from my eyes. The people faded away, the arches, the vaulted roof vanished. I raised my seared eyes to the fathomless glare, and I saw the black stars hanging in the heavens: and the wet winds from the Lake of Hali chilled my face.

And now, far away, over leagues of tossing cloud-waves, I saw the moon dripping with spray; and beyond, the towers of Carcosa rose behind the moon.

Death and the awful abode of lost souls, whither my weakness long ago had sent him, had changed him for every other eye but mine. And now I heard *his voice*, rising, swelling, thundering through the flaring light, and as I fell, the radiance increasing, increasing, poured over me in waves of flame. Then I sank into the depths, and I heard the King in Yellow whispering to my soul: "It is a fearful thing to fall into the hands of the living God!"

The Maker of Moons

I have heard what the Talkers were talking,—the talk
Of the beginning and the end;
But I do not talk of the beginning or the end.

I

CONCERNING Yue-Laou and the Xin I know nothing more than you
shall know. I am miserably anxious to clear the matter up. Perhaps
what I write may save the United States Government money and
lives, perhaps it may arouse the scientific world to action; at any
rate it will put an end to the terrible suspense of two people. Certainty
is better than suspense.

If the Government dares to disregard this warning and refuses to
send a thoroughly equipped expedition at once, the people of the
State may take swift vengeance on the whole region and leave a
blackened devastated waste where to-day forest and flowering
meadow land border the lake in the Cardinal Woods.

You already know part of the story; the New York papers have
been full of alleged details. This much is true: Barris caught the
"Shiner," red handed, or rather yellow handed, for his pockets and
boots and dirty fists were stuffed with lumps of gold. I say gold,
advisedly. You may call it what you please. You also know how
Barris was—but unless I begin at the beginning of my own experiences you will be none the wiser after all.

On the third of August of this present year I was standing in
Tiffany's, chatting with George Godfrey of the designing department.

On the glass counter between us lay a coiled serpent, an exquisite specimen of chiselled gold.

"No," replied Godfrey to my question, "it isn't my work; I wish it was. Why, man, it's a masterpiece!"

"Whose?" I asked.

"Now I should be very glad to know also," said Godfrey. "We bought it from an old jay who says he lives in the country somewhere about the Cardinal Woods. That's near Starlit Lake, I believe—"

"Lake of the Stars?" I suggested

"Some call it Starlit Lake,—it's all the same. Well, my rustic Reuben says that he represents the sculptor of this snake for all practical and business purposes. He got his price too. We hope he'll bring us something more. We have sold this already to the Metropolitan Museum."

I was leaning idly on the glass case, watching the keen eyes of the artist in precious metals as he stooped over the gold serpent.

"A masterpiece!" he muttered to himself, fondling the glittering coil; "look at the texture! whew!" But I was not looking at the serpent. Something was moving,—crawling out of Godfrey's coat pocket,—the pocket nearest to me,—something soft and yellow with crab-like legs all covered with coarse yellow hair.

"What in Heaven's name," said I, "have you got in your pocket? It's crawling out—it's trying to creep up your coat, Godfrey!"

He turned quickly and dragged the creature out with his left hand.

I shrank back as he held the repulsive object dangling before me, and he laughed and placed it on the counter.

"Did you ever see anything like that?" he demanded.

"No," said I truthfully, "and I hope I never shall again. What is it?"

"I don't know. Ask them at the Natural History Museum—they can't tell you. The Smithsonian is all at sea too. It is, I believe, the connecting link between a sea-urchin, a spider, and the devil. It looks venomous but I can't find either fangs or mouth. Is it blind? These things may be eyes but they look as if they were painted. A Japanese sculptor might have produced such an impossible beast, but it is hard to believe that God did. It looks unfinished too. I have a mad idea that this creature is only one of the parts of some larger and more grotesque organism,—it looks so lonely, so hopelessly dependent, so cursedly unfinished. I'm going to use it as a model. If I don't out-Japanese the Japs my name isn't Godfrey."

The creature was moving slowly across the glass case towards me. I drew back.

"Godfrey," I said, "I would execute a man who executed any such work as you propose. What do you want to perpetuate such a reptile for? I can stand the Japanese grotesque but I can't stand that—spider—"

"It's a crab."

"Crab or spider or blind-worm—ugh! What do you want to do it for? It's a nightmare—it's unclean!"

I hated the thing. It was the first living creature that I had ever hated.

For some time I had noticed a damp acrid odour in the air, and Godfrey said it came from the reptile.

"Then kill it and bury it," I said; "and by the way, where did it come from?"

"I don't know that either," laughed Godfrey; "I found it clinging to the box that this gold serpent was brought in. I suppose my old Reuben is responsible."

"If the Cardinal Woods are the lurking places for things like this," said I, "I am sorry that I am going to the Cardinal Woods."

"Are you?" asked Godfrey; "for the shooting?"

"Yes, with Barris and Pierpont. Why don't you kill that creature?"

"Go off on your shooting trip, and let me alone," laughed Godfrey.

I shuddered at the "crab," and bade Godfrey good-bye until December.

That night, Pierpont, Barris, and I sat chatting in the smoking-car of the Quebec Express when the long train pulled out of the Grand Central Depot. Old David had gone forward with the dogs; poor things, they hated to ride in the baggage car, but the Quebec and Northern road provides no sportsman's cars, and David and the three Gordon setters were in for an uncomfortable night.

Except for Pierpont, Barris, and myself, the car was empty. Barris, trim, stout, ruddy, and bronzed, sat drumming on the window ledge, puffing a short fragrant pipe. His gun-case lay beside him on the floor.

"When *I* have white hair and years of discretion," said Pierpont languidly, "I'll not flirt with pretty serving-maids; will you, Roy?"

"No," said I, looking at Barris.

"You mean the maid with the cap in the Pullman car?" asked Barris.

"Yes," said Pierpont.

I smiled, for I had seen it also.

Barris twisted his crisp grey moustache, and yawned.

"You children had better be toddling off to bed," he said. "That lady's-maid is a member of the Secret Service."

"Oh," said Pierpont, "one of your colleagues?"

"You might present us, you know," I said; "the journey is monotonous."

Barris had drawn a telegram from his pocket, and as he sat turning it over and over between his fingers he smiled. After a moment or two he handed it to Pierpont who read it with slightly raised eyebrows.

"It's rot,—I suppose it's cipher," he said; "I see it's signed by General Drummond—"

"Drummond, Chief of the Government Secret Service," said Barris.

"Something interesting?" I enquired, lighting a cigarette.

"Something so interesting," replied Barris, "that I'm going to look into it myself—"

"And break up our shooting trio—"

"No. Do you want to hear about it? Do you Billy Pierpont?"

"Yes," replied that immaculate young man.

Barris rubbed the amber mouth-piece of his pipe on his handkerchief, cleared the stem with a bit of wire, puffed once or twice, and leaned back in his chair.

"Pierpont," he said, "do you remember that evening at the United States Club when General Miles, General Drummond, and I were examining that gold nugget that Captain Mahan had? You examined it also, I believe."

"I did," said Pierpont.

"Was it gold?" asked Barris, drumming on the window.

"It was," replied Pierpont.

"I saw it too," said I; "of course, it was gold."

"Professor La Grange saw it also," said Barris; "he said it was gold."

"Well?" said Pierpont.

"Well," said Barris, "it was not gold."

After a silence Pierpont asked what tests had been made.

"The usual tests," replied Barris. "The United States Mint is satisfied that it is gold, so is every jeweller who has seen it. But it is not gold,—and yet—it is gold."

Pierpont and I exchanged glances.

"Now," said I, "for Barris' usual coup-de-théâtre: what was the nugget?"

"Practically it was pure gold; but," said Barris, enjoying the situation intensely, "really it was not gold. Pierpont, what is gold?"

"Gold's an element, a metal—"

"Wrong! Billy Pierpont," said Barris coolly.

"Gold was an element when I went to school," said I.

"It has not been an element for two weeks," said Barris; "and, except General Drummond, Professor La Grange, and myself, you two youngsters are the only people, except one, in the world who know it,—or have known it."

"Do you mean to say that gold is a composite metal?" said Pierpont slowly.

"I do. La Grange has made it. He produced a scale of pure gold day before yesterday. That nugget was manufactured gold."

Could Barris be joking? Was this a colossal hoax? I looked at Pierpont. He muttered something about that settling the silver question, and turned his head to Barris, but there was that in Barris' face which forbade jesting, and Pierpont and I sat silently pondering.

"Don't ask me how it's made," said Barris, quietly; "I don't know. But I do know that somewhere in the region of the Cardinal Woods there is a gang of people who do know how gold is made, and who make it. You understand the danger this is to every civilized nation. It's got to be stopped of course. Drummond and I have decided that I am the man to stop it. Wherever and whoever these people are— these gold makers,—they must be caught, every one of them,— caught or shot."

"Or shot," repeated Pierpont, who was owner of the Cross-Cut Gold Mine and found his income too small; "Professor La Grange will of course be prudent;—science need not know things that would upset the world!"

"Little Willy," said Barris laughing, "your income is safe."

"I suppose," said I, "some flaw in the nugget gave Professor La Grange the tip."

"Exactly. He cut the flaw out before sending the nugget to be tested. He worked on the flaw and separated gold into its three elements."

"He is a great man," said Pierpont, "but he will be the greatest man in the world if he can keep his discovery to himself."

"Who?" said Barris.

"Professor La Grange."

"Professor La Grange was shot through the heart two hours ago," replied Barris slowly.

II

WE had been at the shooting box in the Cardinal Woods five days when a telegram was brought to Barris by a mounted messenger from the nearest telegraph station, Cardinal Springs, a hamlet on the lumber railroad which joins the Quebec and Northern at Three Rivers Junction, thirty miles below.

Pierpont and I were sitting out under the trees, loading some special shells as experiments; Barris stood beside us, bronzed, erect, holding his pipe carefully so that no sparks should drift into our powder box. The beat of hoofs over the grass aroused us, and when the lank messenger drew bridle before the door, Barris stepped forward and took the sealed telegram. When he had torn it open he went into the house and presently reappeared, reading something that he had written.

"This should go at once," he said, looking the messenger full in the face.

"At once, Colonel Barris," replied the shabby countryman.

Pierpont glanced up and I smiled at the messenger who was gathering his bridle and settling himself in his stirrups. Barris handed him the written reply and nodded good-bye: there was a thud of hoofs on the greensward, a jingle of bit and spur across the gravel, and the messenger was gone. Barris' pipe went out and he stepped to wind-ward to relight it.

"It is queer," said I, "that your messenger—a battered native,—should speak like a Harvard man."

"He is a Harvard man," said Barris.

"And the plot thickens," said Pierpont; "are the Cardinal Woods full of your Secret Service men, Barris?"

"No," replied Barris, "but the telegraph stations are. How many ounces of shot are you using, Roy?"

I told him, holding up the adjustable steel measuring cup. He nodded. After a moment or two he sat down on a camp-stool beside us and picked up a crimper.

"That telegram was from Drummond," he said; "the messenger was one of my men as you two bright little boys divined. Pooh! If he had spoken the Cardinal County dialect you wouldn't have known."

"His make-up was good," said Pierpont.

Barris twirled the crimper and looked at the pile of loaded shells. Then he picked up one and crimped it.

"Let'em alone," said Pierpont, "you crimp too tight."

"Does his little gun kick when the shells are crimped too tight?" enquired Barris tenderly; "well, he shall crimp his own shells then,—where's his little man?"

"His little man," was a weird English importation, stiff, very carefully scrubbed, tangled in his aspirates, named Howlett. As valet, gilly, gun-bearer, and crimper, he aided Pierpont to endure the ennui of existence, by doing for him everything except breathing. Lately, however, Barris' taunts had driven Pierpont to do a few things for himself. To his astonishment he found that cleaning his own gun was not a bore, so he timidly loaded a shell or two, was much pleased with himself, loaded some more, crimped them, and went to breakfast with an appetite. So when Barris asked where "his little man" was, Pierpont did not reply but dug a cupful of shot from the bag and poured it solemnly into the half filled shell.

Old David came out with the dogs and of course there was a pow-wow when "Voyou," my Gordon, wagged his splendid tail across the loading table and sent a dozen unstopped cartridges rolling over the grass, vomiting powder and shot.

"Give the dogs a mile or two," said I; "we will shoot over the Sweet Fern Covert about four o'clock, David."

"Two guns, David," added Barris.

"Are you not going?" asked Pierpont, looking up, as David disappeared with the dogs.

"Bigger game," said Barris shortly. He picked up a mug of ale from the tray which Howlett had just set down beside us and took a long pull. We did the same, silently. Pierpont set his mug on the turf beside him and returned to his loading.

We spoke of the murder of Professor La Grange, of how it had been concealed by the authorities in New York at Drummond's request, of the certainty that it was one of the gang of gold-makers who had done it, and of the possible alertness of the gang.

"Oh, they know that Drummond will be after them sooner or later," said Barris, "but they don't know that the mills of the gods have already begun to grind. Those smart New York papers builded better than they knew when their ferret-eyed reporter poked his red nose into the house on 58th Street and sneaked off with a column on his cuffs about the 'suicide' of Professor La Grange. Billy Pierpont, my revolver is hanging in your room; I'll take yours too—"

"Help yourself," said Pierpont.

"I shall be gone over night," continued Barris; "my poncho and some bread and meat are all I shall take except the 'barkers.'"

"Will they bark to-night?" I asked.

"No, I trust not for several weeks yet. I shall nose about a bit. Roy, did it ever strike you how queer it is that this wonderfully beautiful country should contain no inhabitants?"

"It's like those splendid stretches of pools and rapids which one finds on every trout river and in which one never finds a fish," suggested Pierpont.

"Exactly,—and Heaven alone knows why," said Barris; "I suppose this country is shunned by human beings for the same mysterious reasons."

"The shooting is the better for it," I observed.

"The shooting is good," said Barris, "have you noticed the snipe on the meadow by the lake? Why it's brown with them! That's a wonderful meadow."

"It's a natural one," said Pierpont, "no human being ever cleared that land."

"Then it's supernatural," said Barris; "Pierpont, do you want to come with me?"

Pierpont's handsome face flushed as he answered slowly, "It's awfully good of you,—if I may."

"Bosh," said I, piqued because he had asked Pierpont, "what use is little Willy without his man?"

"True," said Barris gravely, "you can't take Howlett you know."

Pierpont muttered something which ended in "d—n."

"Then," said I, "there will be but one gun on the Sweet Fern Covert this afternoon. Very well, I wish you joy of your cold supper and colder bed. Take your night-gown, Willy, and don't sleep on the damp ground."

"Let Pierpont alone," retorted Barris, "you shall go next time, Roy."

"Oh, all right,—you mean when there's shooting going on?"

"And I?" demanded Pierpont, grieved.

"You too, my son; stop quarrelling! Will you ask Howlett to pack our kits—lightly mind you,—no bottles,—they clink."

"My flask doesn't," said Pierpont, and went off to get ready for a night's stalking of dangerous men.

"It is strange," said I, "that nobody ever settles in this region. How many people live in Cardinal Springs, Barris?"

"Twenty counting the telegraph operator and not counting the lumbermen; they are always changing and shifting. I have six men among them."

"Where have you no men? In the Four Hundred?"

"I have men there also,—chums of Billy's only he doesn't know it. David tells me that there was a strong flight of woodcock last night. You ought to pick up some this afternoon."

Then we chatted about alder-cover and swamp until Pierpont came out of the house and it was time to part.

"Au revoir," said Barris, buckling on his kit, "come along, Pierpont, and don't walk in the damp grass."

"If you are not back by to-morrow noon," said I, "I will take Howlett and David and hunt you up. You say your course is due north?"

"Due north," replied Barris, consulting his compass.

"There is a trail for two miles and a spotted lead for two more," said Pierpont.

"Which we won't use for various reasons," added Barris pleasantly; "don't worry, Roy, and keep your confounded expedition out of the way; there's no danger."

He knew, of course, what he was talking about and I held my peace.

When the tip end of Pierpont's shooting coat had disappeared in the Long Covert, I found myself standing alone with Howlett. He bore my gaze for a moment and then politely lowered his eyes.

"Howlett," said I, "take these shells and implements to the gun room, and drop nothing. Did Voyou come to any harm in the briers this morning?"

"No 'arm, Mr. Cardenhe, sir," said Howlett.

"Then be careful not to drop anything else," said I, and walked away leaving him decorously puzzled. For he had dropped no cartridges. Poor Howlett!

III

About four o'clock that afternoon I met David and the dogs at the spinney which leads into the Sweet Fern Covert. The three setters, Voyou, Gamin, and Mioche were in fine feather,—David had killed a woodcock and a brace of grouse over them that morning,— and they were thrashing about the spinney at short range when I came up, gun under arm and pipe lighted.

"What's the prospect, David," I asked, trying to keep my feet in the tangle of wagging, whining dogs; "hello, what's amiss with Mioche?"

"A brier in his foot sir; I drew it and stopped the wound but I guess the gravel's got in. If you have no objection, sir, I might take him back with me."

"It's safer," I said; "take Gamin too, I only want one dog this afternoon. What is the situation?"

"Fair sir; the grouse lie within a quarter of a mile of the oak second-growth. The woodcock are mostly on the alders. I saw any number of snipe on the meadows. There's something else in by the lake,—I can't just tell what, but the wood-duck set up a clatter when I was in the thicket and they came dashing through the wood as if a dozen foxes was snappin' at their tail feathers.''

"Probably a fox," I said; "leash those dogs,—they must learn to stand it. I'll be back by dinner time.''

"There is one more thing sir," said David, lingering with his gun under his arm.

"Well," said I.

"I saw a man in the woods by the Oak Covert,—at least I think I did.''

"A lumberman?''

"I think not sir—at least,—do they have Chinamen among them?''

"Chinese? No. You didn't see a Chinaman in the woods here?''

"I—I think I did sir,—I can't say positively. He was gone when I ran into the covert.''

"Did the dogs notice it?''

"I can't say—exactly. They acted queer like. Gamin here lay down and whined—it may have been colic—and Mioche whimpered, —perhaps it was the brier.''

"And Voyou?''

"Voyou, he was most remarkable sir, and the hair on his back stood up. I did see a groundhog makin' for a tree near by.''

"Then no wonder Voyou bristled. David, your Chinaman was a stump or tussock. Take the dogs now.''

"I guess it was sir; good afternoon sir," said David, and walked away with the Gordons leaving me alone with Voyou in the spinney.

I looked at the dog and he looked at me.

"Voyou!''

The dog sat down and danced with his fore feet, his beautiful brown eyes sparkling.

"You're a fraud," I said; "which shall it be, the alders or the upland? Upland? Good!—now for the grouse,—heel, my friend, and show your miraculous self-restraint.''

Voyou wheeled into my tracks and followed close, nobly refusing to notice the impudent chipmunks and the thousand and one alluring and important smells which an ordinary dog would have lost no time in investigating.

The brown and yellow autumn woods were crisp with drifting heaps of leaves and twigs that crackled under foot as we turned from the spinney into the forest. Every silent little stream, hurrying toward the lake was gay with painted leaves afloat, scarlet maple or yellow oak. Spots of sunlight fell upon the pools, searching the brown depths, illuminating the gravel bottom where shoals of minnows swam to and fro, and to and fro again, busy with the purpose of their little lives. The crickets were chirping in the long brittle grass on the edge of the woods, but we left them far behind in the silence of the deeper forest.

"Now!" said I to Voyou.

The dog sprang to the front, circled once, zig-zagged through the ferns around us and, all in a moment, stiffened stock still, rigid as sculptured bronze. I stepped forward, raising my gun, two paces, three paces, ten perhaps, before a great cock-grouse blundered up from the brake and burst through the thicket fringe toward the deeper growth. There was a flash and a puff from my gun, a crash of echoes among the low wooded cliffs, and through the faint veil of smoke something dark dropped from mid-air amid a cloud of feathers, brown as the brown leaves under foot.

"Fetch!"

Up from the ground sprang Voyou, and in a moment he came galloping back, neck arched, tail stiff but waving, holding tenderly in his pink mouth a mass of mottled bronzed feathers. Very gravely he laid the bird at my feet and crouched close beside it, his silky ears across his paws, his muzzle on the ground.

I dropped the grouse into my pocket, held for a moment a silent caressing communion with Voyou, then swung my gun under my arm and motioned the dog on.

It must have been five o'clock when I walked into a little opening in the woods and sat down to breathe. Voyou came and sat down in front of me.

"Well?" I enquired.

Voyou gravely presented one paw which I took.

"We will never get back in time for dinner," said I, "so we might as well take it easy. It's all your fault, you know. Is there a brier in your foot?—let's see,—there! it's out my friend and you are free to nose about and lick it. If you loll your tongue out you'll get it all over twigs and moss. Can't you lie down and try to pant less? No, there is no use in sniffing and looking at that fern patch, for we are going to smoke a little, doze a little, and go home by moonlight. Think what a big dinner we will have! Think of Howlett's despair when we are not in time! Think of all the stories you will have to tell to Gamin and Mioche! Think what a good dog you have been! There —you are tired old chap; take forty winks with me."

Voyou was a little tired. He stretched out on the leaves at my feet but whether or not he really slept I could not be certain, until his hind legs twitched and I knew he was dreaming of mighty deeds.

Now I may have taken forty winks, but the sun seemed to be no lower when I sat up and unclosed my lids. Voyou raised his head, saw in my eyes that I was not going yet, thumped his tail half a dozen times on the dried leaves, and settled back with a sigh.

I looked lazily around, and for the first time noticed what a wonderfully beautiful spot I had chosen for a nap. It was an oval glade in the heart of the forest, level and carpeted with green grass. The trees that surrounded it were gigantic; they formed one towering circular wall of verdure, blotting out all except the turquoise blue of the sky-oval above. And now I noticed that in the centre of the greensward lay a pool of water, crystal clear, glimmering like a mirror in the meadow grass, beside a block of granite. It scarcely seemed possible that the symmetry of tree and lawn and lucent pool could have been one of nature's accidents. I had never before seen this glade nor had I ever heard it spoken of by either Pierpont or Barris. It was a marvel, this diamond clear basin, regular and graceful as a Roman fountain, set in the gem of turf. And these great trees,—they also belonged, not in America but in some legend-haunted forest of France, where moss-grown marbles stand neglected in dim glades, and the twilight of the forest shelters fairies and slender shapes from shadow-land.

I lay and watched the sunlight showering the tangled thicket where masses of crimson Cardinal-flowers glowed, or where one long dusty sunbeam tipped the edge of the floating leaves in the pool, turning them to palest gilt. There were birds too, passing through the dim avenues of trees like jets of flame,—the gorgeous Cardinal-Bird in his deep stained crimson robe,—the bird that gave to the woods, to the village fifteen miles away, to the whole country, the name of Cardinal.

I rolled over on my back and looked up at the sky. How pale,—paler than a robin's egg,—it was. I seemed to be lying at the bottom of a well, walled with verdure, high towering on every side. And, as I lay, all about me the air became sweet scented. Sweeter and sweeter and more penetrating grew the perfume, and I wondered what stray breeze, blowing over acres of lilies could have brought it. But there was no breeze; the air was still. A gilded fly alighted on my hand,—a honey-fly. It was as troubled as I by the scented silence.

Then, behind me, my dog growled.

I sat quite still at first, hardly breathing, but my eyes were fixed on a shape that moved along the edge of the pool among the meadow grasses. The dog had ceased growling and was now staring, alert and trembling.

At last I rose and walked rapidly down to the pool, my dog following close to heel.

The figure, a woman's, turned slowly toward us.

IV

SHE was standing still when I approached the pool. The forest around us was so silent that when I spoke the sound of my own voice startled me.

"No," she said,—and her voice was smooth as flowing water, "I have not lost my way. Will he come to me, your beautiful dog?"

Before I could speak, Voyou crept to her and laid his silky head against her knees.

"But surely," said I, "you did not come here alone."

"Alone? I did come alone."

"But the nearest settlement is Cardinal, probably nineteen miles from where we are standing."

"I do not know Cardinal," she said.

"Ste. Croix in Canada is forty miles at least,—how did you come into the Cardinal Woods?" I asked amazed.

"Into the woods?" she repeated a little impatiently.

"Yes."

She did not answer at first but stood caressing Voyou with gentle phrase and gesture.

"Your beautiful dog I am fond of, but I am not fond of being questioned," she said quietly. "My name is Ysonde and I came to the fountain here to see your dog."

I was properly quenched. After a moment or two I did say that in another hour it would be growing dusky, but she neither replied nor looked at me.

"This," I ventured, "is a beautiful pool,—you call it a fountain,— a delicious fountain: I have never before seen it. It is hard to imagine that nature did all this."

"Is it?" she said.

"Don't you think so?" I asked.

"I haven't thought; I wish when you go you would leave me your dog."

"My—my dog?"

"If you don't mind," she said sweetly, and looked at me for the first time in the face.

For an instant our glances met, then she grew grave, and I saw that her eyes were fixed on my forehead. Suddenly she rose and drew nearer, looking intently at my forehead. There was a faint mark there, a tiny crescent, just over my eyebrow. It was a birthmark.

"Is that a scar?" she demanded drawing nearer.

"That crescent shaped mark? No."

"No? Are you sure?" she insisted.

"Perfectly," I replied, astonished.

"A—a birthmark?"

"Yes,—may I ask why?"

As she drew away from me, I saw that the color had fled from her cheeks. For a second she clasped both hands over her eyes as if to shut out my face, then slowly dropping her hands, she sat down on a long square block of stone which half encircled the basin, and on which to my amazement I saw carving. Voyou went to her again and laid his head in her lap.

"What is your name?" she asked at length.

"Roy Cardenhe."

"Mine is Ysonde. I carved these dragon-flies on the stone, these fishes and shells and butterflies you see."

"You! They are wonderfully delicate,—but those are not American dragon-flies—"

"No—they are more beautiful. See, I have my hammer and chisel with me."

She drew from a queer pouch at her side a small hammer and chisel and held them toward me.

"You are very talented," I said, "where did you study?"

"I? I never studied,—I knew how. I saw things and cut them out of stone. Do you like them? Some time I will show you other things that I have done. If I had a great lump of bronze I could make your dog, beautiful as he is."

Her hammer fell into the fountain and I leaned over and plunged my arm into the water to find it.

"It is there, shining on the sand," she said, leaning over the pool with me.

"Where," said I, looking at our reflected faces in the water. For it was only in the water that I had dared, as yet, to look her long in the face.

The pool mirrored the exquisite oval of her head, the heavy hair, the eyes. I heard the silken rustle of her girdle, I caught the flash of a white arm, and the hammer was drawn up dripping with spray.

The troubled surface of the pool grew calm and again I saw her eyes reflected.

"Listen," she said in a low voice, "do you think you will come again to my fountain?"

"I will come," I said. My voice was dull; the noise of water filled my ears.

Then a swift shadow sped across the pool; I rubbed my eyes. Where her reflected face had bent beside mine there was nothing mirrored but the rosy evening sky with one pale star glimmering. I drew myself up and turned. She was gone. I saw the faint star twinkling above me in the afterglow, I saw the tall trees motionless in the still evening air, I saw my dog slumbering at my feet.

The sweet scent in the air had faded, leaving in my nostrils the heavy odor of fern and forest mould. A blind fear seized me, and I caught up my gun and sprang into the darkening woods. The dog followed me, crashing through the undergrowth at my side. Duller and duller grew the light, but I strode on, the sweat pouring from my face and hair, my mind a chaos. How I reached the spinney I can hardly tell. As I turned up the path I caught a glimpse of a human face peering at me from the darkening thicket,—a horrible human face, yellow and drawn with high-boned cheeks and narrow eyes.

Involuntarily I halted; the dog at my heels snarled. Then I sprang straight at it, floundering blindly through the thicket, but the night had fallen swiftly and I found myself panting and struggling in a maze of twisted shrubbery and twining vines, unable to see the very undergrowth that ensnared me.

It was a pale face, and a scratched one that I carried to a late dinner that night. Howlett served me, dumb reproach in his eyes, for the soup had been standing and the grouse was juiceless.

David brought the dogs in after they had had their supper, and I drew my chair before the blaze and set my ale on a table beside me. The dogs curled up at my feet, blinking gravely at the sparks that snapped and flew in eddying showers from the heavy birch logs.

"David," said I, "did you say you saw a Chinaman today?"

"I did sir."

"What do you think about it now?"

"I may have been mistaken sir—"

"But you think not. What sort of whiskey did you put in my flask today?"

"The usual sir."

"Is there much gone?"

"About three swallows sir, as usual."

"You don't suppose there could have been any mistake about that whiskey,—no medicine could have gotten into it for instance."

David smiled and said, "No sir."

"Well," said I, "I have had an extraordinary dream."

When I said "dream," I felt comforted and reassured. I had scarcely dared to say it before, even to myself.

"An extraordinary dream," I repeated; "I fell asleep in the woods about five o'clock, in that pretty glade where the fountain—I mean the pool is. You know the place?"

"I do not sir."

I described it minutely, twice, but David shook his head.

"Carved stone did you say sir? I never chanced on it. You don't mean the New Spring—"

"No, no! This glade is way beyond that. Is it possible that any people inhabit the forest between here and the Canada line?"

"Nobody short of Ste. Croix; at least I have no knowledge of any."

"Of course," said I, "when I thought I saw a Chinaman, it was imagination. Of course I had been more impressed than I was aware of by your adventure. Of course you saw no Chinaman, David."

"Probably not sir," replied David dubiously.

I sent him off to bed, saying I should keep the dogs with me all night; and when he was gone, I took a good long draught of ale, "just to shame the devil," as Pierpont said, and lighted a cigar. Then I thought of Barris and Pierpont, and their cold bed, for I knew they would not dare build a fire, and, in spite of the hot chimney corner and the crackling blaze, I shivered in sympathy.

"I'll tell Barris and Pierpont the whole story and take them to see the carved stone and the fountain," I thought to myself; "what a marvellous dream it was—Ysonde,—if it was a dream."

Then I went to the mirror and examined the faint white mark above my eyebrow.

V

About eight o'clock next morning, as I sat listlessly eyeing my coffee cup which Howlett was filling, Gamin and Mioche set up a howl, and in a moment more I heard Barris' step on the porch.

"Hello, Roy," said Pierpont, stamping into the dining room, "I want my breakfast by jingo! Where's Howlett,—none of your *café au lait* for me,—I want a chop and some eggs. Look at that dog, he'll wag the hinge off his tail in a moment—"

"Pierpont," said I, "this loquacity is astonishing but welcome. Where's Barris? You are soaked from neck to ankle."

Pierpont sat down and tore off his stiff muddy leggings.

"Barris is telephoning to Cardinal Springs,—I believe he wants some of his men,—down! Gamin, you idiot! Howlett, three eggs poached and more toast,—what was I saying? Oh, about Barris;

he's struck something or other which he hopes will locate these gold-making fellows. I had a jolly time,—he'll tell you about it."

"Billy! Billy!" I said in pleased amazement, "you are learning to talk! Dear me! You load your own shells and you carry your own gun and you fire it yourself—hello! here's Barris all over mud. You fellows really ought to change your rig—whew! what a frightful odor!"

"It's probably this," said Barris tossing something onto the hearth where it shuddered for a moment and then began to writhe; "I found it in the woods by the lake. Do you know what it can be, Roy?"

To my disgust I saw it was another of those spidery wormy crab-like creatures that Godfrey had in Tiffany's.

"I thought I recognized that acrid odor," I said; "for the love of the Saints take it away from the breakfast table, Barris!"

"But what is it?" he persisted, unslinging his field-glass and revolver.

"I'll tell you what I know after breakfast," I replied firmly, "Howlett, get a broom and sweep that thing into the road.—What are you laughing at, Pierpont?"

Howlett swept the repulsive creature out and Barris and Pierpont went to change their dew-soaked clothes for dryer raiment. David came to take the dogs for an airing and in a few minutes Barris reappeared and sat down in his place at the head of the table.

"Well," said I, "is there a story to tell?"

"Yes, not much. They are near the lake on the other side of the woods,—I mean these gold-makers. I shall collar one of them this evening. I haven't located the main gang with any certainty,—shove the toast rack this way will you, Roy,—no, I am not at all certain, but I've nailed one anyway. Pierpont was a great help, really, —and, what do you think, Roy? He wants to join the Secret Service!"

"Little Willy!"

"Exactly. Oh I'll dissuade him. What sort of a reptile was that I brought in? Did Howlett sweep it away?"

"He can sweep it back again for all I care," I said indifferently, "I've finished my breakfast."

"No," said Barris, hastily swallowing his coffee, "it's of no importance; you can tell me about the beast—"

"Serve you right if I had it brought in on toast," I returned.

Pierpont came in radiant, fresh from the bath.

"Go on with your story, Roy," he said; and I told them about Godfrey and his reptile pet.

"Now what in the name of common sense can Godfrey find interesting in that creature?" I ended, tossing my cigarette into the fireplace.

"It's Japanese, don't you think?" said Pierpont.

"No," said Barris, "it is not artistically grotesque, it's vulgar and horrible,—it looks cheap and unfinished—"

"Unfinished,—exactly," said I, "like an American humorist—"

"Yes," said Pierpont, "cheap. What about that gold serpent?"

"Oh, the Metropolitan Museum bought it; you must see it, it's marvellous."

Barris and Pierpont had lighted their cigarettes and, after a moment, we all rose and strolled out to the lawn, where chairs and hammocks were placed under the maple trees.

David passed, gun under arm, dogs heeling.

"Three guns on the meadows at four this afternoon," said Pierpont.

"Roy," said Barris as David bowed and started on, "what did you do yesterday?"

This was the question that I had been expecting. All night long I had dreamed of Ysonde and the glade in the woods, where, at the bottom of the crystal fountain, I saw the reflection of her eyes. All the morning while bathing and dressing I had been persuading myself that the dream was not worth recounting and that a search for the glade and the imaginary stone carving would be ridiculous. But now, as Barris asked the question, I suddenly decided to tell him the whole story.

"See here, you fellows," I said abruptly, "I am going to tell you something queer. You can laugh as much as you please too, but first I want to ask Barris a question or two. You have been in China, Barris?"

"Yes," said Barris, looking straight into my eyes.

"Would a Chinaman be likely to turn lumberman?"

"Have you seen a Chinaman?" he asked in a quiet voice.

"I don't know; David and I both imagined we did."

Barris and Pierpont exchanged glances.

"Have you seen one also?" I demanded, turning to include Pierpont.

"No," said Barris slowly; "but I know that there is, or has been, a Chinaman in these woods."

"The devil!" said I.

"Yes," said Barris gravely; "the devil, if you like,—a devil,—a member of the Kuen-Yuin."

I drew my chair close to the hammock where Pierpont lay at full length, holding out to me a ball of pure gold.

"Well?" said I, examining the engraving on its surface, which represented a mass of twisted creatures,—dragons, I supposed.

"Well," repeated Barris, extending his hand to take the golden ball, "this globe of gold engraved with reptiles and Chinese hieroglyphics is the symbol of the Kuen-Yuin."

"Where did you get it?" I asked, feeling that something startling was impending.

"Pierpont found it by the lake at sunrise this morning. It is the symbol of the Kuen-Yuin," he repeated, "the terrible Kuen-Yuin, the sorcerers of China, and the most murderously diabolical sect on earth."

We puffed our cigarettes in silence until Barris rose, and began to pace backward and forward among the trees, twisting his grey moustache.

"The Kuen-Yuin are sorcerers," he said, pausing before the hammock where Pierpont lay watching him; "I mean exactly what I say,—sorcerers. I've seen them,—I've seen them at their devilish business, and I repeat to you solemnly, that as there are angels above, there is a race of devils on earth, and they are sorcerers. Bah!" he cried, "talk to me of Indian magic and Yogis and all that clap-trap! Why, Roy, I tell you that the Kuen-Yuin have absolute control of a hundred millions of people, mind and body, body and soul. Do you know what goes on in the interior of China? Does Europe know,— could any human being conceive of the condition of that gigantic hell-pit? You read the papers, you hear diplomatic twaddle about Li Hung Chang and the Emperor, you see accounts of battles on sea and land, and you know that Japan has raised a toy tempest along the jagged edge of the great unknown. But you never heard before of the Kuen-Yuin; no, nor has any European except a stray missionary or two, and yet I tell you that when the fires from this pit of hell have eaten through the continent to the coast, the explosion will inundate half a world,—and God help the other half."

Pierpont's cigarette went out; he lighted another, and looked hard at Barris.

"But," resumed Barris quietly, " 'sufficient unto the day,' you know,—I didn't intend to say as much as I did,—it would do no good,—even you and Pierpont will forget it,—it seems so impossible and so far away,—like the burning out of the sun. What I want to discuss is the possibility or probability of a Chinaman,—a member of the Kuen-Yuin, being here, at this moment, in the forest."

"If he is," said Pierpont, "possibly the gold-makers owe their discovery to him."

"I do not doubt it for a second," said Barris earnestly.

I took the little golden globe in my hand, and examined the characters engraved upon it.

"Barris," said Pierpont, "I can't believe in sorcery while I am wearing one of Sanford's shooting suits in the pocket of which rests an uncut volume of the 'Duchess.' "

"Neither can I," I said, "for I read the *Evening Post*, and I know Mr. Godkin would not allow it. Hello! What's the matter with this gold ball?"

"What is the matter?" said Barris grimly.

"Why—why—it's changing color—purple, no, crimson—no, it's green I mean—good Heavens! these dragons are twisting under my fingers—"

"Impossible!" muttered Pierpont, leaning over me; "those are not dragons—"

"No!" I cried excitedly; "they are pictures of that reptile that Barris brought back—see—see how they crawl and turn—"

"Drop it!" commanded Barris; and I threw the ball on the turf. In an instant we had all knelt down on the grass beside it, but the globe was again golden, grotesquely wrought with dragons and strange signs.

Pierpont, a little red in the face, picked it up, and handed it to Barris. He placed it on a chair, and sat down beside me.

"Whew!" said I, wiping the perspiration from my face, "how did you play us that trick, Barris?"

"Trick?" said Barris contemptuously.

I looked at Pierpont, and my heart sank. If this was not a trick, what was it? Pierpont returned my glance and colored, but all he said was, "It's devilish queer," and Barris answered, "Yes, devilish." Then Barris asked me again to tell my story, and I did, beginning from the time I met David in the spinney to the moment when I sprang into the darkening thicket where that yellow mask had grinned like a phantom skull.

"Shall we try to find the fountain?" I asked after a pause.

"Yes,—and—er—the lady," suggested Pierpont vaguely.

"Don't be an ass," I said a little impatiently, "you need not come, you know."

"Oh, I'll come," said Pierpont, "unless you think I am indiscreet—"

"Shut up, Pierpont," said Barris, "this thing is serious; I never heard of such a glade or such a fountain, but it's true that nobody knows this forest thoroughly. It's worth while trying for; Roy, can you find your way back to it?"

"Easily," I answered; "when shall we go?"

"It will knock our snipe shooting on the head," said Pierpont, "but when one has the opportunity of finding a live dream-lady—"

I rose, deeply offended, but Pierpont was not very penitent and his laughter was irresistible.

"The lady's yours by right of discovery," he said, "I'll promise not to infringe on your dreams,—I'll dream about other ladies—"

"Come, come," said I, "I'll have Howlett put you to bed in a minute. Barris, if you are ready,—we can get back to dinner—"

Barris had risen and was gazing at me earnestly.

"What's the matter?" I asked nervously, for I saw that his eyes were fixed on my forehead, and I thought of Ysonde and the white crescent scar.

"Is that a birthmark?" said Barris.

"Yes—why, Barris?"

"Nothing,—an interesting coincidence—"

"What!—for Heaven's sake!"

"The scar,—or rather the birthmark. It is the print of the dragon's claw,—the crescent symbol of Yue-Laou—"

"And who the devil is Yue-Laou?" I said crossly.

"Yue-Laou,—the Moon Maker, Dzil-Nbu of the Kuen-Yuin;—
it's Chinese Mythology, but it is believed that Yue-Laou has returned
to rule the Kuen-Yuin—"

"The conversation," interrupted Pierpont, "smacks of peacocks,
feathers and yellow-jackets. The chicken-pox has left its card on Roy,
and Barris is guying us. Come on, you fellows, and make your call
on the dream-lady. Barris, I hear galloping; here come your men."

Two mud splashed riders clattered up to the porch and dismounted
at a motion from Barris. I noticed that both of them carried repeating
rifles and heavy Colt's revolvers.

They followed Barris, deferentially, into the dining-room, and
presently we heard the tinkle of plates and bottles and the low hum
of Barris' musical voice.

Half an hour later they came out again, saluted Pierpont and me,
and galloped away in the direction of the Canadian frontier. Ten
minutes passed, and, as Barris did not appear, we rose and went
into the house, to find him. He was sitting silently before the table,
watching the small golden globe, now glowing with scarlet and
orange fire, brilliant as a live coal. Howlett, mouth ajar, and eyes
starting from the sockets, stood petrified behind him.

"Are you coming?" asked Pierpont, a little startled. Barris did not
answer. The globe slowly turned to pale gold again,—but the face
that Barris raised to ours was white as a sheet. Then he stood up,
and smiled with an effort which was painful to us all.

"Give me a pencil and a bit of paper," he said.

Howlett brought it. Barris went to the window and wrote rapidly.
He folded the paper, placed it in the top drawer of his desk, locked
the drawer, handed me the key, and motioned us to precede him.

When again we stood under the maples, he turned to me with an
impenetrable expression. "You will know when to use the key," he
said: "Come, Pierpont, we must try to find Roy's fountain."

VI

AT two o'clock that afternoon, at Barris' suggestion, we gave up the
search for the fountain in the glade and cut across the forest to the
spinney where David and Howlett were waiting with our guns and
the three dogs.

Pierpont guyed me unmercifully about the "dream-lady" as he called her, and, but for the significant coincidence of Ysonde's and Barris' questions concerning the white scar on my forehead, I should long ago have been perfectly persuaded that I had dreamed the whole thing. As it was, I had no explanation to offer. We had not been able to find the glade although fifty times I came to landmarks which convinced me that we were just about to enter it. Barris was quiet, scarcely uttering a word to either of us during the entire search. I had never before seen him depressed in spirits. However, when we came in sight of the spinney where a cold bit of grouse and a bottle of Burgundy awaited each, Barris seemed to recover his habitual good humor.

"Here's to the dream-lady!" said Pierpont, raising his glass and standing up.

I did not like it. Even if she was only a dream, it irritated me to hear Pierpont's mocking voice. Perhaps Barris understood,—I don't know, but he bade Pierpont drink his wine without further noise, and that young man obeyed with a child-like confidence which almost made Barris smile.

"What about the snipe, David," I asked; "the meadows should be in good condition."

"There is not a snipe on the meadows, sir," said David solemnly.

"Impossible," exclaimed Barris, "they can't have left."

"They have, sir," said David in a sepulchral voice which I hardly recognized.

We all three looked at the old man curiously, waiting for his explanation of this disappointing but sensational report.

David looked at Howlett and Howlett examined the sky.

"I was going," began the old man, with his eyes fastened on Howlett, "I was going along by the spinney with the dogs when I heard a noise in the covert and I seen Howlett come walkin' very fast toward me. In fact," continued David, "I may say he was runnin'. Was you runnin', Howlett?"

Howlett said "Yes," with a decorous cough.

"I beg pardon," said David, "but I'd rather Howlett told the rest. He saw things which I did not."

"Go on, Howlett," commanded Pierpont, much interested.

Howlett coughed again behind his large red hand.

"What David says is true sir," he began; "I h'observed the dogs at a distance 'ow they was a workin' sir, and David stood a lightin' of 's pipe be'ind the spotted beech when I see a 'ead pop up in the covert 'oldin a stick like 'e was h'aimin' at the dogs sir"—

"A head holding a stick?" said Pierpont severely.

"The 'ead 'ad 'ands, sir," explained Howlett, "'ands that 'eld a painted stick,—like that, sir. 'Owlett, thinks I to meself, this 'ere's queer, so I jumps in an' runs, but the beggar 'e seen me an' w'en I comes alongside of David, 'e was gone. ' 'Ello 'Owlett,' sez David, 'what the 'ell'—I beg pardon, sir,—' 'ow did you come 'ere,' sez 'e very loud. 'Run!' sez I, 'the Chinaman is harryin' the dawgs!' 'For Gawd's sake wot Chinaman?' sez David, h'aimin' 'is gun at every bush. Then I thinks I see 'im an' we run an' run, the dawgs a boundin' close to heel sir, but we don't see no Chinaman."

"I'll tell the rest," said David, as Howlett coughed and stepped in a modest corner behind the dogs.

"Go on," said Barris in a strange voice.

"Well sir, when Howlett and I stopped chasin', we was on the cliff overlooking the south meadow. I noticed that there was hundreds of birds there, mostly yellow-legs and plover, and Howlett seen them too. Then before I could say a word to Howlett, something out in the lake gave a splash—a splash as if the whole cliff had fallen into the water. I was that scared that I jumped straight into the bush and Howlett he sat down quick, and all those snipe wheeled up— there was hundreds,— all a squeelin' with fright, and the wood-duck came bowlin' over the meadows as if the old Nick was behind."

David paused and glanced meditatively at the dogs.

"Go on," said Barris in the same strained voice.

"Nothing more sir. The snipe did not come back."

"But that splash in the lake?"

"I don't know what it was sir."

"A salmon? A salmon couldn't have frightened the duck and the snipe that way?"

"No—oh no, sir. If fifty salmon had jumped they couldn't have made that splash. Couldn't they, Howlett?"

"No 'ow," said Howlett.

"Roy," said Barris at length, "what David tells us settles the snipe shooting for to-day. I am going to take Pierpont up to the house. Howlett and David will follow with the dogs,—I have something to say to them. If you care to come, come along; if not, go and shoot a brace of grouse for dinner and be back by eight if you want to see what Pierpont and I discovered last night."

David whistled Gamin and Mioche to heel and followed Howlett and his hamper toward the house. I called Voyou to my side, picked up my gun and turned to Barris.

"I will be back by eight," I said; "you are expecting to catch one of the gold-makers, are you not?"

"Yes," said Barris listlessly.

Pierpont began to speak about the Chinaman but Barris motioned him to follow, and, nodding to me, took the path that Howlett and David had followed toward the house. When they disappeared I tucked my gun under my arm and turned sharply into the forest, Voyou trotting close to my heels.

In spite of myself the continued apparition of the Chinaman made me nervous. If he troubled me again I had fully decided to get the drop on him and find out what he was doing in the Cardinal Woods. If he could give no satisfactory account of himself I would march him in to Barris as a gold-making suspect,—I would march him in anyway, I thought, and rid the forest of his ugly face. I wondered what it was that David had heard in the lake. It must have been a big fish, a salmon, I thought; probably David's and Howlett's nerves were overwrought after their Celestial chase.

A whine from the dog broke the thread of my meditation and I raised my head. Then I stopped short in my tracks.

The lost glade lay straight before me.

Already the dog had bounded into it, across the velvet turf to the carved stone where a slim figure sat. I saw my dog lay his silky head lovingly against her silken kirtle; I saw her face bend above him, and I caught my breath and slowly entered the sun-lit glade.

Half timidly she held out one white hand.

"Now that you have come," she said, "I can show you more of my work. I told you that I could do other things besides these dragon-flies and moths carved here in stone. Why do you stare at me so? Are you ill?"

"Ysonde," I stammered.

"Yes," she said, with a faint color under her eyes.

"I—I never expected to see you again," I blurted out, "—you—I—I—thought I had dreamed—"

"Dreamed, of me? Perhaps you did, is that strange?"

"Strange? N—no—but—where did you go when—when we were leaning over the fountain together? I saw your face,—your face reflected beside mine and then—then suddenly I saw the blue sky and only a star twinkling."

"It was because you fell asleep," she said, "was it not?"

"I—asleep?"

"You slept—I thought you were very tired and I went back—"

"Back?—where?"

"Back to my home where I carve my beautiful images; see, here is one I brought to show you to-day."

I took the sculptured creature that she held toward me, a massive golden lizard with frail claw-spread wings of gold so thin that the sunlight burned through and fell on the ground in flaming gilded patches.

"Good Heavens!" I exclaimed, "this is astounding! Where did you learn to do such work? Ysonde, such a thing is beyond price!"

"Oh, I hope so," she said earnestly, "I can't bear to sell my work, but my step-father takes it and sends it away. This is the second thing I have done and yesterday he said I must give it to him. I suppose he is poor."

"I don't see how he can be poor if he gives you gold to model in," I said, astonished.

"Gold!" she exclaimed, "gold! He has a room full of gold! He makes it."

I sat down on the turf at her feet completely unnerved.

"Why do you look at me so?" she asked, a little troubled.

"Where does your step-father live?" I said at last.

"Here."

"Here!"

"In the woods near the lake. You could never find our house."

"A house!"

"Of course. Did you think I lived in a tree? How silly. I live with my step-father in a beautiful house,—a small house, but very beautiful. He makes his gold there but the men who carry it away never come to the house, for they don't know where it is and if they

did they could not get in. My step-father carries the gold in lumps
to a canvas satchel. When the satchel is full he takes it out into the
woods where the men live and I don't know what they do with it.
I wish he could sell the gold and become rich for then I could go
back to Yian where all the gardens are sweet and the river flows
under the thousand bridges."

"Where is this city?" I asked faintly.

"Yian? I don't know. It is sweet with perfume and the sound of
silver bells all day long. Yesterday I carried a blossom of dried lotus
buds from Yian, in my breast, and all the woods were fragrant. Did
you smell it?"

"Yes."

"I wondered, last night, whether you did. How beautiful your
dog is; I love him. Yesterday I thought most about your dog but
last night—"

"Last night," I repeated below my breath.

"I thought of you. Why do you wear the dragon-claw?"

I raised my hand impulsively to my forehead, covering the scar.

"What do you know of the dragon-claw?" I muttered.

"It is the symbol of Yue-Laou, and Yue-Laou rules the Kuen-
Yuin, my step-father says. My step-father tells me everything that
I know. We lived in Yian until I was sixteen years old. I am eighteen
now; that is two years we have lived in the forest. Look!—see those
scarlet birds! What are they? There are birds of the same color in
Yian."

"Where is Yian, Ysonde?" I asked with deadly calmness.

"Yian? I don't know."

"But you have lived there?"

"Yes, a very long time."

"Is it across the ocean, Ysonde?"

"It is across seven oceans and the great river which is longer than
from the earth to the moon."

"Who told you that?"

"Who? My step-father; he tells me everything."

"Will you tell me his name, Ysonde?"

"I don't know it, he is my step-father, that is all."

"And what is your name?"

"You know it, Ysonde."

"Yes, but what other name."

"That is all, Ysonde. Have you two names? Why do you look at me so impatiently?"

"Does your step-father make gold? Have you seen him make it?"

"Oh yes. He made it also in Yian and I loved to watch the sparks at night whirling like golden bees. Yian is lovely,—if it is all like our garden and the gardens around. I can see the thousand bridges from my garden and the white mountain beyond—"

"And the people—tell me of the people, Ysonde!" I urged gently.

"The people of Yian? I could see them in swarms like ants—oh! many, many millions crossing and recrossing the thousand bridges."

"But how did they look? Did they dress as I do?"

"I don't know. They were very far away, moving specks on the thousand bridges. For sixteen years I saw them every day from my garden but I never went out of my garden into the streets of Yian, for my step-father forbade me."

"You never saw a living creature near by in Yian?" I asked in despair.

"My birds, oh such tall, wise-looking birds, all over grey and rose color."

She leaned over the gleaming water and drew her polished hand across the surface.

"Why do you ask me these questions," she murmured; "are you displeased?"

"Tell me about your step-father," I insisted. "Does he look as I do? Does he dress, does he speak as I do? Is he American?"

"American? I don't know. He does not dress as you do and he does not look as you do. He is old, very, very old. He speaks sometimes as you do, sometimes as they do in Yian. I speak also in both manners."

"Then speak as they do in Yian," I urged impatiently, "speak as —why, Ysonde! why are you crying? Have I hurt you?—I did not intend,—I did not dream of your caring! There Ysonde, forgive me,—see, I beg you on my knees here at your feet."

I stopped, my eyes fastened on a small golden ball which hung from her waist by a golden chain. I saw it trembling against her thigh, I saw it change color, now crimson, now purple, now flaming scarlet. It was the symbol of the Kuen-Yuin.

She bent over me and laid her fingers gently on my arm.

"Why do you ask me such things?" she said, while the tears glistened on her lashes. "It hurts me here,—" she pressed her hand to her breast,—"it pains.—I don't know why. Ah, now your eyes are hard and cold again; you are looking at the golden globe which hangs from my waist. Do you wish to know also what that is?"

"Yes," I muttered, my eyes fixed on the infernal color flames which subsided as I spoke, leaving the ball a pale gilt again.

"It is the symbol of the Kuen-Yuin," she said in a trembling voice; "why do you ask?"

"Is it yours?"

"Y—yes."

"Where did you get it?" I cried harshly.

"My—my step-fa—"

Then she pushed me away from her with all the strength of her slender wrists and covered her face.

If I slipped my arm about her and drew her to me,—if I kissed away the tears that fell slowly between her fingers,—if I told her how I loved her—how it cut me to the heart to see her unhappy,— after all that is my own business. When she smiled through her tears, the pure love and sweetness in her eyes lifted my soul higher than the high moon vaguely glimmering through the sun-lit blue above. My happiness was so sudden, so fierce and overwhelming that I only knelt there, her fingers clasped in mine, my eyes raised to the blue vault and the glimmering moon. Then something in the long grass beside me moved close to my knees and a damp acrid odor filled my nostrils.

"Ysonde!" I cried, but the touch of her hand was already gone and my two clenched fists were cold and damp with dew.

"Ysonde!" I called again, my tongue stiff with fright;—but I called as one awaking from a dream—a horrid dream, for my nostrils quivered with the damp acrid odor and I felt the crab-reptile clinging to my knee. Why had the night fallen so swiftly,—and where was I—where?—stiff, chilled, torn, and bleeding, lying flung like a corpse over my own threshold with Voyou licking my face and Barris stooping above me in the light of a lamp that flared and smoked in the night breeze like a torch. Faugh! the choking stench of the lamp aroused me and I cried out:

"Ysonde!"

"What the devil's the matter with him?" muttered Pierpont, lifting me in his arms like a child, "has he been stabbed, Barris?"

VII

IN a few minutes I was able to stand and walk stiffly into my bedroom where Howlett had a hot bath ready and a hotter tumbler of Scotch. Pierpont sponged the blood from my throat where it had coagulated. The cut was slight, almost invisible, a mere puncture from a thorn. A shampoo cleared my mind, and a cold plunge and alcohol friction did the rest.

"Now," said Pierpont, "swallow your hot Scotch and lie down. Do you want a broiled woodcock? Good, I fancy you are coming about."

Barris and Pierpont watched me as I sat on the edge of the bed, solemnly chewing on the woodcock's wishbone and sipping my Bordeaux, very much at my ease.

Pierpont sighed his relief.

"So," he said pleasantly, "it was a mere case of ten dollars or ten days. I thought you had been stabbed—"

"I was not intoxicated," I replied, serenely picking up a bit of celery.

"Only jagged?" enquired Pierpont, full of sympathy.

"Nonsense," said Barris, "let him alone. Want some more celery, Roy?—it will make you sleep."

"I don't want to sleep," I answered; "when are you and Pierpont going to catch your Goldmaker?"

Barris looked at his watch and closed it with a snap.

"In an hour; you don't propose to go with us?"

"But I do,—toss me a cup of coffee, Pierpont, will you,—that's just what I propose to do. Howlett, bring the new box of Panatella's, —the mild imported;—and leave the decanter. Now Barris, I'll be dressing, and you and Pierpont keep still and listen to what I have to say. Is that door shut tight?"

Barris locked it and sat down.

"Thanks," said I, "Barris, where is the city of Yian?"

An expression akin to terror flashed into Barris' eyes and I saw him stop breathing for a moment.

"There is no such city," he said at length, "have I been talking in my sleep?"

"It is a city," I continued, calmly, "where the river winds under the thousand bridges, where the gardens are sweet scented and the air is filled with the music of silver bells—"

"Stop!" gasped Barris, and rose trembling from his chair. He had grown ten years older.

"Roy," interposed Pierpont coolly, "what the deuce are you harrying Barris for?"

I looked at Barris and he looked at me. After a second or two he sat down again.

"Go on, Roy," he said.

"I must," I answered, "for now I am certain that I have not dreamed."

I told them everything; but, even as I told it, the whole thing seemed so vague, so unreal, that at times I stopped with the hot blood tingling in my ears, for it seemed impossible that sensible men, in the year of our Lord 1896 could seriously discuss such matters.

I feared Pierpont, but he did not even smile. As for Barris, he sat with his handsome head sunk on his breast, his unlighted pipe clasped tight in both hands.

When I had finished, Pierpont turned slowly and looked at Barris. Twice he moved his lips as if about to ask something and then remained mute.

"Yian is a city," said Barris, speaking dreamily; "was that what you wished to know, Pierpont?"

We nodded silently.

"Yian is a city," repeated Barris, "where the great river winds under the thousand bridges,—where the gardens are sweet scented, and the air is filled with the music of silver bells."

My lips formed the question, "Where is this city?"

"It lies," said Barris, almost querulously, "across the seven oceans and the river which is longer than from the earth to the moon."

"What do you mean?" said Pierpont.

"Ah," said Barris, rousing himself with an effort and raising his sunken eyes, "I am using the allegories of another land; let it pass. Have I not told you of the Kuen-Yuin? Yian is the centre of the Kuen-Yuin. It lies hidden in that gigantic shadow called China, vague and vast as the midnight Heavens,—a continent unknown, impenetrable."

"Impenetrable," repeated Pierpont below his breath.

"I have seen it," said Barris dreamily. "I have seen the dead plains of Black Cathay and I have crossed the mountains of Death, whose summits are above the atmosphere. I have seen the shadow of Xangi cast across Abaddon. Better to die a million miles from Yezd and Ater Quedah than to have seen the white water-lotus close in the shadow of Xangi! I have slept among the ruins of Xaindu where the winds never cease and the Wulwulleh is wailed by the dead."

"And Yian," I urged gently.

There was an unearthly look on his face as he turned slowly toward me.

"Yian,—I have lived there—and loved there. When the breath of my body shall cease, when the dragon's claw shall fade from my arm,"—he tore up his sleeve, and we saw a white crescent shining above his elbow,—"when the light of my eyes has faded forever, then, even then I shall not forget the city of Yian. Why, it is my home,— mine! The river and the thousand bridges, the white peak beyond, the sweet-scented gardens, the lilies, the pleasant noise of the summer wind laden with bee music and the music of bells,—all these are mine. Do you think because the Kuen-Yuin feared the dragon's claw on my arm that my work with them is ended? Do you think that because Yue-Laou could give, that I acknowledge his right to take away? Is he Xangi in whose shadow the white water-lotus dares not raise its head? No! No!" he cried violently, "it was not from Yue-Laou, the sorcerer, the Maker of Moons, that my happiness came! It was real, it was not a shadow to vanish like a tinted bubble! Can a sorcerer create and give a man the woman he loves? Is Yue-Laou as great as Xangi then? Xangi is God. In His own time, in His infinite goodness and mercy He will bring me again to the woman I love. And I know she waits for me at God's feet."

In the strained silence that followed I could hear my heart's double beat and I saw Pierpont's face, blanched and pitiful. Barris shook himself and raised his head. The change in his ruddy face frightened me.

"Heed!" he said, with a terrible glance at me; "the print of the dragon's claw is on your forehead and Yue-Laou knows it. If you must love, then love like a man, for you will suffer like a soul in hell, in the end. What is her name again?"

"Ysonde," I answered simply.

VIII

AT nine o'clock that night we caught one of the Goldmakers. I do not know how Barris had laid his trap; all I saw of the affair can be told in a minute or two.

We were posted on the Cardinal road about a mile below the house, Pierpont and I with drawn revolvers on one side, under a butternut tree, Barris on the other, a Winchester across his knees.

I had just asked Pierpont the hour, and he was feeling for his watch when far up the road we heard the sound of a galloping horse, nearer, nearer, clattering, thundering past. Then Barris' rifle spat flame and the dark mass, horse and rider, crashed into the dust. Pierpont had the half stunned horseman by the collar in a second,— the horse was stone dead,—and, as we lighted a pine knot to examine the fellow, Barris' two riders galloped up and drew bridle beside us.

"Hm!" said Barris with a scowl, "it's the 'Shiner,' or I'm a moonshiner."

We crowded curiously around to see the "Shiner." He was red-headed, fat and filthy, and his little red eyes burned in his head like the eyes of an angry pig.

Barris went through his pockets methodically while Pierpont held him and I held the torch. The Shiner was a gold mine; pockets, shirt, boot-legs, hat, even his dirty fists, clutched tight and bleeding, were bursting with lumps of soft yellow gold. Barris dropped this "moonshine gold," as we had come to call it, into the pockets of his shooting-coat, and withdrew to question the prisoner. He came back again in a few minutes and motioned his mounted men to take the

Shiner in charge. We watched them, rifle on thigh, walking their horses slowly away into the darkness, the Shiner, tightly bound, shuffling sullenly between them.

"Who is the Shiner?" asked Pierpont, slipping the revolver into his pocket again.

"A moonshiner, counterfeiter, forger, and highwayman," said Barris, "and probably a murderer. Drummond will be glad to see him, and I think it likely he will be persuaded to confess to him what he refuses to confess to me."

"Wouldn't he talk?" I asked.

"Not a syllable. Pierpont, there is nothing more for you to do."

"For me to do? Are you not coming back with us, Barris?"

"No," said Barris.

We walked along the dark road in silence for a while, I wondering what Barris intended to do, but he said nothing more until we reached our own verandah. Here he held out his hand, first to Pierpont, then to me, saying good-bye as though he were going on a long journey.

"How soon will you be back?" I called out to him as he turned away toward the gate. He came across the lawn again and again took our hands with a quiet affection that I had never imagined him capable of.

"I am going," he said, "to put an end to his gold-making to-night. I know that you fellows have never suspected what I was about on my little solitary evening strolls after dinner. I will tell you. Already I have unobtrusively killed four of these gold-makers,— my men put them underground just below the new wash-out at the four mile stone. There are three left alive,—the Shiner whom we have, another criminal named 'Yellow,' or 'Yaller' in the vernacular, and the third—"

"The third," repeated Pierpont, excitedly.

"The third I have never yet seen. But I know who and what he is, —I know; and if he is of human flesh and blood, his blood will flow to-night."

As he spoke a slight noise across the turf attracted my attention. A mounted man was advancing silently in the starlight over the spongy meadowland. When he came nearer Barris struck a match, and we saw that he bore a corpse across his saddle bow.

"Yaller, Colonel Barris," said the man, touching his slouched hat in salute.

This grim introduction to the corpse made me shudder, and, after a moment's examination of the stiff, wide-eyed dead man, I drew back.

"Identified," said Barris, "take him to the four mile post and carry his effects to Washington,—under seal, mind, Johnstone."

Away cantered the rider with his ghastly burden, and Barris took our hands once more for the last time. Then he went away, gaily, with a jest on his lips, and Pierpont and I turned back into the house.

For an hour we sat moodily smoking in the hall before the fire, saying little until Pierpont burst out with: "I wish Barris had taken one of us with him to-night!"

The same thought had been running in my mind, but I said: "Barris knows what he's about."

This observation neither comforted us nor opened the lane to further conversation, and after a few minutes Pierpont said good night and called for Howlett and hot water. When he had been warmly tucked away by Howlett, I turned out all but one lamp, sent the dogs away with David and dismissed Howlett for the night.

I was not inclined to retire for I knew I could not sleep. There was a book lying open on the table beside the fire and I opened it and read a page or two, but my mind was fixed on other things.

The window shades were raised and I looked out at the star-set firmament. There was no moon that night but the sky was dusted all over with sparkling stars and a pale radiance, brighter even than moonlight, fell over meadow and wood. Far away in the forest I heard the voice of the wind, a soft warm wind that whispered a name, Ysonde.

"Listen," sighed the voice of the wind, and "listen" echoed the swaying trees with every little leaf a-quiver. I listened.

Where the long grasses trembled with the cricket's cadence I heard her name, Ysonde; I heard it in the rustling woodbine where grey moths hovered; I heard it in the drip, drip, drip of the dew from the porch. The silent meadow brook whispered her name, the rippling woodland streams repeated it, Ysonde, Ysonde, until all earth and sky were filled with the soft thrill, Ysonde, Ysonde, Ysonde.

A night-thrush sang in a thicket by the porch and I stole to the verandah to listen. After a while it began again, a little further on. I ventured out into the road. Again I heard it far away in the forest and I followed it, for I knew it was singing of Ysonde.

When I came to the path that leaves the main road and enters the Sweet-Fern Covert below the spinney, I hesitated; but the beauty of the night lured me on and the night-thrushes called me from every thicket. In the starry radiance, shrubs, grasses, field flowers, stood out distinctly, for there was no moon to cast shadows. Meadow and brook, grove and stream, were illuminated by the pale glow. Like great lamps lighted the planets hung from the high domed sky and through their mysterious rays the fixed stars, calm, serene, stared from the heavens like eyes.

I waded on waist deep through fields of dewy golden-rod, through late clover and wild-oat wastes, through crimson fruited sweetbrier, blue-berry, and wild plum, until the low whisper of the Wier Brook warned me that the path had ended.

But I would not stop, for the night air was heavy with the perfume of water-lilies and far away, across the low wooded cliffs and the wet meadowland beyond, there was a distant gleam of silver, and I heard the murmur of sleepy waterfowl. I would go to the lake. The way was clear except for the dense young growth and the snares of the moose-bush.

The night-thrushes had ceased but I did not want for the company of living creatures. Slender, quick darting forms crossed my path at intervals, sleek mink, that fled like shadows at my step, wiry weasels and fat musk-rats, hurrying onward to some tryst or killing.

I never had seen so many little woodland creatures on the move at night. I began to wonder where they all were going so fast, why they all hurried on in the same direction. Now I passed a hare hopping through the brushwood, now a rabbit scurrying by, flag hoisted. As I entered the beech second-growth two foxes glided by me; a little further on a doe crashed out of the underbrush, and close behind her stole a lynx, eyes shining like coals.

He neither paid attention to the doe nor to me, but loped away toward the north.

The lynx was in flight.

"From what?" I asked myself, wondering. There was no forest fire, no cyclone, no flood.

If Barris had passed that way could he have stirred up this sudden exodus? Impossible; even a regiment in the forest could scarcely have put to rout these frightened creatures.

"What on earth," thought I, turning to watch the headlong flight of a fisher-cat, "what on earth has started the beasts out at this time of night?"

I looked up into the sky. The placid glow of the fixed stars comforted me and I stepped on through the narrow spruce belt that leads down to the borders of the Lake of the Stars.

Wild cranberry and moose-bush entwined my feet, dewy branches spattered me with moisture, and the thick spruce needles scraped my face as I threaded my way over mossy logs and deep spongy tussocks down to the level gravel of the lake shore.

Although there was no wind the little waves were hurrying in from the lake and I heard them splashing among the pebbles. In the pale star glow thousands of water-lilies lifted their half-closed chalices toward the sky.

I threw myself full length upon the shore, and, chin on hand, looked out across the lake.

Splash, splash, came the waves along the shore, higher, nearer, until a film of water, thin and glittering as a knife blade, crept up to my elbows. I could not understand it; the lake was rising, but there had been no rain. All along the shore the water was running up; I heard the waves among the sedge grass; the weeds at my side were awash in the ripples. The lilies rocked on the tiny waves, every wet pad rising on the swells, sinking, rising again until the whole lake was glimmering with undulating blossoms. How sweet and deep was the fragrance from the lilies. And now the water was ebbing, slowly, and the waves receded, shrinking from the shore rim until the white pebbles appeared again, shining like froth on a brimming glass.

No animal swimming out in the darkness along the shore, no heavy salmon surging, could have set the whole shore aflood as though the wash from a great boat were rolling in. Could it have been the overflow, through the Weir Brook, of some cloud-burst far back in the forest? This was the only way I could account for it, and yet when I had crossed the Wier Brook I had not noticed that it was swollen.

And as I lay there thinking, a faint breeze sprang up and I saw the surface of the lake whiten with lifted lily pads.

All around me the alders were sighing; I heard the forest behind me stir; the crossed branches rubbing softly, bark against bark. Something—it may have been an owl—sailed out of the night, dipped, soared, and was again engulfed, and far across the water I heard its faint cry, Ysonde.

Then first, for my heart was full, I cast myself down upon my face, calling on her name. My eyes were wet when I raised my head,—for the spray from the shore was drifting in again,—and my heart beat heavily; "No more, no more." But my heart lied, for even as I raised my face to the calm stars, I saw her standing still, close beside me; and very gently I spoke her name, Ysonde. She held out both hands.

"I was lonely," she said, "and I went to the glade, but the forest is full of frightened creatures and they frightened me. Has anything happened in the woods? The deer are running toward the heights."

Her hand still lay in mine as we moved along the shore, and the lapping of the water on rock and shallow was no lower than our voices.

"Why did you leave me without a word, there at the fountain in the glade?" she said.

"I leave you!—"

"Indeed you did, running swiftly with your dog, plunging through thickets and brush,—oh—you frightened me."

"Did I leave you so?"

"Yes—after—"

"After?"

"You had kissed me—"

Then we leaned down together and looked into the black water set with stars, just as we had bent together over the fountain in the glade.

"Do you remember?" I asked.

"Yes. See, the water is inlaid with silver stars,—everywhere white lilies floating and the stars below, deep, deep down."

"What is the flower you hold in your hand?"

"White water-lotus."

"Tell me about Yue-Laou, Dzil Nbu of the Kuen-Yuin," I whispered, lifting her head so I could see her eyes.

"Would it please you to hear?"

"Yes, Ysonde."

"All that I know is yours, now, as I am yours, all that I am. Bend closer. Is it of Yue-Laou you would know? Yue-Laou is Dzil-Nbu of the Kuen-Yuin. He lived in the Moon. He is old—very, very old, and once, before he came to rule the Kuen-Yuin, he was the old man who unites with a silken cord all predestined couples, after which nothing can prevent their union. But all that is changed since he came to rule the Kuen-Yuin. Now he has perverted the Xin,—the good genii of China,—and has fashioned from their warped bodies a monster which he calls the Xin. This monster is horrible, for it not only lives in its own body, but it has thousands of loathsome satellites,—living creatures without mouths, blind, that move when the Xin moves, like a mandarin and his escort. They are part of the Xin although they are not attached. Yet if one of these satellites is injured the Xin writhes with agony. It is fearful—this huge living bulk and these creatures spread out like severed fingers that wriggle around a hideous hand."

"Who told you this?"

"My step-father."

"Do you believe it?"

"Yes. I have seen one of the Xin's creatures."

"Where, Ysonde?"

"Here in these woods."

"Then you believe there is a Xin here?"

"There must be,—perhaps in the lake—"

"Oh, Xins inhabit lakes?"

"Yes, and the seven seas. I am not afraid here."

"Why?"

"Because I wear the symbol of the Kuen-Yuin."

"Then I am not safe," I smiled.

"Yes you are, for I hold you in my arms. Shall I tell you more about the Xin? When the Xin is about to do to death a man, the Yeth-hounds gallop through the night—"

"What are the Yeth-hounds, Ysonde?"

"The Yeth-hounds are dogs without heads. They are the spirits of murdered children, which pass through the woods at night, making a wailing noise."

"Do you believe this?"

"Yes, for I have worn the yellow lotus—"

"The yellow lotus—"

"Yellow is the symbol of faith—"

"Where?"

"In Yian," she said faintly.

After a while I said, "Ysonde, you know there is a God?"

"God and Xangi are one."

"Have you ever heard of Christ?"

"No," she answered softly.

The wind began again among the tree tops. I felt her hands closing in mine.

"Ysonde," I asked again, "do you believe in sorcerers?"

"Yes, the Kuen-Yuin are sorcerers; Yue-Laou is a sorcerer."

"Have you seen sorcery?"

"Yes, the reptile satellite of the Xin—"

"Anything else?"

"My charm,—the golden ball, the symbol of the Kuen-Yuin. Have you seen it change,—have you seen the reptiles writhe—?"

"Yes," said I shortly, and then remained silent, for a sudden shiver of apprehension had seized me. Barris also had spoken gravely, ominously of the sorcerers, the Kuen-Yuin, and I had seen with my own eyes the graven reptiles turning and twisting on the glowing globe.

"Still," said I aloud, "God lives and sorcery is but a name."

"Ah," murmured Ysonde, drawing closer to me, "they say, in Yian, the Kuen-Yuin live; God is but a name."

"They lie," I whispered fiercely.

"Be careful," she pleaded, "they may hear you. Remember that you have the mark of the dragon's claw on your brow."

"What of it?" I asked, thinking also of the white mark on Barris' arm.

"Ah don't you know that those who are marked with the dragon's claw are followed by Yue-Laou, for good or for evil,—and the evil means death if you offend him?"

"Do you believe that!" I asked impatiently.

"I know it," she sighed.

"Who told you all this? Your step-father? What in Heaven's name is he then,—a Chinaman!"

"I don't know; he is not like you."

"Have—have you told him anything about me?"

"He knows about you—no, I have told him nothing,—ah, what is this—see—it is a cord, a cord of silk about your neck—and about mine!"

"Where did that come from?" I asked astonished.

"It must be—it must be Yue-Laou who binds me to you,—it is as my step-father said—he said Yue-Laou would bind us—"

"Nonsense," I said almost roughly, and seized the silken cord, but to my amazement it melted in my hand like smoke.

"What is all this damnable jugglery!" I whispered angrily, but my anger vanished as the words were spoken, and a convulsive shudder shook me to the feet. Standing on the shore of the lake, a stone's throw away, was a figure, twisted and bent,—a little old man, blowing sparks from a live coal which he held in his naked hand. The coal glowed with increasing radiance, lighting up the skull-like face above it, and threw a red glow over the sands at his feet. But the face! —the ghastly Chinese face on which the light flickered,—and the snaky slitted eyes, sparkling as the coal glowed hotter. Coal! It was not a coal but a golden globe staining the night with crimson flames, —it was the symbol of the Kuen-Yuin.

"See! See!" gasped Ysonde, trembling violently, "see the moon rising from between his fingers! Oh I thought it was my step-father and it is Yue-Laou the Maker of Moons—no! no! it is my step-father—ah God! they are the same!"

Frozen with terror I stumbled to my knees, groping for my revolver which bulged in my coat pocket; but something held me—something which bound me like a web in a thousand strong silky meshes. I struggled and turned but the web grew tighter; it was over us—all around us, drawing, pressing us into each other's arms until we lay side by side, bound hand and body and foot, palpitating, panting like a pair of netted pigeons.

And the creature on the shore below! What was my horror to see a moon, huge, silvery, rise like a bubble from between his fingers, mount higher, higher into the still air and hang aloft in the midnight sky, while another moon rose from his fingers, and another and yet another until the vast span of Heaven was set with moons and the earth sparkled like a diamond in the white glare.

A great wind began to blow from the east and it bore to our ears a long mournful howl,—a cry so unearthly that for a moment our hearts stopped.

"The Yeth-hounds!" sobbed Ysonde, "do you hear!—they are passing through the forest! The Xin is near!"

Then all around us in the dry sedge grasses came a rustle as if some small animals were creeping, and a damp acrid odor filled the air. I knew the smell, I saw the spidery crab-like creatures swarm out around me and drag their soft yellow hairy bodies across the shrinking grasses. They passed, hundreds of them, poisoning the air, tumbling, writhing, crawling with their blind mouthless heads raised. Birds, half asleep and confused by the darkness fluttered away before them in helpless fright, rabbits sprang from their forms, weasels glided away like flying shadows. What remained of the forest creatures rose and fled from the loathsome invasion; I heard the squeak of a terrified hare, the snort of stampeding deer, and the lumbering gallop of a bear; and all the time I was choking, half suffocated by the poisoned air.

Then, as I struggled to free myself from the silken snare about me, I cast a glance of deadly fear at the sorcerer below, and at the same moment I saw him turn in his tracks.

"Halt!" cried a voice from the bushes.

"Barris!" I shouted, half leaping up in my agony.

I saw the sorcerer spring forward, I heard the bang! bang! bang! of a revolver, and, as the sorcerer fell on the water's edge, I saw Barris jump out into the white glare and fire again, once, twice, three times, into the writhing figure at his feet.

Then an awful thing occurred. Up out of the black lake reared a shadow, a nameless shapeless mass, headless, sightless, gigantic, gaping from end to end.

A great wave struck Barris and he fell, another washed him up on the pebbles, another whirled him back into the water and then,— and then the thing fell over him,—and I fainted.

*   *   *

This, then, is all that I know concerning Yue-Laou and the Xin. I do not fear the ridicule of scientists or of the press for I have told the truth. Barris is gone and the thing that killed him is alive to-day in the Lake of the Stars while the spider-like satellites roam through the Cardinal Woods. The game has fled, the forests around the lake are empty of any living creatures save the reptiles that creep when the Xin moves in the depths of the lake.

General Drummond knows what he has lost in Barris, and we, Pierpont and I, know what we have lost also. His will we found in the drawer, the key of which he had handed me. It was wrapped in a bit of paper on which was written;

Yue-Laou the sorcerer is here in the Cardinal Woods. I must kill him or he will kill me. He made and gave to me the woman I loved,—he made her, —I saw him,—he made her out of a white water-lotus bud. When our child was born, he came again before me and demanded from me the woman I loved. Then, when I refused, he went away, and that night my wife and child vanished from my side, and I found upon her pillow a white lotus bud. Roy, the woman of your dream, Ysonde, may be my child. God help you if you love her for Yue-Laou will give,—and take away, as though he were Xangi, which is God. I will kill Yue-Laou before I leave this forest,— or he will kill me.

FRANKLYN BARRIS.

Now the world knows what Barris thought of the Kuen-Yuin and of Yue-Laou. I see that the newspapers are just becoming excited over the glimpses that Li-Hung-Chang has afforded them of Black Cathay and the demons of the Kuen-Yuin. The Kuen-Yuin are on the move.

Pierpont and I have dismantled the shooting-box in the Cardinal Woods. We hold ourselves ready at a moment's notice to join and lead the first Government party to drag the Lake of the Stars and cleanse the forest of the crab reptiles. But it will be necessary that a large force assembles, and a well-armed force, for we never have found the body of Yue-Laou, and, living or dead, I fear him. Is he living?

Pierpont, who found Ysonde and myself lying unconscious on the lake shore, the morning after, saw no trace of corpse or blood on the sands. He may have fallen into the lake, but I fear and Ysonde fears that he is alive. We never were able to find either her dwelling place or the glade and the fountain again. The only thing that remains of her former life is the gold serpent in the Metropolitan Museum and her golden globe, the symbol of the Kuen-Yuin; but the latter no longer changes color.

David and the dogs are waiting for me in the court yard as I write. Pierpont is in the gun room loading shells, and Howlett brings him mug after mug of my ale from the wood. Ysonde bends over my desk,—I feel her hand on my arm, and she is saying, "Don't you think you have done enough to-day, dear? How can you write such silly nonsense without a shadow of truth or foundation?"

A Pleasant Evening

Et pis, doucett'ment on s'endort,
On fait sa carne, on fait sa sorgue,
On ronfle, et, comme un tuyau d'orgue,
L'tuyau s'met à ronfler pus fort. . . .
                              ARISTIDE BRUANT.

I

As I stepped upon the platform of a Broadway cable-car at Forty-second Street, somebody said; "hello, Hilton, Jamison's looking for you."

"Hello, Curtis," I replied, "what does Jamison want?"

"He wants to know what you've been doing all the week," said Curtis, hanging desperately to the railing as the car lurched forward; "he says you seem to think that the *Manhattan Illustrated Weekly* was created for the sole purpose of providing salary and vacations for you."

"The shifty old tom-cat!" I said, indignantly, "he knows well enough where I've been. Vacation! Does he think the State Camp in June is a snap?"

"Oh," said Curtis, "you've been to Peekskill?"

"I should say so," I replied, my wrath rising as I thought of my assignment.

"Hot?" inquired Curtis, dreamily.

"One hundred and three in the shade," I answered. "Jamison wanted three full pages and three half pages, all for process work,

and a lot of line drawings into the bargain. I could have faked them
—I wish I had. I was fool enough to hustle and break my neck to
get some honest drawings, and that's the thanks I get!"

"Did you have a camera?"

"No. I will next time—I'll waste no more conscientious work on
Jamison," I said sulkily.

"It doesn't pay," said Curtis. "When I have military work
assigned me, I don't do the dashing sketch-artist act, you bet; I go
to my studio, light my pipe, pull out a lot of old *Illustrated London
News*, select several suitable battle scenes by Caton Woodville—
and use 'em too."

The car shot around the neck-breaking curve at Fourteenth
Street.

"Yes," continued Curtis, as the car stopped in front of the Morton
House for a moment, then plunged forward again amid a furious
clanging of gongs, "it doesn't pay to do decent work for the fat-
headed men who run the *Manhattan Illustrated*. They don't appreciate
it."

"I think the public does," I said, "but I'm sure Jamison doesn't.
It would serve him right if I did what most of you fellows do—take a
lot of Caton Woodville's and Thulstrup's drawings, change the
uniforms, 'chic' a figure or two, and turn in a drawing labelled
'from life.' I'm sick of this sort of thing anyway. Almost every day
this week I've been chasing myself over that tropical camp, or
galloping in the wake of those batteries. I've got a full page of the
'camp by moonlight,' full pages of 'artillery drill' and 'light battery
in action,' and a dozen smaller drawings that cost me more groans
and perspiration than Jamison ever knew in all his lymphatic life!"

"Jamison's got wheels," said Curtis,—"more wheels than there
are bicycles in Harlem. He wants you to do a full page by Saturday."

"A what?" I exclaimed, aghast.

"Yes he does—he was going to send Jim Crawford, but Jim
expects to go to California for the winter fair, and you've got to do it."

"What is it?" I demanded savagely.

"The animals in Central Park," chuckled Curtis.

I was furious. The animals! Indeed! I'd show Jamison that I was
entitled to some consideration! This was Thursday; that gave me a
day and a half to finish a full-page drawing for the paper, and, after

my work at the State Camp I felt that I was entitled to a little rest. Anyway I objected to the subject. I intended to tell Jamison so— I intended to tell him firmly. However, many of the things that we often intended to tell Jamison were never told. He was a peculiar man, fat-faced, thin-lipped, gentle-voiced, mild-mannered, and soft in his movements as a pussy cat. Just why our firmness should give way when we were actually in his presence, I have never quite been able to determine. He said very little—so did we, although we often entered his presence with other intentions.

The truth was that the *Manhattan Illustrated Weekly* was the best paying, best illustrated paper in America, and we young fellows were not anxious to be cast adrift. Jamison's knowledge of art was probably as extensive as the knowledge of any "Art editor" in the city. Of course that was saying nothing, but the fact merited careful consideration on our part, and we gave it much consideration.

This time, however, I decided to let Jamison know that drawings are not produced by the yard, and that I was neither a floor-walker nor a hand-me-down. I would stand up for my rights; I'd tell old Jamison a few things to set the wheels under his silk hat spinning, and if he attempted any of his pussy-cat ways on me, I'd give him a few plain facts that would curl what hair he had left.

Glowing with a splendid indignation I jumped off the car at the City Hall, followed by Curtis, and a few minutes later entered the office of the *Manhattan Illustrated News.*

"Mr. Jamison would like to see you, sir," said one of the compositors as I passed into the long hallway. I threw my drawings on the table and passed a handkerchief over my forehead.

"Mr. Jamison would like to see you, sir," said a small freckle-faced boy with a smudge of ink on his nose.

"I know it," I said, and started to remove my gloves.

"Mr. Jamison would like to see you, sir," said a lank messenger who was carrying a bundle of proofs to the floor below.

"The deuce take Jamison," I said to myself. I started toward the dark passage that leads to the abode of Jamison, running over in my mind the neat and sarcastic speech which I had been composing during the last ten minutes.

Jamison looked up and nodded softly as I entered the room. I forgot my speech.

"Mr. Hilton," he said, "we want a full page of the Zoo before it is removed to Bronx Park. Saturday afternoon at three o'clock the drawing must be in the engraver's hands. Did you have a pleasant week in camp?"

"It was hot," I muttered, furious to find that I could not remember my little speech.

"The weather," said Jamison, with soft courtesy, "is oppressive everywhere. Are your drawings in, Mr. Hilton?"

"Yes. It was infernally hot and I worked like the devil—"

"I suppose you were quite overcome. Is that why you took a two days' trip to the Catskills? I trust the mountain air restored you— but—was it prudent to go to Cranston's for the cotillion Tuesday? Dancing in such uncomfortable weather is really unwise. Good-morning, Mr. Hilton, remember the engraver should have your drawings on Saturday by three."

I walked out, half hypnotized, half enraged. Curtis grinned at me as I passed—I could have boxed his ears.

"Why the mischief should I lose my tongue whenever that old tom-cat purrs!" I asked myself as I entered the elevator and was shot down to the first floor. "I'll not put up with this sort of thing much longer—how in the name of all that's foxy did he know that I went to the mountains? I suppose he thinks I'm lazy because I don't wish to be boiled to death. How did he know about the dance at Cranston's? Old cat!"

The roar and turmoil of machinery and busy men filled my ears as I crossed the avenue and turned into the City Hall Park.

From the staff on the tower the flag drooped in the warm sunshine with scarcely a breeze to lift its crimson bars. Overhead stretched a splendid cloudless sky, deep, deep blue, thrilling, scintillating in the gemmed rays of the sun.

Pigeons wheeled and circled about the roof of the grey Post Office or dropped out of the blue above to flutter around the fountain in the square.

On the steps of the City Hall the unlovely politician lounged, exploring his heavy underjaw with wooden toothpick, twisting his drooping black moustache, or distributing tobacco juice over marble steps and close-clipped grass.

My eyes wandered from these human vermin to the calm scornful face of Nathan Hale, on his pedestal, and then to the grey-coated Park policeman whose occupation was to keep little children from the cool grass.

A young man with thin hands and blue circles under his eyes was slumbering on a bench by the fountain, and the policeman walked over to him and struck him on the soles of his shoes with a short club.

The young man rose mechanically, stared about, dazed by the sun, shivered, and limped away. I saw him sit down on the steps of the white marble building, and I went over and spoke to him. He neither looked at me, nor did he notice the coin I offered.

"You're sick," I said, "you had better go to the hospital."

"Where?" he asked vacantly—"I've been, but they wouldn't receive me."

He stooped and tied the bit of string that held what remained of his shoe to his foot.

"You are French," I said.

"Yes."

"Have you no friends? Have you been to the French Consul?"

"The Consul!" he replied; "no, I haven't been to the French Consul."

After a moment I said, "You speak like a gentleman."

He rose to his feet and stood very straight, looking me, for the first time, directly in the eyes.

"Who are you ?" I asked abruptly.

"An outcast," he said, without emotion, and limped off thrusting his hands into his ragged pockets.

"Huh!" said the Park policeman who had come up behind me in time to hear my question and the vagabond's answer; "don't you know who that hobo is?—An' you a newspaper man!"

"Who is he, Cusick?" I demanded, watching the thin shabby figure moving across Broadway toward the river.

"On the level you don't know, Mr. Hilton?" repeated Cusick, suspiciously.

"No, I don't; I never before laid eyes on him."

"Why," said the sparrow policeman, "that's 'Soger Charlie';— you remember—that French officer what sold secrets to the Dutch Emperor."

"And was to have been shot? I remember now, four years ago—and he escaped—you mean to say that is the man?"

"Everybody knows it," sniffed Cusick, "I'd a-thought you newspaper gents would have knowed it first."

"What was his name?" I asked after a moment's thought.

"Soger Charlie—"

"I mean his name at home."

"Oh, some French dago name. No Frenchman will speak to him here; sometimes they curse him and kick him. I guess he's dyin' by inches."

I remembered the case now. Two young French cavalry officers were arrested, charged with selling plans of fortifications and other military secrets to the Germans. On the eve of their conviction, one of them, Heaven only knows how, escaped and turned up in New York. The other was duly shot. The affair had made some noise, because both young men were of good families. It was a painful episode, and I had hastened to forget it. Now that it was recalled to my mind, I remembered the newspaper accounts of the case, but I had forgotten the names of the miserable young men.

"Sold his country," observed Cusick, watching a group of children out of the corner of his eyes—"you can't trust no Frenchman nor dagoes nor Dutchmen either. I guess Yankees are about the only white men."

I looked at the noble face of Nathan Hale and nodded.

"Nothin' sneaky about us, eh, Mr. Hilton?"

I thought of Benedict Arnold and looked at my boots.

Then the policeman said, "Well, solong, Mr. Hilton," and went away to frighten a pasty-faced little girl who had climbed upon the railing and was leaning down to sniff the fragrant grass.

"Cheese it, de cop!" cried her shrill-voiced friends, and the whole bevy of small ragamuffins scuttled away across the square.

With a feeling of depression I turned and walked toward Broadway, where the long yellow cable-cars swept up and down, and the din of gongs and the deafening rumble of heavy trucks echoed from the marble walls of the Court House to the granite mass of the Post Office.

Throngs of hurrying busy people passed up town and down town, slim sober-faced clerks, trim cold-eyed brokers, here and there a red-necked politician linking arms with some favourite heeler, here and there a City Hall lawyer, sallow-faced and saturnine. Sometimes a fireman, in his severe blue uniform, passed through the crowd, sometimes a blue-coated policeman, mopping his clipped hair, holding his helmet in his white-gloved hand. There were women too, pale-faced shop girls with pretty eyes, tall blonde girls who might be typewriters and might not, and many, many older women whose business in that part of the city no human being could venture to guess, but who hurried up town and down town, all occupied with *something* that gave to the whole restless throng a common likeness—the expression of one who hastens toward a hopeless goal.

I knew some of those who passed me. There was little Jocelyn of the *Mail and Express*; there was Hood, who had more money than he wanted and was going to have less than he wanted when he left Wall Street; there was Colonel Tidmouse of the 45th Infantry, N.G.S.N.Y., probably coming from the office of the *Army and Navy Journal*, and there was Dick Harding who wrote the best stories of New York life that have been printed. People said his hat no longer fitted,—especially people who also wrote stories of New York life and whose hats threatened to fit as long as they lived.

I looked at the statue of Nathan Hale, then at the human stream that flowed around his pedestal.

"Quand même," I muttered and walked out into Broadway, signalling to the gripman of an uptown cable-car.

II

I passed into the Park by the Fifth Avenue and 59th Street gate; I could never bring myself to enter it through the gate that is guarded by the hideous pigmy statue of Thorwaldsen.

The afternoon sun poured into the windows of the New Netherlands Hotel, setting every orange-curtained pane a-glitter, and tipping the wings of the bronze dragons with flame.

Gorgeous masses of flowers blazed in the sunshine from the grey terraces of the Savoy, from the high grilled court of the Vanderbilt palace, and from the balconies of the Plaza opposite.

The white marble façade of the Metropolitan Club was a grateful relief in the universal glare, and I kept my eyes on it until I had crossed the dusty street and entered the shade of the trees.

Before I came to the Zoo I smelled it. Next week it was to be removed to the fresh cool woods and meadows in Bronx Park, far from the stifling air of the city, far from the infernal noise of the Fifth Avenue omnibuses.

A noble stag stared at me from his enclosure among the trees as I passed down the winding asphalt walk. "Never mind, old fellow," said I, "you will be splashing about in the Bronx River next week and cropping maple shoots to your heart's content."

On I went, past herds of staring deer, past great lumbering elk, and moose, and long-faced African antelopes, until I came to the dens of the great carnivora.

The tigers sprawled in the sunshine, blinking and licking their paws; the lions slept in the shade or squatted on their haunches, yawning gravely. A slim panther travelled to and fro behind her barred cage, pausing at times to peer wistfully out into the free sunny world. My heart ached for caged wild things, and I walked on, glancing up now and then to encounter the blank stare of a tiger or the mean shifty eyes of some ill-smelling hyena.

Across the meadow I could see the elephants swaying and swinging their great heads, the sober bison solemnly slobbering over their cuds, the sarcastic countenances of camels, the wicked little zebras, and a lot more animals of the camel and llama tribe, all resembling each other, all equally ridiculous, stupid, deadly uninteresting.

Somewhere behind the old arsenal an eagle was screaming, probably a Yankee eagle; I heard the "tchug! tchug!" of a blowing hippopotamus, the squeal of a falcon, and the snarling yap! of quarrelling wolves.

"A pleasant place for a hot day!" I pondered bitterly, and I thought some things about Jamison that I shall not insert in this volume. But I lighted a cigarette to deaden the aroma from the hyenas, unclasped my sketching block, sharpened my pencil, and fell to work on a family group of hippopotami.

They may have taken me for a photographer, for they all wore smiles as if "welcoming a friend," and my sketch block presented a series of wide open jaws, behind which shapeless bulky bodies vanished in alarming perspective.

The alligators were easy; they looked to me as though they had not moved since the founding of the Zoo, but I had a bad time with the big bison, who persistently turned his tail to me, looking stolidly around his flank to see how I stood it. So I pretended to be absorbed in the antics of two bear cubs, and the dreary old bison fell into the trap, for I made some good sketches of him and laughed in his face as I closed the book.

There was a bench by the abode of the eagles, and I sat down on it to draw the vultures and condors, motionless as mummies among the piled rocks. Gradually I enlarged the sketch, bringing in the gravel plaza, the steps leading up to Fifth Avenue, the sleepy park policeman in front of the arsenal—and a slim, white-browed girl, dressed in shabby black, who stood silently in the shade of the willow trees.

After a while I found that the sketch, instead of being a study of the eagles, was in reality a composition in which the girl in black occupied the principal point of interest. Unwittingly I had subordinated everything else to her, the brooding vultures, the trees and walks, and the half indicated groups of sun-warmed loungers.

She stood very still, her pallid face bent, her thin white hands loosely clasped before her. "Rather dejected reverie," I thought, "probably she's out of work." Then I caught a glimpse of a sparkling diamond ring on the slender third finger of her left hand.

"She'll not starve with such a stone as that about her," I said to myself, looking curiously at her dark eyes and sensitive mouth. They were both beautiful, eyes and mouth—beautiful, but touched with pain.

After a while I rose and walked back to make a sketch or two of the lions and tigers. I avoided the monkeys—I can't stand them, and they never seem funny to me, poor dwarfish, degraded caricatures of all that is ignoble in ourselves.

"I've enough now," I thought; "I'll go home and manufacture a full page that will probably please Jamison." So I strapped the elastic band around my sketching block, replaced pencil and rubber in my waistcoat pocket, and strolled off toward the Mall to smoke a cigarette in the evening glow before going back to my studio to work until midnight, up to the chin in charcoal grey and Chinese white.

Across the long meadow I could see the roofs of the city faintly looming above the trees. A mist of amethyst, ever deepening, hung low on the horizon, and through it, steeple and dome, roof and tower, and the tall chimneys where thin fillets of smoke curled idly, were transformed into pinnacles of beryl and flaming minarets, swimming in filmy haze. Slowly the enchantment deepened; all that was ugly and shabby and mean had fallen away from the distant city, and now it towered into the evening sky, splendid, gilded, magnificent, purified in the fierce furnace of the setting sun.

The red disk was half hidden now; the tracery of trees, feathery willow and budding birch, darkened against the glow; the fiery rays shot far across the meadow, gilding the dead leaves, staining with soft crimson the dark moist tree trunks around me.

Far across the meadow a shepherd passed in the wake of a huddling flock, his dog at his heels, faint moving blots of grey.

A squirrel sat up on the gravel walk in front of me, ran a few feet, and sat up again, so close that I could see the palpitation of his sleek flanks.

Somewhere in the grass a hidden field insect was rehearsing last summer's solos; I heard the tap! tap! tat-tat-t-t-tat! of a wood-pecker among the branches overhead and the querulous note of a sleepy robin.

The twilight deepened; out of the city the music of bells floated over wood and meadow; faint mellow whistles sounded from the river craft along the north shore, and the distant thunder of a gun announced the close of a June day.

The end of my cigarette began to glimmer with a redder light; shepherd and flock were blotted out in the dusk, and I only knew they were still moving when the sheep bells tinkled faintly.

Then suddenly that strange uneasiness that all have known—that half-awakened sense of having seen it all before, of having been through it all, came over me, and I raised my head and slowly turned.

A figure was seated at my side. My mind was struggling with the instinct to remember. Something so vague and yet so familiar—something that eluded thought yet challenged it, something—God knows what! troubled me. And now, as I looked, without interest, at the dark figure beside me, an apprehension, totally involuntary, an impatience to *understand,* came upon me, and I sighed and turned restlessly again to the fading west.

I thought I heard my sigh re-echoed—I scarcely heeded; and in a moment I sighed again, dropping my burned-out cigarette on the gravel beneath my feet.

"Did you speak to me?" said some one in a low voice, so close that I swung around rather sharply.

"No," I said after a moment's silence.

It was a woman. I could not see her face clearly, but I saw on her clasped hands, which lay listlessly in her lap, the sparkle of a great diamond. I knew her at once. It did not need a glance at the shabby dress of black, the white face, a pallid spot in the twilight, to tell me that I had her picture in my sketch-book.

"Do—do you mind if I speak to you?" she asked timidly. The hopeless sadness in her voice touched me, and I said: "Why, no, of course not. Can I do anything for you?"

"Yes," she said, brightening a little, "if you—you only would."

"I will if I can," said I, cheerfully; "what is it? Out of ready cash?"

"No, not that," she said, shrinking back.

I begged her pardon, a little surprised, and withdrew my hand from my change pocket.

"It is only—only that I wish you to take these,"—she drew a thin packet from her breast,—"these two letters."

"I?" I asked astonished.

"Yes, if you will."

"But what am I to do with them?" I demanded.

"I can't tell you; I only know that I must give them to you. Will you take them?"

"Oh, yes, I'll take them," I laughed, "am I to read them?" I added to myself, "It's some clever begging trick."

"No," she answered slowly, "you are not to read them; you are to give them to somebody."

"To whom? Anybody?"

"No, not to anybody. You will know whom to give them to when the time comes."

"Then I am to keep them until further instructions?"

"Your own heart will instruct you," she said, in a scarcely audible voice. She held the thin packet toward me, and to humour her I took it. It was wet.

"The letters fell into the sea," she said. "There was a photograph which should have gone with them but the salt water washed it blank. Will you care if I ask you something else?"

"I? Oh, no."

"Then give me the picture that you made of me to-day."

I laughed again, and demanded how she knew I had drawn her.

"Is it like me?" she said.

"I think it is very like you," I answered truthfully.

"Will you not give it to me?"

Now it was on the tip of my tongue to refuse, but I reflected that I had enough sketches for a full page without that one, so I handed it to her, nodded that she was welcome, and stood up. She rose also, the diamond flashing on her finger.

"You are sure that you are not in want?" I asked, with a tinge of good-natured sarcasm.

"Hark!" she whispered; "listen!—do you hear the bells of the convent!"

I looked out into the misty night.

"There are no bells sounding," I said, "and anyway there are no convent bells here. We are in New York, mademoiselle"—I had noticed her French accent—"we are in Protestant Yankee-land, and the bells that ring are much less mellow than the bells of France."

I turned pleasantly to say good-night. She was gone.

III

"Have you ever drawn a picture of a corpse?" inquired Jamison next morning as I walked into his private room with a sketch of the proposed full page of the Zoo.

"No, and I don't want to," I replied, sullenly.

"Let me see your Central Park page," said Jamison in his gentle voice, and I displayed it. It was about worthless as an artistic production, but it pleased Jamison, as I knew it would.

"Can you finish it by this afternoon?" he asked, looking up at me with persuasive eyes.

"Oh, I suppose so," I said, wearily; "anything else, Mr. Jamison?"

"The corpse," he replied, "I want a sketch by to-morrow—finished."

"What corpse?" I demanded, controlling my indignation as I met Jamison's soft eyes.

There was a mute duel of glances. Jamison passed his hand across his forehead with a slight lifting of the eyebrows.

"I shall want it as soon as possible," he said in his caressing voice.

What I thought was, "Damned purring pussy-cat!" What I said was, "Where is this corpse?"

"In the Morgue—have you read the morning papers? No? Ah, —as you very rightly observe you are too busy to read the morning papers. Young men must learn industry first, of course, of course. What you are to do is this: the San Francisco police have sent out an alarm regarding the disappearance of a Miss Tufft—the millionaire's daughter, you know. To-day a body was brought to the Morgue here in New York, and it has been identified as the missing young lady,—by a diamond ring. Now I am convinced that it isn't, and I'll show you why, Mr. Hilton."

He picked up a pen and made a sketch of a ring on a margin of that morning's *Tribune*.

"That is the description of her ring as sent on from San Francisco. You notice the diamond is set in the centre of the ring where the two gold serpents' *tails* cross!

"Now the ring on the finger of the woman in the Morgue is like this," and he rapidly sketched another ring where the diamond rested in the *fangs* of the two gold serpents.

"That is the difference," he said in his pleasant, even voice.

"Rings like that are not uncommon," said I, remembering that I had seen such a ring on the finger of the white-faced girl in the Park the evening before. Then a sudden thought took shape—perhaps that was the girl whose body lay in the Morgue!

"Well," said Jamison, looking up at me, "what are you thinking about?"

"Nothing," I answered, but the whole scene was before my eyes, the vultures brooding among the rocks, the shabby black dress, and the pallid face,—and the ring, glittering on that slim white hand!

"Nothing," I repeated, "when shall I go, Mr. Jamison? Do you want a portrait—or what?"

"Portrait,—careful drawing of the ring, and,—er—a centre piece of the Morgue at night. Might as well give people the horrors while we're about it."

"But," said I, "the policy of this paper—"

"Never mind, Mr. Hilton," purred Jamison, "I am able to direct the policy of this paper."

"I don't doubt you are," I said angrily.

"I am," he repeated, undisturbed and smiling; "you see this Tufft case interests society. I am—er—also interested."

He held out to me a morning paper and pointed to a heading.

I read: "Miss Tufft Dead! Her Fiancé was Mr. Jamison, the well known Editor."

"What!" I cried in horrified amazement. But Jamison had left the room, and I heard him chatting and laughing softly with some visitors in the press-room outside.

I flung down the paper and walked out.

"The cold-blooded toad!" I exclaimed again and again;—"making capital out of his fiancée's disappearance! Well, I—I'm d—nd! I knew he was a bloodless, heartless, grip-penny, but I never thought—I never imagined—" Words failed me.

Scarcely conscious of what I did I drew a *Herald* from my pocket and saw the column entitled: "Miss Tufft Found! Identified by a Ring. Wild Grief of Mr. Jamison, her Fiancé."

That was enough. I went out into the street and sat down in City Hall Park. And, as I sat there, a terrible resolution came to me; I would draw that dead girl's face in such a way that it would chill Jamison's sluggish blood, I would crowd the black shadows of the Morgue with forms and ghastly faces, and every face should bear something in it of Jamison. Oh, I'd rouse him from his cold snaky apathy! I'd confront him with Death in such an awful form, that, passionless, base, inhuman as he was, he'd shrink from it as he would from a dagger thrust. Of course I'd lose my place, but that did not bother me, for I had decided to resign anyway, not having a taste for the society of human reptiles. And, as I sat there in the sunny park, furious, trying to plan a picture whose sombre horror should leave in his mind an ineffaceable scar, I suddenly thought of the pale black-robed girl in Central Park. Could it be her poor slender body that lay among the shadows of the grim Morgue! ·If ever brooding despair was stamped on any face, I had seen its print on hers when she spoke to me in the Park and gave me the letters. The letters! I had not thought of them since, but now I drew them from my pocket and looked at the addresses.

"Curious," I thought, "the letters are still damp; they smell of salt water too."

I looked at the address again, written in the long fine hand of an educated woman who had been bred in a French convent. Both letters bore the same address, in French:

CAPTAIN D'YNIOL.
(Kindness of a Stranger.)

"Captain d'Yniol," I repeated aloud—"confound it, I've heard that name! Now, where the deuce—where in the name of all that's queer—" Somebody who had sat down on the bench beside me placed a heavy hand on my shoulder.

It was the Frenchman, "Soger Charlie."

"You spoke my name," he said in apathetic tones.

"Your name!"

"Captain d'Yniol," he repeated; "it is my name."

I recognized him in spite of the black goggles he was wearing, and, at the same moment, it flashed into my mind that d'Yniol was the name of the traitor who had escaped. Ah, I remembered now!

"I am Captain d'Yniol," he said again, and I saw his fingers closing on my coat sleeve.

It may have been my involuntary movement of recoil,—I don't know,—but the fellow dropped my coat and sat straight up on the bench.

"I am Captain d'Yniol," he said for the third time, "charged with treason and under sentence of death."

"And innocent!" I muttered, before I was even conscious of having spoken. What was it that wrung those involuntary words from my lips, I shall never know, perhaps—but it was I, not he, who trembled, seized with a strange agitation, and it was I, not he, whose hand was stretched forth impulsively, touching his.

Without a tremor he took my hand, pressed it almost impercep-
tibly, and dropped it. Then I held both letters toward him, and, as
he neither looked at them nor at me, I placed them in his hand.
Then he started.

"Read them," I said, "they are for you."

"Letters!" he gasped in a voice that sounded like nothing human.

"Yes, they are for you,—I know it now—"

"Letters!—letters directed to *me*?"

"Can you not see?" I cried.

Then he raised one frail hand and drew the goggles from his eyes,
and, as I looked, I saw two tiny white specks exactly in the centre of
both pupils.

"Blind!" I faltered.

"I have been unable to read for two years," he said.

After a moment he placed the tip of one finger on the letters.

"They are wet," I said; "shall—would you like to have me read
them?" For a long time he sat silently in the sunshine, fumbling with
his cane, and I watched him without speaking. At last he said, "Read,
Monsieur," and I took the letters and broke the seals.

The first letter contained a sheet of paper, damp and discoloured,
on which a few lines were written:

My darling, I knew you were innocent—

Here the writing ended, but, in the blur beneath, I read:

Paris shall know—France shall know, for at last I have the proofs and I
am coming to find you, my soldier, and to place them in your own dear brave
hands. They know, now, at the War Ministry—they have a copy of the
traitor's confession—but they dare not make it public—they dare not with-
stand the popular astonishment and rage. Therefore I sail on Monday from
Cherbourg by the Green Cross Line, to bring you back to your own again,
where you will stand before all the world, without fear, without reproach.

ALINE.

"This—this is terrible!" I stammered; "can God live and see
such things done!"

But with his thin hand he gripped my arm again, bidding me read
the other letter; and I shuddered at the menace in his voice.

Then, with his sightless eyes on me, I drew the other letter
from the wet, stained envelope. And before I was aware—before I

understood the purport of what I saw, I had read aloud these half effaced lines:

"The *Lorient* is sinking—an iceberg—mid-ocean—good-bye—you are innocent—I love—"

"The *Lorient*!" I cried; "it was the French steamer that was never heard from—the *Lorient* of the Green Cross Line! I had forgotten—I—"

The loud crash of a revolver stunned me; my ears rang and ached with it as I shrank back from a ragged dusty figure that collapsed on the bench beside me, shuddered a moment, and tumbled to the asphalt at my feet.

The trampling of the eager hard-eyed crowd, the dust and taint of powder in the hot air, the harsh alarm of the ambulance clattering up Mail Street,—these I remember, as I knelt there, helplessly holding the dead man's hands in mine.

"Soger Charlie," mused the sparrow policeman, "shot his-self, didn't he, Mr. Hilton? You seen him, sir,—blowed the top of his head off, didn't he, Mr. Hilton?"

"Soger Charlie," they repeated, "a French dago what shot his-self;" and the words echoed in my ears long after the ambulance rattled away, and the increasing throng dispersed, sullenly, as a couple of policemen cleared a space around the pool of thick blood on the asphalt.

They wanted me as a witness, and I gave my card to one of the policemen who knew me. The rabble transferred its fascinated stare to me, and I turned away and pushed a path between frightened shop girls and ill-smelling loafers, until I lost myself in the human torrent of Broadway.

The torrent took me with it where it flowed—East? West?—I did not notice nor care, but I passed on through the throng, listless, deadly weary of attempting to solve God's justice—striving to understand His purpose—His laws—His judgments which are "true and righteous altogether."

IV

"More to be desired are they than gold, yea, than much fine gold. Sweeter also than honey and the honey-comb!"

I turned sharply toward the speaker who shambled at my elbow. His sunken eyes were dull and lustreless, his bloodless face gleamed pallid as a death mask above the blood-red jersey—the emblem of the soldiers of Christ.

I don't know why I stopped, lingering, but, as he passed, I said, "Brother, I also was meditating upon God's wisdom and His testimonies."

The pale fanatic shot a glance at me, hesitated, and fell into my own pace, walking by my side. Under the peak of his Salvation Army cap his eyes shone in the shadow with a strange light.

"Tell me more," I said, sinking my voice below the roar of traffic, the clang! clang! of the cable-cars, and the noise of feet on the worn pavements—"tell me of His testimonies."

"Moreover by them is Thy servant warned and in keeping of them there is great reward. Who can understand His errors? Cleanse Thou me from secret faults. Keep back Thy servant also from presumptuous sins. Let them not have dominion over me. Then shall I be upright and I shall be innocent from the great transgression. Let the words of my mouth and the meditation of my heart be acceptable in Thy sight,—O Lord! My strength and my Redeemer!"

"It is Holy Scripture that you quote," I said; "I also can read that when I choose. But it cannot clear for me the reasons—it cannot make me understand—"

"What?" he asked, and muttered to himself.

"That, for instance," I replied, pointing to a cripple, who had been *born* deaf and dumb and horridly misshapen,—a wretched diseased lump on the sidewalk below St. Paul's Churchyard,—a sore-eyed thing that mouthed and mowed and rattled pennies in a tin cup as though the sound of copper could stem the human pack that passed hot on the scent of gold.

Then the man who shambled beside me turned and looked long and earnestly into my eyes. And after a moment a dull recollection stirred within me—a vague something that seemed like the awakening memory of a past, long, long forgotten, dim, dark, too subtle, too frail, too indefinite—ah! the old feeling that all men have known— the old strange uneasiness, that useless struggle to remember when and where it all occurred before.

And the man's head sank on his crimson jersey, and he muttered, muttered to himself of God and love and compassion, until I saw that the fierce heat of the city had touched his brain, and I went away and left him prating of mysteries that none but such as he dare name.

So I passed on through dust and heat; and the hot breath of men touched my cheek and eager eyes looked into mine. Eyes, eyes, that met my own and looked through them, beyond—far beyond to where gold glittered amid the mirage of eternal hope. Gold! It was in the air where the soft sunlight gilded the floating moats, it was under foot in the dust that the sun made gilt, it glimmered from every window pane where the long red beams struck golden sparks above the gasping gold-hunting hordes of Wall Street.

High, high, in the deepening sky the tall buildings towered, and the breeze from the bay lifted the sun-dyed flags of commerce until they waved above the turmoil of the hives below—waved courage and hope and strength to those who lusted after gold.

The sun dipped low behind Castle William as I turned listlessly into the Battery, and the long straight shadows of the trees stretched away over greensward and asphalt walk.

Already the electric lights were glimmering among the foliage although the bay shimmered like polished brass and the topsails of the ships glowed with a deeper hue, where the red sun rays fall athwart the rigging.

Old men tottered along the sea-wall, tapping the asphalt with worn canes, old women crept to and fro in the coming twilight,—old women who carried baskets that gaped for charity or bulged with mouldy stuffs,—food, clothing?—I could not tell; I did not care to know.

The heavy thunder from the parapets of Castle William died away over the placid bay, the last red arm of the sun shot up out of the sea, and wavered and faded into the sombre tones of the afterglow. Then came the night, timidly at first, touching sky and water with grey fingers, folding the foliage into soft massed shapes, creeping onward, onward, more swiftly now, until colour and form had gone from all the earth and the world was a world of shadows.

And, as I sat there on the dusky sea-wall, gradually the bitter thoughts faded and I looked out into the calm night with something of that peace that comes to all when day is ended.

The death at my very elbow of the poor blind wretch in the Park had left a shock, but now my nerves relaxed their tension and I began to think about it all,—about the letters and the strange woman who had given them to me. I wondered where she had found them, —whether they really were carried by some vagrant current in to the shore from the wreck of the fated *Lorient*.

Nothing but these letters had human eyes encountered from the *Lorient*, although we believed that fire or berg had been her portion; for there had been no storms when the *Lorient* steamed away from Cherbourg.

And what of the pale-faced girl in black who had given these letters to me, saying that my own heart would teach me where to place them?

I felt in my pockets for the letters where I had thrust them all crumpled and wet. They were there, and I decided to turn them over to the police. Then I thought of Cusick and the City Hall Park and these set my mind running on Jamison and my own work,—ah! I had forgotten that,—I had forgotten that I had sworn to stir Jamison's cold, sluggish blood! Trading on his fiancée's reported suicide,—or murder! True, he had told me that he was satisfied that the body at the Morgue was not Miss Tufft's because the ring did not correspond with his fiancée's ring. But what sort of man was that!— to go crawling and nosing about morgues and graves for a full-page illustration which might sell a few extra thousand papers. I had never known he was such a man. It was strange too—for that was not the sort of illustration that the *Weekly* used; it was against all precedent—against the whole policy of the paper. He would lose a hundred subscribers where he would gain one by such work.

"The callous brute!" I muttered to myself, "I'll wake him up —I'll—"

I sat straight up on the bench and looked steadily at a figure which was moving toward me under the spluttering electric light.

It was the woman I had met in the Park.

She came straight up to me, her pale face gleaming like marble in the dark, her slim hands outstretched.

"I have been looking for you all day—all day," she said, in the same low thrilling tones,—"I want the letters back; have you them here?"

"Yes," I said, "I have them here,—take them in Heaven's name; they have done enough evil for one day!"

She took the letters from my hand; I saw the ring, made of the double serpents, flashing on her slim finger, and I stepped closer, and looked her in the eyes.

"Who are you?" I asked.

"I? My name is of no importance to you," she answered.

"You are right," I said, "I do not care to know your name. That ring of yours—"

"What of my ring?" she murmured.

"Nothing,—a dead woman lying in the Morgue wears such a ring. Do you know what your letters have done? No? Well I read them to a miserable wretch and he blew his brains out!"

"You read them to a man!"

"I did. He killed himself."

"Who was that man?"

"Captain d'Yniol—"

With something between a sob and a laugh she seized my hand and covered it with kisses, and I, astonished and angry, pulled my hand away from her cold lips and sat down on the bench.

"You needn't thank me," I said sharply; "if I had known that, —but no matter. Perhaps after all the poor devil is better off somewhere in other regions with his sweetheart who was drowned,—yes, I imagine he is. He was blind and ill,—and broken-hearted."

"Blind?" she asked gently.

"Yes. Did you know him?"

"I knew him."

"And his sweetheart, Aline?"

"Aline," she repeated softly,—"she is dead. I come to thank you in her name."

"For what?—for his death?"

"Ah, yes, for that."

"Where did you get those letters?" I asked her, suddenly.

She did not answer, but stood fingering the wet letters.

Before I could speak again she moved away into the shadows of the trees, lightly, silently, and far down the dark walk I saw her diamond flashing.

Grimly brooding, I rose and passed through the Battery to the steps of the Elevated Road. These I climbed, bought my ticket, and stepped out to the damp platform. When a train came I crowded in with the rest, still pondering on my vengeance, feeling and believing that I was to scourge the conscience of the man who speculated on death.

And at last the train stopped at 28th Street, and I hurried out and down the steps and away to the Morgue.

When I entered the Morgue, Skelton, the keeper, was standing before a slab that glistened faintly under the wretched gas jets. He heard my footsteps, and turned around to see who was coming. Then he nodded, saying: "Mr. Hilton, just take a look at this here stiff—I'll be back in a moment—this is the one that all the papers take to be Miss Tufft,—but they're all off, because this stiff has been here now for two weeks."

I drew out my sketching-block and pencils.

"Which is it, Skelton?" I asked, fumbling for my rubber.

"This one, Mr. Hilton, the girl what's smilin'. Picked up off Sandy Hook, too. Looks as if she was asleep, eh?"

"What's she got in her hand—clenched tight? Oh,—a letter. Turn up the gas, Skelton, I want to see her face."

The old man turned the gas jet, and the flame blazed and whistled in the damp, fetid air. Then suddenly my eyes fell on the dead.

Rigid, scarcely breathing, I stared at the ring, made of two twisted serpents set with a great diamond,—I saw the wet letters crushed in her slender hand,—I looked, and—God help me!—I looked upon the dead face of the girl with whom I had been speaking on the Battery!

"Dead for a month at least," said Skelton, calmly.

Then, as I felt my senses leaving me, I screamed out, and at the same instant somebody from behind seized my shoulder and shook me savagely—shook me until I opened my eyes again and gasped and coughed.

"Now then, young feller!" said a Park policeman bending over me, "if you go to sleep on a bench, somebody'll lift your watch!"

I turned, rubbing my eyes desperately.

Then it was all a dream—and no shrinking girl had come to me with damp letters,—I had not gone to the office—there was no such person as Miss Tufft,—Jamison was not an unfeeling villain,—no, indeed!—he treated us all much better than we deserved, and he was kind and generous too. And the ghastly suicide! Thank God that also was a myth,—and the Morgue and the Battery at night where that pale-faced girl had—ugh!

I felt for my sketch-block, found it; turned the pages of all the animals that I had sketched, the hippopotami, the buffalo, the tigers —ah! where was that sketch in which I had made the woman in shabby black the principal figure, with the brooding vultures all around and the crowd in the sunshine—? It was gone.

I hunted everywhere, in every pocket. It was gone.

At last I rose and moved along the narrow asphalt path in the falling twilight.

And as I turned into the broader walk, I was aware of a group, a policeman holding a lantern, some gardeners, and a knot of loungers gathered about something,—a dark mass on the ground.

"Found 'em just so," one of the gardeners was saying, "better not touch 'em until the coroner comes."

The policeman shifted his bull's-eye a little; the rays fell on two faces, on two bodies, half supported against a park bench. On the finger of the girl glittered a splendid diamond, set between the fangs of two gold serpents. The man had shot himself; he clasped two wet letters in his hand. The girl's clothing and hair were wringing wet, and her face was the face of a drowned person.

"Well, sir," said the policeman, looking at me; "you seem to know these two people—by your looks—"

"I never saw them before," I gasped, and walked on, trembling in every nerve.

For among the folds of her shabby black dress I had noticed the end of a paper,—my sketch that I had missed!

The Messenger

Little gray messenger,
Robed like painted Death,
Your robe is dust.
Whom do you seek
Among the lilies and closed buds
    At dusk?

Among lilies and closed buds
    At dusk,
Whom do you seek,
Little gray messenger,
Robed in the awful panoply
Of painted Death?

    All-wise,
Hast thou seen all there is to see with thy two eyes?
Dost thou know all there is to know, and so,
    Omniscient,
Darest thou still to say thy brother lies?
              R.W.C.

I

"THE bullet entered here," said Max Fortin, and he placed his middle finger over a smooth hole exactly in the centre of the forehead.

I sat down upon a mound of dry seaweed and unslung my fowling piece.

The little chemist cautiously felt the edges of the shot-hole, first with his middle finger, then with his thumb.

"Let me see the skull again," said I.

Max Fortin picked it up from the sod.

"It's like all the others," he observed. I nodded, without offering to take it from him. After a moment he thoughtfully replaced it upon the grass at my feet.

"It's like all the others," he repeated, wiping his glasses on his handkerchief. "I thought you might care to see one of the skulls, so I brought this over from the gravel pit. The men from Bannalec are digging yet. They ought to stop."

"How many skulls are there altogether?" I inquired.

"They found thirty-eight skulls; there are thirty-nine noted in the list. They lie piled up in the gravel pit on the edge of Le Bihan's wheat field. The men are at work yet. Le Bihan is going to stop them."

"Let's go over," said I; and I picked up my gun and started across the cliffs, Fortin on one side, Môme on the other.

"Who has the list?" I asked, lighting my pipe. "You say there is a list?"

"The list was found rolled up in a brass cylinder," said the little chemist. He added: "You should not smoke here. You know that if a single spark drifted into the wheat—"

"Ah, but I have a cover to my pipe," said I, smiling.

Fortin watched me as I closed the pepper-box arrangement over the glowing bowl of the pipe. Then he continued:

"The list was made out on thick yellow paper; the brass tube has preserved it. It is as fresh to-day as it was in 1760. You shall see it."

"Is that the date?"

"The list is dated 'April, 1760.' The Brigadier Durand has it. It is not written in French."

"Not written in French!" I exclaimed.

"No," replied Fortin solemnly, "it is written in Breton."

"But," I protested, "the Breton language was never written or printed in 1760."

"Except by priests," said the chemist.

"I have heard of but one priest who ever wrote the Breton language," I began.

Fortin stole a glance at my face.

"You mean—the Black Priest?" he asked.

I nodded.

Fortin opened his mouth to speak again, hesitated, and finally shut his teeth obstinately over the wheat stem that he was chewing.

"And the Black Priest?" I suggested encouragingly. But I knew it was useless; for it is easier to move the stars from their courses than to make an obstinate Breton talk. We walked on for a minute or two in silence.

"Where is the Brigadier Durand?" I asked, motioning Môme to come out of the wheat, which he was trampling as though it were heather. As I spoke we came in sight of the farther edge of the wheat field and the dark, wet mass of cliffs beyond.

"Durand is down there—you can see him; he stands just behind the Mayor of St. Gildas."

"I see," said I; and we struck straight down, following a sun-baked cattle path across the heather.

When we reached the edge of the wheat field, Le Bihan, the Mayor of St. Gildas, called to me, and I tucked my gun under my arm and skirted the wheat to where he stood.

"Thirty-eight skulls," he said in his thin, high-pitched voice; "there is but one more, and I am opposed to further search. I suppose Fortin told you?"

I shook hands with him, and returned the salute of the Brigadier Durand.

"I am opposed to further search," repeated Le Bihan, nervously picking at the mass of silver buttons which covered the front of his velvet and broadcloth jacket like a breastplate of scale armour.

Durand pursed up his lips, twisted his tremendous mustache, and hooked his thumbs in his sabre belt.

"As for me," he said, "I am in favour of further search."

"Further search for what—for the thirty-ninth skull?" I asked.

Le Bihan nodded. Durand frowned at the sunlit sea, rocking like a bowl of molten gold from the cliffs to the horizon. I followed his eyes. On the dark glistening cliffs, silhouetted against the glare of the sea, sat a cormorant, black, motionless, its horrible head raised toward heaven.

"Where is that list, Durand?" I asked.

The gendarme rummaged in his despatch pouch and produced a brass cylinder about a foot long. Very gravely he unscrewed the head and dumped out a scroll of thick yellow paper closely covered with writing on both sides. At a nod from Le Bihan he handed me the scroll. But I could make nothing of the coarse writing, now faded to a dull brown.

"Come, come, Le Bihan," I said impatiently, "translate it, won't you? You and Max Fortin make a lot of mystery out of nothing, it seems."

Le Bihan went to the edge of the pit where the three Bannalec men were digging, gave an order or two in Breton, and turned to me.

As I came to the edge of the pit the Bannalec men were removing a square piece of sail-cloth from what appeared to be a pile of cobblestones.

"Look!" said Le Bihan shrilly. I looked. The pile below was a heap of skulls. After a moment I clambered down the gravel sides of the pit and walked over to the men of Bannalec. They saluted me gravely, leaning on their picks and shovels, and wiping their sweating faces with sunburned hands.

"How many?" said I in Breton.

"Thirty-eight," they replied.

I glanced around. Beyond the heap of skulls lay two piles of human bones. Beside these was a mound of broken, rusted bits of iron and steel. Looking closer, I saw that this mound was composed of rusty bayonets, sabre blades, scythe blades, with here and there a tarnished buckle attached to a bit of leather hard as iron.

I picked up a couple of buttons and a belt plate. The buttons bore the royal arms of England; the belt plate was emblazoned with the English arms, and also with the number "27."

"I have heard my grandfather speak of the terrible English regiment, the 27th Foot, which landed and stormed the fort up there," said one of the Bannalec men.

"Oh!" said I; "then these are the bones of English soldiers?"

"Yes," said the men of Bannalec.

Le Bihan was calling to me from the edge of the pit above, and I handed the belt plate and buttons to the men and climbed the side of the excavation.

"Well," said I, trying to prevent Môme from leaping up and licking my face as I emerged from the pit, "I suppose you know what these bones are. What are you going to do with them?"

"There was a man," said Le Bihan angrily, "an Englishman, who passed here in a dog-cart on his way to Quimper about an hour ago, and what do you suppose he wished to do?"

"Buy the relics?" I asked, smiling.

"Exactly—the pig!" piped the mayor of St. Gildas. "Jean Marie Tregunc, who found the bones, was standing there where Max Fortin stands, and do you know what he answered? He spat upon the ground, and said: 'Pig of an Englishman, do you take me for a desecrator of graves?'"

I knew Tregunc, a sober, blue-eyed Breton, who lived from one year's end to the other without being able to afford a single bit of meat for a meal.

"How much did the Englishman offer Tregunc?" I asked.

"Two hundred francs for the skulls alone."

I thought of the relic hunters and the relic buyers on the battle-fields of our civil war.

"Seventeen hundred and sixty is long ago," I said.

"Respect for the dead can never die," said Fortin.

"And the English soldiers came here to kill your fathers and burn your homes," I continued.

"They were murderers and thieves, but—they are dead," said Tregunc, coming up from the beach below, his long sea rake balanced on his dripping jersey.

"How much do you earn every year, Jean Marie?" I asked, turning to shake hands with him.

"Two hundred and twenty francs, monsieur."

"Forty-five dollars a year," I said. "Bah! you are worth more, Jean. Will you take care of my garden for me? My wife wished me to ask you. I think it would be worth one hundred francs a month to you and to me. Come on, Le Bihan—come along, Fortin—and you, Durand. I want somebody to translate that list into French for me."

Tregunc stood gazing at me, his blue eyes dilated.

"You may begin at once," I said, smiling, "if the salary suits you?"

"It suits," said Tregunc, fumbling for his pipe in a silly way that annoyed Le Bihan.

"Then go and begin your work," cried the mayor impatiently; and Tregunc started across the moors toward St. Gildas, taking off his velvet-ribboned cap to me and gripping his sea rake very hard.

"You offer him more than my salary," said the mayor, after a moment's contemplation of his silver buttons.

"Pooh!" said I, "what do you do for your salary except play dominoes with Max Fortin at the Groix Inn?"

Le Bihan turned red, but Durand rattled his sabre and winked at Max Fortin, and I slipped my arm through the arm of the sulky magistrate, laughing.

"There's a shady spot under the cliff," I said; "come on, Le Bihan, and read me what is in the scroll."

In a few moments we reached the shadow of the cliff, and I threw myself upon the turf, chin on hand, to listen.

The gendarme, Durand, also sat down, twisting his mustache into needlelike points. Fortin leaned against the cliff, polishing his glasses and examining us with vague, near-sighted eyes; and Le Bihan, the mayor, planted himself in our midst, rolling up the scroll and tucking it under his arm.

"First of all," he began in a shrill voice, "I am going to light my pipe, and while lighting it I shall tell you what I have heard about the attack on the fort yonder. My father told me; his father told him."

He jerked his head in the direction of the ruined fort, a small, square stone structure on the sea cliff, now nothing but crumbling walls. Then he slowly produced a tobacco pouch, a bit of flint and tinder, and a long-stemmed pipe fitted with a microscopical bowl of baked clay. To fill such a pipe requires ten minutes' close attention. To smoke it to a finish takes but four puffs. It is very Breton, this Breton pipe. It is the crystallization of everything Breton.

"Go on," said I, lighting a cigarette.

"The fort," said the mayor, "was built by Louis XIV, and was dismantled twice by the English. Louis XV restored it in 1739. In 1760 it was carried by assault by the English. They came across from the island of Groix—three shiploads—and they stormed the fort and sacked St. Julien yonder, and they started to burn St. Gildas— you can see the marks of their bullets on my house yet; but the men of Bannalec and the men of Lorient fell upon them with pike and scythe and blunderbuss, and those who did not run away lie there below in the gravel pit now—thirty-eight of them."

"And the thirty-ninth skull?" I asked, finishing my cigarette.

The mayor had succeeded in filling his pipe, and now he began to put his tobacco pouch away.

"The thirty-ninth skull," he mumbled, holding the pipestem between his defective teeth—"the thirty-ninth skull is no business of mine. I have told the Bannalec men to cease digging."

"But what is—whose is the missing skull?" I persisted curiously.

The mayor was busy trying to strike a spark to his tinder. Presently he set it aglow, applied it to his pipe, took the prescribed four puffs, knocked the ashes out of the bowl, and gravely replaced the pipe in his pocket.

"The missing skull?" he asked.

"Yes," said I impatiently.

The mayor slowly unrolled the scroll and began to read, translating from the Breton into French. And this is what he read:

On the Cliffs of St. Gildas,
April 13, 1760.

On this day, by order of the Count of Soisic, general in chief of the Breton forces now lying in Kerselec Forest, the bodies of thirty-eight English soldiers of the 27th, 50th, and 72nd regiments of Foot were buried in this spot, together with their arms and equipments.

The mayor paused and glanced at me reflectively.

"Go on, Le Bihan," I said.

"With them," continued the mayor, turning the scroll and reading on the other side, "was buried the body of that vile traitor who betrayed the fort to the English. The manner of his death was as follows: By order of the most noble Count of Soisic, the traitor was first branded upon the forehead with the brand of an arrowhead. The iron burned through the flesh, and was pressed heavily so that the brand should even burn into the bone of the skull. The traitor was then led out and bidden to kneel. He admitted having guided the English from the island of Groix. Although a priest and a Frenchman, he had violated his priestly office to aid him in discovering the password to the fort. This password he extorted during confession from a young Breton girl who was in the habit of rowing across from the island of Groix to visit her husband in the fort. When the fort fell, this young girl, crazed by the death of her husband, sought the Count of Soisic and told how the priest had forced her to confess to him all she knew about the fort. The priest was arrested at St. Gildas as he was about to cross the river to Lorient. When arrested he cursed the girl, Marie Trevec—"

"What!" I exclaimed, "Marie Trevec!"

"Marie Trevec," repeated Le Bihan; "the priest cursed Marie Trevec, and all her family and descendants. He was shot as he knelt, having a mask of leather over his face, because the Bretons who composed the squad of execution refused to fire at a priest unless his face was concealed. The priest was l'Abbé Sorgue, commonly known as the Black Priest on account of his dark face and swarthy eyebrows. He was buried with a stake through his heart."

Le Bihan paused, hesitated, looked at me, and handed the manuscript back to Durand. The gendarme took it and slipped it into the brass cylinder.

"So," said I, "the thirty-ninth skull is the skull of the Black Priest."

"Yes," said Fortin. "I hope they won't find it."

"I have forbidden them to proceed," said the mayor querulously. "You heard me, Max Fortin."

I rose and picked up my gun. Môme came and pushed his head into my hand.

"That's a fine dog," observed Durand, also rising.

"Why don't you wish to find his skull?" I asked Le Bihan. "It would be curious to see whether the arrow brand really burned into the bone."

"There is something in that scroll that I didn't read to you," said the mayor grimly. "Do you wish to know what it is?"

"Of course," I replied in surprise.

"Give me the scroll again, Durand," he said; then he read from the bottom: "I, l'Abbé Sorgue, forced to write the above by my executioners, have written it in my own blood; and with it I leave my curse. My curse on St. Gildas, on Marie Trevec, and on her descendants. I will come back to St. Gildas when my remains are disturbed. Woe to that Englishman whom my branded skull shall touch!"

"What rot!" I said. "Do you believe it was really written in his own blood?"

"I am going to test it," said Fortin, "at the request of Monsieur le Maire. I am not anxious for the job, however."

"See," said Le Bihan, holding out the scroll to me, "it is signed, l'Abbé Sorgue.' "

I glanced curiously over the paper.

"It must be the Black Priest," I said. "He was the only man who wrote in the Breton language. This is a wonderfully interesting discovery, for now, at last, the mystery of the Black Priest's disappearance is cleared up. You will, of course, send this scroll to Paris, Le Bihan?"

"No," said the mayor obstinately, "it shall be buried in the pit below where the rest of the Black Priest lies."

I looked at him and recognized that argument would be useless. But still I said, "It will be a loss to history, Monsieur Le Bihan."

"All the worse for history, then," said the enlightened Mayor of St. Gildas.

We had sauntered back to the gravel pit while speaking. The men of Bannalec were carrying the bones of the English soldiers toward the St. Gildas cemetery, on the cliffs to the east, where already a knot of white-coiffed women stood in attitudes of prayer; and I saw the sombre robe of a priest among the crosses of the little graveyard.

"They were thieves and assassins; they are dead now," muttered Max Fortin.

"Respect the dead," repeated the Mayor of St. Gildas, looking after the Bannalec men.

"It was written in that scroll that Marie Trevec, of Groix Island, was cursed by the priest—she and her descendants," I said, touching Le Bihan on the arm. "There was a Marie Trevec who married an Yves Trevec of St. Gildas—"

"It is the same," said Le Bihan, looking at me obliquely.

"Oh!" said I; "then they were ancestors of my wife."

"Do you fear the curse?" asked Le Bihan.

"What?" I laughed.

"There was the case of the Purple Emperor," said Max Fortin timidly.

Startled for a moment, I faced him, then shrugged my shoulders and kicked at a smooth bit of rock which lay near the edge of the pit, almost embedded in gravel.

"Do you suppose the Purple Emperor drank himself crazy because he was descended from Marie Trevec?" I asked contemptuously.

"Of course not," said Max Fortin hastily.

"Of course not," piped the mayor. "I only—Hello! what's that you're kicking?"

"What?" said I, glancing down, at the same time involuntarily giving another kick. The smooth bit of rock dislodged itself and rolled out of the loosened gravel at my feet.

"The thirty-ninth skull!" I exclaimed. "By jingo, it's the noddle of the Black Priest! See! there is the arrowhead branded on the front!"

The mayor stepped back. Max Fortin also retreated. There was a pause, during which I looked at them, and they looked anywhere but at me.

"I don't like it," said the mayor at last, in a husky, high voice. "I don't like it! The scroll says he will come back to St. Gildas when his remains are disturbed. I—I don't like it, Monsieur Darrel—"

"Bosh!" said I; "the poor wicked devil is where he can't get out. For Heaven's sake, Le Bihan, what is this stuff you are talking in the year of grace 1896?"

The mayor gave me a look.

"And he says 'Englishman.' You are an Englishman, Monsieur Darrel," he announced.

"You know better. You know I'm an American."

"It's all the same," said the Mayor of St. Gildas, obstinately.

"No, it isn't!" I answered, much exasperated, and deliberately pushed the skull till it rolled into the bottom of the gravel pit below.

"Cover it up," said I; "bury the scroll with it too, if you insist, but I think you ought to send it to Paris. Don't look so gloomy, Fortin, unless you believe in were-wolves and ghosts. Hey! what the —what the devil's the matter with you, anyway? What are you staring at, Le Bihan?"

"Come, come," muttered the mayor in a low, tremulous voice, "it's time we got out of this. Did you see? Did you see, Fortin?"

"I saw," whispered Max Fortin, pallid with fright.

The two men were almost running across the sunny pasture now, and I hastened after them, demanding to know what was the matter.

"Matter!" chattered the mayor, gasping with exasperation and terror. "The skull is rolling uphill again!" and he burst into a terrified gallop. Max Fortin followed close behind.

I watched them stampeding across the pasture, then turned toward the gravel pit, mystified, incredulous. The skull was lying on the edge of the pit, exactly where it had been before I pushed it over the edge. For a second I stared at it; a singular chilly feeling crept up my spinal column, and I turned and walked away, sweat starting from the root of every hair on my head. Before I had gone twenty paces the absurdity of the whole thing struck me. I halted, hot with shame and annoyance, and retraced my steps.

There lay the skull.

"I rolled a stone down instead of the skull," I muttered to myself. Then with the butt of my gun I pushed the skull over the edge of the pit and watched it roll to the bottom; and as it struck the bottom of the pit, Môme, my dog, suddenly whipped his tail between his legs, whimpered, and made off across the moor.

"Môme!" I shouted, angry and astonished; but the dog only fled the faster, and I ceased calling from sheer surprise.

"What the mischief is the matter with that dog!" I thought. He had never before played me such a trick.

Mechanically I glanced into the pit, but I could not see the skull. I looked down. The skull lay at my feet again, touching them.

"Good heavens!" I stammered, and struck at it blindly with my gunstock. The ghastly thing flew into the air, whirling over and over, and rolled again down the sides of the pit to the bottom. Breathlessly I stared at it, then, confused and scarcely comprehending, I stepped back from the pit, still facing it, one, ten, twenty paces, my eyes almost starting from my head, as though I expected to see the thing roll up from the bottom of the pit under my very gaze. At last I turned my back to the pit and strode out across the gorse-covered moorland toward my home. As I reached the road that winds from St. Gildas to St. Julien I gave one hasty glance at the pit over my shoulder. The sun shone hot on the sod about the excavation. There was something white and bare and round on the turf at the edge of the pit. It might have been a stone; there were plenty of them lying about.

II

WHEN I entered my garden I saw Môme sprawling on the stone doorstep. He eyed me sideways and flopped his tail.

"Are you not mortified, you idiot dog?" I said, looking about the upper windows for Lys.

Môme rolled over on his back and raised one deprecating fore-paw, as though to ward off calamity.

"Don't act as though I was in the habit of beating you to death," I said, disgusted. I had never in my life raised whip to the brute. "But you are a fool dog," I continued. "No, you needn't come to be babied and wept over; Lys can do that, if she insists, but I am ashamed of you, and you can go to the devil."

Môme slunk off into the house, and I followed, mounting directly to my wife's boudoir. It was empty.

"Where has she gone?" I said, looking hard at Môme, who had followed me. "Oh! I see you don't know. Don't pretend you do. Come off that lounge! Do you think Lys wants tan-coloured hairs all over her lounge?"

I rang the bell for Catherine and 'Fine, but they didn't know where "madame" had gone; so I went into my room, bathed, exchanged my somewhat grimy shooting clothes for a suit of warm, soft knickerbockers, and, after lingering some extra moments over my toilet—for I was particular, now that I had married Lys—I went down to the garden and took a chair out under the fig-trees.

"Where can she be?" I wondered. Môme came sneaking out to be comforted, and I forgave him for Lys's sake, whereupon he frisked.

"You bounding cur," said I, "now what on earth started you off across the moor? If you do it again I'll push you along with a charge of dust shot."

As yet I had scarcely dared think about the ghastly hallucination of which I had been a victim, but now I faced it squarely, flushing a little with mortification at the thought of my hasty retreat from the gravel pit.

"To think," I said aloud, "that those old woman's tales of Max Fortin and Le Bihan should have actually made me see what didn't exist at all! I lost my nerve like a schoolboy in a dark bedroom." For I knew now that I had mistaken a round stone for a skull each time, and had pushed a couple of big pebbles into the pit instead of the skull itself.

"By jingo!" said I, "I'm nervous; my liver must be in a devil of a condition if I see such things when I'm awake! Lys will know what to give me."

I felt mortified and irritated and sulky, and thought disgustedly of Le Bihan and Max Fortin.

But after a while I ceased speculating, dismissed the mayor, the chemist, and the skull from my mind, and smoked pensively, watching the sun low dipping in the western ocean. As the twilight fell for a moment over ocean and moorland, a wistful, restless happiness filled my heart, the happiness that all men know—all men who have loved.

Slowly the purple mist crept out over the sea; the cliffs darkened; the forest was shrouded.

Suddenly the sky above burned with the afterglow, and the world was alight again.

Cloud after cloud caught the rose dye; the cliffs were tinted with it; moor and pasture, heather and forest burned and pulsated with the gentle flush. I saw the gulls turning and tossing above the sand bar, their snowy wings tipped with pink; I saw the sea swallows sheering the surface of the still river, stained to its placid depths with warm reflections of the clouds. The twitter of drowsy hedge birds broke out in the stillness; a salmon rolled its shining side above tide-water.

The interminable monotone of the ocean intensified the silence. I sat motionless, holding my breath as one who listens to the first low rumour of an organ. All at once the pure whistle of a nightingale cut the silence, and the first moonbeam silvered the wastes of mist-hung waters.

I raised my head.

Lys stood before me in the garden.

When we had kissed each other, we linked arms and moved up and down the gravel walks, watching the moonbeams sparkle on the sand bar as the tide ebbed and ebbed. The broad beds of white pinks about us were atremble with hovering white moths; the October roses hung all abloom, perfuming the salt wind.

"Sweetheart," I said, "where is Yvonne? Has she promised to spend Christmas with us?

"Yes, Dick; she drove me down from Plougat this afternoon. She sent her love to you. I am not jealous. What did you shoot?"

"A hare and four partridges. They are in the gun room. I told Catherine not to touch them until you had seen them."

Now I suppose I knew that Lys could not be particularly enthusiastic over game or guns; but she pretended she was, and always scornfully denied that it was for my sake and not for the pure love of sport. So she dragged me off to inspect the rather meagre game bag, and she paid me pretty compliments and gave a little cry of delight and pity as I lifted the enormous hare out of the sack by his ears.

"He'll eat no more of our lettuce," I said, attempting to justify the assassination.

"Unhappy little bunny—and what a beauty! O Dick, you are a splendid shot, are you not?"

I evaded the question and hauled out a partridge.

"Poor little dead things!" said Lys in a whisper; "it seems a pity—doesn't it, Dick? But then you are so clever—"

"We'll have them broiled," I said guardedly; "tell Catherine."

Catherine came in to take away the game, and presently 'Fine Lelocard, Lys's maid, announced dinner, and Lys tripped away to her boudoir.

I stood an instant contemplating her blissfully, thinking, "My boy, you're the happiest fellow in the world—you're in love with your wife!"

I walked into the dining room, beamed at the plates, walked out again; met Tregunc in the hallway, beamed on him; glanced into the kitchen, beamed at Catherine, and went up stairs, still beaming.

Before I could knock at Lys's door it opened, and Lys came hastily out. When she saw me she gave a little cry of relief, and nestled close to my breast.

"There is something peering in at my window," she said.

"What!" I cried angrily.

"A man, I think, disguised as a priest, and he has a mask on. He must have climbed up by the bay tree."

I was down the stairs and out of doors in no time. The moonlit garden was absolutely deserted. Tregunc came up, and together we searched the hedge and shrubbery around the house and out to the road.

"Jean Marie," said I at length, "loose my bulldog—he knows you—and take your supper on the porch where you can watch. My wife says the fellow is disguised as a priest, and wears a mask."

Tregunc showed his white teeth in a smile. "He will not care to venture in here again, I think, Monsieur Darrel."

I went back and found Lys seated quietly at the table.

"The soup is ready, dear," she said. "Don't worry; it was only some foolish lout from Bannalec. No one in St. Gildas or St. Julien would do such a thing."

I was too much exasperated to reply at first, but Lys treated it as a stupid joke, and after a while I began to look at it in that light.

Lys told me about Yvonne, and reminded me of my promise to have Herbert Stuart down to meet her.

"You wicked diplomat!" I protested. "Herbert is in Paris, and hard at work for the Salon."

"Don't you think he might spare a week to flirt with the prettiest girl in Finistère?" inquired Lys innocently.

"Prettiest girl! Not much!" I said.

"Who is, then?" urged Lys.

I laughed a trifle sheepishly.

"I suppose you mean me, Dick," said Lys, colouring up.

"Now I bore you, don't I?"

"Bore me? Ah, no, Dick."

After coffee and cigarettes were served I spoke about Tregunc, and Lys approved.

"Poor Jean! he will be glad, won't he? What a dear fellow you are!"

"Nonsense," said I; "we need a gardener; you said so yourself, Lys."

But Lys leaned over and kissed me, and then bent down and hugged Môme, who whistled through his nose in sentimental appreciation.

"I am a very happy woman," said Lys.

"Môme was a very bad dog to-day," I observed.

"Poor Môme!" said Lys, smiling.

When dinner was over and Môme lay snoring before the blaze—for the October nights are often chilly in Finistère—Lys curled up in the chimney corner with her embroidery, and gave me a swift glance from under her drooping lashes.

"You look like a schoolgirl, Lys," I said teasingly. "I don't believe you are sixteen yet."

She pushed back her heavy burnished hair thoughtfully. Her wrist was as white as surf foam.

"Have we been married four years? I don't believe it," I said.

She gave me another swift glance and touched the embroidery on her knee, smiling faintly.

"I see," said I, also smiling at the embroidered garment. "Do you think it will fit?"

"Fit?" repeated Lys. Then she laughed.

"And," I persisted, "are you perfectly sure that you—er—we shall need it?"

"Perfectly," said Lys. A delicate colour touched her cheeks and neck. She held up the little garment, all fluffy with misty lace and wrought with quaint embroidery.

"It is very gorgeous," said I; "don't use your eyes too much, dearest. May I smoke a pipe?"

"Of course," she said, selecting a skein of pale blue silk.

For a while I sat and smoked in silence, watching her slender fingers among the tinted silks and thread of gold.

Presently she spoke: "What did you say your crest is, Dick?"

"My crest? Oh, something or other rampant on a something or other—"

"Dick!"

"Dearest?"

"Don't be flippant."

"But I really forget. It's an ordinary crest; everybody in New York has them. No family should be without 'em."

"You are disagreeable, Dick. Send Josephine upstairs for my album."

"Are you going to put that crest on the—the—whatever it is?"

"I am; and my own crest, too."

I thought of the Purple Emperor and wondered a little.

"You didn't know I had one, did you?" she smiled.

"What is it?" I replied evasively.

"You shall see. Ring for Josephine."

I rang, and, when 'Fine appeared, Lys gave her some orders in a low voice, and Josephine trotted away, bobbing her white-coiffed head with a "Bien, madame!"

After a few minutes she returned, bearing a tattered, musty volume, from which the gold and blue had mostly disappeared.

I took the book in my hands and examined the ancient emblazoned covers.

"Lilies!" I exclaimed.

"Fleur-de-lis," said my wife demurely.

"Oh!" said I, astonished, and opened the book.

"You have never before seen this book?" asked Lys, with a touch of malice in her eyes.

"You know I haven't. Hello! what's this? Oho! So there should be a *de* before Trevec? Lys de Trevec? Then why in the world did the Purple Emperor—"

"Dick!" cried Lys.

"All right," said I. "Shall I read about the Sieur de Trevec who rode to Saladin's tent alone to seek for medicine for St. Louis? or shall I read about—what is it? Oh, here it is, all down in black and white—about the Marquis de Trevec who drowned himself before Alva's eyes rather than surrender the banner of the fleur-de-lis to Spain? It's all written here. But, dear, how about that soldier named Trevec who was killed in the old fort on the cliff yonder?"

"He dropped the *de*, and the Trevecs since then have been Republicans," said Lys—"all except me."

"That's quite right," said I; "it is time that we Republicans should agree upon some feudal system. My dear, I drink to the king!" and I raised my wine-glass and looked at Lys.

"To the king," said Lys, flushing. She smoothed out the tiny garment on her knees; she touched the glass with her lips; her eyes were very sweet. I drained the glass to the king.

After a silence I said: "I will tell the king stories. His Majesty shall be amused."

"His Majesty," repeated Lys softly.

"Or hers," I laughed. "Who knows?"

"Who knows?" murmured Lys, with a gentle sigh.

"I know some stories about Jack the Giant-Killer," I announced. "Do you, Lys?"

"I? No, not about a giant-killer, but I know all about the were-wolf, and Jeanne-la-Flamme, and the Man in Purple Tatters, and—O dear me! I know lots more."

"You are very wise," said I. "I shall teach his Majesty English."

"And I Breton," cried Lys jealously.

"I shall bring playthings to the king," said I—"big green lizards from the gorse, little gray mullets to swim in glass globes, baby rabbits from the forest of Kerselec—"

"And I," said Lys, "will bring the first primrose, the first branch of aubepine, the first jonquil, to the king—my king."

"Our king," said I; and there was peace in Finistère.

I lay back, idly turning the leaves of the curious old volume.

"I am looking," said I, "for the crest."

"The crest, dear? It is a priest's head with an arrow-shaped mark on the forehead, on a field—"

I sat up and stared at my wife.

"Dick, whatever is the matter?" she smiled. "The story is there in that book. Do you care to read it? No? Shall I tell it to you? Well, then: It happened in the third crusade. There was a monk whom men called the Black Priest. He turned apostate, and sold himself to the enemies of Christ. A Sieur de Trevec burst into the Saracen camp, at the head of only one hundred lances, and carried the Black Priest away out of the very midst of their army."

"So that is how you came by the crest," I said quietly; but I thought of the branded skull in the gravel pit, and wondered.

"Yes," said Lys. "The Sieur de Trevec cut the Black Priest's head off, but first he branded him with an arrow mark on the forehead. The book says it was a pious action, and the Sieur de Trevec got great merit by it. But I think it was cruel, the branding," she sighed.

"Did you ever hear of any other Black Priest?"

"Yes. There was one in the last century, here in St. Gildas. He cast a white shadow in the sun. He wrote in the Breton language. Chronicles, too, I believe. I never saw them. His name was the same as that of the old chronicler, and of the other priest, Jacques Sorgue. Some said he was a lineal descendant of the traitor. Of course the first Black Priest was bad enough for anything. But if he did have a child, it need not have been the ancestor of the last Jacques Sorgue. They say this one was a holy man. They say he was so good he was not allowed to die, but was caught up to heaven one day," added Lys, with believing eyes.

I smiled.

"But he disappeared," persisted Lys.

"I'm afraid his journey was in another direction," I said jestingly, and thoughtlessly told her the story of the morning. I had utterly forgotten the masked man at her window, but before I finished I remembered him fast enough, and realized what I had done as I saw her face whiten.

"Lys," I urged tenderly, "that was only some clumsy clown's trick. You said so yourself. You are not superstitious, my dear?"

Her eyes were on mine. She slowly drew the little gold cross from her bosom and kissed it. But her lips trembled as they pressed the symbol of faith.

III

About nine o'clock the next morning I walked into the Groix Inn and sat down at the long discoloured oaken table, nodding good-day to Marianne Bruyère, who in turn bobbed her white coiffe at me.

"My clever Bannalec maid," said I, "what is good for a stirrup-cup at the Groix Inn?"

"Schist?" she inquired in Breton.

"With a dash of red wine, then," I replied.

She brought the delicious Quimperlé cider, and I poured a little Bordeaux into it. Marianne watched me with laughing black eyes.

"What makes your cheeks so red, Marianne?" I asked. "Has Jean Marie been here?"

"We are to be married, Monsieur Darrel," she laughed.

"Ah! Since when has Jean Marie Tregunc lost his head?"

"His head? Oh, Monsieur Darrel—his heart, you mean!"

"So I do," said I. "Jean Marie is a practical fellow."

"It is all due to your kindness—" began the girl, but I raised my hand and held up the glass.

"It's due to himself. To your happiness, Marianne;" and I took a hearty draught of the schist. "Now," said I, "tell me where I can find Le Bihan and Max Fortin."

"Monsieur Le Bihan and Monsieur Fortin are above in the broad room. I believe they are examining the Red Admiral's effects."

"To send them to Paris? Oh, I know. May I go up, Marianne?"

"And God go with you," smiled the girl.

When I knocked at the door of the broad room above little Max Fortin opened it. Dust covered his spectacles and nose; his hat, with the tiny velvet ribbons fluttering, was all awry.

"Come in, Monsieur Darrel," he said; "the mayor and I are packing up the effects of the Purple Emperor and of the poor Red Admiral."

"The collections?" I asked, entering the room. "You must be very careful in packing those butterfly cases; the slightest jar might break wings and antennæ, you know."

Le Bihan shook hands with me and pointed to the great pile of boxes.

"They're all cork lined," he said, "but Fortin and I are putting felt around each box. The Entomological Society of Paris pays the freight."

The combined collections of the Red Admiral and the Purple Emperor made a magnificent display.

I lifted and inspected case after case set with gorgeous butterflies and moths, each specimen carefully labelled with the name in Latin. There were cases filled with crimson tiger moths all aflame with colour; cases devoted to the common yellow butterflies; symphonies in orange and pale yellow; cases of soft gray and dun-coloured sphinx moths; and cases of garish nettle-bred butterflies of the numerous family of *Vanessa*.

All alone in a great case by itself was pinned the purple emperor, the Apatura Iris, that fatal specimen that had given the Purple Emperor his name and quietus.

I remembered the butterfly, and stood looking at it with bent eyebrows.

Le Bihan glanced up from the floor where he was nailing down the lid of a box full of cases.

"It is settled, then," said he, "that madame, your wife, gives the Purple Emperor's entire collection to the city of Paris?"

I nodded.

"Without accepting anything for it?"

"It is a gift," I said.

"Including the purple emperor there in the case? That butterfly is worth a great deal of money," persisted Le Bihan.

"You don't suppose that we would wish to sell that specimen, do you?" I answered a trifle sharply.

"If I were you I should destroy it," said the mayor in his high-pitched voice.

"That would be nonsense," said I—"like your burying the brass cylinder and scroll yesterday."

"It was not nonsense," said Le Bihan doggedly, "and I should prefer not to discuss the subject of the scroll."

I looked at Max Fortin, who immediately avoided my eyes.

"You are a pair of superstitious old women," said I, digging my hands into my pockets; "you swallow every nursery tale that is invented."

"What of it?" said Le Bihan sulkily; "there's more truth than lies in most of 'em."

"Oh!" I sneered, "does the Mayor of St. Gildas and St. Julien believe in the Loup-garou?"

"No, not in the Loup-garou."

"In what, then—Jeanne-la-Flamme?"

"That," said Le Bihan with conviction, "is history."

"The devil it is!" said I; "and perhaps, monsieur the mayor, your faith in giants is unimpaired?"

"There were giants—everybody knows it," growled Max Fortin.

"And you a chemist!" I observed scornfully.

"Listen, Monsieur Darrel," squeaked Le Bihan; "you know yourself that the Purple Emperor was a scientific man. Now suppose I should tell you that he always refused to include in his collection a Death's Messenger?"

"A what?" I exclaimed.

"You know what I mean—that moth that flies by night; some call it the Death's Head, but in St. Gildas we call it 'Death's Messenger.'"

"Oh!" said I, "you mean that big sphinx moth that is commonly known as the 'death's-head moth.' Why the mischief should the people here call it death's messenger?"

"For hundreds of years it has been known as death's messenger in St. Gildas," said Max Fortin. "Even Froissart speaks of it in his commentaries on Jacques Sorgue's Chronicles. The book is in your library."

"Sorgue? And who was Jacques Sorgue? I never read his book."

"Jacques Sorgue was the son of some unfrocked priest—I forget. It was during the crusades."

"Good Heavens!" I burst out, "I've been hearing of nothing but crusades and priests and death and sorcery ever since I kicked that skull into the gravel pit, and I am tired of it, I tell you frankly. One would think we lived in the dark ages. Do you know what year of our Lord it is, Le Bihan?"

"Eighteen hundred and ninety-six," replied the mayor.

"And yet you two hulking men are afraid of a death's-head moth."

"I don't care to have one fly into the window," said Max Fortin; "it means evil to the house and the people in it."

"God alone knows why he marked one of his creatures with a yellow death's head on the back," observed Le Bihan piously, "but I take it that he meant it as a warning; and I propose to profit by it," he added triumphantly.

"See here, Le Bihan," I said; "by a stretch of imagination one can make out a skull on the thorax of a certain big sphinx moth. What of it?"

"It is a bad thing to touch," said the mayor, wagging his head.

"It squeaks when handled," added Max Fortin.

"Some creatures squeak all the time," I observed, looking hard at Le Bihan.

"Pigs," added the mayor.

"Yes, and asses," I replied. "Listen, Le Bihan: do you mean to tell me that you saw that skull roll uphill yesterday?"

The mayor shut his mouth tightly and picked up his hammer.

"Don't be obstinate," I said; "I asked you a question."

"And I refuse to answer," snapped Le Bihan. "Fortin saw what I saw; let him talk about it."

I looked searchingly at the little chemist.

"I don't say that I saw it actually roll up out of the pit, all by itself," said Fortin with a shiver, "but—but then, how did it come up out of the pit, if it didn't roll up all by itself?"

"It didn't come up at all; that was a yellow cobblestone that you mistook for the skull again," I replied. "You were nervous, Max."

"A—a very curious cobblestone, Monsieur Darrel," said Fortin.

"I also was a victim to the same hallucination," I continued, "and I regret to say that I took the trouble to roll two innocent cobblestones into the gravel pit, imagining each time that it was the skull I was rolling."

"It was," observed Le Bihan with a morose shrug.

"It just shows," said I, ignoring the mayor's remark, "how easy it is to fix up a train of coincidences so that the result seems to savour of the supernatural. Now, last night my wife imagined that she saw a priest in a mask peer in at her window—"

Fortin and Le Bihan scrambled hastily from their knees, dropping hammer and nails.

"W-h-a-t—what's that?" demanded the mayor.

I repeated what I had said. Max Fortin turned livid.

"My God!" muttered Le Bihan, "the Black Priest is in St. Gildas!"

"D-don't you—you know the old prophecy?" stammered Fortin; "Froissart quotes it from Jacques Sorgue:

> When the Black Priest rises from the dead,
> St. Gildas folk shall shriek in bed;
> When the Black Priest rises from his grave,
> May the good God St. Gildas save!"

"Aristide Le Bihan," I said angrily, "and you, Max Fortin, I've got enough of this nonsense! Some foolish lout from Bannalec has been in St. Gildas playing tricks to frighten old fools like you. If you have nothing better to talk about than nursery legends I'll wait until you come to your senses. Good-morning." And I walked out, more disturbed than I cared to acknowledge to myself.

The day had become misty and overcast. Heavy, wet clouds hung in the east. I heard the surf thundering against the cliffs, and the gray gulls squealed as they tossed and turned high in the sky. The tide was creeping across the river sands, higher, higher, and I saw the seaweed floating on the beach, and the *lançons* springing from the foam, silvery threadlike flashes in the gloom. Curlew were flying up the river in twos and threes; the timid sea swallows skimmed across the moors toward some quiet, lonely pool, safe from the coming tempest. In every hedge field birds were gathering, huddling together, twittering restlessly.

When I reached the cliffs I sat down, resting my chin on my clenched hands. Already a vast curtain of rain, sweeping across the

ocean miles away, hid the island of Groix. To the east, behind
the white semaphore on the hills, black clouds crowded up over the
horizon. After a little the thunder boomed, dull, distant, and slender
skeins of lightning unravelled across the crest of the coming storm.
Under the cliff at my feet the surf rushed foaming over the shore, and
the *lançons* jumped and skipped and quivered until they seemed to be
but the reflections of the meshed lightning.

I turned to the east. It was raining over Groix, it was raining at
Sainte Barbe, it was raining now at the semaphore. High in the
storm whirl a few gulls pitched; a nearer cloud trailed veils of rain
in its wake; the sky was spattered with lightning; the thunder boomed.

As I rose to go, a cold raindrop fell upon the back of my hand, and
another, and yet another on my face. I gave a last glance at the sea,
where the waves were bursting into strange white shapes that seemed
to fling out menacing arms toward me. Then something moved on the
cliff, something black as the black rock it clutched—a filthy cormorant, craning its hideous head at the sky.

Slowly I plodded homeward across the sombre moorland, where
the gorse stems glimmered with a dull metallic green, and the heather,
no longer violet and purple, hung drenched and dun-coloured
among the dreary rocks. The wet turf creaked under my heavy boots,
the black-thorn scraped and grated against knee and elbow. Over
all lay a strange light, pallid, ghastly, where the sea spray whirled
across the landscape and drove into my face until it grew numb
with the cold. In broad bands, rank after rank, billow on billow, the
rain burst out across the endless moors, and yet there was no wind
to drive it at such a pace.

Lys stood at the door as I turned into the garden, motioning me
to hasten; and then for the first time I became conscious that I was
soaked to the skin.

"How ever in the world did you come to stay out when such a
storm threatened?" she said. "Oh, you are dripping! Go quickly
and change; I have laid your warm underwear on the bed, Dick."

I kissed my wife, and went upstairs to change my dripping clothes
for something more comfortable.

When I returned to the morning room there was a driftwood fire
on the hearth, and Lys sat in the chimney corner embroidering.

"Catherine tells me that the fishing fleet from Lorient is out. Do you think they are in danger, dear?" asked Lys, raising her blue eyes to mine as I entered.

"There is no wind, and there will be no sea," said I, looking out of the window. Far across the moor I could see the black cliffs looming in the mist.

"How it rains!" murmured Lys; "come to the fire, Dick."

I threw myself on the fur rug, my hands in my pockets, my head on Lys's knees.

"Tell me a story," I said. "I feel like a boy of ten."

Lys raised a finger to her scarlet lips. I always waited for her to do that.

"Will you be very still, then?" she said.

"Still as death."

"Death," echoed a voice, very softly.

"Did you speak, Lys?" I asked, turning so that I could see her face.

"No; did you, Dick?"

"Who said 'death'?" I asked, startled.

"Death," echoed a voice, softly.

I sprang up and looked about. Lys rose too, her needles and embroidery falling to the floor. She seemed about to faint, leaning heavily on me, and I led her to the window and opened it a little way to give her air. As I did so the chain lightning split the zenith, the thunder crashed, and a sheet of rain swept into the room, driving with it something that fluttered—something that flapped, and squeaked, and beat upon the rug with soft, moist wings.

We bent over it together, Lys clinging to me, and we saw that it was a death's-head moth drenched with rain.

The dark day passed slowly as we sat beside the fire, hand in hand, her head against my breast, speaking of sorrow and mystery and death. For Lys believed that there were things on earth that none might understand, things that must be nameless forever and ever, until God rolls up the scroll of life and all is ended. We spoke of hope and fear and faith, and the mystery of the saints; we spoke of the beginning and the end, of the shadow of sin, of omens, and of love. The moth still lay on the floor, quivering its sombre wings in the warmth of the fire, the skull and ribs clearly etched upon its neck and body.

"If it is a messenger of death to this house," I said, "why should we fear, Lys?"

"Death should be welcome to those who love God," murmured Lys, and she drew the cross from her breast and kissed it.

"The moth might die if I threw it out into the storm," I said after a silence.

"Let it remain," sighed Lys.

Late that night my wife lay sleeping, and I sat beside her bed and read in the Chronicle of Jacques Sorgue. I shaded the candle, but Lys grew restless, and finally I took the book down into the morning room, where the ashes of the fire rustled and whitened on the hearth.

The death's-head moth lay on the rug before the fire where I had left it. At first I thought it was dead, but, when I looked closer I saw a lambent fire in its amber eyes. The straight white shadow it cast across the floor wavered as the candle flickered.

The pages of the Chronicle of Jacques Sorgue were damp and sticky; the illuminated gold and blue initials left flakes of azure and gilt where my hand brushed them.

"It is not paper at all; it is thin parchment," I said to myself; and I held the discoloured page close to the candle flame and read, translating laboriously:

"I, Jacques Sorgue, saw all these things. And I saw the Black Mass celebrated in the chapel of St. Gildas-on-the-Cliff. And it was said by the Abbé Sorgue, my kinsman: for which deadly sin the apostate priest was seized by the most noble Marquis of Plougastel and by him condemned to be burned with hot irons, until his seared soul quit its body and fly to its master the devil. But when the Black Priest lay in the crypt of Plougastel, his master Satan came at night and set him free, and carried him across land and sea to Mahmoud, which is Soldan or Saladin. And I, Jacques Sorgue, travelling afterward by sea, beheld with my own eyes my kinsman, the Black Priest of St. Gildas, borne along in the air upon a vast black wing, which was the wing of his master Satan. And this was seen also by two men of the crew."

I turned the page. The wings of the moth on the floor began to quiver. I read on and on, my eyes blurring under the shifting candle flame. I read of battles and of saints, and I learned how the great Soldan made his pact with Satan, and then I came to the Sieur de

Trevec, and read how he seized the Black Priest in the midst of Saladin's tents and carried him away and cut off his head, first branding him on the forehead. "And before he suffered," said the Chronicle, "he cursed the Sieur de Trevec and his descendants, and he said he would surely return to St. Gildas. 'For the violence you do to me, I will do violence to you. For the evil I suffer at your hands, I will work evil on you and your descendants. Woe to your children, Sieur de Trevec!'" There was a whirr, a beating of strong wings, and my candle flashed up as in a sudden breeze. A humming filled the room; the great moth darted hither and thither, beating, buzzing, on ceiling and wall. I flung down my book and stepped forward. Now it lay fluttering upon the window sill, and for a moment I had it under my hand, but the thing squeaked and I shrank back. Then suddenly it darted across the candle flame; the light flared and went out, and at the same moment a shadow moved in the darkness outside. I raised my eyes to the window. A masked face was peering in at me.

Quick as thought I whipped out my revolver and fired every cartridge, but the face advanced beyond the window, the glass melting away before it like mist, and through the smoke of my revolver I saw something creep swiftly into the room. Then I tried to cry out, but the thing was at my throat, and I fell backward among the ashes of the hearth.

When my eyes unclosed I was lying on the hearth, my head among the cold ashes. Slowly I got on my knees, rose painfully, and groped my way to a chair. On the floor lay my revolver, shining in the pale light of early morning. My mind clearing by degrees, I looked, shuddering, at the window. The glass was unbroken. I stooped stiffly, picked up my revolver and opened the cylinder. Every cartridge had been fired. Mechanically I closed the cylinder and placed the revolver in my pocket. The book, the Chronicles of Jacques Sorgue, lay on the table beside me, and as I started to close it I glanced at the page. It was all splashed with rain, and the lettering had run, so that the page was merely a confused blur of gold and red and black. As I stumbled toward the door I cast a fearful glance over my shoulder. The death's-head moth crawled shivering on the rug.

IV

THE sun was about three hours high. I must have slept, for I was aroused by the sudden gallop of horses under our window. People were shouting and calling in the road. I sprang up and opened the sash. Le Bihan was there, an image of helplessness, and Max Fortin stood beside him, polishing his glasses. Some gendarmes had just arrived from Quimperlé, and I could hear them around the corner of the house, stamping, and rattling their sabres and carbines, as they led their horses into my stable.

Lys sat up, murmuring half-sleepy, half-anxious questions.

"I don't know," I answered. "I am going out to see what it means."

"It is like the day they came to arrest you," Lys said, giving me a troubled look. But I kissed her, and laughed at her until she smiled too. Then I flung on coat and cap and hurried down the stairs.

The first person I saw standing in the road was the Brigadier Durand.

"Hello!" said I, "have you come to arrest me again? What the devil is all this fuss about, anyway?"

"We were telegraphed for an hour ago," said Durand briskly, "and for a sufficient reason, I think. Look there, Monsieur Darrel!"

He pointed to the ground almost under my feet.

"Good heavens!" I cried, "where did that puddle of blood come from?"

"That's what I want to know, Monsieur Darrel. Max Fortin found it at daybreak. See, it's splashed all over the grass, too. A trail of it leads into your garden, across the flower beds to your very window, the one that opens from the morning room. There is another trail leading from this spot across the road to the cliffs, then to the gravel pit, and thence across the moor to the forest of Kerselec. We are going to mount in a minute and search the bosquets. Will you join us? Bon Dieu! but the fellow bled like an ox. Max Fortin says it's human blood, or I should not have believed it."

The little chemist of Quimperlé came up at that moment, rubbing his glasses with a coloured handkerchief.

"Yes, it is human blood," he said, "but one thing puzzles me: the corpuscles are yellow. I never saw any human blood before with yellow corpuscles. But your English Doctor Thompson asserts that he has—"

"Well, it's human blood, anyway—isn't it?" insisted Durand, impatiently.

"Ye-es," admitted Max Fortin.

"Then it's my business to trail it," said the big gendarme, and he called his men and gave the order to mount.

"Did you hear anything last night?" asked Durand of me.

"I heard the rain. I wonder the rain did not wash away these traces."

"They must have come after the rain ceased. See this thick splash, how it lies over and weighs down the wet grass blades. Pah!"

It was a heavy, evil-looking clot, and I stepped back from it, my throat closing in disgust.

"My theory," said the brigadier, "is this: Some of those Biribi fishermen, probably the Icelanders, got an extra glass of cognac into their hides and quarrelled on the road. Some of them were slashed, and staggered to your house. But there is only one trail, and yet— and yet, how could all that blood come from only one person? Well, the wounded man, let us say, staggered first to your house and then back here, and he wandered off, drunk and dying, God knows where. That's my theory."

"A very good one," said I calmly. "And you are going to trail him?"

"Yes."

"When?"

"At once. Will you come?"

"Not now. I'll gallop over by-and-bye. You are going to the edge of the Kerselec forest?"

"Yes; you will hear us calling. Are you coming, Max Fortin? And you, Le Bihan? Good; take the dog-cart."

The big gendarme tramped around the corner to the stable and presently returned mounted on a strong gray horse; his sabre shone on his saddle; his pale yellow and white facings were spotless. The little crowd of white-coiffed women with their children fell back, as Durand touched spurs and clattered away followed by his two troopers. Soon after Le Bihan and Max Fortin also departed in the mayor's dingy dog-cart.

"Are you coming?" piped Le Bihan shrilly.

"In a quarter of an hour," I replied, and went back to the house.

When I opened the door of the morning room the death's-head moth was beating its strong wings against the window. For a second I hesitated, then walked over and opened the sash. The creature fluttered out, whirred over the flower beds a moment, then darted across the moorland toward the sea. I called the servants together and questioned them. Josephine, Catherine, Jean Marie Tregunc, not one of them had heard the slightest disturbance during the night. Then I told Jean Marie to saddle my horse, and while I was speaking Lys came down.

"Dearest," I began, going to her.

"You must tell me everything you know, Dick," she interrupted, looking me earnestly in the face.

"But there is nothing to tell—only a drunken brawl, and some one wounded."

"And you are going to ride—where, Dick?"

"Well, over to the edge of Kerselec forest. Durand and the mayor, and Max Fortin, have gone on, following a—a trail."

"What trail?"

"Some blood."

"Where did they find it?"

"Out in the road there." Lys crossed herself.

"Does it come near our house?"

"Yes."

"How near?"

"It comes up to the morning-room window," said I, giving in.

Her hand on my arm grew heavy. "I dreamed last night—"

"So did I—" but I thought of the empty cartridges in my revolver, and stopped.

"I dreamed that you were in great danger, and I could not move hand or foot to save you; but you had your revolver, and I called out to you to fire—"

"I did fire!" I cried excitedly.

"You—you fired?"

I took her in my arms. "My darling," I said, "something strange has happened—something that I can not understand as yet. But, of course, there is an explanation. Last night I thought I fired at the Black Priest."

"Ah!" gasped Lys.

"Is that what you dreamed?"

"Yes, yes, that was it! I begged you to fire—"

"And I did."

Her heart was beating against my breast. I held her close in silence.

"Dick," she said at length, "perhaps you killed the—the thing."

"If it was human I did not miss," I answered grimly. "And it was human," I went on, pulling myself together, ashamed of having so nearly gone to pieces. "Of course it was human! The whole affair is plain enough. Not a drunken brawl, as Durand thinks; it was a drunken lout's practical joke, for which he has suffered. I suppose I must have filled him pretty full of bullets, and he has crawled away to die in Kerselec forest. It's a terrible affair; I'm sorry I fired so hastily; but that idiot Le Bihan and Max Fortin have been working on my nerves till I am as hysterical as a school-girl," I ended angrily.

"You fired—but the window glass was not shattered," said Lys in a low voice.

"Well, the window was open, then. And as for the—the rest— I've got nervous indigestion, and a doctor will settle the Black Priest for me, Lys."

I glanced out of the window at Tregunc waiting with my horse at the gate.

"Dearest, I think I had better go to join Durand and the others."

"I will go too."

"Oh, no!"

"Yes, Dick."

"Don't, Lys."

"I shall suffer every moment you are away."

"The ride is too fatiguing, and we can't tell what unpleasant sight you may come upon. Lys, you don't really think there is anything supernatural in this affair?"

"Dick," she answered gently, "I am a Bretonne." With both arms around my neck, my wife said, "Death is the gift of God. I do not fear it when we are together. But alone—oh, my husband, I should fear a God who could take you away from me!"

We kissed each other soberly, simply, like two children. Then Lys hurried away to change her gown, and I paced up and down the garden waiting for her.

She came, drawing on her slender gauntlets. I swung her into the saddle, gave a hasty order to Jean Marie, and mounted.

Now, to quail under thoughts of terror on a morning like this, with Lys in the saddle beside me, no matter what had happened or might happen, was impossible. Moreover, Môme came sneaking after us. I asked Tregunc to catch him, for I was afraid he might be brained by our horses' hoofs if he followed, but the wily puppy dodged and bolted after Lys, who was trotting along the high-road. "Never mind," I thought; "if he's hit he'll live, for he has no brains to lose."

Lys was waiting for me in the road beside the Shrine of Our Lady of St. Gildas when I joined her. She crossed herself, I doffed my cap, then we shook out our bridles and galloped toward the forest of Kerselec.

We said very little as we rode. I always loved to watch Lys in the saddle. Her exquisite figure and lovely face were the incarnation of youth and grace; her curling hair glistened like threaded gold.

Out of the corner of my eye I saw the spoiled puppy Môme come bounding cheerfully alongside, oblivious of our horses' heels. Our road swung close to the cliffs. A filthy cormorant rose from the black rocks and flapped heavily across our path. Lys' horse reared, but she pulled him down, and pointed at the bird with her riding crop.

"I see," said I; "it seems to be going our way. Curious to see a cormorant in a forest, isn't it?"

"It is a bad sign," said Lys. "You know the Morbihan proverb: 'When the cormorant turns from the sea, Death laughs in the forest, and wise woodsmen build boats.'"

"I wish," said I sincerely, "that there were fewer proverbs in Brittany."

We were in sight of the forest now; across the gorse I could see the sparkle of gendarmes' trappings, and the glitter of Le Bihan's silver-buttoned jacket. The hedge was low and we took it without difficulty, and trotted across the moor to where Le Bihan and Durand stood gesticulating.

They bowed ceremoniously to Lys as we rode up.

"The trail is horrible—it is a river," said the mayor in his squeaky voice. "Monsieur Darrel, I think perhaps madame would scarcely care to come any nearer."

Lys drew bridle and looked at me.

"It is horrible!" said Durand, walking up beside me; "it looks as though a bleeding regiment had passed this way. The trail winds and winds about there in the thickets; we lose it at times, but we always find it again. I can't understand how one man—no, nor twenty—could bleed like that!"

A halloo, answered by another, sounded from the depths of the forest.

"It's my men; they are following the trail," muttered the brigadier. "God alone knows what is at the end!"

"Shall we gallop back, Lys?" I asked.

"No; let us ride along the western edge of the woods and dismount. The sun is so hot now, and I should like to rest for a moment," she said.

"The western forest is clear of anything disagreeable," said Durand.

"Very well," I answered; "call me, Le Bihan, if you find anything."

Lys wheeled her mare, and I followed across the springy heather, Môme trotting cheerfully in the rear.

We entered the sunny woods about a quarter of a kilometre from where we left Durand. I took Lys from her horse, flung both bridles over a limb, and, giving my wife my arm, aided her to a flat mossy rock which overhung a shallow brook gurgling among the beach trees. Lys sat down and drew off her gauntlets. Môme pushed his head into her lap, received an undeserved caress, and came doubtfully toward me. I was weak enough to condone his offence, but I made him lie down at my feet, greatly to his disgust.

I rested my head on Lys's knees, looking up at the sky through the crossed branches of the trees.

"I suppose I have killed him," I said. "It shocks me terribly, Lys."

"You could not have known, dear. He may have been a robber, and—if—not—Did—have you ever fired your revolver since that day four years ago, when the Red Admiral's son tried to kill you? But I know you have not."

"No," said I, wondering. "It's a fact, I have not. Why?"

"And don't you remember that I asked you to let me load it for you the day when Yves went off, swearing to kill you and his father?"

"Yes, I do remember. Well?"

"Well, I—I took the cartridges first to St. Gildas chapel and dipped them in holy water. You must not laugh, Dick," said Lys gently, laying her cool hands on my lips.

"Laugh, my darling!"

Overhead the October sky was pale amethyst, and the sunlight burned like orange flame through the yellow leaves of beach and oak. Gnats and midges danced and wavered overhead; a spider dropped from a twig halfway to the ground and hung suspended on the end of his gossamer thread.

"Are you sleepy, dear?" asked Lys, bending over me.

"I am—a little; I scarcely slept two hours last night," I answered.

"You may sleep, if you wish," said Lys, and touched my eyes caressingly.

"Is my head heavy on your knees?"

"No, Dick."

I was already in a half doze; still I heard the brook babbling under the beeches and the humming of forest flies overhead. Presently even these were stilled.

The next thing I knew I was sitting bolt upright, my ears ringing with a scream, and I saw Lys cowering beside me, covering her white face with both hands.

As I sprang to my feet she cried again and clung to my knees. I saw my dog rush growling into a thicket, then I heard him whimper, and he came backing out, whining, ears flat, tail down. I stooped and disengaged Lys's hand.

"Don't go, Dick!" she cried. "O God, it's the Black Priest!"

In a moment I had leaped across the brook and pushed my way into the thicket. It was empty. I stared about me; I scanned every tree trunk, every bush. Suddenly I saw him. He was seated on a fallen log, his head resting in his hands, his rusty black robe gathered around him. For a moment my hair stirred under my cap; sweat started on forehead and cheek-bone; then I recovered my reason, and understood that the man was human and was probably wounded to death. Ay, to death; for there, at my feet, lay the wet trail of blood, over leaves and stones, down into the little hollow, across to the figure in black resting silently under the trees.

I saw that he could not escape even if he had the strength, for before him, almost at his very feet, lay a deep, shining swamp.

As I stepped forward my foot broke a twig. At the sound the figure started a little, then its head fell forward again. Its face was masked. Walking up to the man, I bade him tell where he was wounded. Durand and the others broke through the thicket at the same moment and hurried to my side.

"Who are you who hide a masked face in a priest's robe?" said the gendarme loudly.

There was no answer.

"See—see the stiff blood all over his robe!" muttered Le Bihan to Fortin.

"He will not speak," said I.

"He may be too badly wounded," whispered Le Bihan.

"I saw him raise his head," I said; "my wife saw him creep up here."

Durand stepped forward and touched the figure.

"Speak!" he said.

"Speak!" quavered Fortin.

Durand waited a moment, then with a sudden upward movement he stripped off the mask and threw back the man's head. We were looking into the eye sockets of a skull. Durand stood rigid; the mayor shrieked. The skeleton burst out from its rotting robes and collapsed on the ground before us. From between the staring ribs and the grinning teeth spurted a torrent of black blood, showering the shrinking grasses; then the thing shuddered, and fell over into the black ooze of the bog. Little bubbles of iridescent air appeared from the mud; the bones were slowly engulfed, and, as the last fragments sank out of sight, up from the depths and along the bank crept a creature, shiny, shivering, quivering its wings.

It was a death's-head moth.

I wish I had time to tell you how Lys outgrew superstitions—for she never knew the truth about the affair, and she never will know, since she has promised not to read this book. I wish I might tell you about the king and his coronation, and how the coronation robe fitted. I wish that I were able to write how Yvonne and Herbert Stuart rode to a boar hunt in Quimperlé, and how the hounds raced the quarry right through the town, overturning three gendarmes, the notary, and an old woman. But I am becoming garrulous, and Lys is calling me to come and hear the king say that he is sleepy. And his Highness shall not be kept waiting.

The Key
to Grief

The wild hawk to the wind-swept sky
The deer to the wholesome wold,
And the heart of a man to the heart of a maid,
As it was in the days of old.
                    KIPLING

I

THEY were doing their work very badly. They got the rope around
his neck, and tied his wrists with moose-bush withes, but again he
fell, sprawling, turning, twisting over the leaves, tearing up everything around him like a trapped panther.

He got the rope away from them; he clung to it with bleeding
fists; he set his white teeth in it, until the jute strands relaxed, unravelled, and snapped, gnawed through by his white teeth.

Twice Tully struck him with a gum hook. The dull blows fell on
flesh rigid as stone.

Panting, foul with forest mould and rotten leaves, hands and face
smeared with blood, he sat up on the ground, glaring at the circle of
men around him.

"Shoot him!" gasped Tully, dashing the sweat from his bronzed
brow; and Bates, breathing heavily, sat down on a log and dragged
a revolver from his rear pocket. The man on the ground watched
him; there was froth in the corners of his mouth.

"Git back!" whispered Bates, but his voice and hand trembled.
"Kent," he stammered, "won't ye hang?"

The man on the ground glared.

"Ye've got to die, Kent," he urged; "they all say so. Ask Lefty Sawyer; ask Dyce; ask Carrots.—He's got to swing fur it—ain't he, Tully?—Kent, fur God's sake, swing fur these here gents!"

The man on the ground panted; his bright eyes never moved.

After a moment Tully sprang on him again. There was a flurry of leaves, a crackle, a gasp and a grunt, then the thumping and thrashing of two bodies writhing in the brush. Dyce and Carrots jumped on the prostrate men. Lefty Sawyer caught the rope again, but the jute strands gave way and he stumbled. Tully began to scream, "He's chokin' me!" Dyce staggered out into the open, moaning over a broken wrist.

"Shoot!" shouted Lefty Sawyer, and dragged Tully aside. "Shoot, Jim Bates! Shoot straight, b'God!"

"Git back!" gasped Bates, rising from the fallen log.

The crowd parted right and left; a quick report rang out—another —another. Then from the whirl of smoke a tall form staggered, dealing blows—blows that sounded sharp as the crack of a whip.

"He's off! Shoot straight!" they cried.

There was a gallop of heavy boots in the woods. Bates, faint and dazed, turned his head.

"Shoot!" shrieked Tully.

But Bates was sick; his smoking revolver fell to the ground; his white face and pale eyes contracted. It lasted only a moment; he started after the others, plunging, wallowing through thickets of osier and hemlock underbrush.

Far ahead he heard Kent crashing on like a young moose in November, and he knew he was making for the shore. The others knew too. Already the gray gleam of the sea cut a straight line along the forest edge; already the soft clash of the surf on the rocks broke faintly through the forest silence.

"He's got a canoe there!" bawled Tully. "He'll be into it!"

And he was into it, kneeling in the bow, driving his paddle to the handle. The rising sun gleamed like red lightning on the flashing blade; the canoe shot to the crest of a wave, hung, bows dripping in the wind, dropped into the depths, glided, tipped, rolled, shot up again, staggered, and plunged on.

Tully ran straight out into the cove surf; the water broke against his chest, bare and wet with sweat. Bates sat down on a worn black rock and watched the canoe listlessly.

The canoe dwindled to a speck of gray and silver; and when Carrots, who had run back to the gum camp for a rifle, returned, the speck on the water might have been easier to hit than a loon's head at twilight. So Carrots, being thrifty by nature, fired once, and was satisfied to save the other cartridges. The canoe was still visible, making for the open sea. Somewhere beyond the horizon lay the keys, a string of rocks bare as skulls, black and slimy where the sea cut their base, white on the crests with the excrement of sea birds.

"He's makin' fur the Key to Grief!" whispered Bates to Dyce.

Dyce, moaning, and nursing his broken wrist, turned a sick face out to sea.

The last rock seaward was the Key to Grief, a splintered pinnacle polished by the sea. From the Key to Grief, seaward a day's paddle, if a man dared, lay the long wooded island in the ocean known as Grief on the charts of the bleak coast.

In the history of the coast, two men had made the voyage to the Key to Grief, and from there to the island. One of these was a rum-crazed pelt hunter, who lived to come back; the other was a college youth; they found his battered canoe at sea, and a day later his battered body was flung up in the cove.

So, when Bates whispered to Dyce, and when Dyce called to the others, they knew that the end was not far off for Kent and his canoe; and they turned away into the forest, sullen, but satisfied that Kent would get his dues when the devil got his.

Lefty spoke vaguely of the wages of sin. Carrots, with an eye to thrift, suggested a plan for an equitable division of Kent's property.

When they reached the gum camp they piled Kent's personal effects on a blanket.

Carrots took the inventory: a revolver, two gum hooks, a fur cap, a nickel-plated watch, a pipe, a pack of new cards, a gum sack, forty pounds of spruce gum, and a frying pan.

Carrots shuffled the cards, picked out the joker, and flipped it pensively into the fire. Then he dealt cold decks all around.

When the goods and chattels of their late companion had been divided by chance—for there was no chance to cheat—somebody remembered Tully.

"He's down there on the coast, starin' after the canoe," said Bates huskily.

He rose and walked toward a heap on the ground covered by a blanket. He started to lift the blanket, hesitated, and finally turned away. Under the blanket lay Tully's brother, shot the night before by Kent.

"Guess we'd better wait till Tully comes," said Carrots uneasily. Bates and Kent had been campmates. An hour later Tully walked into camp.

He spoke to no one that day. In the morning Bates found him down on the coast digging, and said: "Hello, Tully! Guess we ain't much hell on lynchin'!"

"Naw," said Tully. "Git a spade."

"Goin' to plant him there?"

"Yep."

"Where he kin hear them waves?"

"Yep."

"Purty spot."

"Yep."

"Which way will he face?"

"Where he kin watch fur that damned canoe!" cried Tully fiercely.

"He—he can't see," ventured Bates uneasily. "He's dead, ain't he?"

"He'll heave up that there sand when the canoe comes back! An' it's a-comin'! An' Bud Kent'll be in it, dead or alive! Git a spade!"

The pale light of superstition flickered in Bate's eyes. He hesitated.

"The—the dead can't see," he began; "kin they?"

Tully turned a distorted face toward him.

"Yer lie!" he roared. "My brother kin see, dead or livin'! An' he'll see the hangin' of Bud Kent! An' he'll git up outer the grave fur to see it, Bill Bates! I'm tellin' ye! I'm tellin' ye! Deep as I'll plant him, he'll heave that there sand and call to me, when the canoe comes in! I'll hear him; I'll be here! An' we'll live to see the hangin' of Bud Kent!"

About sundown they planted Tully's brother, face to the sea.

II

ON the Key to Grief the green waves rub all day. White at the summit, black at the base, the shafted rocks rear splintered pinnacles, slanting like channel buoys. On the polished pillars sea birds brood —white-winged, bright-eyed sea birds, that nestle and preen and flap and clatter their orange-coloured beaks when the sifted spray drives and drifts across the reef.

As the sun rose, painting crimson streaks criss-cross over the waters, the sea birds sidled together, huddling row on row, steeped in downy drowse.

Where the sun of noon burnished the sea, an opal wave washed, listless, noiseless; a sea bird stretched one listless wing.

And into the silence of the waters a canoe glided, bronzed by the sunlight, jewelled by the salt drops stringing from prow to thwart, seaweed a-trail in the diamond-flashing wake, and in the bow a man dripping with sweat.

Up rose the gulls, sweeping in circles, turning, turning over rock and sea, and their clamour filled the sky, starting little rippling echoes among the rocks.

The canoe grated on a shelf of ebony; the seaweed rocked and washed; the little sea crabs sheered sideways, down, down into limpid depths of greenest shadows. Such was the coming of Bud Kent to the Key to Grief.

He drew the canoe halfway up the shelf of rock and sat down, breathing heavily, one brown arm across the bow. For an hour he sat there. The sweat dried under his eyes. The sea birds came back, filling the air with soft querulous notes.

There was a livid mark around his neck, a red, raw circle. The salt wind stung it; the sun burned it into his flesh like a collar of red-hot steel. He touched it at times; once he washed it with cold salt water.

Far in the north a curtain of mist hung on the sea, dense, motionless as the fog on the Grand Banks. He never moved his eyes from it; he knew what it was. Behind it lay the Island of Grief.

All the year round the Island of Grief is hidden by the banks of mist, ramparts of dead white fog encircling it on every side. Ships give it wide berth. Some speak of warm springs on the island whose waters flow far out to sea, rising in steam eternally.

The pelt hunter had come back with tales of forests and deer and flowers everywhere; but he had been drinking much, and much was forgiven him.

The body of the college youth tossed up in the cove on the mainland was battered out of recognition, but some said, when found, one hand clutched a crimson blossom half wilted, but broad as a sap pan.

So Kent lay motionless beside his canoe, burned with thirst, every nerve vibrating, thinking of all these things. It was not fear that whitened the firm flesh under the tan; it was the fear of fear. He must not think—he must throttle dread; his eyes must never falter, his head never turn from that wall of mist across the sea. With set teeth he crushed back terror; with glittering eyes he looked into the hollow eyes of fright. And so he conquered fear.

He rose. The sea birds whirled up into the sky, pitching, tossing, screaming, till the sharp flapping of their pinions set the snapping echoes flying among the rocks.

Under the canoe's sharp prow the kelp bobbed and dipped and parted; the sunlit waves ran out ahead, glittering, dancing. Splash! splash! bow and stern! And now he knelt again, and the polished paddle swung and dipped, and swept and swung and dipped again.

Far behind, the clamour of the sea birds lingered in his ears, till the mellow dip of the paddle drowned all sound and the sea was a sea of silence.

No wind came to cool the hot sweat on cheek and breast. The sun blazed a path of flame before him, and he followed out into the waste of waters. The still ocean divided under the bows and rippled innocently away on either side, tinkling, foaming, sparkling like the current in a woodland brook. He looked around at the world of flattened water, and the fear of fear rose up and gripped his throat again. Then he lowered his head, like a tortured bull, and shook the fear of fear from his throat, and drove the paddle into the sea as a butcher stabs, to the hilt.

So at last he came to the wall of mist. It was thin at first, thin and cool, but it thickened and grew warmer, and the fear of fear dragged at his head, but he would not look behind.

Into the fog the canoe shot; the gray water ran by, high as the gunwales, oily, silent. Shapes flickered across the bows, pillars of mist that rode the waters, robed in films of tattered shadows. Gigantic forms towered to dizzy heights above him, shaking out shredded shrouds of cloud. The vast draperies of the fog swayed and hung and trembled as he brushed them; the white twilight deepened to a sombre gloom. And now it grew thinner; the fog became a mist, and the mist a haze, and the haze floated away and vanished into the blue of the heavens.

All around lay a sea of pearl and sapphire, lapping, lapping on a silver shoal.

So he came to the Island of Grief.

III

On the silver shoal the waves washed and washed, breaking like crushed opals where the sands sang with the humming froth.

Troops of little shore birds, wading on the shoal, tossed their sun-tipped wings and scuttled inland, where, dappled with shadow from the fringing forest, the white beach of the island stretched.

The water all around was shallow, limpid as crystal, and he saw the ribbed sand shining on the bottom, where purple seaweed floated, and delicate sea creatures darted and swarmed and scattered again at the dip of his paddle.

Like velvet rubbed on velvet the canoe brushed across the sand. He staggered to his feet, stumbled out, dragged the canoe high up under the trees, turned it bottom upward, and sank beside it, face downward in the sand. Sleep came to drive away the fear of fear, but hunger, thirst, and fever fought with sleep, and he dreamed— dreamed of a rope that sawed his neck, of the fight in the woods, and the shots. He dreamed, too, of the camp, of his forty pounds of spruce gum, of Tully, and of Bates. He dreamed of the fire and the smoke-scorched kettle, of the foul odour of musty bedding, of the greasy cards, and of his own new pack, hoarded for weeks to please the others. All this he dreamed, lying there face downward in the sand; but he did not dream of the face of the dead.

The shadows of the leaves moved on his blond head, crisp with clipped curls. A butterfly flitted around him, alighting now on his legs, now on the back of his bronzed hands. All the afternoon the bees hung droning among the wildwood blossoms; the leaves above scarcely rustled; the shore birds brooded along the water's edge; the thin tide, sleeping on the sand, mirrored the sky.

Twilight paled the zenith; a breeze moved in the deeper woods; a star glimmered, went out, glimmered again, faded, and glimmered.

Night came. A moth darted to and fro under the trees; a beetle hummed around a heap of seaweed and fell scrambling in the sand. Somewhere among the trees a sound had become distinct, the song of a little brook, melodious, interminable. He heard it in his dream; it threaded all his dreams like a needle of silver, and like a needle it pricked him—pricked his dry throat and cracked lips. It could not awake him; the cool night swathed him head and foot.

Toward dawn a bird woke up and piped. Other birds stirred, restless, half awakened; a gull spread a cramped wing on the shore, preened its feathers, scratched its tufted neck, and took two drowsy steps toward the sea.

The sea breeze stirred out behind the mist bank; it raised the feathers on the sleeping gulls; it set the leaves whispering. A twig snapped, broke off, and fell. Kent stirred, sighed, trembled, and awoke.

The first thing he heard was the song of the brook, and he stumbled straight into the woods. There it lay, a thin, deep stream in the gray morning light, and he stretched himself beside it and laid his cheek in it. A bird drank in the pool, too—a little fluffy bird, bright-eyed and fearless.

His knees were firmer when at last he rose, heedless of the drops that beaded lips and chin. With his knife he dug and scraped at some white roots that hung half meshed in the bank of the brook, and when he had cleaned them in the pool he ate them.

The sun stained the sky when he went down to the canoe, but the eternal curtain of fog, far out at sea, hid it as yet from sight.

He lifted the canoe, bottom upwards, to his head, and, paddle and pole in either hand, carried it into the forest.

After he had set it down he stood a moment, opening and shutting his knife. Then he looked up into the trees. There were birds there, if he could get at them. He looked at the brook. There were prints of his fingers in the sand; there, too, was the print of something else—a deer's pointed hoof.

He had nothing but his knife. He opened it again and looked at it.

That day he dug for clams and ate them raw. He waded out into the shallows, too, and jabbed at fish with his setting pole, but hit nothing except a yellow crab.

Fire was what he wanted. He hacked and chipped at flinty-looking pebbles, and scraped tinder from a stick of sun-dried driftwood. His knuckles bled, but no fire came.

That night he heard deer in the woods, and could not sleep for thinking, until the dawn came up behind the wall of mist, and he rose with it to drink his fill at the brook and tear raw clams with his white teeth. Again he fought for fire, craving it as he had never craved water, but his knuckles bled, and the knife scraped on the flint in vain.

His mind, perhaps, had suffered somewhat. The white beach seemed to rise and fall like a white carpet on a gusty hearth. The birds, too, that ran along the sand, seemed big and juicy, like partridges; and he chased them, hurling shells and bits of driftwood at them till he could scarcely keep his feet for the rising, plunging beach—or carpet, whichever it was. That night the deer aroused him at intervals. He heard them splashing and grunting and crackling along the brook. Once he arose and stole after them, knife in hand, till a false step into the brook awoke him to his folly, and he felt his way back to the canoe, trembling.

Morning came, and again he drank at the brook, lying on the sand where countless heart-shaped hoofs had passed leaving clean imprints; and again he ripped the raw clams from their shells and swallowed them, whimpering.

All day long the white beach rose and fell and heaved and flattened under his bright dry eyes. He chased the shore birds at times, till the unsteady beach tripped him up and he fell full length in the sand. Then he would rise moaning, and creep into the shadow of the wood, and watch the little song-birds in the branches, moaning, always moaning.

His hands, sticky with blood, hacked steel and flint together, but so feebly that now even the cold sparks no longer came.

He began to fear the advancing night; he dreaded to hear the big warm deer among the thickets. Fear clutched him suddenly, and he lowered his head and set his teeth and shook fear from his throat again.

Then he started aimlessly into the woods, crowding past bushes, scraping trees, treading on moss and twig and mouldy stump, his bruised hands swinging, always swinging.

The sun set in the mist as he came out of the woods on to another beach—a warm, soft beach, crimsoned by the glow in the evening clouds.

And on the sand at his feet lay a young girl asleep, swathed in the silken garment of her own black hair, round limbed, brown, smooth as the bloom on the tawny beach.

A gull flapped overhead, screaming. Her eyes, deeper than night, unclosed. Then her lips parted in a cry, soft with sleep, "Ihó!"

She rose, rubbing her velvet eyes. "Ihó!" she cried in wonder; "Inâh!"

The gilded sand settled around her little feet. Her cheeks crimsoned.

"E-hó! E-hó!" she whispered, and hid her face in her hair.

IV

THE bridge of the stars spans the sky seas; the sun and the moon are the travellers who pass over it. This was also known in the lodges of the Isantee, hundreds of years ago. Chaské told it to Hârpam, and when Hârpam knew he told it to Hapéda; and so the knowledge spread to Hârka, and from Winona to Wehârka, up and down, across and ever across, woof and web, until it came to the Island of Grief. And how? God knows!

Wehârka, prattling in the tules, may have told Ne-kâ; and Ne-kâ, high in the November clouds, may have told Kay-óshk, who told it to Shinge-bis, who told it to Skeé-skah, who told it to Sé-só-Kah.

Ihó! Inâh! Behold the wonder of it! And this is the fate of all knowledge that comes to the Island of Grief.

As the red glow died in the sky, and the sand swam in shadows, the girl parted the silken curtains of her hair and looked at him.

"Ehó!" she whispered again in soft delight.

For now it was plain to her that he was the sun! He had crossed the bridge of stars in the blue twilight; he had come!

"E-tó!"

She stepped nearer, shivering, faint with the ecstasy of this holy miracle wrought before her.

He was the Sun! His blood streaked the sky at dawn; his blood stained the clouds at even. In his eyes the blue of the sky still lingered, smothering two blue stars; and his body was as white as the breast of the Moon.

She opened both arms, hands timidly stretched, palm upward. Her face was raised to his, her eyes slowly closed; the deep-fringed lids trembled.

Like a young priestess she stood, motionless save for the sudden quiver of a limb, a quick pulse-flutter in the rounded throat. And so she worshipped, naked and unashamed, even after he, reeling, fell heavily forward on his face; even when the evening breeze stealing over the sands stirred the hair on his head, as winds stir the fur of a dead animal in the dust.

When the morning sun peered over the wall of mist, and she saw it was the sun, and she saw him, flung on the sand at her feet, then she knew that he was a man, only a man, pallid as death and smeared with blood.

And yet—miracle of miracles!—the divine wonder in her eyes deepened, and her body seemed to swoon, and fall a-trembling, and swoon again.

For, although it was but a man who lay at her feet, it had been easier for her to look upon a god.

He dreamed that he breathed fire—fire, that he craved as he had never craved water. Mad with delirium, he knelt before the flames, rubbing his torn hands, washing them in the crimson-scented flames. He had water, too, cool scented water, that sprayed his burning flesh, that washed in his eyes, his hair, his throat. After that came hunger, a fierce rending agony, that scorched and clutched and tore at his entrails; but that, too, died away, and he dreamed that he had eaten and all his flesh was warm. Then he dreamed that he slept; and when he slept he dreamed no more.

One day he awoke and found her stretched beside him, soft palms tightly closed, smiling, asleep.

V

Now the days began to run more swiftly than the tide along the tawny beach; and the nights, star-dusted and blue, came and vanished and returned, only to exhale at dawn like perfume from a violet.

They counted hours as they counted the golden bubbles, winking with a million eyes along the foam-flecked shore; and the hours ended, and began, and glimmered, iridescent, and ended as bubbles end in a tiny rainbow haze.

There was still fire in the world; it flashed up at her touch and where she chose. A bow strung with the silk of her own hair, an arrow winged like a sea bird and tipped with shell, a line from the silver tendon of a deer, a hook of polished bone—these were the mysteries he learned, and learned them laughing, her silken head bent close to his.

The first night that the bow was wrought and the glossy string attuned, she stole into the moonlit forest to the brook; and there they stood, whispering, listening, and whispering, though neither understood the voice they loved.

In the deeper woods, Kaug, the porcupine, scraped and snuffed. They heard Wabóse, the rabbit, pit-a-pat, pit-a-pat, loping across dead leaves in the moonlight. Skeé-skah, the wood-duck, sailed past, noiseless, gorgeous as a floating blossom.

Out on the ocean's placid silver, Shinge-bis, the diver, shook the scented silence with his idle laughter, till Kay-óshk, the gray gull, stirred in his slumber. There came a sudden ripple in the stream, a mellow splash, a soft sound on the sand.

"Ihó! Behold!"

"I see nothing."

The beloved voice was only a wordless melody to her.

"Ihó! Ta-hinca, the red deer! E-hó! The buck will follow!"

"Ta-hinca," he repeated, notching the arrow.

"E-tó! Ta-mdóka!"

So he drew the arrow to the head, and the gray gull feathers brushed his ear, and the darkness hummed with the harmony of the singing string.

Thus died Ta-mdóka, the buck deer of seven prongs.

VI

As an apple tossed spinning into the air, so spun the world above the hand that tossed it into space.

And one day in early spring, Sé-só-Kah, the robin, awoke at dawn, and saw a girl at the foot of the blossoming tree holding a babe cradled in the silken sheets of her hair.

At its feeble cry, Kaug, the porcupine, raised his quilled head. Wabosé, the rabbit, sat still with palpitating sides. Kay-óshk, the gray gull, tiptoed along the beach.

Kent knelt with one bronzed arm around them both.

"Ihó! Inâh!" whispered the girl, and held the babe up in the rosy flames of dawn.

But Kent trembled as he looked, and his eyes filled. On the pale green moss their shadows lay—three shadows. But the shadow of the babe was white as froth.

Because it was the firstborn son, they named it Chaské; and the girl sang as she cradled it there in the silken vestments of her hair; all day long in the sunshine she sang:

> Wâ-wa, wâ-wa, wâ-we—yeá;
> Kah-wéen, nee-zhéka Ke-diaus-âi,
> Ke-gâh nau-wâi, ne-mé-go S'weén,
> Ne-bâun, ne-bâun, ne-dâun-is âis.
> E-we wâ-wa, wâ-we—yeá;
> E-we wâ-wa, wâ-we—yeá.

Out in the calm ocean, Shinge-bis, the diver, listened, preening his satin breast in silence. In the forest, Ta-hinca, the red deer, turned her delicate head to the wind.

That night Kent thought of the dead, for the first time since he had come to the Key of Grief.

"Aké-u! aké-u!" chirped Sé-só-Kah, the robin. But the dead never come again.

"Beloved, sit close to us," whispered the girl, watching his troubled eyes. "Ma-cânte maséca."

But he looked at the babe and its white shadow on the moss, and he only sighed: "Ma-cânte maséca, beloved! Death sits watching us across the sea."

Now for the first time he knew more than the fear of fear; he knew fear. And with fear came grief.

He never before knew that grief lay hidden there in the forest. Now he knew it. Still, that happiness, eternally reborn when two small hands reached up around his neck, when feeble fingers clutched his hand—that happiness that Sé-só-Kah understood, chirping to his brooding mate—that Ta-mdóka knew, licking his dappled fawns— that happiness gave him heart to meet grief calmly, in dreams or in the forest depths, and it helped him to look into the hollow eyes of fear.

He often thought of the camp now; of Bates, his blanket mate; of Dyce, whose wrist he had broken with a blow; of Tully, whose brother he had shot. He even seemed to hear the shot, the sudden report among the hemlocks; again he saw the haze of smoke, he caught a glimpse of a tall form falling through the bushes.

He remembered every minute incident of the trial: Bates's hand laid on his shoulder; Tully, red-bearded and wild-eyed, demanding his death; while Dyce spat and spat and smoked and kicked at the blackened log-ends projecting from the fire. He remembered, too, the verdict, and Tully's terrible laugh; and the new jute rope that they stripped off the market-sealed gum packs.

He thought of these things, sometimes wading out on the shoals, shell-tipped fish spear poised: at such times he would miss his fish. He thought of it sometimes when he knelt by the forest stream listening for Ta-hinca's splash among the cresses: at such moments the feathered shaft whistled far from the mark, and Ta-mdóka stamped and snorted till even the white fisher, stretched on a rotting log, flattened his whiskers and stole away into the forest's blackest depths.

When the child was a year old, hour for hour notched at sunset and sunrise, it prattled with the birds, and called to Ne-Kâ, the wild goose, who called again to the child from the sky: "Northward! northward, beloved!"

When winter came—there is no frost on the Island of Grief— Ne-Kâ, the wild goose, passing high in the clouds, called: "Southward! southward, beloved!" And the child answered in a soft whisper of an unknown tongue, till the mother shivered, and covered it with her silken hair.

"O beloved!" said the girl, "Chaské calls to all things living—to Kaug, the porcupine, to Wabóse, to Kay-óshk, the gray gull—he calls, and they understand."

Kent bent and looked into her eyes.

"Hush, beloved; it is not *that* I fear."

"Then what, beloved?"

"His shadow. It is white as surf foam. And at night—I—I have seen—"

"Oh, what?"

"The air about him aglow like a pale rose."

"Ma cânté maséca. The earth alone lasts. I speak as one dying—I know, O beloved!"

Her voice died away like a summer wind.

"Beloved!" he cried.

But there before him she was changing; the air grew misty, and her hair wavered like shreds of fog, and her slender form swayed, and faded, and swerved, like the mist above a pond.

In her arms the babe was a figure of mist, rosy, vague as a breath on a mirror.

"The earth alone lasts. Inâh! It is the end, O beloved!"

The words came from the mist—a mist as formless as the ether—a mist that drove in and crowded him, that came from the sea, from the clouds, from the earth at his feet. Faint with terror, he staggered forward calling, "Beloved! And thou, Chaské, O beloved! Aké u! Aké u!"

Far out at sea a rosy star glimmered an instant in the mist and went out.

A sea bird screamed, soaring over the waste of fog-smothered waters. Again he saw the rosy star; it came nearer; its reflection glimmered in the water.

"Chaské!" he cried.

He heard a voice, dull in the choking mist.

"O beloved, I am here!" he called again.

There was a sound on the shoal, a flicker in the fog, the flare of a torch, a face white, livid, terrible—the face of the dead.

He fell upon his knees; he closed his eyes and opened them. Tully stood beside him with a coil of rope.

Ihó! Behold the end! The earth alone lasts. The sand, the opal wave on the golden beach, the sea of sapphire, the dusted starlight, the wind, and love, shall die. Death also shall die, and lie on the shores of the skies like the bleached skull there on the Key to Grief, polished, empty, with its teeth embedded in the sand.

The
Harbor-Master

Where the slanting forest eaves,
Shingled tight with greenest leaves,
Sweep the scented meadow-sedge,
Let us snoop along the edge;
Let us pry in hidden nooks,
Laden with our nature books,
Scaring birds with happy cries,
Chloroforming butterflies,
Rooting up each woodland plant,
Pinning beetle, fly, and ant,
So we may identify
What we've ruined, by-and-by.

I

BECAUSE it all seems so improbable—so horribly impossible to me
now, sitting here safe and sane in my own library—I hesitate to
record an episode which already appears to me less horrible than
grotesque. Yet, unless this story is written now, I know I shall never
have the courage to tell the truth about the matter—not from fear
of ridicule, but because I myself shall soon cease to credit what I now
know to be true. Yet scarcely a month has elapsed since I heard the
stealthy purring of what I belived to be the shoaling undertow—
scarcely a month ago, with my own eyes, I saw that which, even now,
I am beginning to believe never existed. As for the harbor-master—
and the blow I am now striking at the old order of things— But of
that I shall not speak now, or later; I shall try to tell the story simply
and truthfully, and let my friends testify as to my probity and the
publishers of this book corroborate them.

On the 29th of February I resigned my position under the government and left Washington to accept an offer from Professor Farrago —whose name he kindly permits me to use—and on the first day of April I entered upon my new and congenial duties as general superintendent of the water-fowl department connected with the Zoological Gardens then in course of erection at Bronx Park, New York.

For a week I followed the routine, examining the new foundations, studying the architect's plans, following the surveyors through the Bronx thickets, suggesting arrangements for water-courses and pools destined to be included in the enclosures for swans, geese, pelicans, herons, and such of the waders and swimmers as we might expect to acclimate in Bronx Park.

It was at that time the policy of the trustees and officers of the Zoological Gardens neither to employ collectors nor to send out expeditions in search of specimens. The society decided to depend upon voluntary contributions, and I was always busy, part of the day, in dictating answers to correspondents who wrote offering their services as hunters of big game, collectors of all sorts of fauna, trappers, snarers, and also to those who offered specimens for sale, usually at exorbitant rates.

To the proprietors of five-legged kittens, mangy lynxes, moth-eaten coyotes, and dancing bears I returned courteous but uncompromising refusals—of course, first submitting all such letters, together with my replies, to Professor Farrago.

One day towards the end of May, however, just as I was leaving Bronx Park to return to town, Professor Lesard, of the reptilian department, called out to me that Professor Farrago wanted to see me a moment; so I put my pipe into my pocket again and retraced my steps to the temporary, wooden building occupied by Professor Farrago, general superintendent of the Zoological Gardens. The professor, who was sitting at his desk before a pile of letters and replies submitted for approval by me, pushed his glasses down and looked over them at me with a whimsical smile that suggested amusement, impatience, annoyance, and perhaps a faint trace of apology.

"Now, here's a letter," he said, with a deliberate gesture towards a sheet of paper impaled on a file—"a letter that I suppose you remember." He disengaged the sheet of paper and handed it to me.

"Oh yes," I replied, with a shrug; "of course the man is mistaken
—or—"

"Or what?" demanded Professor Farrago, tranquilly, wiping his
glasses.

"—Or a liar," I replied.

After a silence he leaned back in his chair and bade me read the
letter to him again, and I did so with a contemptuous tolerance for
the writer, who must have been either a very innocent victim or a
very stupid swindler. I said as much to Professor Farrago, but, to my
surprise, he appeared to waver.

"I suppose," he said, with his near-sighted, embarrassed smile,
"that nine hundred and ninety-nine men in a thousand would throw
that letter aside and condemn the writer as a liar or a fool?"

"In my opinion," said I, "he's one or the other."

"He isn't—in mine," said the professor, placidly.

"What!" I exclaimed. "Here is a man living all alone on a strip
of rock and sand between the wilderness and the sea, who wants you
to send somebody to take charge of a bird that doesn't exist!"

"How do you know," asked Professor Farrago, "that the bird in
question does not exist?"

"It is generally accepted," I replied, sarcastically, "that the
great auk has been extinct for years. Therefore I may be pardoned
for doubting that our correspondent possesses a pair of them alive."

"Oh, you young fellows," said the professor, smiling wearily,
"you embark on a theory for destinations that don't exist."

He leaned back in his chair, his amused eyes searching space for
the imagery that made him smile.

"Like swimming squirrels, you navigate with the help of Heaven
and a stiff breeze, but you never land where you hope to—do
you?"

Rather red in the face, I said: "Don't you believe the great auk to
be extinct?"

"Audubon saw the great auk."

"Who has seen a single specimen since?"

"Nobody—except our correspondent here," he replied, laughing.

I laughed, too, considering the interview at an end, but the professor went on, coolly:

"Whatever it is that our correspondent has—and I am daring to believe that it *is* the great auk itself—I want you to secure it for the society."

When my astonishment subsided my first conscious sentiment was one of pity. Clearly, Professor Farrago was on the verge of dotage—ah, what a loss to the world!

I believe now that Professor Farrago perfectly interpreted my thoughts, but he betrayed neither resentment nor impatience. I drew a chair up beside his desk—there was nothing to do but to obey, and this fool's errand was none of my conceiving.

Together we made out a list of articles necessary for me and itemized the expenses I might incur, and I set a date for my return, allowing no margin for a successful termination to the expedition.

"Never mind that," said the professor. "What I want you to do is to get those birds here safely. Now, how many men will you take?"

"None," I replied, bluntly; "it's a useless expense, unless there is something to bring back. If there is I'll wire you, you may be sure."

"Very well," said Professor Farrago, good-humoredly, "you shall have all the assistance you may require. Can you leave to-night?"

The old gentleman was certainly prompt. I nodded, half-sulkily, aware of his amusement.

"So," I said, picking up my hat, "I am to start north to find a place called Black Harbor, where there is a man named Halyard who possesses, among other household utensils, two extinct great auks—"

We were both laughing by this time. I asked him why on earth he credited the assertion of a man he had never before heard of.

"I suppose," he replied, with the same half-apologetic, half-humorous smile, "it is instinct. I feel, somehow, that this man Halyard *has* got an auk—perhaps two. I can't get away from the idea that we are on the eve of acquiring the rarest of living creatures. It's odd for a scientist to talk as I do; doubtless you're shocked—admit it, now!"

But I was not shocked; on the contrary, I was conscious that the same strange hope that Professor Farrago cherished was beginning, in spite of me, to stir my pulses, too.

"If he has—" I began, then stopped.

The professor and I looked hard at each other in silence.

"Go on," he said, encouragingly.

But I had nothing more to say, for the prospect of beholding with my own eyes a living specimen of the great auk produced a series of conflicting emotions within me which rendered speech profanely superfluous.

As I took my leave Professor Farrago came to the door of the temporary, wooden office and handed me the letter written by the man Halyard. I folded it and put it into my pocket, as Halyard might require it for my own identification.

"How much does he want for the pair?" I asked.

"Ten thousand dollars. Don't demur—if the birds are really—"

"I know," I said, hastily, not daring to hope too much.

"One thing more," said Professor Farrago, gravely; "you know, in that last paragraph of his letter, Halyard speaks of something else in the way of specimens—an undiscovered species of amphibious biped—just read that paragraph again, will you?"

I drew the letter from my pocket and read as he directed:

When you have seen the two living specimens of the great auk, and have satisfied yourself that I tell the truth, you may be wise enough to listen without prejudice to a statement I shall make concerning the existence of the strangest creature ever fashioned. I will merely say, at this time, that the creature referred to is an amphibious biped and inhabits the ocean near this coast. More I cannot say, for I personally have not seen the animal, but I have a witness who has, and there are many who affirm that they have seen the creature. You will naturally say that my statement amounts to nothing; but when your representative arrives, if he be free from prejudice, I expect his reports to you concerning this sea-biped will confirm the solemn statements of a witness I *know* to be unimpeachable.

Yours truly, BURTON HALYARD.

BLACK HARBOR.

"Well," I said, after a moment's thought, "here goes for the wild-goose chase."

"Wild auk, you mean," said Professor Farrago, shaking hands with me. "You will start to-night, won't you?"

"Yes, but Heaven knows how I'm ever going to land in this man Halyard's door-yard. Good-bye!"

"About that sea-biped—" began Professor Farrago, shyly.

"Oh, don't!" I said; "I can swallow the auks, feathers and claws, but if this fellow Halyard is hinting he's seen an amphibious creature resembling a man—"

"—Or a woman," said the professor, cautiously.

I retired, disgusted, my faith shaken in the mental vigor of Professor Farrago.

II

THE three days' voyage by boat and rail was irksome. I bought my kit at Sainte Croix, on the Central Pacific Railroad, and on June 1st I began the last stage of my journey *via* the Sainte Isole broad-gauge, arriving in the wilderness by daylight. A tedious forced march by blazed trail, freshly spotted on the wrong side, of course, brought me to the northern terminus of the rusty, narrow-gauge lumber railway which runs from the heart of the hushed pine wilderness to the sea.

Already a long train of battered flat-cars, piled with sluice-props and roughly hewn sleepers, was moving slowly off into the brooding forest gloom, when I came in sight of the track; but I developed a gratifying and unexpected burst of speed, shouting all the while. The train stopped; I swung myself aboard the last car, where a pleasant young fellow was sitting on the rear brake, chewing spruce and reading a letter.

"Come aboard, sir," he said, looking up with a smile; "I guess you're the man in a hurry."

"I'm looking for a man named Halyard," I said, dropping rifle and knapsack on the fresh-cut, fragrant pile of pine. "Are you Halyard?"

"No, I'm Francis Lee, bossing the mica pit at Port-of-Waves," he replied, "but this letter is from Halyard, asking me to look out for a man in a hurry from Bronx Park, New York."

"I'm that man," said I, filling my pipe and offering him a share of the weed of peace, and we sat side by side smoking very amiably, until a signal from the locomotive sent him forward and I was left alone, lounging at ease, head pillowed on both arms, watching the blue sky flying through the branches overhead.

Long before we came in sight of the ocean I smelled it; the fresh, salt aroma stole into my senses, drowsy with the heated odor of pine and hemlock, and I sat up, peering ahead into the dusky sea of pines.

Fresher and fresher came the wind from the sea, in puffs, in mild, sweet breezes, in steady, freshening currents, blowing the feathery crowns of the pines, setting the balsam's blue tufts rocking.

Lee wandered back over the long line of flats, balancing himself nonchalantly as the cars swung around a sharp curve, where water dripped from a newly propped sluice that suddenly emerged from the depths of the forest to run parallel to the railroad track.

"Built it this spring," he said, surveying his handiwork, which seemed to undulate as the cars swept past. "It runs to the cove—or ought to—" He stopped abruptly with a thoughtful glance at me.

"So you're going over to Halyard's?" he continued, as though answering a question asked by himself.

I nodded.

"You've never been there—of course?"

"No," I said, "and I'm not likely to go again."

I would have told him why I was going if I had not already begun to feel ashamed of my idiotic errand.

"I guess you're going to look at those birds of his," continued Lee, placidly.

"I guess I am," I said, sulkily, glancing askance to see whether he was smiling.

But he only asked me, quite seriously, whether a great auk was really a very rare bird; and I told him that the last one ever seen had been found dead off Labrador in January, 1870. Then I asked him whether these birds of Halyard's were really great auks, and he replied, somewhat indifferently, that he supposed they were—at least, nobody had ever before seen such birds near Port-of-Waves.

"There's something else," he said, running a pine-sliver through his pipe-stem—"something that interests us all here more than auks, big or little. I suppose I might as well speak of it, as you are bound to hear about it sooner or later."

He hesitated, and I could see that he was embarrassed, searching for the exact words to convey his meaning.

"If," said I, "you have anything in this region more important to science that the great auk, I should be very glad to know about it."

Perhaps there was the faintest tinge of sarcasm in my voice, for he shot a sharp glance at me and then turned slightly. After a moment, however, he put his pipe into his pocket, laid hold of the brake with both hands, vaulted to his perch aloft, and glanced down at me.

"Did you ever hear of the harbor-master?" he asked, maliciously.

"Which harbor-master?" I inquired.

"You'll know before long," he observed, with a satisfied glance into perspective.

This rather extraordinary observation puzzled me. I waited for him to resume, and, as he did not, I asked him what he meant.

"If I knew," he said, "I'd tell you. But, come to think of it, I'd be a fool to go into details with a scientific man. You'll hear about the harbor-master—perhaps you will see the harbor-master. In that event I should be glad to converse with you on the subject."

I could not help laughing at his prim and precise manner, and after a moment, he also laughed, saying:

"It hurts a man's vanity to know he knows a thing that somebody else knows he doesn't know. I'm damned if I say another word about the harbor-master until you've been to Halyard's!"

"A harbor-master," I persisted, "is an official who superintends the mooring of ships—isn't he?"

But he refused to be tempted into conversation, and we lounged silently on the lumber until a long, thin whistle from the locomotive and a rush of stinging salt-wind brought us to our feet. Through the trees I could see the bluish-black ocean, stretching out beyond black headlands to meet the clouds; a great wind was roaring among the trees as the train slowly came to a stand-still on the edge of the primeval forest.

Lee jumped to the ground and aided me with my rifle and pack, and then the train began to back away along a curved side-track which, Lee said, led to the mica-pit and company stores.

"Now what will you do?" he asked, pleasantly. "I can give you a good dinner and a decent bed to-night if you like—and I'm sure Mrs. Lee would be very glad to have you stop with us as long as you choose."

I thanked him, but said that I was anxious to reach Halyard's before dark, and he very kindly led me along the cliffs and pointed out the path.

"This man Halyard," he said, "is an invalid. He lives at a cove called Black Harbor, and all his truck goes through to him over the company's road. We receive it here, and send a pack-mule through once a month. I've met him; he's a bad-tempered hypochondriac,

a cynic at heart, and a man whose word is never doubted. If he says
he has a great auk, you may be satisfied he has."

My heart was beating with excitement at the prospect; I looked
out across the wooded headlands and tangled stretches of dune and
hollow, trying to realize what it might mean to me, to Professor
Farrago, to the world, if I should lead back to New York a live auk.

"He's a crank," said Lee; "frankly, I don't like him. If you find it
unpleasant there, come back to us."

"Does Halyard live alone?" I asked.

"Yes—except for a professional trained nurse—poor thing!"

"A man?"

"No," said Lee, disgustedly.

Presently he gave me a peculiar glance; hesitated, and finally said:
"Ask Halyard to tell you about his nurse and—the harbor-master.
Good-bye—I'm due at the quarry. Come and stay with us whenever
you care to; you will find a welcome at Port-of-Waves."

We shook hands and parted on the cliff, he turning back into the
forest along the railway, I starting northward, pack slung, rifle over
my shoulder. Once I met a group of quarrymen, faces burned brick-
red, scarred hands swinging as they walked. And, as I passed them
with a nod, turning, I saw that they also had turned to look after me,
and I caught a word or two of their conversation, whirled back to me
on the sea-wind.

They were speaking of the harbor-master.

III

Towards sunset I came out on a sheer granite cliff where the sea-
birds were whirling and clamoring, and the great breakers dashed
rolling in double-thundered reverberations on the sun-dyed, crimson
sands below the rock.

Across the half-moon of beach towered another cliff, and, behind
this, I saw a column of smoke rising in the still air. It certainly came
from Halyard's chimney, although the opposite cliff prevented me
from seeing the house itself.

I rested a moment to refill my pipe, then resumed rifle and pack,
and cautiously started to skirt the cliffs. I had descended half-way

towards the beach, and was examining the cliff opposite, when something on the very top of the rock arrested my attention—a man darkly outlined against the sky. The next moment, however, I knew it could not be a man, for the object suddenly glided over the face of the cliff and slid down the sheer, smooth face like a lizard. Before I could get a square look at it, the thing crawled into the surf—or, at least, it seemed to—but the whole episode occurred so suddenly, so unexpectedly, that I was not sure I had seen anything at all.

However, I was curious enough to climb the cliff on the land side and make my way towards the spot where I imagined I saw the man. Of course, there was nothing there—not a trace of a human being, I mean. Something *had* been there—a sea-otter, possibly—for the remains of a freshly killed fish lay on the rock, eaten to the back-bone and tail.

The next moment, below me, I saw the house, a freshly painted, trim, flimsy structure, modern, and very much out of harmony with the splendid savagery surrounding it. It struck a nasty, cheap note in the noble, gray monotony of headland and sea.

The descent was easy enough. I crossed the crescent beach, hard as pink marble, and found a little trodden path among the rocks, that led to the front porch of the house.

There were two people on the porch—I heard their voices before I saw them—and when I set my foot upon the wooden steps, I saw one of them, a woman, rise from her chair and step hastily towards me.

"Come back!" cried the other, a man with a smooth-shaven, deeply lined face, and a pair of angry, blue eyes; and the woman stepped back quietly, acknowledging my lifted hat with a silent inclination.

The man, who was reclining in an invalid's rolling-chair, clapped both large, pale hands to the wheels and pushed himself out along the porch. He had shawls pinned about him, an untidy, drab-colored hat on his head, and, when he looked down at me, he scowled.

"I know who you are," he said, in his acid voice; "you're one of the Zoological men from Bronx Park. You look like it, anyway."

"It is easy to recognize you from your reputation," I replied irritated at his discourtesy.

"Really," he replied, with something between a sneer and a laugh, "I'm obliged for your frankness. You're after my great auks, are you not?"

"Nothing else would have tempted me into this place," I replied, sincerely.

"Thank Heaven for that," he said. "Sit down a moment; you've interrupted us." Then, turning to the young woman, who wore the neat gown and tiny cap of a professional nurse, he bade her resume what she had been saying. She did so, with a deprecating glance at me, which made the old man sneer again.

"It happened so suddenly," she said, in her low voice, "that I had no chance to get back. The boat was drifting in the cove; I sat in the stern, reading, both oars shipped, and the tiller swinging. Then I heard a scratching under the boat, but thought it might be seaweed —and, next moment, came those soft thumpings, like the sound of a big fish rubbing its nose against a float."

Halyard clutched the wheels of his chair and stared at the girl in grim displeasure.

"Didn't you know enough to be frightened?" he demanded.

"No—not then," she said, coloring faintly; "but when, after a few moments, I looked up and saw the harbor-master running up and down the beach, I was horribly frightened."

"Really?" said Halyard, sarcastically; "it was about time." Then, turning to me, he rasped out: "And that young lady was obliged to row all the way to Port-of-Waves and call to Lee's quarrymen to take her boat in."

Completely mystified, I looked from Halyard to the girl, not in the least comprehending what all this meant.

"That will do," said Halyard, ungraciously, which curt phrase was apparently the usual dismissal for the nurse.

She rose, and I rose, and she passed me with an inclination, stepping noiselessly into the house.

"I want beef-tea!" bawled Halyard after her; then he gave me an unamiable glance.

"I was a well-bred man," he sneered; "I'm a Harvard graduate, too, but I live as I like, and I do what I like, and I say what I like."

"You certainly are not reticent," I said, disgusted.

"Why should I be?" he rasped; "I pay that young woman for my irritability; it's a bargain between us."

"In your domestic affairs," I said, "there is nothing that interests me. I came to see those auks."

"You probably believe them to be razor-billed auks," he said, contemptuously. "But they're not; they're great auks."

I suggested that he permit me to examine them, and he replied, indifferently, that they were in a pen in his backyard, and that I was free to step around the house when I cared to.

I laid my rifle and pack on the veranda, and hastened off with mixed emotions, among which hope no longer predominated. No man in his senses would keep two such precious prizes in a pen in his backyard, I argued, and I was perfectly prepared to find anything from a puffin to a penguin in that pen.

I shall never forget, as long as I live, my stupor of amazement when I came to the wire-covered enclosure. Not only were there two great auks in the pen, alive, breathing, squatting in bulky majesty on their seaweed bed, but one of them was gravely contemplating two newly hatched chicks, all bill and feet, which nestled sedately at the edge of a puddle of salt-water, where some small fish were swimming.

For a while excitement blinded, nay, deafened me. I tried to realize that I was gazing upon the last individuals of an all but extinct race—the sole survivors of the gigantic auk, which, for thirty years, has been accounted an extinct creature.

I believe that I did not move muscle nor limb until the sun had gone down and the crowding darkness blurred my straining eyes and blotted the great, silent, bright-eyed birds from sight.

Even then I could not tear myself away from the enclosure; I listened to the strange, drowsy note of the male bird, the fainter responses of the female, the thin plaints of the chicks, huddling under her breast; I heard their flipper-like, embryotic wings beating sleepily as the birds stretched and yawned their beaks and clacked them, preparing for slumber.

"If you please," came a soft voice from the door, "Mr. Halyard awaits your company to dinner."

IV

I DINED well—or, rather, I might have enjoyed my dinner if Mr. Halyard had been eliminated; and the feast consisted exclusively of a joint of beef, the pretty nurse, and myself. She was exceedingly attractive—with a disturbing fashion of lowering her head and raising her dark eyes when spoken to.

As for Halyard, he was unspeakable, bundled up in his snuffy shawls, and making uncouth noises over his gruel. But it is only just to say that his table was worth sitting down to and his wine was sound as a bell.

"Yah!" he snapped, "I'm sick of this cursed soup—and I'll trouble you to fill my glass—"

"It is dangerous for you to touch claret," said the pretty nurse.

"I might as well die at dinner as anywhere," he observed.

"Certainly," said I, cheerfully passing the decanter, but he did not appear overpleased with the attention.

"I can't smoke, either," he snarled, hitching the shawls around until he looked like Richard the Third.

However, he was good enough to shove a box of cigars at me, and I took one and stood up, as the pretty nurse slipped past and vanished into the little parlor beyond.

We sat there for a while without speaking. He picked irritably at the bread-crumbs on the cloth, never glancing in my direction; and I, tired from my long foot-tour, lay back in my chair, silently appreciating one of the best cigars I ever smoked.

"Well," he rasped out at length, "what do you think of my auks —and my veracity?"

I told him that both were unimpeachable.

"Didn't they call me a swindler down there at your museum?" he demanded.

I admitted that I had heard the term applied. Then I made a clean breast of the matter, telling him that it was I who had doubted; that my chief, Professor Farrago, had sent me against my will, and that I was ready and glad to admit that he, Mr. Halyard, was a benefactor of the human race.

"Bosh!" he said. "What good does a confounded wobbly, bandy-toed bird do to the human race?"

But he was pleased, nevertheless; and presently he asked me, not unamiably, to punish his claret again.

"I'm done for," he said; "good things to eat and drink are no good to me. Some day I'll get mad enough to have a fit, and then—"

He paused to yawn.

"Then," he continued, "that little nurse of mine will drink up my claret and go back to civilization, where people are polite."

Somehow or other, in spite of the fact that Halyard was an old pig, what he had said touched me. There was certainly not much left in life for him—as he regarded life.

"I'm going to leave her this house," he said, arranging his shawls. "She doesn't know it. I'm going to leave her my money, too. She doesn't know that. Good Lord! What kind of a woman can she be to stand my bad temper for a few dollars a month!"

"I think," said I, "that it's partly because she's poor, partly because she's sorry for you."

He looked up with a ghastly smile.

"You think she really is sorry?"

Before I could answer he went on: "I'm no mawkish sentimentalist, and I won't allow anybody to be sorry for me—do you hear?"

"Oh, I'm not sorry for you!" I said, hastily, and, for the first time since I had seen him, he laughed heartily, without a sneer.

We both seemed to feel better after that; I drank his wine and smoked his cigars, and he appeared to take a certain grim pleasure in watching me.

"There's no fool like a young fool," he observed, presently.

As I had no doubt he referred to me, I paid him no attention.

After fidgeting with his shawls, he gave me an oblique scowl and asked me my age.

"Twenty-four," I replied.

"Sort of a tadpole, aren't you?" he said.

As I took no offence, he repeated the remark.

"Oh, come," said I, "there's no use in trying to irritate me. I see through you; a row acts like a cocktail on you—but you'll have to stick to gruel in my company."

"I call that impudence!" he rasped out, wrathfully.

"I don't care what you call it," I replied, undisturbed, "I am not going to be worried by you. Anyway," I ended, "it is my opinion that you could be very good company if you chose."

The proposition appeared to take his breath away—at least, he said nothing more; and I finished my cigar in peace and tossed the stump into a saucer.

"Now," said I, "what price do you set upon your birds, Mr. Halyard?"

"Ten thousand dollars," he snapped, with an evil smile.

"You will receive a certified check when the birds are delivered," I said, quietly.

"You don't mean to say that you agree to that outrageous bargain —and I won't take a cent less, either—Good Lord!—haven't you any spirit left?" he cried, half rising from his pile of shawls.

His piteous eagerness for a dispute sent me into laughter impossible to control, and he eyed me, mouth open, animosity rising visibly.

Then he seized the wheels of his invalid chair and trundled away, too mad to speak; and I strolled out into the parlor, still laughing.

The pretty nurse was there, sewing under a hanging lamp.

"If I am not indiscreet—" I began.

"Indiscretion is the better part of valor," said she, dropping her head but raising her eyes.

So I sat down with a frivolous smile peculiar to the appreciated.

"Doubtless," said I, "you are hemming a 'kerchief."

"Doubtless I am not," she said; "this is a night-cap for Mr. Halyard."

A mental vision of Halyard in a night-cap, very mad, nearly set me laughing again.

"Like the King of Yvetot, he wears his crown in bed," I said, flippantly.

"The King of Yvetot might have made that remark," she observed, re-threading her needle.

It is unpleasant to be reproved. How large and red and hot a man's ears feel.

To cool them, I strolled out to the porch; and, after a while, the pretty nurse came out, too, and sat down in a chair not far away. She probably regretted her lost opportunity to be flirted with.

"I have so little company—it is a great relief to see somebody from the world," she said. "If you can be agreeable, I wish you would."

The idea that she had come out to see me was so agreeable that I remained speechless until she said: "Do tell me what people are doing in New York."

So I seated myself on the steps and talked about the portion of the world inhabited by me, while she sat sewing in the dull light that straggled out from the parlor windows.

She had a certain coquetry of her own, using the usual methods with an individuality that was certainly fetching. For instance, when she lost her needle—and, another time, when we both, on hands and knees, hunted for her thimble.

However, directions for these pastimes may be found in contemporary classics.

I was as entertaining as I could be—perhaps not quite as entertaining as a young man usually thinks he is. However, we got on very well together until I asked her tenderly who the harbor-master might be, whom they all discussed so mysteriously.

"I do not care to speak about it," she said, with a primness of which I had not suspected her capable.

Of course I could scarcely pursue the subject after that—and, indeed, I did not intend to—so I began to tell her how I fancied I had seen a man on the cliff that afternoon, and how the creature slid over the sheer rock like a snake.

To my amazement, she asked me to kindly discontinue the account of my adventures, in an icy tone, which left no room for protest.

"It was only a sea-otter," I tried to explain, thinking perhaps she did not care for snake stories.

But the explanation did not appear to interest her, and I was mortified to observe that my impression upon her was anything but pleasant.

"She doesn't seem to like me and my stories," thought I, "but she is too young, perhaps, to appreciate them."

So I forgave her—for she was even prettier than I had thought her at first—and I took my leave, saying that Mr. Halyard would doubtless direct me to my room.

Halyard was in his library, cleaning a revolver, when I entered.

"Your room is next to mine," he said; "pleasant dreams, and kindly refrain from snoring."

"May I venture an absurd hope that you will do the same!" I replied, politely.

That maddened him, so I hastily withdrew.

I had been asleep for at least two hours when a movement by my bedside and a light in my eyes awakened me. I sat bolt upright

in bed, blinking at Halyard, who, clad in a dressing-gown and
wearing a night-cap, had wheeled himself into my room with one
hand, while with the other he solemnly waved a candle over my head.

"I'm so cursed lonely," he said—"come, there's a good fellow—
talk to me in your own original, impudent way."

I objected strenuously, but he looked so worn and thin, so lonely
and bad-tempered, so lovelessly grotesque, that I got out of bed and
passed a spongeful of cold water over my head.

Then I returned to bed and propped the pillows up for a back-rest,
ready to quarrel with him if it might bring some little pleasure into
his morbid existence.

"No," he said, amiably, "I'm too worried to quarrel, but I'm
much obliged for your kindly offer. I want to tell you something."

"What?" I asked, suspiciously.

"I want to ask you if you ever saw a man with gills like a fish?"

"Gills?" I repeated.

"Yes, gills! Did you?"

"No," I replied, angrily, "and neither did you."

"No, I never did," he said, in a curiously placid voice, "but there's
a man with gills like a fish who lives in the ocean out there. Oh, you
needn't look that way—nobody ever thinks of doubting my word,
and I tell you that there's a man—or a thing that looks like a man—
as big as you are, too—all slate-colored—with nasty red gills like a
fish!—and I've a witness to prove what I say!"

"Who?" I asked, sarcastically.

"The witness? My nurse."

"Oh! She saw a slate-colored man with gills?"

"Yes, she did. So did Francis Lee, superintendent of the Mica
Quarry Company at Port-of-Waves. So have a dozen men who work
in the quarry. Oh, you needn't laugh, young man. It's an old story
here, and anybody can tell you about the harbor-master."

"The harbor-master!" I exclaimed.

"Yes, that slate-colored thing with gills, that looks like a man—
and—by Heaven! *is* a man—that's the harbor-master. Ask any
quarryman at Port-of-Waves what it is that comes purring around
their boats at the wharf and unties painters and changes the mooring
of every cat-boat in the cove at night! Ask Francis Lee what it was
he saw running and leaping up and down the shoal at sunset last

Friday! Ask anybody along the coast what sort of a thing moves about the cliffs like a man and slides over them into the sea like an otter—"

"I saw it do that!" I burst out.

"Oh, did you? Well, *what was it?*"

Something kept me silent, although a dozen explanations flew to my lips.

After a pause, Halyard said: "You saw the harbor-master, that's what you saw!"

I looked at him without a word.

"Don't mistake me," he said, pettishly; "I don't think that the harbor-master is a spirit or a sprite or a hobgoblin, or any sort of damned rot. Neither do I believe it to be an optical illusion."

"What do you think it is?" I asked.

"I think it's a man—I think it's a branch of the human race— that's what I think. Let me tell you something: the deepest spot in the Atlantic Ocean is a trifle over five miles deep—and I suppose you know that this place lies only about a quarter of a mile off this headland. The British exploring vessel, *Gull*, Captain Marotte, discovered and sounded it, I believe. Anyway, it's there, and it's my belief that the profound depths are inhabited by the remnants of the last race of amphibious human beings!"

This was childish; I did not bother to reply.

"Believe it or not, as you will," he said, angrily; "one thing I know, and that is this: the harbor-master has taken to hanging around my cove, and he is attracted by my nurse! I won't have it! I'll blow his fishy gills out of his head if I ever get a shot at him! I don't care whether it's homicide or not—anyway, it's a new kind of murder and it attracts me!"

I gazed at him incredulously, but he was working himself into a passion, and I did not choose to say what I thought.

"Yes, this slate-colored thing with gills goes purring and grinning and spitting about after my nurse—when she walks, when she rows, when she sits on the beach! Gad! It drives me nearly frantic. I won't tolerate it, I tell you!"

"No," said I, "I wouldn't either." And I rolled over in bed convulsed with laughter.

The next moment I heard my door slam. I smothered my mirth

and rose to close the window, for the land-wind blew cold from the
forest, and a drizzle was sweeping the carpet as far as my bed.

That luminous glare which sometimes lingers after the stars go
out, threw a trembling, nebulous radiance over sand and cove. I
heard the seething currents under the breakers' softened thunder—
louder than I ever heard it. Then, as I closed my window, lingering
for a last look at the crawling tide, I saw a man standing, ankle-deep,
in the surf, all alone there in the night. But—was it a man? For the
figure suddenly began running over the beach on all fours like a
beetle, waving its limbs like feelers. Before I could throw open the
window again it darted into the surf, and, when I leaned out into
the chilling drizzle, I saw nothing save the flat ebb crawling on the
coast—I heard nothing save the purring of bubbles on seething sands.

V

It took me a week to perfect my arrangements for transporting the
great auks, by water, to Port-of-Waves, where a lumber schooner
was to be sent from Petite Sainte Isole, chartered by me for a voyage
to New York.

I had constructed a cage made of osiers, in which my auks were
to squat until they arrived at Bronx Park. My telegrams to Professor
Farrago were brief. One merely said "Victory!" Another explained
that I wanted no assistance; and a third read: "Schooner chartered.
Arrive New York July 1st. Send furniture-van to foot of Bluff
Street."

My week as a guest of Mr. Halyard proved interesting. I wrangled
with that invalid to his heart's content, I worked all day on my osier
cage, I hunted the thimble in the moonlight with the pretty nurse.
We sometimes found it.

As for the thing they called the harbor-master, I saw it a dozen
times, but always either at night or so far away and so close to the
sea that of course no trace of it remained when I reached the spot,
rifle in hand.

I had quite made up my mind that the so-called harbor-master
was a demented darky—wandered from, Heaven knows where—
perhaps shipwrecked and gone mad from his sufferings. Still, it was

far from pleasant to know that the creature was strongly attracted by the pretty nurse.

She, however, persisted in regarding the harbor-master as a sea-creature; she earnestly affirmed that it had gills, like a fish's gills, that it had a soft, fleshy hole for a mouth, and its eyes were luminous and lidless and fixed.

"Besides," she said, with a shudder, "it's all slate color, like a porpoise, and it looks as wet as a sheet of india-rubber in a dissecting-room."

The day before I was to set sail with my auks in a cat-boat bound for Port-of-Waves, Halyard trundled up to me in his chair and announced his intention of going with me.

"Going where?" I asked.

"To Port-of-Waves and then to New York," he replied, tranquilly.

I was doubtful, and my lack of cordiality hurt his feelings.

"Oh, of course, if you need the sea-voyage—" I began.

"I don't; I need you," he said, savagely; "I need the stimulus of our daily quarrel. I never disagreed so pleasantly with anybody in my life; it agrees with me; I am a hundred per cent better than I was last week."

I was inclined to resent this, but something in the deep-lined face of the invalid softened me. Besides, I had taken a hearty liking to the old pig.

"I don't want any mawkish sentiment about it," he said, observing me closely; "I won't permit anybody to feel sorry for me—do you understand?"

"I'll trouble you to use a different tone in addressing me," I replied, hotly; "I'll feel sorry for you if I choose to!" And our usual quarrel proceeded, to his deep satisfaction.

By six o'clock next evening I had Halyard's luggage stowed away in the cat-boat, and the pretty nurse's effects corded down, with the newly hatched auk-chicks in a hat-box on top. She and I placed the osier cage aboard, securing it firmly, and then, throwing table-cloths over the auks' heads, we led those simple and dignified birds down the path and across the plank at the little wooden pier. Together we locked up the house, while Halyard stormed at us both and wheeled himself furiously up and down the beach below. At the last moment she forgot her thimble. But we found it, I forget where.

"Come on!" shouted Halyard, waving his shawls furiously; "what the devil are you about up there?"

He received our explanation with a sniff, and we trundled him aboard without further ceremony.

"Don't run me across the plank like a steamer trunk!" he shouted, as I shot him dexterously into the cock-pit. But the wind was dying away, and I had no time to dispute with him then.

The sun was setting above the pine-clad ridge as our sail flapped and partly filled, and I cast off, and began a long tack, east by south, to avoid the spouting rocks on our starboard bow.

The sea-birds rose in clouds as we swung across the shoal, the black surf-ducks scuttered out to sea, the gulls tossed their sun-tipped wings in the ocean, riding the rollers like bits of froth.

Already we were sailing slowly out across that great hole in the ocean, five miles deep, the most profound sounding ever taken in the Atlantic. The presence of great heights or great depths, seen or unseen, always impresses the human mind—perhaps oppresses it. We were very silent; the sunlight stain on cliff and beach deepened to crimson, then faded into sombre purple bloom that lingered long after the rose-tint died out in the zenith.

Our progress was slow; at times, although the sail filled with the rising land breeze, we scarcely seemed to move at all.

"Of course," said the pretty nurse, "we couldn't be aground in the deepest hole in the Atlantic."

"Scarcely," said Halyard, sarcastically, "unless we're grounded on a whale."

"What's that soft thumping?" I asked. "Have we run afoul of a barrel or log?"

It was almost too dark to see, but I leaned over the rail and swept the water with my hand.

Instantly something smooth glided under it, like the back of a great fish, and I jerked my hand back to the tiller. At the same moment the whole surface of the water seemed to begin to purr, with a sound like the breaking of froth in a champagne-glass.

"What's the matter with you?" asked Halyard, sharply.

"A fish came up under my hand," I said; "a porpoise or something—"

With a low cry, the pretty nurse clasped my arm in both her hands.

"Listen!" she whispered. "It's purring around the boat."

"What the devil's purring?" shouted Halyard. "I won't have anything purring around me!"

At that moment, to my amazement, I saw that the boat had stopped entirely, although the sail was full and the small pennant fluttered from the mast-head. Something, too, was tugging at the rudder, twisting and jerking it until the tiller strained and creaked in my hand. All at once it snapped; the tiller swung useless and the boat whirled around, heeling in the stiffening wind, and drove shoreward.

It was then that I, ducking to escape the boom, caught a glimpse of something ahead—something that a sudden wave seemed to toss on deck and leave there, wet and flapping—a man with round, fixed, fishy eyes, and soft, slaty skin.

But the horror of the thing were the two gills that swelled and relaxed spasmodically, emitting a rasping, purring sound—two gasping, blood-red gills, all fluted and scolloped and distended.

Frozen with amazement and repugnance, I stared at the creature; I felt the hair stirring on my head and the icy sweat on my forehead.

"It's the harbor-master!" screamed Halyard.

The harbor-master had gathered himself into a wet lump, squatting motionless in the bows under the mast; his lidless eyes were phosphorescent, like the eyes of living codfish. After a while I felt that either fright or disgust was going to strangle me where I sat, but it was only the arms of the pretty nurse clasped around me in a frenzy of terror.

There was not a fire-arm aboard that we could get at. Halyard's hand crept backward where a steel-shod boat-hook lay, and I also made a clutch at it. The next moment I had it in my hand, and staggered forward, but the boat was already tumbling shoreward among the breakers, and the next I knew the harbor-master ran at me like a colossal rat, just as the boat rolled over and over through the surf, spilling freight and passengers among the sea-weed-covered rocks.

When I came to myself I was thrashing about knee-deep in a rocky pool, blinded by the water and half suffocated, while under my feet, like a stranded porpoise, the harbor-master made the water boil in his efforts to upset me. But his limbs seemed soft and boneless;

he had no nails, no teeth, and he bounced and thumped and flapped and splashed like a fish, while I rained blows on him with the boat-hook that sounded like blows on a football. And all the while his gills were blowing out and frothing, and purring, and his lidless eyes looked into mine, until, nauseated and trembling, I dragged myself back to the beach, where already the pretty nurse alternately wrung her hands and her petticoats in ornamental despair.

Beyond the cove, Halyard was bobbing up and down, afloat in his invalid's chair, trying to steer shoreward. He was the maddest man I ever saw.

"Have you killed that rubber-headed thing yet?" he roared.

"I can't kill it," I shouted, breathlessly. "I might as well try to kill a football!"

"Can't you punch a hole in it?" he bawled. "If I can only get at him—"

His words were drowned in a thunderous splashing, a roar of great, broad flippers beating the sea, and I saw the gigantic forms of my two great auks, followed by their chicks, blundering past in a shower of spray, driving headlong out into the ocean.

"Oh, Lord!" I said. "I can't stand that," and, for the first time in my life, I fainted peacefully—and appropriately—at the feet of the pretty nurse.

It is within the range of possibility that this story may be doubted. It doesn't matter; nothing can add to the despair of a man who has lost two great auks.

As for Halyard, nothing affects him—except his involuntary sea-bath, and that did him so much good that he writes me from the South that he's going on a walking-tour through Switzerland—if I'll join him. I might have joined him if he had not married the pretty nurse. I wonder whether— But, of course, this is no place for speculation.

In regard to the harbor-master, you may believe it or not, as you choose. But if you hear of any great auks being found, kindly throw a table-cloth over their heads and notify the authorities at the new Zoological Gardens in Bronx Park, New York. The reward is ten thousand dollars.

In Quest
of the Dingue

I

BEFORE I proceed any further, common decency requires me to reassure my readers concerning my intentions, which, Heaven knows,
are far from flippant.

To separate fact from fancy has always been difficult for me, but
now that I have had the honor to be chosen secretary of the Zoological
Gardens in Bronx Park, I realize keenly that unless I give up writing
fiction nobody will believe what I write about science. Therefore
it is to a serious and unimaginative public that I shall hereafter
address myself; and I do it in the modest confidence that I shall
neither be distrusted nor doubted, although unfortunately I still
write in that irrational style which suggests covert frivolity, and for
which I am undergoing a course of treatment in English literature
at Columbia College. Now, having promised to avoid originality
and confine myself to facts, I shall tell what I have to tell concerning
the dingue, the mammoth, and—*something else.*

For some weeks it had been rumored that Professor Farrago,
president of the Bronx Park Zoological Society, would resign, to
accept an enormous salary as manager of Barnum & Bailey's circus.
He was now with the circus in London, and had promised to cable
his decision before the day was over.

I hoped he would decide to remain with us. I was his secretary and particular favorite, and I viewed, without enthusiasm, the advent of a new president, who might shake us all out of our congenial and carefully excavated ruts. However, it was plain that the trustees of the society expected the resignation of Professor Farrago, for they had been in secret session all day, considering the names of possible candidates to fill Professor Farrago's large, old-fashioned shoes. These preparations worried me, for I could scarcely expect another chief as kind and considerate as Professor Leonidas Farrago.

That afternoon in June I left my office in the Administration Building in Bronx Park and strolled out under the trees for a breath of air. But the heat of the sun soon drove me to seek shelter under a little square arbor, a shady retreat covered with purple wistaria and honeysuckle. As I entered the arbor I noticed that there were three other people seated there—an elderly lady with masculine features and short hair, a younger lady sitting beside her, and, farther away, a rough-looking young man reading a book.

For a moment I had an indistinct impression of having met the elder lady somewhere, and under circumstances not entirely agreeable, but beyond a stony and indifferent glance she paid no attention to me. As for the younger lady, she did not look at me at all. She was very young, with pretty eyes, a mass of silky brown hair, and a skin as fresh as a rose which had just been rained on.

With that delicacy peculiar to lonely scientific bachelors, I modestly sat down beside the rough young man, although there was more room beside the younger lady. "Some lazy loafer reading a penny dreadful," I thought, glancing at him, then at the title of his book. Hearing me beside him, he turned around and blinked over his shabby shoulder, and the movement uncovered the page he had been silently conning. The volume in his hands was Darwin's famous monograph on the monodactyl.

He noticed the astonishment on my face and smiled uneasily, shifting the short clay pipe in his mouth.

"I guess," he observed, "that this here book is too much for me, mister."

"It's rather technical," I replied, smiling.

"Yes," he said, in vague admiration; "it's fierce, ain't it?"

After a silence I asked him if he would tell me why he had chosen Darwin as a literary pastime.

"Well," he said, placidly, "I was tryin' to read about annermals, but I'm up against a word-slinger this time all right. Now here's a gum-twister," and he painfully spelled out m-o-n-o-d-a-c-t-y-l, breathing hard all the while.

"Monodactyl," I said, "means a single-toed creature."

He turned the page with alacrity. "Is that the beast he's talkin' about?" he asked.

The illustration he pointed out was a wood-cut representing Darwin's reconstruction of the dingue from the fossil bones in the British Museum. It was a well-executed wood-cut, showing a dingue in the foreground and, to give scale, a mammoth in the middle distance.

"Yes," I replied, "that is the dingue."

"I've seen one," he observed, calmly.

I smiled and explained that the dingue had been extinct for some thousands of years.

"Oh, I guess not," he replied, with cool optimism. Then he placed a grimy forefinger on the mammoth.

"I've seen them things, too," he remarked.

Again I patiently pointed out his error, and suggested that he referred to the elephant.

"Elephant be blowed!" he replied, scornfully. "I guess I know what I seen. An' I seen that there thing you call a dingue, too."

Not wishing to prolong a futile discussion, I remained silent. After a moment he wheeled around, removing his pipe from his hard mouth.

"Did you ever hear tell of Graham's Glacier?" he demanded.

"Certainly," I replied, astonished; "it's the southern-most glacier in British America."

"Right," he said. "And did you ever hear tell of the Hudson Mountings, mister?"

"Yes," I replied.

"What's behind 'em?" he snapped out.

"Nobody knows," I answered. "They are considered impassable."

"They ain't, though," he said, doggedly; "I've been behind 'em."

"Really!" I replied, tiring of his yarn.

"Ya-as, reely," he repeated, sullenly. Then he began to fumble and search through the pages of his book until he found what he wanted. "Mister," he said, "jest read that out loud, please."

The passage he indicated was the famous chapter beginning:

Is the mammoth extinct? Is the dingue extinct? Probably. And yet the aborigines of British America maintain the contrary. Probably both the mammoth and the dingue are extinct; but until expeditions have penetrated and explored not only the unknown region in Alaska but also that hidden table-land beyond the Graham Glacier and the Hudson Mountains, it will not be possible to definitely announce the total extinction of either the mammoth or the dingue.

When I had read it, slowly, for his benefit, he brought his hand down smartly on one knee and nodded rapidly.

"Mister," he said, "that gent knows a thing or two, and don't you forgit it!" Then he demanded, abruptly, how I knew he hadn't been behind the Graham Glacier.

I explained.

"Shucks!" he said; "there's a road five miles wide inter that there table-land. Mister, I ain't been in New York long; I come inter port a week ago on the *Arctic Belle*, whaler. I was in the Hudson range when that there Graham Glacier bust up—"

"What!" I exclaimed.

"Didn't you know it?" he asked. "Well, mebbe it ain't in the papers, but it busted all right—blowed up by a earthquake an' volcano combine. An', mister, it was oreful. My, how I did run!"

"Do you mean to tell me that some convulsion of the earth has shattered the Graham Glacier?" I asked.

"Convulsions? Ya-as, an' fits, too," he said, sulkily. "The hull blame thing dropped inter a hole. An' say, mister, home an' mother is good enough fur me now."

I stared at him stupidly.

"Once," he said, "I ketched pelts fur them sharps at Hudson Bay, like any yaller husky, but the things I seen arter that convulsion-fit—the *things I seen behind the Hudson Mountings*—don't make me hanker arter no life on the pe-rarie wild, lemme tell yer. I may be a Mother Carey chicken, but this chicken has got enough."

After a long silence I picked up his book again and pointed at the picture of the mammoth.

"What color is it?" I asked.

"Kinder red an' brown," he answered, promptly. "It's woolly, too."

Astounded, I pointed to the dingue.

"One-toed," he said, quickly; "makes a noise like a bell when scutterin' about."

Intensely excited, I laid my hand on his arm. "My society will give you a thousand dollars," I said, "if you pilot me inside the Hudson table-land and show me either a mammoth or a dingue!"

He looked me calmly in the eye.

"Mister," he said, slowly, "have you got a million for to squander on me?"

"No," I said, suspiciously.

"Because," he went on, "it wouldn't be enough. Home an' mother suits me now."

He picked up his book and rose. In vain I asked his name and address; in vain I begged him to dine with me—to become my honored guest.

"Nit," he said, shortly, and shambled off down the path.

But I was not going to lose him like that. I rose and deliberately started to stalk him. It was easy. He shuffled along, pulling on his pipe, and I after him.

It was growing a little dark, although the sun still reddened the tops of the maples. Afraid of losing him in the falling dusk, I once more approached him and laid my hand upon his ragged sleeve.

"Look here," he cried, wheeling about, "I want you to quit follerin' me. Don't I tell you money can't make me go back to them mountings!" And as I attempted to speak, he suddenly tore off his cap and pointed to his head. His hair was white as snow.

"That's what come of monkeyin' inter your cursed mountings," he shouted, fiercely. "There's things in there what no Christian oughter see. Lemme alone er I'll bust yer."

He shambled on, doubled fists swinging by his side. The next moment, setting my teeth obstinately, I followed him and caught him by the park gate. At my hail he whirled around with a snarl, but I grabbed him by the throat and backed him violently against the park wall.

"You invaluable ruffian," I said, "now you listen to me. I live in that big stone building, and I'll give you a thousand dollars to take me behind the Graham Glacier. Think it over and call on me when you are in a pleasanter frame of mind. If you don't come by noon to-morrow I'll go to the Graham Glacier without you."

He was attempting to kick me all the time, but I managed to avoid him, and when I had finished I gave him a shove which almost loosened his spinal column. He went reeling out across the sidewalk, and when he had recovered his breath and his balance he danced with displeasure and displayed a vocabulary that astonished me. However, he kept his distance.

As I turned back into the park, satisfied that he would not follow, the first person I saw was the elderly, stony-faced lady of the wistaria arbor advancing on tiptoe. Behind her came the younger lady with cheeks like a rose that had been rained on.

Instantly it occurred to me that they had followed us, and at the same moment I knew who the stony-faced lady was. Angry, but polite, I lifted my hat and saluted her, and she, probably furious at having been caught tiptoeing after me, cut me dead. The younger lady passed me with face averted, but even in the dusk I could see the tip of one little ear turn scarlet.

Walking on hurriedly, I entered the Administration Building, and found Professor Lesard, of the reptilian department, preparing to leave.

"Don't you do it," I said, sharply; "I've got exciting news."

"I'm only going to the theatre," he replied. "It's a good show— Adam and Eve; there's a snake in it, you know. It's in my line."

"I can't help it," I said; and I told him briefly what had occurred in the arbor.

"But that's not all," I continued, savagely. "Those women followed us, and who do you think one of them turned out to be? Well, it was Professor Smawl, of Barnard College, and I'll bet every pair of boots I own that she starts for the Graham Glacier within a week. Idiot that I was!" I exclaimed, smiting my head with both hands. "I never recognized her until I saw her tiptoeing and craning her neck to listen. Now she knows about the glacier; she heard every word that young ruffian said, and she'll go to the glacier if it's only to forestall me."

Professor Lesard looked anxious. He knew that Miss Smawl, professor of natural history at Barnard College, had long desired an appointment at the Bronx Park gardens. It was even said she had a chance of succeeding Professor Farrago as president, but that, of course, must have been a joke. However, she haunted the gardens, annoying the keepers by persistently poking the animals with her umbrella. On one occasion she sent us word that she desired to enter the tigers' enclosure for the purpose of making experiments in hypnotism. Professor Farrago was absent, but I took it upon myself to send back word that I feared the tigers might injure her. The miserable small boy who took my message informed her that I was afraid she might injure the tigers, and the unpleasant incident almost cost me my position.

"I am quite convinced," said I to Professor Lesard, "that Miss Smawl is perfectly capable of abusing the information she overheard, and of starting herself to explore a region that, by all the laws of decency, justice, and prior claim, belongs to me."

"Well," said Lesard, with a peculiar laugh, "it's not certain whether you can go at all."

"Professor Farrago will authorize me," I said, confidently.

"Professor Farrago has resigned," said Lesard. It was a bolt from a clear sky.

"Good Heavens!" I blurted out. "What will become of the rest of us, then?"

"I don't know," he replied. "The trustees are holding a meeting over in the Administration Building to elect a new president for us. It depends on the new president what becomes of us."

"Lesard," I said, hoarsely, "you don't suppose that they could possibly elect Miss Smawl as our president, do you?"

He looked at me askance and bit his cigar.

"I'd be in a nice position, wouldn't I?" said I, anxiously.

"The lady would probably make you walk the plank for that tiger business," he replied.

"But I didn't do it," I protested, with sickly eagerness. "Besides, I explained to her—"

He said nothing, and I stared at him, appalled by the possibility of reporting to Professor Smawl for instructions next morning.

"See here, Lesard," I said, nervously, "I wish you would step over to the Administration Building and ask the trustees if I may prepare for this expedition. Will you?"

He glanced at me sympathetically. It was quite natural for me to wish to secure my position before the new president was elected—especially as there was a chance of the new president being Miss Smawl.

"You are quite right," he said; "the Graham Glacier would be the safest place for you if our next president is to be the Lady of the Tigers." And he started across the park puffing his cigar.

I sat down on the doorstep to wait for his return, not at all charmed with the prospect. It made me furious, too, to see my ambition nipped with the frost of a possible veto from Miss Smawl.

"If she is elected," thought I, "there is nothing for me but to resign—to avoid the inconvenience of being shown the door. Oh, I wish I had allowed her to hypnotize the tigers!"

Thoughts of crime flitted through my mind. Miss Smawl would not remain president—or anything else very long—if she persisted in her desire for the tigers. And then when she called for help I would pretend not to hear.

Aroused from my criminal meditation by the return of Professor Lesard, I jumped up and peered into his perplexed eyes. "They've elected a president," he said, "but they won't tell us who the president is until to-morrow."

"You don't think—" I stammered.

"I don't know. But I know this: the new president sanctions the expedition to the Graham Glacier, and directs you to choose an assistant and begin preparations for four people."

Overjoyed, I seized his hand and said, "Hurray!" in a voice weak with emotion. "The old dragon isn't elected this time," I added, triumphantly.

"By-the-way," he said, "who was the other dragon with her in the park this evening?"

I described her in a more modulated voice.

"Whew!" observed Professor Lesard, "that must be her assistant, Professor Dorothy Van Twiller! She's the prettiest blue-stocking in town."

With this curious remark my confrère followed me into my room and wrote down the list of articles I dictated to him. The list included complete camping equipment for myself and three other men.

"Am I one of those other men?" inquired Lesard, with an unhappy smile.

Before I could reply my door was shoved open and a figure appeared at the threshold, cap in hand.

"What do you want?" I asked, sternly; but my heart was beating high with triumph.

The figure shuffled; then came a subdued voice:

"Mister, I guess I'll go back to the Graham Glacier along with you. I'm Billy Spike, an' it kinder scares me to go back to them Hudson Mountains, but somehow, mister, when you choked me and kinder walked me off on my ear, why, mister, I kinder took to you like."

There was absolute silence for a minute; then he said:

"So if you go, I guess I'll go, too, mister."

"For a thousand dollars?"

"Fur nawthin'," he muttered—"or what you like."

"All right, Billy," I said, briskly; "just look over those rifles and ammunition and see that everything's sound."

He slowly lifted his tough young face and gave me a doglike glance. They were hard eyes, but there was gratitude in them.

"You'll get your throat slit," whispered Lesard.

"Not while Billy's with me," I replied, cheerfully.

Late that night, as I was preparing for pleasant dreams, a knock came on my door and a telegraph-messenger handed me a note, which I read, shivering in my bare feet, although the thermometer marked eighty Fahrenheit:

You will immediately leave for the Hudson Mountains *via* Wellman Bay, Labrador, there to await further instructions. Equipment for yourself and one assistant will include following articles [here began a list of camping utensils, scientific paraphernalia, and provisions]. The steamer *Penguin* sails at five o'clock to-morrow morning. Kindly find yourself on board at that hour. Any excuse for not complying with these orders will be accepted as your resignation.

SUSAN SMAWL,
PRESIDENT BRONX ZOOLOGICAL SOCIETY.

"Lesard!" I shouted, trembling with fury.

He appeared at his door, chastely draped in pajamas; and he read the insolent letter with terrified alacrity.

"What are you going to do—resign?" he asked, much frightened.

"Do!" I snarled, grinding my teeth; "I'm going—that's what I'm going to do!"

"But—but you can't get ready and catch that steamer, too," he stammered.

He did not know me.

II

AND so it came about that one calm evening towards the end of June, William Spike and I went into camp under the southerly shelter of that vast granite wall called the Hudson Mountains, there to await the promised "further instructions."

It had been a tiresome trip by steamer to Anticosti, from there by schooner to Widgeon Bay, then down the coast and up the Cape Clear River to Port Porpoise. There we bought three pack-mules and started due north on the Great Fur Trail. The second day out we passed Fort Boisé, the last outpost of civilization, and on the sixth day we were travelling eastward under the granite mountain parapets.

On the evening of the sixth day out from Fort Boisé we went into camp for the last time before entering the unknown land.

I could see it already through my field-glasses, and while William was building the fire I climbed up among the rocks above and sat down, glasses levelled, to study the prospect.

There was nothing either extraordinary or forbidding in the landscape which stretched out beyond; to the right the solid palisade of granite cut off the view; to the left the palisade continued, an endless barrier of sheer cliffs crowned with pine and hemlock. But the interesting section of the landscape lay almost directly in front of me —a rent in the mountain-wall through which appeared to run a level, arid plain, miles wide, and as smooth and even as a highroad.

There could be no doubt concerning the significance of that rent in the solid mountain-wall; and, moreover, it was exactly as William Spike had described it. However, I called to him and he came up from the smoky camp-fire, axe on shoulder.

"Yep," he said, squatting beside me; "the Graham Glacier used to meander through that there hole, but somethin' went wrong with the earth's in'ards an' there was a bust-up.''

"And you saw it, William?" I said, with a sigh of envy.

"Hey? Seen it? Sure I seen it! I was to Spoutin' Springs, twenty mile west, with a bale o' blue fox an' otter pelt. Fust I knew them geysers begun for to groan egregious like, an' I seen the caribou gallopin' hell-bent south. 'This climate,' sez I, 'is too bracin' for me,' so I struck a back trail an' landed onto a hill. Then them geysers blowed up, one arter the next, an' I heard somethin' kinder cave in between here an' China. I disremember things what happened. Somethin' throwed me down, but I couldn't stay there, for the blamed ground was runnin' like a river—all wavy-like, an' the sky hit me on the back o' me head.''

"And then?" I urged, in that new excitement which every repetition of the story revived. I had heard it all twenty times since we left New York, but mere repetition could not apparently satisfy me.

"Then," continued William, "the whole world kinder went off like a fire-cracker, an' I come too, an' ran like—"

"I know," said I, cutting him short, for I had become wearied of the invariable profanity which lent a lurid ending to his narrative.

"After that," I continued, "you went through the rent in the mountains?"

"Sure."

"And you saw a dingue and a creature that resembled a mammoth?"

"Sure," he repeated, sulkily.

"And you saw something else?" I always asked this question; it fascinated me to see the sullen fright flicker in William's eyes, and the mechanical backward glance, as though what he had seen might still be behind him.

He had never answered this third question but once, and that time he fairly snarled in my face as he growled: "I seen what no Christian oughter see."

So when I repeated: "And you saw something else, William?" he gave me a wicked, frightened leer, and shuffled off to feed the mules. Flattery, entreaties, threats left him unmoved; he never told me what the third thing was that he had seen behind the Hudson Mountains.

William had retired to mix up with his mules; I resumed my binoculars and my silent inspection of the great, smooth path left by the Graham Glacier when something or other exploded that vast mass of ice into vapor.

The arid plain wound out from the unknown country like a river, and I thought then, and think now, that when the glacier was blown into vapor the vapor descended in the most terrific rain the world has ever seen, and poured through the newly blasted mountain-gateway, sweeping the earth to bed-rock. To corroborate this theory, miles to the southward I could see the débris winding out across the land towards Wellman Bay, but as the terminal moraine of the vanished glacier formerly ended there I could not be certain that my theory was correct. Owing to the formation of the mountains I could not see more than half a mile into the unknown country. What I could see appeared to be nothing but the continuation of the glacier's path, scored out by the cloud-burst, and swept as smooth as a floor.

Sitting there, my heart beating heavily with excitement, I looked through the evening glow at the endless, pine-crowned mountain-wall with its giant's gateway pierced for me! And I thought of all the explorers and the unknown heroes—trappers, Indians, humble naturalists, perhaps—who had attempted to scale that sheer barri-cade and had died there or failed, beaten back from those eternal cliffs. Eternal? No! For the Eternal Himself had struck the rock, and it had sprung asunder, thundering obedience.

In the still evening air the smoke from the fire below mounted in a straight, slender pillar, like the smoke from those ancient altars builded before the first blood had been shed on earth.

The evening wind stirred the pines; a tiny spring brook made thin harmony among the rocks; a murmur came from the quiet camp. It was William adjuring his mules. In the deepening twilight I descended the hillock, stepping cautiously among the rocks.

Then, suddenly, as I stood outside the reddening ring of firelight, far in the depths of the unknown country, far behind the mountain-wall, a sound grew on the quiet air. William heard it and turned his face to the mountains. The sound faded to a vibration which was felt, not heard. Then once more I began to divine a vibration in the air, gathering in distant volume until it became a sound, lasting the space of a spoken word, fading to vibration, then silence.

Was it a cry?

I looked at William inquiringly. He had quietly fainted away.

I got him to the little brook and poked his head into the icy water, and after a while he sat up pluckily.

To an indignant question he replied: "Naw, I ain't a-cussin' you. Lemme be or I'll have fits."

"Was it that sound that scared you?" I asked.

"Ya-as," he replied with a dauntless shiver.

"Was it the voice of the mammoth?" I persisted, excitedly. "Speak, William, or I'll drag you about and kick you!"

He replied that it was neither a mammoth nor a dingue, and added a strong request for privacy, which I was obliged to grant, as I could not torture another word out of him.

I slept little that night; the exciting proximity of the unknown land was too much for me. But although I lay awake for hours, I heard nothing except the tinkle of water among the rocks and the plover calling from some hidden marsh. At daybreak I shot a ptarmigan which had walked into camp, and the shot set the echoes yelling among the mountains.

William, sullen and heavy-eyed, dressed the bird, and we broiled it for breakfast.

Neither he nor I alluded to the sound we had heard the night before; he boiled water and cleaned up the mess-kit, and I pottered about among the rocks for another ptarmigan. Wearying of this, presently, I returned to the mules and William, and sat down for a smoke.

"It strikes me," I said, "that our instructions to 'await further orders' are idiotic. How are we to receive 'further orders' here?"

William did not know.

"You don't suppose," said I, in sudden disgust, "that Miss Smawl believes there is a summer hotel and daily mail service in the Hudson Mountains?"

William thought perhaps she did suppose something of the sort.

It irritated me beyond measure to find myself at last on the very border of the unknown country, and yet checked, held back, by the irresponsible orders of a maiden lady named Smawl. However, my salary depended upon the whim of that maiden lady, and although

I fussed and fumed and glared at the mountains through my glasses,
I realized that I could not stir without the permission of Miss Smawl.
At times this grotesque situation became almost unbearable, and I
often went away by myself and indulged in fantasies, firing my gun
off and pretending I had hit Miss Smawl by mistake. At such moments
I would imagine I was free at last to plunge into the strange country,
and I would squat on a rock and dream of bagging my first
mammoth.

The time passed heavily; the tension increased with each new day.
I shot ptarmigan and kept our table supplied with brook-trout.
William chopped wood, conversed with his mules, and cooked very
badly.

"See here," I said, one morning; "we have been in camp a week
to-day, and I can't stand your cooking another minute!"

William, who was washing a saucepan, looked up and begged me
sarcastically to accept the *cordon bleu*. But I know only how to cook
eggs, and there were no eggs within some hundred miles.

To get the flavor of the breakfast out of my mouth I walked up to
my favorite hillock and sat down for a smoke. The next moment,
however, I was on my feet, cheering excitedly and shouting for
William.

"Here come 'further instructions' at last!" I cried, pointing to
the southward, where two dots on the grassy plain were impercep-
tibly moving in our direction.

"People on mules," said William, without enthusiasm.

"They must be messengers for us!" I cried, in chaste joy. "Three
cheers for the northward trail, William, and the mischief take Miss—
Well, never mind now," I added.

"On them approachin' mules," observed William, "there is
wimmen."

I stared at him for a second, then attempted to strike him. He
dodged wearily and repeated his incredible remark: "Ya-as, there
is—wimmen—two female ladies onto them there mules."

"Bring me my glasses!" I said, hoarsely; "bring me those glasses,
William, because I shall destroy you if you don't!"

Somewhat awed by my calm fury, he hastened back to camp and
returned with the binoculars. It was a breathless moment. I adjusted
the lenses with a steady hand and raised them.

Now, of all unexpected sights my fate may reserve for me in the future, I trust—nay, I know—that none can ever prove as unwelcome as the sight I perceived through my binoculars. For upon the backs of those distant mules were two women, and the first one was Miss Smawl!

Upon her head she wore a helmet, from which fluttered a green veil. Otherwise she was clothed in tweeds; and at moments she beat upon her mule with a thick umbrella.

Surfeited with the sickening spectacle, I sat down on a rock and tried to cry.

"I told yer so," observed William; but I was too tired to attack him.

When the caravan rode into camp I was myself again, smilingly prepared for the worst, and I advanced, cap in hand, followed furtively by William.

"Welcome," I said, violently injecting joy into my voice. "Welcome, Professor Smawl, to the Hudson Mountains!"

"Kindly take my mule," she said, climbing down to mother earth.

"William," I said, with dignity, "take the lady's mule."

Miss Smawl gave me a stolid glance, then made directly for the camp-fire, where a kettle of game-broth simmered over the coals. The last I saw of her she was smelling of it, and I turned my back and advanced towards the second lady pilgrim, prepared to be civil until snubbed.

Now, it is quite certain that never before had William Spike or I beheld so much feminine loveliness in one human body on the back of a mule. She was clad in the daintiest of shooting-kilts, yet there was nothing mannish about her except the way she rode the mule, and that only accentuated her adorable femininity.

I remembered what Professor Lesard had said about blue stockings —but Miss Dorothy Van Twiller's were gray, turned over at the tops, and disappearing into canvas spats buckled across a pair of slim shooting-boots.

"Welcome," said I, attempting to restrain a too violent cordiality. "Welcome, Professor Van Twiller, to the Hudson Mountains."

"Thank you," she replied, accepting my assistance very sweetly; "it is a pleasure to meet a human being again."

I glanced at Miss Smawl. She was eating game-broth, but she resembled a human being in a general way.

"I should very much like to wash my hands," said Professor Van Twiller, drawing the buckskin gloves from her slim fingers.

I brought towels and soap and conducted her to the brook.

She called to Professor Smawl to join her, and her voice was crystalline; Professor Smawl declined, and her voice was batrachian.

"She is so hungry!" observed Miss Van Twiller. "I am very thankful we are here at last, for we've had a horrid time. You see, we neither of us know how to cook."

I wondered what they would say to William's cooking, but I held my peace and retired, leaving the little brook to mirror the sweetest face that was ever bathed in water.

III

THAT afternoon our expedition, in two sections, moved forward. The first section comprised myself and all the mules; the second section was commanded by Professor Smawl, followed by Professor Van Twiller, armed with a tiny shot-gun. William, loaded down with the ladies' toilet articles, skulked in the rear. I say skulked; there was no other word for it.

"So you're a guide, are you?" observed Professor Smawl when William, cap in hand, had approached her with well-meant advice. "The woods are full of lazy guides. Pick up those Gladstone bags! I'll do the guiding for this expedition."

Made cautious by William's humiliation, I associated with the mules exclusively. Nevertheless, Professor Smawl had her hard eyes on me, and I realized she meant mischief.

The encounter took place just as I, driving the five mules, entered the great mountain gateway, thrilled with anticipation which almost amounted to foreboding. As I was about to set foot across the imaginary frontier which divided the world from the unknown land, Professor Smawl hailed me and I halted until she came up.

"As commander of this expedition," she said, somewhat out of breath, "I desire to be the first living creature who has ever set foot behind the Graham Glacier. Kindly step aside, young sir!"

"Madam," said I, rigid with disappointment, "my guide, William Spike, entered that unknown land a year ago."

"He *says* he did," sneered Professor Smawl.

"As you like," I replied; "but it is scarcely generous to forestall the person whose stupidity gave you the clew to this unexplored region."

"You mean yourself?" she asked, with a stony stare.

"I do," said I, firmly.

Her little, hard eyes grew harder, and she clutched her umbrella until the steel ribs crackled.

"Young man," she said, insolently; "if I could have gotten rid of you I should have done so the day I was appointed president. But Professor Farrago refused to resign unless your position was assured, subject, of course, to your good behavior. Frankly, I don't like you, and I consider your views on science ridiculous, and if an opportunity presents itself I will be most happy to request your resignation. Kindly collect your mules and follow me."

Mortified beyond measure, I collected my mules and followed my president into the strange country behind the Hudson Mountains—I who had aspired to lead, compelled to follow in the rear, driving mules.

The journey was monotonous at first, but we shortly ascended a ridge from which we could see, stretching out below us, the wilderness where, save the feet of William Spike, no human feet had passed.

As for me, tingling with enthusiasm, I forgot my chagrin, I forgot the gross injustice, I forgot my mules. "Excelsior!" I cried, running up and down the ridge in uncontrollable excitement at the sublime spectacle of forest, mountain, and valley all set with little lakes.

"Excelsior!" repeated an excited voice at my side, and Professor Van Twiller sprang to the ridge beside me, her eyes bright as stars.

Exalted, inspired by the mysterious beauty of the view, we clasped hands and ran up and down the grassy ridge.

"That will do," said Professor Smawl, coldly, as we raced about like a pair of distracted kittens. The chilling voice broke the spell; I dropped Professor Van Twiller's hand and sat down on a boulder, aching with wrath.

Late that afternoon we halted beside a tiny lake, deep in the unknown wilderness, where purple and scarlet bergamot choked the shores and the spruce-partridge strutted fearlessly under our very feet. Here we pitched our two tents. The afternoon sun slanted through the pines; the lake glittered; acres of golden brake perfumed the forest silence, broken only at rare intervals by the distant thunder of a partridge drumming.

Professor Smawl ate heavily and retired to her tent to lie torpid until evening. William drove the unloaded mules into an intervale full of sun-cured, fragrant grasses; I sat down beside Professor Van Twiller.

The wilderness is electric. Once within the influence of its currents, human beings become positively or negatively charged, violently attracting or repelling each other.

"There is something the matter with this air," said Professor Van Twiller. "It makes me feel as though I were desperately enamoured of the entire human race."

She leaned back against a pine, smiling vaguely, and crossing one knee over the other.

Now I am not bold by temperament, and, normally, I fear ladies. Therefore it surprised me to hear myself begin a frivolous *causerie*, replying to her pretty epigrams with epigrams of my own, advancing to the borderland of badinage, fearlessly conducting her and myself over that delicate frontier to meet upon the terrain of undisguised flirtation.

It was clear that she was out for a holiday. The seriousness and restraints of twenty-two years she had left behind her in the civilized world, and now, with a shrug of her young shoulders, she unloosened her burden of reticence, dignity, and responsibility and let the whole load fall with a discreet thud.

"Even hares go mad in March," she said, seriously. "I know you intend to flirt with me—and I don't care. Anyway, there's nothing else to do, is there?"

"Suppose," said I, solemnly, "I should take you behind that big tree and attempt to kiss you!"

The prospect did not appear to appall her, so I looked around with that sneaking yet conciliatory caution peculiar to young men who are novices in the art. Before I had satisfied myself that neither William nor the mules were observing us, Professor Van Twiller rose to her feet and took a short step backward.

"Let's set traps for a dingue," she said, "will you?"

I looked at the big tree, undecided. "Come on," she said; "I'll show you how." And away we went into the woods, she leading, her kilts flashing through the golden half-light.

Now I had not the faintest notion how to trap the dingue, but Professor Van Twiller asserted that it formerly fed on the tender tips of the spruce, quoting Darwin as her authority.

So we gathered a bushel of spruce-tips, piled them on the bank of a little stream, then built a miniature stockade around the bait, a foot high. I roofed this with hemlock, then laboriously whittled out and adjusted a swinging shutter for the entrance, setting it on springy twigs.

"The dingue, you know, was supposed to live in the water," she said, kneeling beside me over our trap.

I took her little hand and thanked her for the information.

"Doubtless," she said, enthusiastically, "a dingue will come out of the lake to-night to feed on our spruce-tips. Then," she added, "we've got him."

"True!" I said, earnestly, and pressed her fingers very gently.

Her face was turned a little away; I don't remember what she said; I don't remember that she said anything. A faint rose-tint stole over her cheek. A few moments later she said: "You must not do that again."

It was quite late when we strolled back to camp. Long before we came in sight of the twin tents we heard a deep voice bawling our names. It was Professor Smawl, and she pounced upon Dorothy and drove her ignominiously into the tent.

"As for you," she said, in hollow tones, "you may explain your conduct at once, or place your resignation at my disposal."

But somehow or other I appeared to be temporarily lost to shame, and I only smiled at my infuriated president, and entered my own tent with a step that was distinctly frolicsome.

"Billy," said I to William Spike, who regarded me morosely from the depths of the tent, "I'm going out to bag a mammoth to-morrow, so kindly clean my elephant-gun and bring an axe to chop out the tusks."

That night Professor Smawl complained bitterly of the cooking, but as neither Dorothy nor I knew how to improve it, she revenged herself on us by eating everything on the table and retiring to bed, taking Dorothy with her.

I could not sleep very well; the mosquitoes were intrusive, and Professor Smawl dreamed she was a pack of wolves and yelped in her sleep.

"Bird, ain't she?" said William, roused from slumber by her weird noises.

Dorothy, much frightened, crawled out of her tent, where her blanket-mate still dreamed dyspeptically, and William and I made her comfortable by the camp-fire.

It takes a pretty girl to look pretty half asleep in a blanket.

"Are you sure you are quite well?" I asked her.

To make sure, I tested her pulse. For an hour it varied more or less, but without alarming either of us. Then she went back to bed and I sat alone by the camp-fire.

Towards midnight I suddenly began to feel that strange, distant vibration that I had once before felt. As before, the vibration grew on the still air, increasing in volume until it became a sound, then died out into silence.

I rose and stole into my tent.

William, white as death, lay in his corner, weeping in his sleep.

I roused him remorselessly, and he sat up scowling, but refused to tell me what he had been dreaming.

"Was it about that third thing you saw—" I began. But he snarled up at me like a startled animal, and I was obliged to go to bed and toss about and speculate.

The next morning it rained. Dorothy and I visited our dingue-trap but found nothing in it. We were inclined, however, to stay out in the rain behind a big tree, but Profesor Smawl vetoed that proposition and sent me off to supply the larder with fresh meat.

I returned, mad and wet, with a dozen partridges and a white hare —brown at that season—and William cooked them vilely.

"I can taste the feathers!" said Professor Smawl, indignantly.

"There is no accounting for taste," I said, with a polite gesture of deprecation; "personally, I find feathers unpalatable."

"You may hand in your resignation this evening!" cried Professor Smawl, in hollow tones of passion.

I passed her the pancakes with a cheerful smile, and flippantly pressed the hand next to me. Unexpectedly it proved to be William's sticky fist, and Dorothy and I laughed until her tears ran into Professor Smawl's coffee-cup—an accident which kindled her wrath to red heat, and she requested my resignation five times during the evening.

The next day it rained again, more or less. Professor Smawl complained of the cooking, demanded my resignation, and finally marched out to explore, lugging the reluctant William with her. Dorothy and I sat down behind the largest tree we could find.

I don't remember what we were saying when a peculiar sound interrupted us, and we listened earnestly.

It was like a bell in the woods, ding-dong! ding-dong! ding-dong! —a low, mellow, golden harmony, coming nearer, then stopping.

I clasped Dorothy in my arms in my excitement.

"It is the note of the dingue!" I whispered, "and that explains its name, handed down from remote ages along with the names of the behemoth and the coney. It was because of its bell-like cry that it was named! Darling!" I cried, forgetting our short acquaintance, "we have made a discovery that the whole world will ring with!"

Hand in hand we tiptoed through the forest to our trap. There was something in it that took fright at our approach and rushed panic-stricken round and round the interior of the trap, uttering its alarm-note, which sounded like the jangling of a whole string of bells.

I seized the strangely beautiful creature; it neither attempted to bite nor scratch, but crouched in my arms, trembling and eyeing me.

Delighted with the lovely, tame animal, we bore it tenderly back to the camp and placed it on my blanket. Hand in hand we stood before it, awed by the sight of this beast, so long believed to be extinct.

"It is too good to be true," sighed Dorothy, clasping her white hands under her chin and gazing at the dingue in rapture.

"Yes," said I, solemnly, "you and I, my child, are face to face with the fabled dingue—*Dingus solitarius!* Let us continue to gaze at it, reverently, prayerfully, humbly—"

Dorothy yawned—probably with excitement.

We were still mutely adoring the dingue when Professor Smawl burst into the tent at a hand-gallop, bawling hoarsely for her kodak and note-book.

Dorothy seized her triumphantly by the arm and pointed at the dingue, which appeared to be frightened to death.

"What!" cried Professor Smawl, scornfully; "*that* a dingue? Rubbish!"

"Madam," I said, firmly, "it is a dingue! It's a monodactyl! See! It has but a single toe!"

"Bosh!" she retorted; "it's got four!"

"Four!" I repeated, blankly.

"Yes; one on each foot!"

"Of course," I said; "you didn't suppose a monodactyl meant a beast with one leg and one toe!"

But she laughed hatefully and declared it was a woodchuck.

We squabbled for a while until I saw the significance of her attitude. The unfortunate woman wished to find a dingue first and be accredited with the discovery.

I lifted the dingue in both hands and shook the creature gently, until the chiming ding-dong of its protestations filled our ears like sweet bells jangled out of tune.

Pale with rage at this final proof of the dingue's identity, she seized her camera and note-book.

"I haven't any time to waste over that musical woodchuck!" she shouted, and bounced out of the tent.

"What have you discovered, dear?" cried Dorothy, running after her.

"A mammoth!" bawled Professor Smawl, triumphantly; "and I'm going to photograph him!"

Neither Dorothy nor I believed her. We watched the flight of the infatuated woman in silence.

And now, at last, the tragic shadow falls over my paper as I write. I was never passionately attached to Professor Smawl, yet I would gladly refrain from chronicling the episode that must follow if, as I have hitherto attempted, I succeed in sticking to the unornamented truth.

I have said that neither Dorothy nor I believed her. I don't know why, unless it was that we had not yet made up our minds to believe that the mammoth still existed on earth. So, when Professor Smawl disappeared in the forest, scuttling through the underbrush like a demoralized hen, we viewed her flight with unconcern. There was a large tree in the neighborhood—a pleasant shelter in case of rain. So we sat down behind it, although the sun was shining fiercely.

It was one of those peaceful afternoons in the wilderness when the whole forest dreams, and the shadows are asleep and every little leaflet takes a nap. Under the still tree-tops the dappled sunlight, motionless, soaked the sod; the forest-flies no longer whirled in circles, but sat sunning their wings on slender twig-tips.

The heat was sweet and spicy; the sun drew out the delicate essence of gum and sap, warming volatile juices until they exhaled through the aromatic bark.

The sun went down into the wilderness; the forest stirred in its sleep; a fish splashed in the lake. The spell was broken. Presently the wind began to rise somewhere far away in the unknown land. I heard it coming, nearer, nearer—a brisk wind that grew heavier and blew harder as it neared us—a gale that swept distant branches—a furious gale that set limbs clashing and cracking, nearer and nearer. Crack! and the gale grew to a hurricane, trampling trees like dead twigs! Crack! Crackle! Crash! Crash!

Was it the wind?

With the roaring in my ears I sprang up, staring into the forest vista, and at the same instant, out of the crashing forest, sped Professor Smawl, skirts tucked up, thin legs flying like bicycle-spokes. I shouted, but the crashing drowned my voice. Then all at once the solid earth began to shake, and with the rush and roar of a tornado a gigantic living thing burst out of the forest before our eyes—a vast shadowy bulk that rocked and rolled along, mowing down trees in its course.

Two great crescents of ivory curved from its head; its back swept through the tossing tree-tops. Once it bellowed like a gun fired from a high bastion.

The apparition passed with the noise of thunder rolling on towards the ends of the earth. Crack! crash! went the trees, the tempest swept away in a rolling volley of reports, distant, more distant, until, long after the tumult had deadened, then ceased, the stunned forest echoed with the fall of mangled branches slowly dropping.

That evening an agitated young couple sat close together in the deserted camp, calling timidly at intervals for Professor Smawl and William Spike. I say timidly, because it is correct; we did not care to have a mammoth respond to our calls. The lurking echoes across the lake answered our cries; the full moon came up over the forest to look at us. We were not much to look at. Dorothy was moistening my shoulder with unfeigned tears, and I, afraid to light the fire, sat hunched up under the common blanket, wildly examining the darkness around us.

Chilled to the spinal marrow, I watched the gray lights whiten in the east. A single bird awoke in the wilderness. I saw the nearer trees looming in the mist, and the silver fog rolling on the lake.

All night long the darkness had vibrated with the strange monotone which I had heard the first night, camping at the gate of the unknown land. My brain seemed to echo that subtle harmony which rings in the auricular labyrinth after sound has ceased.

There are ghosts of sound which return to haunt long after sound is dead. It was these voiceless spectres of a voice long dead that stirred the transparent silence, intoning toneless tones.

I think I make myself clear.

It was an uncanny night; morning whitened the east; gray daylight stole into the woods, blotting the shadows to paler tints. It was nearly mid-day before the sun became visible through the fine-spun web of mist—a pale spot of gilt in the zenith.

By this pallid light I labored to strike the two empty tents, gather up our equipments and pack them on our five mules. Dorothy aided me bravely, whimpering when I spoke of Professor Smawl and William Spike, but abating nothing of her industry until we had the mules loaded and I was ready to drive them, Heaven knows whither.

"Where shall we go?" quavered Dorothy, sitting on a log with the dingue in her lap.

One thing was certain; this mammoth-ridden land was no place for women, and I told her so.

We placed the dingue in a basket and tied it around the leading mule's neck. Immediately the dingue, alarmed, began dingling like a cow-bell. It acted like a charm on the other mules, and they gravely filed off after their leader, following the bell. Dorothy and I, hand in hand, brought up the rear.

I shall never forget that scene in the forest—the gray arch of the heavens swimming in mist through which the sun peered shiftily, the tall pines wavering through the fog, the preoccupied mules marching single file, the foggy bell-note of the gentle dingue in its swinging basket, and Dorothy, limp kilts dripping with dew, plodding through the white dusk.

We followed the terrible tornado-path which the mammoth had left in its wake, but there were no traces of its human victims—neither one jot of Professor Smawl nor one solitary tittle of William Spike.

And now I would be glad to end this chapter if I could; I would gladly leave myself as I was, there in the misty forest, with an arm encircling the slender body of my little companion, and the mules moving in a monotonous line, and the dingue discreetly jingling—but again that menacing shadow falls across my page, and truth bids me tell all, and I, the slave of accuracy, must remember my vows as the dauntless disciple of truth.

Towards sunset—or that pale parody of sunset which set the forest swimming in a ghastly, colorless haze—the mammoth's trail of ruin brought us suddenly out of the trees to the shore of a great sheet of water.

It was a desolate spot; northward a chaos of sombre peaks rose, piled up like thunder-clouds along the horizon; east and south the darkening wilderness spread like a pall. Westward, crawling out into the mist from our very feet, the gray waste of water moved under the dull sky, and flat waves slapped the squatting rocks, heavy with slime.

And now I understood why the trail of the mammoth continued straight into the lake, for on either hand black, filthy tamarack swamps lay under ghostly sheets of mist. I strove to creep out into the bog, seeking a footing, but the swamp quaked and the smooth surface trembled like jelly in a bowl. A stick thrust into the slime sank into unknown depths.

Vaguely alarmed, I gained the firm land again and looked around, believing there was no road open but the desolate trail we had traversed. But I was in error; already the leading mule was wading out into the water, and the others, one by one, followed.

How wide the lake might be we could not tell, because the band of fog hung across the water like a curtain. Yet out into this flat, shallow void our mules went steadily, slop! slop! slop! in single file. Already they were growing indistinct in the fog, so I bade Dorothy hasten and take off her shoes and stockings.

She was ready before I was, I having to unlace my shooting-boots, and she stepped out into the water, kilts fluttering, moving her white feet cautiously. In a moment I was beside her, and we waded forward, sounding the shallow water with our poles.

When the water had risen to Dorothy's knees I hesitated, alarmed. But when we attempted to retrace our steps we could not find the shore again, for the blank mist shrouded everything, and the water deepened at every step.

I halted and listened for the mules. Far away in the fog I heard a dull splashing, receding as I listened. After a while all sound died away, and a slow horror stole over me—a horror that froze the little net-work of veins in every limb. A step to the right and the water rose to my knees; a step to the left and the cold, thin circle of the flood chilled my breast. Suddenly Dorothy screamed, and the next moment a far cry answered—a far, sweet cry that seemed to come from the sky, like the rushing harmony of the world's swift winds. Then the curtain of fog before us lighted up from behind; shadows moved on the misty screen, outlines of trees and grassy shores, and tiny birds flying. Thrown on the vapory curtain, in silhouette, a man and a woman passed under the lovely trees, arms about each other's necks; near them the shadows of five mules grazed peacefully; a dingue gambolled close by.

"It is a mirage!" I muttered, but my voice made no sound. Slowly the light behind the fog died out; the vapor around us turned to rose, then dissolved, while mile on mile of a limitless sea spread away till, like a quick line pencilled at a stroke, the horizon cut sky and sea in half, and before us lay an ocean from which towered a mountain of snow—or a gigantic berg of milky ice—for it was moving.

"Good Heavens," I shrieked; "it is alive!"

At the sound of my crazed cry the mountain of snow became a pillar, towering to the clouds, and a wave of golden glory drenched the figure to its knees! Figure? Yes—for a colossal arm shot across the sky, then curved back in exquisite grace to a head of awful beauty—a woman's head, with eyes like the blue lake of heaven—ay, a woman's splendid form, upright from the sky to the earth, knee-deep in the sea. The evening clouds drifted across her brow; her shimmering hair lighted the world beneath with sunset. Then, shading her white brow with one hand, she bent, and, with the other hand dipped in the sea, she sent a wave rolling at us. Straight out of the horizon it sped—a ripple that grew to a wave, then to a furious breaker which caught us up in a whirl of foam, bearing us onward, faster, faster, swiftly flying through leagues of spray until consciousness ceased and all was blank.

Yet ere my senses fled I heard again that strange cry—that sweet, thrilling harmony rushing out over the foaming waters, filling earth and sky with its soundless vibrations.

And I knew it was the hail of the Spirit of the North warning us back to life again.

Looking back, now, over the days that passed before we staggered into the Hudson Bay outpost at Gravel Cove, I am inclined to believe that neither Dorothy nor I were clothed entirely in our proper minds —or, if we were, our minds, no doubt, must have been in the same condition as our clothing. I remember shooting ptarmigan, and that we ate them; flashes of memory recall the steady downpour of rain through the endless twilight of shaggy forests; dim days on the foggy tundra, mud-holes from which the wild ducks rose in thousands; then the stunted hemlocks, then the forest again. And I do not even recall the moment when, at last, stumbling into the smooth path left by the Graham Glacier, we crawled through the mountain-wall, out of the unknown land, and once more into a world protected by the Lord Almighty.

A hunting-party of Elbon Indians brought us in to the post, and everybody was most kind—that I remember, just before going into several weeks of unpleasant delirium mercifully mitigated with unconsciousness.

Curiously enough, Professor Van Twiller was not very much battered, physically, for I had carried her for days, pickaback. But the awful experience had produced a shock which resulted in a nervous condition that lasted so long after she returned to New York that the wealthy and eminent specialist who attended her insisted upon taking her to the Riviera and marrying her. I sometimes wonder—but, as I have said, such reflections have no place in these austere pages.

However, anybody, I fancy, is at liberty to speculate upon the fate of the late Professor Smawl and William Spike, and upon the mules and the gentle dingue. Personally, I am convinced that the suggestive silhouettes I saw on that ghastly curtain of fog were cast by beatified beings in some earthly paradise—a mirage of bliss of which we caught but the colorless shadow-shapes floating 'twixt sea and sky.

At all events, neither Professor Smawl nor her William Spike ever returned; no exploring expedition has found a trace of mule or lady, of William or the dingue. The new expedition to be organized by Barnard College may penetrate still farther. I suppose that, when the time comes, I shall be expected to volunteer. But Professor Van Twiller is married, and William and Professor Smawl ought to be, and altogether, considering the mammoth and that gigantic and splendid apparition that bent from the zenith to the ocean and sent a tidal-wave rolling from the palm of one white hand—I say, taking all these various matters under consideration, I think I shall decide to remain in New York and continue writing for the scientific periodicals.

Is the
Ux Extinct?

I

WHEN the delegates were appointed to the International Scientific
Congress at the Paris Exposition of 1900, how little did anybody
imagine that the great conference would end in the most gigantic
scandal that ever stirred two continents?

Yet, had it not been for the pair of American newspapers published
in Paris, this scandal would never have been aired, for the continen-
tal press is so well muzzled that when it bites its teeth merely meet
in the empty atmosphere with a discreet snap.

But to the Yankee nothing excepting the Monroe Doctrine is sacred,
and the unsopped watch-dogs of the press bite right and left,
unmuzzled. The biter bites—it is his profession—and that ends the
affair; the bitee is bitten, and, in the deplorable argot of the hour,
"it is up to him."

So now that the scandal has been well aired and hung out to dry
in the teeth of decency and the four winds, and as all the details have
been cheerfully and grossly exaggerated, it is, perhaps, the proper
moment for the truth to be written by the only person whose knowledge of all the facts in the affair entitles him to speak for himself as
well as for those honorable ladies and gentlemen whose names and
titles have been so mercilessly criticised.

These, then, are the simple facts:

The International Scientific Congress, now adjourned *sine die*,

met at nine o'clock in the morning, May 3, 1900, in the Tasmanian
Pavilion of the Paris Exposition. There were present the most
famous scientists of Great Britain, France, Germany, Russia, Italy,
Switzerland, and the United States.

His Royal Highness the Crown-Prince of Monaco presided.

It is not necessary, now, to repeat the details of that preliminary
meeting. It is sufficient to say that committees representing the
various known sciences were named and appointed by the Prince of
Monaco, who had been unanimously elected permanent chairman
of the conference. It is the composition of a single committee that
concerns us now, and that committee, representing the science
which treats of bird life, was made up as follows:

Chairman—His Royal Highness the Crown-Prince of Monaco.
Members—Sir Peter Grebe, Great Britain; Baron de Becasse,
France; his Royal Highness King Christian, of Finland; the Countess
d'Alzette, of Belgium; and I, from the United States, representing
the Smithsonian Institution and the Bronx Park Zoological Society
of New York.

This, then, was the composition of that now notorious ornithological committee, a modest, earnest, self-effacing little band of
workers, bound together—in the beginning—by those ties of mutual
respect and esteem which unite all laborers in the vineyard of
science.

From the first meeting of our committee, science, the great
leveller, left no artificial barriers of rank or title standing between us.
We were enthusiasts in our love for ornithology; we found new
inspiration in the democracy of our common interests.

As for me, I chatted with my fellows, feeling no restraint myself
and perceiving none. The King of Finland and I discussed his latest
monograph on the speckled titmouse, and I was glad to agree with
the King in all his theories concerning the nesting habits of that
important bird.

Sir Peter Grebe, a large, red gentleman in tweeds, read us some
notes he had made on the domestic hen and her reasons for running
ahead of a horse and wagon instead of stepping aside to let the disturbing vehicle pass.

The Crown-Prince of Monaco took issue with Sir Peter; so did
the Baron de Becasse; and we were entertained by a friendly and

marvellously interesting three-cornered dispute, shared in by three of the most profound thinkers of the century.

I shall never forget the brilliancy of that argument, nor the modest, good-humored retorts which gave us all a glimpse into depths of erudition which impressed us profoundly and set the seal on the bonds which held us so closely together.

Alas, that the seal should ever have been broken! Alas, that the glittering apple of discord should have been flung into our midst!— no, not flung, but gently rolled under our noses by the gloved fingers of the lovely Countess d'Alzette.

"Messieurs," said the fair Countess, when all present, excepting she and I, had touched upon or indicated the subjects which they had prepared to present to the congress—"messieurs mes confrères, I have been requested by our distinguished chairman, the Crown-Prince of Monaco, to submit to your judgment the subject which, by favor of the King of the Belgians, I have prepared to present to the International Scientific Congress."

She made a pretty courtesy as she named her own sovereign, and we all rose out of respect to that most austere and moral ruler the King of Belgium.

"But," she said, with a charming smile of depreciation, "I am very, very much afraid that the subject which I have chosen may not meet with your approval, gentlemen."

She stood there in her dainty Parisian gown and bonnet, shaking her pretty head uncertainly, a smile on her lips, her small, gloved fingers interlocked.

"Oh, I know how dreadful it would be if this great congress should be compelled to listen to any hoax like that which Monsieur de Rougemont imposed on the British Royal Society," she said, gravely; "and because the subject of my paper is as strange as the strangest phenomenon alleged to have been noted by Monsieur de Rougemont, I hesitate—"

She glanced at the silent listeners around her. Sir Peter's red face had hardened; the King of Finland frowned slightly; the Crown-Prince of Monaco and Baron de Becasse wore anxious smiles. But when her violet eyes met mine I gave her a glance of encouragement, and that glance, I am forced to confess, was not dictated by scientific approval, but by something that never entirely dries up in the mustiest and dustiest of savants—the old Adam implanted in us all.

Now, I knew perfectly well what her subject must be; so did every man present. For it was no secret that his Majesty of Belgium had been swindled by some natives in Tasmania, and had paid a very large sum of money for a skin of that gigantic bird, the ux, which has been so often reported to exist among the inaccessible peaks of the Tasmanian Mountains. Needless, perhaps, to say that the skin proved a fraud, being nothing more than a Barnum contrivance made up out of the skins of a dozen ostriches and cassowaries, and most cleverly put together by Chinese workmen; at least, such was the report made on it by Sir Peter Grebe, who had been sent by the British Society to Antwerp to examine the acquisition. Needless, also, perhaps, to say that King Leopold, of Belgium, stoutly maintained that the skin of the ux was genuine from beak to claw.

For six months there had been a most serious difference of opinion among European ornithologists concerning the famous ux in the Antwerp Museum; and this difference had promised to result in an open quarrel between a few Belgian savants on one side and all Europe and Great Britain on the other.

Scientists have a deep-rooted horror of anything that touches on charlatanism; the taint of trickery not only alarms them, but drives them away from any suspicious subject, and usually ruins, scientifically speaking, the person who has introduced the subject for discussion.

Therefore, it took no little courage for the Countess d'Alzette to touch, with her dainty gloves, a subject which every scientist in Europe, with scarcely an exception, had pronounced fraudulent and unworthy of investigation. And to bring it before the great International Congress required more courage still; for the person who could face, in executive session, the most brilliant intellects in the world, and openly profess faith in a Barnumized bird skin, either had no scientific reputation to lose or was possessed of a bravery far above that of the savants who composed the audience.

Now, when the pretty Countess caught a flash of encouragement in my glance she turned rosy with gratification and surprise. Clearly, she had not expected to find a single ally in the entire congress. Her quick smile of gratitude touched me, and made me ashamed, too, for I had encouraged her out of the pure love of mischief, hoping to hear the whole matter threshed before the congress and so have it settled once for all. It was a thoughtless thing to do on my part. I should have remembered the consequences to the Countess if it were proven that she had been championing a fraud. The ruffled dignity of the congress would never forgive her; her scientific career would practically be at an end, because her theories and observations could no longer command respect or even the attention of those who knew that she herself had once been deceived by a palpable fraud.

I looked at her guiltily, already ashamed of myself for encouraging her to her destruction. How lovely and innocent she appeared, standing there reading her notes in a low, clear voice, fresh as a child's, with now and then a delicious upward sweep of her long, dark lashes.

With a start I came to my senses and bestowed a pinch on myself. This was neither the time nor the place to sentimentalize over a girlish beauty whose small, Parisian head was crammed full of foolish, brave theories concerning an imposition which her aged sovereign had been unable to detect.

I saw the gathering frown on the King of Finland's dark face; I saw Sir Peter Grebe grow redder and redder, and press his thick lips together to control the angry "Bosh!" which need not have been uttered to have been understood. The Baron de Becasse wore a painfully neutral smile, which froze his face into a quaint gargoyle; the Crown-Prince of Monaco looked at his polished finger-nails with a startled yet abstracted resignation. Clearly the young Countess had not a sympathizer in the committee.

Something—perhaps it was the latent chivalry which exists imbedded in us all, perhaps it was pity, perhaps a glimmering dawn of belief in the ux skin—set my thoughts working very quickly.

The Countess d'Alzette finished her notes, then glanced around with a deprecating smile, which died out on her lips when she perceived the silent and stony hostility of her fellow-scientists. A quick expression of alarm came into her lovely eyes. Would they vote against giving her a hearing before the congress? It required a unanimous vote to reject a subject. She turned her eyes on me.

I rose, red as fire, my head humming with a chaos of ideas all disordered and vague, yet whirling along in a single, resistless current. I had come to the congress prepared to deliver a monograph on the great auk; but now the subject went overboard as the birds themselves had, and I found myself pleading with the committee to give the Countess a hearing on the ux.

"Why not?" I exclaimed, warmly. "It is established beyond question that the ux does exist in Tasmania. Wallace saw several uxen, through his telescope, walking about upon the inaccessible heights of the Tasmanian Mountains. Darwin acknowledged that the bird exists; Professor Farrago has published a pamphlet containing an accumulation of all data bearing upon the ux. Why should not Madame la Comtesse be heard by the entire congress?"

I looked at Sir Peter Grebe.

"Have *you* seen this alleged bird skin in the Antwerp Museum?" he asked, perspiring with indignation.

"Yes, I have," said I. "It has been patched up, but how are we to know that the skin did not require patching? I have not found that ostrich skin has been used. It is true that the Tasmanians may have shot the bird to pieces and mended the skin with bits of cassowary hide here and there. But the greater part of the skin, and the beak and claws, are, in my estimation, well worth the serious attention of savants. To pronounce them fraudulent is, in my opinion, rash and premature."

I mopped my brow; I was in for it now. I had thrown in my reputation with the reputation of the Countess.

The displeasure and astonishment of my confrères was unmistakable. In the midst of a strained silence I moved that a vote be taken upon the advisability of a hearing before the congress on the subject of the ux. After a pause the young Countess, pale and determined, seconded my motion. The result of the balloting was a forgone conclusion; the Countess had one vote—she herself refraining from voting—and the subject was entered on the committee-book as acceptable and a date set for the hearing before the International Congress.

The effect of this vote on our little committee was most marked. Constraint took the place of cordiality, polite reserve replaced that guileless and open-hearted courtesy with which our proceedings had begun.

With icy politeness, the Crown-Prince of Monaco asked me to state the subject of the paper I proposed to read before the congress, and I replied quietly that, as I was partly responsible for advocating the discussion of the ux, I proposed to associate myself with the Countess d'Alzette in that matter—if Madame la Comtesse would accept the offer of a brother savant.

"Indeed I will," she said, impulsively, her blue eyes soft with gratitude.

"Very well," observed Sir Peter Grebe, swallowing his indignation and waddling off towards the door; "I shall resign my position on this committee—yes, I will, I tell you!"—as the King of Finland laid a fatherly hand on Sir Peter's sleeve—"I'll not be made responsible for this damn—"

He choked, sputtered, then bowed to the horrified Countess, asking pardon, and declaring that he yielded to nobody in respect for the gentler sex. And he retired with the Baron de Becasse.

But out in the hallway I heard him explode. "Confound it! This is no place for petticoats, Baron! And as for that Yankee ornithologist, he's hung himself with the Countess's corset-string—yes, he has! Don't tell me, Baron! The young idiot was all right until the Countess looked at him, I tell you. Gad! how she crumpled him up with those blue eyes of hers! What the devil do women come into such committees for? Eh? It's an outrage, I tell you! Why, the whole world will jeer at us if we sit and listen to her monograph on that fraudulent bird!"

The young Countess, who was writing near the window, could not have heard this outburst; but I heard it, and so did King Christian and the Crown-Prince of Monaco.

"Lord," thought I, "the Countess and I are in the frying-pan this time. I'll do what I can to keep us both out of the fire."

When the King and the Crown-Prince had made their adieux to the Countess, and she had responded, pale and serious, they came over to where I was standing, looking out on the Seine.

"Though we must differ from you," said the King, kindly, "we wish you all success in this dangerous undertaking."

I thanked him.

"You are a young man to risk a reputation already established," remarked the Crown-Prince; then added: "You are braver than I.

Ridicule is a barrier to all knowledge, and, though we know that, we seekers after truth always bring up short at that barrier and dismount, not daring to put our hobbies to the fence."

"One can but come a cropper," said I.

"And risk staking our hobbies? No, no, that would make us ridiculous; and ridicule kills in Europe."

"It's somewhat deadly in America, too," I said, smiling.

"The more honor to you," said the Crown-Prince, gravely.

"Oh, I am not the only one," I answered, lightly. "There is my confrère, Professor Hyssop, who studies apparitions and braves a contempt and ridicule which none of us would dare challenge. We Yankees are learning slowly. Some day we will find the lost key to the future while Europe is sneering at those who are trying to pick the lock."

When King Christian, of Finland, and the Crown-Prince of Monaco had taken their hats and sticks and departed, I glanced across the room at the young Countess, who was now working rapidly on a type-writer, apparently quite oblivious of my presence.

I looked out of the window again, and my gaze wandered over the exposition grounds. Gilt and scarlet and azure the palaces rose in every direction, under a wilderness of fluttering flags. Towers, minarets, turrets, golden spires cut the blue sky; in the west the gaunt Eiffel Tower sprawled across the glittering Esplanade; behind it rose the solid golden dome of the Emperor's tomb, gilded once more by the Almighty's sun, to amuse the living rabble while the dead slumbered in his imperial crypt, himself now but a relic for the amusement of the people whom he had despised. O tempora! O mores! O Napoleon!

Down under my window, in the asphalted court, the King of Finland was entering his beautiful victoria. An adjutant, wearing a cocked hat and brilliant uniform, mounted the box beside the green-and-gold coachman; the two postilions straightened up in their saddles; the four horses danced. Then, when the Crown-Prince of Monaco had taken a seat beside the King, the carriage rolled away, and far down the quay I watched it until the flutter of the green-and-white plumes in the adjutant's cocked hat was all I could see of vanishing royalty.

I was still musing there by the window, listening to the click and ringing of the type-writer, when I suddenly became aware that the clicking had ceased, and, turning, I saw the young Countess standing beside me.

"Thank you for your chivalrous impulse to help me," she said, frankly, holding out her bare hand.

I bent over it.

"I had not realized how desperate my case was," she said, with a smile. "I supposed that they would at least give me a hearing. How can I thank you for your brave vote in my favor?"

"By giving me your confidence in this matter," said I, gravely. "If we are to win, we must work together and work hard, madame. We are entering a struggle, not only to prove the genuineness of a bird skin and the existence of a bird which neither of us has ever seen, but also a struggle which will either make us famous forever or render it impossible for either of us ever again to face a scientific audience."

"I know it," she said, quietly. "And I understand all the better how gallant a gentleman I have had the fortune to enlist in my cause. Believe me, had I not absolute confidence in my ability to prove the existence of the ux I should not, selfish as I am, have accepted your chivalrous offer to stand or fall with me."

The subtle emotion in her voice touched a responsive chord in me. I looked at her earnestly; she raised her beautiful eyes to mine.

"Will you help me?" she asked.

Would I help her? Faith, I'd pass the balance of my life turning flip-flaps to please her. I did not attempt to undeceive myself; I realized that the lightning had struck me—that I was desperately in love with the young Countess from the tip of her bonnet to the toe of her small, polished shoe. I was curiously cool about it, too, although my heart gave a thump that nigh choked me, and I felt myself going red from temple to chin.

If the Countess d'Alzette noticed it she gave no sign, unless the pink tint under her eyes, deepening, was a subtle signal of understanding to the signal in my eyes.

"Suppose," she said, "that I failed, before the congress, to prove my theory? Suppose my investigations resulted in the exposure of a fraud and my name was held up to ridicule before all Europe? What would become of you, monsieur?"

I was silent.

"You are already celebrated as the discoverer of the mammoth and the great auk," she persisted. "You are young, enthusiastic, renowned, and you have a future before you that anybody in the world might envy."

I said nothing.

"And yet," she said, softly, "you risk all because you will not leave a young woman friendless among her confrères. It is not wise, monsieur; it is gallant and generous and impulsive, but it is not wisdom. Don Quixote rides no more in Europe, my friend."

"He stays at home—seventy million of a little him—in America," said I.

After a moment she said, "I believe you, monsieur."

"It is true enough," I said, with a laugh. "We are the only people who tilt at windmills these days—we and our cousins, the British, who taught us."

I bowed gayly, and added:

"With your colors to wear, I shall have the honor of breaking a lance against the biggest windmill in the world."

"You mean the Citadel of Science," she said, smiling.

"And its rock-ribbed respectability," I replied.

She looked at me thoughtfully, rolling and unrolling the scroll in her hands. Then she sighed, smiled, and brightened, handing me the scroll.

"Read it carefully," she said; "it is an outline of the policy I suggest that we follow. You will be surprised at some of the statements. Yet every word is the truth. And, monsieur, your reward for the devotion you have offered will be no greater than you deserve, when you find yourself doubly famous for our joint monograph on the ux. Without your vote in the committee I should have been denied a hearing, even though I produced proofs to support my theory. I appreciate that; I do most truly appreciate the courage which prompted you to defend a woman at the risk of your own ruin. Come to me this evening at nine. I hold for you in store a surprise and pleasure which you do not dream of."

"Ah, but I do," I said, slowly, under the spell of her delicate beauty and enthusiasm.

"How can you?" she said, laughing. "You don't know what awaits you at nine this evening?"

"You," I said, fascinated.

The color swept her face; she dropped me a deep courtesy.

"At nine, then," she said. "No. 8 Rue d'Alouette."

I bowed, took my hat, gloves, and stick, and attended her to her carriage below.

Long after the blue-and-black victoria had whirled away down the crowded quay I stood looking after it, mazed in the web of that ancient enchantment whose spell fell over the first man in Eden, and whose sorcery shall not fail till the last man returns his soul.

II

I LUNCHED at my lodgings on the Quai Malthus, and I had but little appetite, having fed upon such an unexpected variety of emotions during the morning.

Now, although I was already heels over head in love, I do not believe that loss of appetite was the result of that alone. I was slowly beginning to realize what my recent attitude might cost me, not only in an utter collapse of my scientific career, and the consequent material ruin which was likely to follow, but in the loss of all my friends at home. The Zoological Society of Bronx Park and the Smithsonian Institution of Washington had sent me as their trusted delegate, leaving it entirely to me to choose the subject on which I was to speak before the International Congress. What, then, would be their attitude when they learned that I had chosen to uphold the dangerous theory of the existence of the ux?

Would they repudiate me and send another delegate to replace me? Would they merely wash their hands of me and let me go to my own destruction?

"I will know soon enough," thought I, "for this morning's proceedings will have been cabled to New York ere now, and read at the breakfast-tables of every old, moss-grown naturalist in America before I see the Countess d'Alzette this evening." And I drew from my pocket the roll of paper which she had given me, and, lighting a cigar, lay back in my chair to read it.

The manuscript had been beautifully type-written, and I had no trouble in following her brief, clear account of the circumstances under which the notorious ux-skin had been obtained. As for the story itself, it was somewhat fishy, but I manfully swallowed my growing nervousness and comforted myself with the belief of Darwin in the existence of the ux, and the subsequent testimony of Wallace, who simply stated what he had seen through his telescope, and then left it to others to identify the enormous birds he described as he had observed them stalking about on the snowy peaks of the Tasmanian Alps.

My own knowledge of the ux was confined to a single circumstance. When, in 1897, I had gone to Tasmania with Professor Farrago, to make a report on the availability of the so-called "Tasmanian devil," as a substitute for the mongoose in the West Indies, I of course heard a great deal of talk among the natives concerning the birds which they affirmed haunted the summits of the mountains.

Our time in Tasmania was too limited to admit of an exploration then. But although we were perfectly aware that the summits of the Tasmanian Alps are inaccessible, we certainly should have attempted to gain them had not the time set for our departure arrived before we had completed the investigation for which we were sent.

One relic, however, I carried away with me. It was a single greenish bronzed feather, found high up in the mountains by a native, and sold to me for a somewhat large sum of money.

Darwin believed the ux to be covered with greenish plumage; Wallace was too far away to observe the color of the great birds; but all the natives of Tasmania unite in affirming that the plumage of the ux is green.

It was not only the color of this feather that made me an eager purchaser, it was the extraordinary length and size. I knew of no living bird large enough to wear such a feather. As for the color, that might have been tampered with before I bought it, and, indeed, testing it later, I found on the fronds traces of sulphate of copper. But the same thing has been found in the feathers of certain birds whose color is metallic green, and it has been proven that such birds pick up and swallow shining bits of copper pyrites.

Why should not the ux do the same thing?

Still, my only reason for believing in the existence of the bird was this single feather. I had easily proved that it belonged to no known species of bird. I also proved it to be similar to the tail-feathers of the ux-skin in Antwerp. But the feathers on the Antwerp specimen were gray, and the longest of them was but three feet in length, while my huge, bronze-green feather measured eleven feet from tip to tip.

One might account for it supposing the Antwerp skin to be that of a young bird, or of a moulting bird, or perhaps of a different sex from the bird whose feather I had secured.

Still, these ideas were not proven. Nothing concerning the birds had been proven. I had but a single fact to lean on, and that was that the feather I possessed could not have belonged to any known species of bird. Nobody but myself knew of the existence of this feather. And now I meant to cable to Bronx Park for it, and to place this evidence at the disposal of the beautiful Countess d'Alzette.

My cigar had gone out, as I sat musing, and I relighted it and resumed my reading of the type-written notes, lazily, even a trifle sceptically, for all the evidence that she had been able to collect to substantiate her theory of the existence of the ux was not half as important as the evidence I was to produce in the shape of that enormous green feather.

I came to the last paragraph, smoking serenely, and leaning back comfortably, one leg crossed over the other. Then, suddenly, my attention became riveted on the words under my eyes. Could I have read them aright? Could I believe what I read in ever-growing astonishment which culminated in an excitement that stirred the very hair on my head?

The ux exists. There is no longer room for doubt. Ocular proof I can now offer in the shape of *five living eggs* of this gigantic bird. All measures have been taken to hatch these eggs; they are now in the vast incubator. It is my plan to have them hatch, one by one, under the very eyes of the International Congress. It will be the greatest triumph that science has witnessed since the discovery of the New World.

[Signed] SUZANNE D'ALZETTE.

"Either," I cried out, in uncontrollable excitement—"either that girl is mad or she is the cleverest woman on earth."

After a moment I added:

"In either event I am going to marry her."

III

THAT evening, a few minutes before nine o'clock, I descended from a cab in front of No. 8 Rue d'Alouette, and was ushered into a pretty reception-room by an irreproachable servant, who disappeared directly with my card.

In a few moments the young Countess came in, exquisite in her silvery dinner-gown, eyes bright, white arms extended in a charming, impulsive welcome. The touch of her silky fingers thrilled me; I was dumb under the enchantment of her beauty; and I think she understood my silence, for her blue eyes became troubled and the happy parting of her lips changed to a pensive curve.

Presently I began to tell her about my bronzed-green feather; at my first word she looked up brightly, almost gratefully, I fancied; and in another moment we were deep in eager discussion of the subject which had first drawn us together.

What evidence I possessed to sustain our theory concerning the existence of the ux I hastened to reveal; then, heart beating excitedly, I asked her about the eggs and where they were at present, and whether she believed it possible to bring them to Paris—all these questions in the same breath—which brought a happy light into her eyes and a delicious ripple of laughter to her lips.

"Why, of course it is possible to bring the eggs here," she cried. "Am I sure? Parbleu! The eggs are already here, monsieur!"

"Here!" I exclaimed. "In Paris?"

"In Paris? Mais oui; and in my own house—*this very house*, monsieur. Come, you shall behold them with your own eyes!"

Her eyes were brilliant with excitement; impulsively she stretched out her rosy hand. I took it; and she led me quickly back through the drawing-room, through the dining-room, across the butler's pantry, and into a long, dark hallway. We were almost running now —I keeping tight hold of her soft little hand, she, raising her gown a trifle, hurrying down the hallway, silken petticoats rustling like a silk banner in the wind. A turn to the right brought us to the cellar-stairs; down we hastened, and then across the cemented floor towards a long, glass-fronted shelf, pierced with steam-pipes.

"A match," she whispered, breathlessly.

I struck a wax match and touched it to the gas-burner overhead.

Never, never can I forget what that flood of gas-light revealed. In a row stood five large, glass-mounted incubators; behind the glass doors lay, in dormant majesty, five enormous eggs. The eggs were pale-green—lighter, somewhat, than robins' eggs, but not as pale as herons' eggs. Each egg appeared to be larger than a large hogs-head, and was partly embedded in bales of cotton-wool.

Five little silver thermometers inside the glass doors indicated a temperature of 95° Fahrenheit. I noticed that there was an automatic arrangement connected with the pipes which regulated the temperature.

I was too deeply moved for words. Speech seemed superfluous as we stood there, hand in hand, contemplating those gigantic, pale-green eggs.

There is something in a silent egg which moves one's deeper emotions—something solemn in its embryotic inertia, something awesome in its featureless immobility.

I know of nothing on earth which is so totally lacking in expression as an egg. The great desert Sphinx, brooding through its veil of sand, has not that tremendous and meaningless dignity which wraps the colorless oval effort of a single domestic hen.

I held the hand of the young Countess very tightly. Her fingers closed slightly.

Then and there, in the solemn presence of those emotionless eggs, I placed my arm around her supple waist and kissed her.

She said nothing. Presently she stooped to observe the thermometer. Naturally, it registered 95° Fahrenheit.

"Suzanne," I said, softly.

"Oh, we must go up-stairs," she whispered, breathlessly; and, picking up her silken skirts, she fled up the cellar-stairs.

I turned out the gas, with that instinct of economy which early wastefulness has implanted in me, and followed the Countess Suzanne through the suite of rooms and into the small reception-hall where she had first received me.

She was sitting on a low divan, head bent, slowly turning a sapphire ring on her finger, round and round.

I looked at her romantically, and then—

"Please don't," she said.

The correct reply to this is:

"Why not?"—very tenderly spoken.

"Because," she replied, which was also the correct and regular answer.

"Suzanne," I said, slowly and passionately.

She turned the sapphire ring on her finger. Presently she tired of this, so I lifted her passive hand very gently and continued turning the sapphire ring on her finger, slowly, to harmonize with the cadence of our unspoken thoughts.

Towards midnight I went home, walking with great care through a new street in Paris, paved exclusively with rose-colored blocks of air.

IV

At nine o'clock in the evening, July 31, 1900, the International Congress was to assemble in the great lecture-hall of the Belgian Scientific Pavilion, which adjourned the Tasmanian Pavilion, to hear the Countess Suzanne d'Alzette read her paper on the ux.

That morning the Countess and I, with five furniture vans, had transported the five great incubators to the platform of the lecture-hall, and had engaged an army of plumbers and gas-fitters to make the steam-heating connections necessary to maintain in the incubators a temperature of 100° Fahrenheit.

A heavy green curtain hid the stage from the body of the lecture-hall. Behind this curtain the five enormous eggs reposed, each in its incubator.

The Countess Suzanne was excited and calm by turns, her cheeks were pink, her lips scarlet, her eyes bright as blue planets at midnight.

Without faltering she rehearsed her discourse before me, reading from her type-written manuscript in a clear voice, in which I could scarcely discern a tremor. Then we went through the dumb show of exhibiting the uxen eggs to a frantically applauding audience; she responded to countless supposititious encores, I leading her out repeatedly before the green curtain to face the great, damp, darkened auditorium.

Then, in response to repeated imaginary recalls, she rehearsed the extemporaneous speech, thanking the distinguished audience for their patience in listening to an unknown confrère, and confessing her obligations to me (here I appeared and bowed in self-abasement) for my faith in her and my aid in securing for her a public hearing before the most highly educated audience in the world.

After that we retired behind the curtain to sit on an empty box and eat sandwiches and watch the last lingering plumbers pasting up the steam connections with a pot of molten lead.

The plumbers were Americans, brought to Paris to make repairs on the American buildings during the exposition, and we conversed with them affably as they pottered about, plumber-like, poking under the flooring with lighted candles, rubbing their thumbs up and down musty old pipes, and prying up planks in dark corners.

They informed us that they were union men and that they hoped we were too. And I replied that union was certainly my ultimate purpose, at which the young Countess smiled dreamily at vacancy.

We did not dare leave the incubators. The plumbers lingered on, hour after hour, while we sat and watched the little silver thermometers, and waited.

It was time for the Countess Suzanne to dress, and still the plumbers had not finished; so I sent a messenger for her maid, to bring her trunk to the lecture-hall, and I despatched another messenger to my lodgings for my evening clothes and fresh linen.

There were several dressing-rooms off the stage. Here, about six o'clock, the Countess retired with her maid, to dress, leaving me to watch the plumbers and the thermometers.

When the Countess Suzanne returned, radiant and lovely in an evening gown of black lace, I gave her the roses I had brought for her and hurried off to dress in my turn, leaving her to watch the thermometers.

I was not absent more than half an hour, but when I returned I found the Countess anxiously conversing with the plumbers and pointing despairingly at the thermometers, which now registered only 95°.

"You must keep up the temperature!" I said. "Those eggs are due to hatch within a few hours. What's the trouble with the heat?"

The plumber did not know, but thought the connections were defective.

"But that's why we called you in!" exclaimed the Countess. "Can't you fix things securely?"

"Oh, we'll fix things, lady," replied the plumber, condescendingly, and he ambled away to rub his thumb up and down a pipe.

As we alone were unable to move and handle the enormous eggs, the Countess, whose sweet character was a stranger to vindictiveness or petty resentment, had written to the members of the ornithological committee, revealing the marvellous fortune which had crowned her efforts in the search for evidence to sustain her theory concerning the ux, and inviting these gentlemen to aid her in displaying the great eggs to the assembled congress.

This she had done the night previous. Every one of the gentlemen invited had come post-haste to her "hotel," to view the eggs with their own sceptical and astonished eyes; and the fair young Countess and I tasted our first triumph in her cellar, whither we conducted Sir Peter Grebe, the Crown-Prince of Monaco, Baron de Becasse, and his Majesty King Christian of Finland.

Scepticism and incredulity gave place to excitement and unbounded enthusiasm. The old King embraced the Countess; Baron de Becasse attempted to kiss me; Sir Peter Grebe made a handsome apology for his folly and vowed that he would do open penance for his sins. The poor Crown-Prince, who was of a nervous temperament, sat on the cellar-stairs and wept like a child.

His grief at his own pig-headedness touched us all profoundly.

So it happened that these gentlemen were coming tonight to give their aid to us in moving the priceless eggs, and lend their countenance and enthusiastic support to the young Countess in her maiden effort.

Sir Peter Grebe arrived first, all covered with orders and decorations, and greeted us affectionately, calling the Countess the "sweetest lass in France," and me his undutiful Yankee cousin who had landed feet foremost at the expense of the British Empire.

The King of Finland, the Crown-Prince, and Baron de Becasse arrived together, a composite mass of medals, sashes, and academy palms. To see them moving boxes about, straightening chairs, and pulling out rugs reminded me of those golden embroidered gentlemen who run out into the arena and roll up carpets after the acrobats have finished their turn in the Nouveau Cirque.

I was aiding the King of Finland to move a heavy keg of nails, when the Countess called out to me in alarm, saying that the thermometers had dropped to 80° Fahrenheit.

I spoke sharply to the plumbers, who were standing in a circle behind the dressing-rooms; but they answered sullenly that they could do no more work that day.

Indignant and alarmed, I ordered them to come out to the stage, and, after some hesitation, they filed out, a sulky, silent lot of workmen, with their tools already gathered up and tied in their kits. At once I noticed that a new man had appeared among them—a red-faced, stocky man wearing a frock-coat and a shiny silk hat.

"Who is the master-workman here?" I asked.

"I am," said a man in blue overalls.

"Well," said I, "why don't you fix those steam-fittings?"

There was a silence. The man in the silk hat smirked.

"Well?" said I.

"Come, come, that's all right," said the man in the silk hat. "These men know their business without you tellin' them."

"Who are you?" I demanded, sharply.

"Oh, I'm just a walkin' delegate," he replied, with a sneer. "There's a strike in New York and I come over here to tie this here exposition up. See?"

"You mean to say you won't let these men finish their work?" I asked, thunderstruck.

"That's about it, young man," he said, coolly.

Furious, I glanced at my watch, then at the thermometers, which now registered only 75°. Already I could hear the first-comers of the audience arriving in the body of the hall. Already a stage-hand was turning up the footlights and dragging chairs and tables hither and thither.

"What will you take to stay and attend to those steam-pipes?" I demanded, desperately.

"It can't be done nohow," observed the man in the silk hat. "That New York strike is good for a month yet." Then, turning to the workmen, he nodded and, to my horror, the whole gang filed out after him, turning deaf ears to my entreaties and threats.

There was a deathly silence, then Sir Peter exploded into a vivid shower of words. The Countess, pale as a ghost, gave me a heart-breaking look. The Crown-Prince wept.

"Great Heaven!" I cried; "the thermometers have fallen to 70°!"

The King of Finland sat down on a chair and pressed his hands over his eyes. Baron de Becasse ran round and round, uttering subdued and plaintive screams; Sir Peter swore steadily.

"Gentlemen," I cried, desperately, "we must save those eggs! They are on the very eve of hatching! Who will volunteer?"

"To do what?" moaned the Crown-Prince.

"I'll show you," I exclaimed, running to the incubators and beckoning to the Baron to aid me.

In a moment we had rolled out the great egg, made a nest on the stage floor with the bales of cotton-wool, and placed the egg in it. One after another we rolled out the remaining eggs, building for each its nest of cotton; and at last the five enormous eggs lay there in a row behind the green curtain.

"Now," said I, excitedly, to the King, "you must get up on that egg and try to keep it warm."

The King began to protest, but I would take no denial, and presently his Majesty was perched up on the great egg, gazing foolishly about at the others, who were now all climbing up on their allotted eggs.

"Great Heaven!" muttered the King, as Sir Peter settled down comfortably on his egg, "I am willing to give life and fortune for the sake of science, but I can't bear to hatch out eggs like a bird!"

The Crown-Prince was now sitting patiently beside the Baron de Becasse.

"I feel in my bones," he murmured, "that I'm about to hatch something. Can't you hear a tapping on the shell of your egg, Baron?"

"Parbleu!" replied the Baron. "The shell is moving under me."

It certainly was; for, the next moment, the Baron fell into his egg with a crash and a muffled shriek, and floundered out, dripping, yellow as a canary.

"N'importe!" he cried, excitedly. "Allons! Save the eggs! Hurrah! Vive la science!" And he scrambled up on the fourth egg and sat there, arms folded, sublime courage transfiguring him from head to foot.

We all gave him a cheer, which was hushed as the stage-manager ran in, warning us that the audience was already assembled and in place.

"You're not going to raise the curtain while we're sitting, are you?" demanded the King of Finland, anxiously.

"No, no," I said; "sit tight, your Majesty. Courage, gentlemen! Our vindication is at hand!"

The Countess glanced at me with startled eyes; I took her hand, saluted it respectfully, and then quietly led her before the curtain, facing an ocean of upturned faces across the flaring footlights.

She stood a moment to acknowledge the somewhat ragged applause, a calm smile on her lips. All her courage had returned; I saw that at once.

Very quietly she touched her lips to the *eau-sucrée*, laid her manuscript on the table, raised her beautiful head, and began:

"That the ux is a living bird I am here before you to prove—"

A sharp report behind the curtain drowned her voice. She paled; the audience rose amid cries of excitement.

"What was it?" she asked, faintly.

"Sir Peter has hatched out his egg," I whispered. "Hark! There goes another egg!" And I ran behind the curtain.

Such a scene as I beheld was never dreamed of on land or sea. Two enormous young uxen, all over gigantic pin-feathers, were wandering stupidly about. Mounted on one was Sir Peter Grebe, eyes starting from his apoplectic visage; on the other, clinging to the bird's neck, hung the Baron de Becasse.

Before I could move, the two remaining eggs burst, and a pair of huge, scrawny fledgelings rose among the débris, bearing off on their backs the King and Crown-Prince.

"Help!" said the King of Finland, faintly. "I'm falling off!"

I sprang to his aid, but tripped on the curtain-spring. The next instant the green curtain shot up, and there, revealed to that vast and distinguished audience, roamed four enormous chicks, bearing on their backs the most respected and exclusive aristocracy of Europe.

The Countess Suzanne turned with a little shriek of horror, then sat down in her chair, laid her lovely head on the table, and very quietly fainted away, unconscious of the frantic cheers which went roaring to the roof.

This, then, is the *true* history of the famous exposition scandal. And, as I have said, had it not been for the presence in that audience of two American reporters nobody would have known what all the world now knows—nobody would have read of the marvellous feats of bareback riding indulged in by the King of Finland—nobody would have read how Sir Peter Grebe steered his mount safely past the footlights only to come to grief over the prompter's box.

But this *is* scandal. And, as for the charming Countess Suzanne d'Alzette, the public has heard all that it is entitled to hear, and much that it is not entitled to hear.

However, on second thoughts, perhaps the public is entitled to hear a little more. I will therefore say this much—the shock of astonishment which stunned me when the curtain flew up, revealing the King-bestridden uxen, was nothing to the awful blow which smote me when the Count d'Alzette leaped from the orchestra, over the footlights, and bore away with him the fainting form of his wife, the lovely Countess d'Alzette.

I sometimes wonder—but, as I have repeatedly observed, this dull and pedantic narrative of fact is no vehicle for sentimental soliloquy. It is, then, merely sufficient to say that I took the earliest steamer for kinder shores, spurred on to haste by a venomous cablegram from the Smithsonian, repudiating me, and by another from Bronx Park, ordering me to spend the winter in some inexpensive, poisonous, and unobtrusive spot, and make a collection of isopods. The island of Java appeared to me to be as poisonously unobtrusive and inexpensive a region as I had ever heard of; a steamer sailed from Antwerp for Batavia in twenty-four hours. Therefore, as I say, I took the night-train for Brussels, and the steamer from Antwerp the following evening.

Of my uneventful voyage, of the happy and successful quest, there is little to relate. The Javanese are frolicsome and hospitable. There was a girl there with features that were as delicate as though chiselled out of palest amber; and I remember she wore a most wonderful jewelled, helmet-like head-dress, and jingling bangles on her ankles, and when she danced she made most graceful and poetic gestures with her supple wrists—but that has nothing to do with isopods, absolutely nothing.

A CATALOG OF SELECTED
DOVER BOOKS
IN ALL FIELDS OF INTEREST

A CATALOG OF SELECTED DOVER
BOOKS IN ALL FIELDS OF INTEREST

CONCERNING THE SPIRITUAL IN ART, Wassily Kandinsky. Pioneering work by father of abstract art. Thoughts on color theory, nature of art. Analysis of earlier masters. 12 illustrations. 80pp. of text. 5⅜ x 8½.   0-486-23411-8

CELTIC ART: The Methods of Construction, George Bain. Simple geometric techniques for making Celtic interlacements, spirals, Kells-type initials, animals, humans, etc. Over 500 illustrations. 160pp. 9 x 12. (Available in U.S. only.)   0-486-22923-8

AN ATLAS OF ANATOMY FOR ARTISTS, Fritz Schider. Most thorough reference work on art anatomy in the world. Hundreds of illustrations, including selections from works by Vesalius, Leonardo, Goya, Ingres, Michelangelo, others. 593 illustrations. 192pp. 7⅛ x 10¼.   0-486-20241-0

CELTIC HAND STROKE-BY-STROKE (Irish Half-Uncial from "The Book of Kells"): An Arthur Baker Calligraphy Manual, Arthur Baker. Complete guide to creating each letter of the alphabet in distinctive Celtic manner. Covers hand position, strokes, pens, inks, paper, more. Illustrated. 48pp. 8¼ x 11.   0-486-24336-2

EASY ORIGAMI, John Montroll. Charming collection of 32 projects (hat, cup, pelican, piano, swan, many more) specially designed for the novice origami hobbyist. Clearly illustrated easy-to-follow instructions insure that even beginning papercrafters will achieve successful results. 48pp. 8¼ x 11.   0-486-27298-2

BLOOMINGDALE'S ILLUSTRATED 1886 CATALOG: Fashions, Dry Goods and Housewares, Bloomingdale Brothers. Famed merchants' extremely rare catalog depicting about 1,700 products: clothing, housewares, firearms, dry goods, jewelry, more. Invaluable for dating, identifying vintage items. Also, copyright-free graphics for artists, designers. Co-published with Henry Ford Museum & Greenfield Village. 160pp. 8¼ x 11.   0-486-25780-0

THE ART OF WORLDLY WISDOM, Baltasar Gracian. "Think with the few and speak with the many," "Friends are a second existence," and "Be able to forget" are among this 1637 volume's 300 pithy maxims. A perfect source of mental and spiritual refreshment, it can be opened at random and appreciated either in brief or at length. 128pp. 5⅜ x 8½.   0-486-44034-6

JOHNSON'S DICTIONARY: A Modern Selection, Samuel Johnson (E. L. McAdam and George Milne, eds.). This modern version reduces the original 1755 edition's 2,300 pages of definitions and literary examples to a more manageable length, retaining the verbal pleasure and historical curiosity of the original. 480pp. 5³⁄₁₆ x 8¼.   0-486-44089-3

ADVENTURES OF HUCKLEBERRY FINN, Mark Twain, Illustrated by E. W. Kemble. A work of eternal richness and complexity, a source of ongoing critical debate, and a literary landmark, Twain's 1885 masterpiece about a barefoot boy's journey of self-discovery has enthralled readers around the world. This handsome clothbound reproduction of the first edition features all 174 of the original black-and-white illustrations. 368pp. 5⅜ x 8½.   0-486-44322-1

STICKLEY CRAFTSMAN FURNITURE CATALOGS, Gustav Stickley and L. & J. G. Stickley. Beautiful, functional furniture in two authentic catalogs from 1910. 594 illustrations, including 277 photos, show settles, rockers, armchairs, reclining chairs, bookcases, desks, tables. 183pp. 6½ x 9¼.   0-486-23838-5

AMERICAN LOCOMOTIVES IN HISTORIC PHOTOGRAPHS: 1858 to 1949, Ron Ziel (ed.). A rare collection of 126 meticulously detailed official photographs, called "builder portraits," of American locomotives that majestically chronicle the rise of steam locomotive power in America. Introduction. Detailed captions. xi+ 129pp. 9 x 12.   0-486-27393-8

AMERICA'S LIGHTHOUSES: An Illustrated History, Francis Ross Holland, Jr. Delightfully written, profusely illustrated fact-filled survey of over 200 American light-houses since 1716. History, anecdotes, technological advances, more. 240pp. 8 x 10¾.
                    0-486-25576-X

TOWARDS A NEW ARCHITECTURE, Le Corbusier. Pioneering manifesto by founder of "International School." Technical and aesthetic theories, views of industry, eco-nomics, relation of form to function, "mass-production split" and much more. Profusely illustrated. 320pp. 6⅛ x 9¼. (Available in U.S. only.)   0-486-25023-7

HOW THE OTHER HALF LIVES, Jacob Riis. Famous journalistic record, expos-ing poverty and degradation of New York slums around 1900, by major social reformer. 100 striking and influential photographs. 233pp. 10 x 7⅞.   0-486-22012-5

FRUIT KEY AND TWIG KEY TO TREES AND SHRUBS, William M. Harlow. One of the handiest and most widely used identification aids. Fruit key covers 120 deciduous and evergreen species; twig key 160 deciduous species. Easily used. Over 300 photographs. 126pp. 5⅜ x 8½.   0-486-20511-8

COMMON BIRD SONGS, Dr. Donald J. Borror. Songs of 60 most common U.S. birds: robins, sparrows, cardinals, bluejays, finches, more–arranged in order of increasing complexity. Up to 9 variations of songs of each species.
                    Cassette and manual 0-486-99911-4

ORCHIDS AS HOUSE PLANTS, Rebecca Tyson Northen. Grow cattleyas and many other kinds of orchids–in a window, in a case, or under artificial light. 63 illus-trations. 148pp. 5⅜ x 8½.   0-486-23261-1

MONSTER MAZES, Dave Phillips. Masterful mazes at four levels of difficulty. Avoid deadly perils and evil creatures to find magical treasures. Solutions for all 32 exciting illustrated puzzles. 48pp. 8¼ x 11.   0-486-26005-4

MOZART'S DON GIOVANNI (DOVER OPERA LIBRETTO SERIES), Wolfgang Amadeus Mozart. Introduced and translated by Ellen H. Bleiler. Standard Italian libretto, with complete English translation. Convenient and thoroughly portable–an ideal companion for reading along with a recording or the performance itself. Introduction. List of characters. Plot summary. 121pp. 5¼ x 8½. 0-486-24944-1

FRANK LLOYD WRIGHT'S DANA HOUSE, Donald Hoffmann. Pictorial essay of residential masterpiece with over 160 interior and exterior photos, plans, eleva-tions, sketches and studies. 128pp. 9¹/₄ x 10¾.   0-486-29120-0

THE CLARINET AND CLARINET PLAYING, David Pino. Lively, comprehensive work features suggestions about technique, musicianship, and musical interpretation, as well as guidelines for teaching, making your own reeds, and preparing for public performance. Includes an intriguing look at clarinet history. "A godsend," *The Clarinet*, Journal of the International Clarinet Society. Appendixes. 7 illus. 320pp. 5⅜ x 8½. 0-486-40270-3

HOLLYWOOD GLAMOR PORTRAITS, John Kobal (ed.). 145 photos from 1926-49. Harlow, Gable, Bogart, Bacall; 94 stars in all. Full background on photographers, technical aspects. 160pp. 8⅜ x 11¼. 0-486-23352-9

THE RAVEN AND OTHER FAVORITE POEMS, Edgar Allan Poe. Over 40 of the author's most memorable poems: "The Bells," "Ulalume," "Israfel," "To Helen," "The Conqueror Worm," "Eldorado," "Annabel Lee," many more. Alphabetic lists of titles and first lines. 64pp. 5$\frac{3}{16}$ x 8¼. 0-486-26685-0

PERSONAL MEMOIRS OF U. S. GRANT, Ulysses Simpson Grant. Intelligent, deeply moving firsthand account of Civil War campaigns, considered by many the finest military memoirs ever written. Includes letters, historic photographs, maps and more. 528pp. 6⅛ x 9¼. 0-486-28587-1

ANCIENT EGYPTIAN MATERIALS AND INDUSTRIES, A. Lucas and J. Harris. Fascinating, comprehensive, thoroughly documented text describes this ancient civilization's vast resources and the processes that incorporated them in daily life, including the use of animal products, building materials, cosmetics, perfumes and incense, fibers, glazed ware, glass and its manufacture, materials used in the mummification process, and much more. 544pp. 6⅛ x 9¼. (Available in U.S. only.) 0-486-40446-3

RUSSIAN STORIES/RUSSKIE RASSKAZY: A Dual-Language Book, edited by Gleb Struve. Twelve tales by such masters as Chekhov, Tolstoy, Dostoevsky, Pushkin, others. Excellent word-for-word English translations on facing pages, plus teaching and study aids, Russian/English vocabulary, biographical/critical introductions, more. 416pp. 5⅜ x 8½. 0-486-26244-8

PHILADELPHIA THEN AND NOW: 60 Sites Photographed in the Past and Present, Kenneth Finkel and Susan Oyama. Rare photographs of City Hall, Logan Square, Independence Hall, Betsy Ross House, other landmarks juxtaposed with contemporary views. Captures changing face of historic city. Introduction. Captions. 128pp. 8¼ x 11. 0-486-25790-8

NORTH AMERICAN INDIAN LIFE: Customs and Traditions of 23 Tribes, Elsie Clews Parsons (ed.). 27 fictionalized essays by noted anthropologists examine religion, customs, government, additional facets of life among the Winnebago, Crow, Zuni, Eskimo, other tribes. 480pp. 6⅛ x 9¼. 0-486-27377-6

TECHNICAL MANUAL AND DICTIONARY OF CLASSICAL BALLET, Gail Grant. Defines, explains, comments on steps, movements, poses and concepts. 15-page pictorial section. Basic book for student, viewer. 127pp. 5⅜ x 8½. 0-486-21843-0

THE MALE AND FEMALE FIGURE IN MOTION: 60 Classic Photographic Sequences, Eadweard Muybridge. 60 true-action photographs of men and women walking, running, climbing, bending, turning, etc., reproduced from rare 19th-century masterpiece. vi + 121pp. 9 x 12. 0-486-24745-7

ANIMALS: 1,419 Copyright-Free Illustrations of Mammals, Birds, Fish, Insects, etc., Jim Harter (ed.). Clear wood engravings present, in extremely lifelike poses, over 1,000 species of animals. One of the most extensive pictorial sourcebooks of its kind. Captions. Index. 284pp. 9 x 12. 0-486-23766-4

1001 QUESTIONS ANSWERED ABOUT THE SEASHORE, N. J. Berrill and Jacquelyn Berrill. Queries answered about dolphins, sea snails, sponges, starfish, fishes, shore birds, many others. Covers appearance, breeding, growth, feeding, much more. 305pp. 5¼ x 8¼. 0-486-23366-9

ATTRACTING BIRDS TO YOUR YARD, William J. Weber. Easy-to-follow guide offers advice on how to attract the greatest diversity of birds: birdhouses, feeders, water and waterers, much more. 96pp. 5³⁄₁₆ x 8¼. 0-486-28927-3

MEDICINAL AND OTHER USES OF NORTH AMERICAN PLANTS: A Historical Survey with Special Reference to the Eastern Indian Tribes, Charlotte Erichsen-Brown. Chronological historical citations document 500 years of usage of plants, trees, shrubs native to eastern Canada, northeastern U.S. Also complete identifying information. 343 illustrations. 544pp. 6½ x 9¼. 0-486-25951-X

STORYBOOK MAZES, Dave Phillips. 23 stories and mazes on two-page spreads: Wizard of Oz, Treasure Island, Robin Hood, etc. Solutions. 64pp. 8¼ x 11. 0-486-23628-5

AMERICAN NEGRO SONGS: 230 Folk Songs and Spirituals, Religious and Secular, John W. Work. This authoritative study traces the African influences of songs sung and played by black Americans at work, in church, and as entertainment. The author discusses the lyric significance of such songs as "Swing Low, Sweet Chariot," "John Henry," and others and offers the words and music for 230 songs. Bibliography. Index of Song Titles. 272pp. 6½ x 9¼. 0-486-40271-1

MOVIE-STAR PORTRAITS OF THE FORTIES, John Kobal (ed.). 163 glamor, studio photos of 106 stars of the 1940s: Rita Hayworth, Ava Gardner, Marlon Brando, Clark Gable, many more. 176pp. 8⅜ x 11¼. 0-486-23546-7

YEKL and THE IMPORTED BRIDEGROOM AND OTHER STORIES OF YIDDISH NEW YORK, Abraham Cahan. Film Hester Street based on Yekl (1896). Novel, other stories among first about Jewish immigrants on N.Y.'s East Side. 240pp. 5⅜ x 8½. 0-486-22427-9

SELECTED POEMS, Walt Whitman. Generous sampling from Leaves of Grass. Twenty-four poems include "I Hear America Singing," "Song of the Open Road," "I Sing the Body Electric," "When Lilacs Last in the Dooryard Bloom'd," "O Captain! My Captain!"–all reprinted from an authoritative edition. Lists of titles and first lines. 128pp. 5³⁄₁₆ x 8¼. 0-486-26878-0

SONGS OF EXPERIENCE: Facsimile Reproduction with 26 Plates in Full Color, William Blake. 26 full-color plates from a rare 1826 edition. Includes "The Tyger," "London," "Holy Thursday," and other poems. Printed text of poems. 48pp. 5¼ x 7. 0-486-24636-1

THE BEST TALES OF HOFFMANN, E. T. A. Hoffmann. 10 of Hoffmann's most important stories: "Nutcracker and the King of Mice," "The Golden Flowerpot," etc. 458pp. 5⅜ x 8½. 0-486-21793-0

THE BOOK OF TEA, Kakuzo Okakura. Minor classic of the Orient: entertaining, charming explanation, interpretation of traditional Japanese culture in terms of tea ceremony. 94pp. 5⅜ x 8½. 0-486-20070-1

FRENCH STORIES/CONTES FRANÇAIS: A Dual-Language Book, Wallace Fowlie. Ten stories by French masters, Voltaire to Camus: "Micromegas" by Voltaire; "The Atheist's Mass" by Balzac; "Minuet" by de Maupassant; "The Guest" by Camus, six more. Excellent English translations on facing pages. Also French-English vocabulary list, exercises, more. 352pp. 5⅜ x 8½. 0-486-26443-2

CHICAGO AT THE TURN OF THE CENTURY IN PHOTOGRAPHS: 122 Historic Views from the Collections of the Chicago Historical Society, Larry A. Viskochil. Rare large-format prints offer detailed views of City Hall, State Street, the Loop, Hull House, Union Station, many other landmarks, circa 1904-1913. Introduction. Captions. Maps. 144pp. 9⅜ x 12¼. 0-486-24656-6

OLD BROOKLYN IN EARLY PHOTOGRAPHS, 1865-1929, William Lee Younger. Luna Park, Gravesend race track, construction of Grand Army Plaza, moving of Hotel Brighton, etc. 157 previously unpublished photographs. 165pp. 8⅞ x 11¾. 0-486-23587-4

THE MYTHS OF THE NORTH AMERICAN INDIANS, Lewis Spence. Rich anthology of the myths and legends of the Algonquins, Iroquois, Pawnees and Sioux, prefaced by an extensive historical and ethnological commentary. 36 illustrations. 480pp. 5⅜ x 8½. 0-486-25967-6

AN ENCYCLOPEDIA OF BATTLES: Accounts of Over 1,560 Battles from 1479 B.C. to the Present, David Eggenberger. Essential details of every major battle in recorded history from the first battle of Megiddo in 1479 B.C. to Grenada in 1984. List of Battle Maps. New Appendix covering the years 1967-1984. Index. 99 illustrations. 544pp. 6½ x 9¼. 0-486-24913-1

SAILING ALONE AROUND THE WORLD, Captain Joshua Slocum. First man to sail around the world, alone, in small boat. One of great feats of seamanship told in delightful manner. 67 illustrations. 294pp. 5⅜ x 8½. 0-486-20326-3

ANARCHISM AND OTHER ESSAYS, Emma Goldman. Powerful, penetrating, prophetic essays on direct action, role of minorities, prison reform, puritan hypocrisy, violence, etc. 271pp. 5⅜ x 8½. 0-486-22484-8

MYTHS OF THE HINDUS AND BUDDHISTS, Ananda K. Coomaraswamy and Sister Nivedita. Great stories of the epics; deeds of Krishna, Shiva, taken from puranas, Vedas, folk tales; etc. 32 illustrations. 400pp. 5⅜ x 8½. 0-486-21759-0

MY BONDAGE AND MY FREEDOM, Frederick Douglass. Born a slave, Douglass became outspoken force in antislavery movement. The best of Douglass' autobiographies. Graphic description of slave life. 464pp. 5⅜ x 8½. 0-486-22457-0

FOLLOWING THE EQUATOR: A Journey Around the World, Mark Twain. Fascinating humorous account of 1897 voyage to Hawaii, Australia, India, New Zealand, etc. Ironic, bemused reports on peoples, customs, climate, flora and fauna, politics, much more. 197 illustrations. 720pp. 5⅜ x 8½. 0-486-26113-1

THE PEOPLE CALLED SHAKERS, Edward D. Andrews. Definitive study of Shakers: origins, beliefs, practices, dances, social organization, furniture and crafts, etc. 33 illustrations. 351pp. 5⅜ x 8½. 0-486-21081-2

THE MYTHS OF GREECE AND ROME, H. A. Guerber. A classic of mythology, generously illustrated, long prized for its simple, graphic, accurate retelling of the principal myths of Greece and Rome, and for its commentary on their origins and significance. With 64 illustrations by Michelangelo, Raphael, Titian, Rubens, Canova, Bernini and others. 480pp. 5⅜ x 8½. 0-486-27584-1

PSYCHOLOGY OF MUSIC, Carl E. Seashore. Classic work discusses music as a medium from psychological viewpoint. Clear treatment of physical acoustics, auditory apparatus, sound perception, development of musical skills, nature of musical feeling, host of other topics. 88 figures. 408pp. 5⅜ x 8½. 0-486-21851-1

LIFE IN ANCIENT EGYPT, Adolf Erman. Fullest, most thorough, detailed older account with much not in more recent books, domestic life, religion, magic, medicine, commerce, much more. Many illustrations reproduce tomb paintings, carvings, hieroglyphs, etc. 597pp. 5⅜ x 8½. 0-486-22632-8

SUNDIALS, Their Theory and Construction, Albert Waugh. Far and away the best, most thorough coverage of ideas, mathematics concerned, types, construction, adjusting anywhere. Simple, nontechnical treatment allows even children to build several of these dials. Over 100 illustrations. 230pp. 5⅜ x 8½. 0-486-22947-5

THEORETICAL HYDRODYNAMICS, L. M. Milne-Thomson. Classic exposition of the mathematical theory of fluid motion, applicable to both hydrodynamics and aerodynamics. Over 600 exercises. 768pp. 6⅛ x 9¼. 0-486-68970-0

OLD-TIME VIGNETTES IN FULL COLOR, Carol Belanger Grafton (ed.). Over 390 charming, often sentimental illustrations, selected from archives of Victorian graphics–pretty women posing, children playing, food, flowers, kittens and puppies, smiling cherubs, birds and butterflies, much more. All copyright-free. 48pp. 9¼ x 12¼. 0-486-27269-9

PERSPECTIVE FOR ARTISTS, Rex Vicat Cole. Depth, perspective of sky and sea, shadows, much more, not usually covered. 391 diagrams, 81 reproductions of drawings and paintings. 279pp. 5⅜ x 8½. 0-486-22487-2

DRAWING THE LIVING FIGURE, Joseph Sheppard. Innovative approach to artistic anatomy focuses on specifics of surface anatomy, rather than muscles and bones. Over 170 drawings of live models in front, back and side views, and in widely varying poses. Accompanying diagrams. 177 illustrations. Introduction. Index. 144pp. 8⅜ x11¼. 0-486-26723-7

GOTHIC AND OLD ENGLISH ALPHABETS: 100 Complete Fonts, Dan X. Solo. Add power, elegance to posters, signs, other graphics with 100 stunning copyright-free alphabets: Blackstone, Dolbey, Germania, 97 more–including many lower-case, numerals, punctuation marks. 104pp. 8⅛ x 11. 0-486-24695-7

THE BOOK OF WOOD CARVING, Charles Marshall Sayers. Finest book for beginners discusses fundamentals and offers 34 designs. "Absolutely first rate . . . well thought out and well executed."–E. J. Tangerman. 118pp. 7¾ x 10⅝. 0-486-23654-4

ILLUSTRATED CATALOG OF CIVIL WAR MILITARY GOODS: Union Army Weapons, Insignia, Uniform Accessories, and Other Equipment, Schuyler, Hartley, and Graham. Rare, profusely illustrated 1846 catalog includes Union Army uniform and dress regulations, arms and ammunition, coats, insignia, flags, swords, rifles, etc. 226 illustrations. 160pp. 9 x 12. 0-486-24939-5

WOMEN'S FASHIONS OF THE EARLY 1900s: An Unabridged Republication of "New York Fashions, 1909," National Cloak & Suit Co. Rare catalog of mail-order fashions documents women's and children's clothing styles shortly after the turn of the century. Captions offer full descriptions, prices. Invaluable resource for fashion, costume historians. Approximately 725 illustrations. 128pp. 8⅜ x 11¼. 0-486-27276-1

HOW TO DO BEADWORK, Mary White. Fundamental book on craft from simple projects to five-bead chains and woven works. 106 illustrations. 142pp. 5⅜ x 8.
0-486-20697-1

THE 1912 AND 1915 GUSTAV STICKLEY FURNITURE CATALOGS, Gustav Stickley. With over 200 detailed illustrations and descriptions, these two catalogs are essential reading and reference materials and identification guides for Stickley furniture. Captions cite materials, dimensions and prices. 112pp. 6½ x 9¼. 0-486-26676-1

EARLY AMERICAN LOCOMOTIVES, John H. White, Jr. Finest locomotive engravings from early 19th century: historical (1804–74), main-line (after 1870), special, foreign, etc. 147 plates. 142pp. 11⅜ x 8¼. 0-486-22772-3

LITTLE BOOK OF EARLY AMERICAN CRAFTS AND TRADES, Peter Stockham (ed.). 1807 children's book explains crafts and trades: baker, hatter, cooper, potter, and many others. 23 copperplate illustrations. 140pp. 4⅝ x 6.
0-486-23336-7

VICTORIAN FASHIONS AND COSTUMES FROM HARPER'S BAZAR, 1867–1898, Stella Blum (ed.). Day costumes, evening wear, sports clothes, shoes, hats, other accessories in over 1,000 detailed engravings. 320pp. 9⅜ x 12¼.
0-486-22990-4

THE LONG ISLAND RAIL ROAD IN EARLY PHOTOGRAPHS, Ron Ziel. Over 220 rare photos, informative text document origin (1844) and development of rail service on Long Island. Vintage views of early trains, locomotives, stations, passengers, crews, much more. Captions. 8⅞ x 11¾. 0-486-26301-0

VOYAGE OF THE LIBERDADE, Joshua Slocum. Great 19th-century mariner's thrilling, first-hand account of the wreck of his ship off South America, the 35-foot boat he built from the wreckage, and its remarkable voyage home. 128pp. 5⅜ x 8½.
0-486-40022-0

TEN BOOKS ON ARCHITECTURE, Vitruvius. The most important book ever written on architecture. Early Roman aesthetics, technology, classical orders, site selection, all other aspects. Morgan translation. 331pp. 5⅜ x 8½. 0-486-20645-9

THE HUMAN FIGURE IN MOTION, Eadweard Muybridge. More than 4,500 stopped-action photos, in action series, showing undraped men, women, children jumping, lying down, throwing, sitting, wrestling, carrying, etc. 390pp. 7⅞ x 10⅝.
0-486-20204-6 Clothbd.

TREES OF THE EASTERN AND CENTRAL UNITED STATES AND CANADA, William M. Harlow. Best one-volume guide to 140 trees. Full descriptions, woodlore, range, etc. Over 600 illustrations. Handy size. 288pp. 4½ x 6⅜. 0-486-20395-6

GROWING AND USING HERBS AND SPICES, Milo Miloradovich. Versatile handbook provides all the information needed for cultivation and use of all the herbs and spices available in North America. 4 illustrations. Index. Glossary. 236pp. 5⅜ x 8½.
0-486-25058-X

BIG BOOK OF MAZES AND LABYRINTHS, Walter Shepherd. 50 mazes and labyrinths in all–classical, solid, ripple, and more–in one great volume. Perfect inexpensive puzzler for clever youngsters. Full solutions. 112pp. 8⅛ x 11. 0-486-22951-3

PIANO TUNING, J. Cree Fischer. Clearest, best book for beginner, amateur. Simple repairs, raising dropped notes, tuning by easy method of flattened fifths. No previous skills needed. 4 illustrations. 201pp. 5⅜ x 8½. 0-486-23267-0

HINTS TO SINGERS, Lillian Nordica. Selecting the right teacher, developing confidence, overcoming stage fright, and many other important skills receive thoughtful discussion in this indispensible guide, written by a world-famous diva of four decades' experience. 96pp. 5⅜ x 8½. 0-486-40094-8

THE COMPLETE NONSENSE OF EDWARD LEAR, Edward Lear. All nonsense limericks, zany alphabets, Owl and Pussycat, songs, nonsense botany, etc., illustrated by Lear. Total of 320pp. 5⅜ x 8½. (Available in U.S. only.) 0-486-20167-8

VICTORIAN PARLOUR POETRY: An Annotated Anthology, Michael R. Turner. 117 gems by Longfellow, Tennyson, Browning, many lesser-known poets. "The Village Blacksmith," "Curfew Must Not Ring Tonight," "Only a Baby Small," dozens more, often difficult to find elsewhere. Index of poets, titles, first lines. xxiii + 325pp. 5⅝ x 8¼. 0-486-27044-0

DUBLINERS, James Joyce. Fifteen stories offer vivid, tightly focused observations of the lives of Dublin's poorer classes. At least one, "The Dead," is considered a masterpiece. Reprinted complete and unabridged from standard edition. 160pp. 5³⁄₁₆ x 8¼. 0-486-26870-5

GREAT WEIRD TALES: 14 Stories by Lovecraft, Blackwood, Machen and Others, S. T. Joshi (ed.). 14 spellbinding tales, including "The Sin Eater," by Fiona McLeod, "The Eye Above the Mantel," by Frank Belknap Long, as well as renowned works by R. H. Barlow, Lord Dunsany, Arthur Machen, W. C. Morrow and eight other masters of the genre. 256pp. 5⅜ x 8½. (Available in U.S. only.) 0-486-40436-6

THE BOOK OF THE SACRED MAGIC OF ABRAMELIN THE MAGE, translated by S. MacGregor Mathers. Medieval manuscript of ceremonial magic. Basic document in Aleister Crowley, Golden Dawn groups. 268pp. 5⅜ x 8½. 0-486-23211-5

THE BATTLES THAT CHANGED HISTORY, Fletcher Pratt. Eminent historian profiles 16 crucial conflicts, ancient to modern, that changed the course of civilization. 352pp. 5⅜ x 8½. 0-486-41129-X

NEW RUSSIAN-ENGLISH AND ENGLISH-RUSSIAN DICTIONARY, M. A. O'Brien. This is a remarkably handy Russian dictionary, containing a surprising amount of information, including over 70,000 entries. 366pp. 4½ x 6⅛. 0-486-20208-9

NEW YORK IN THE FORTIES, Andreas Feininger. 162 brilliant photographs by the well-known photographer, formerly with *Life* magazine. Commuters, shoppers, Times Square at night, much else from city at its peak. Captions by John von Hartz. 181pp. 9¼ x 10¾. 0-486-23585-8

INDIAN SIGN LANGUAGE, William Tomkins. Over 525 signs developed by Sioux and other tribes. Written instructions and diagrams. Also 290 pictographs. 111pp. 6⅛ x 9¼. 0-486-22029-X

ANATOMY: A Complete Guide for Artists, Joseph Sheppard. A master of figure drawing shows artists how to render human anatomy convincingly. Over 460 illustrations. 224pp. 8⅜ x 11¼. 0-486-27279-6

MEDIEVAL CALLIGRAPHY: Its History and Technique, Marc Drogin. Spirited history, comprehensive instruction manual covers 13 styles (ca. 4th century through 15th). Excellent photographs; directions for duplicating medieval techniques with modern tools. 224pp. 8⅜ x 11¼. 0-486-26142-5

DRIED FLOWERS: How to Prepare Them, Sarah Whitlock and Martha Rankin. Complete instructions on how to use silica gel, meal and borax, perlite aggregate, sand and borax, glycerine and water to create attractive permanent flower arrangements. 12 illustrations. 32pp. 5⅜ x 8½. 0-486-21802-3

EASY-TO-MAKE BIRD FEEDERS FOR WOODWORKERS, Scott D. Campbell. Detailed, simple-to-use guide for designing, constructing, caring for and using feeders. Text, illustrations for 12 classic and contemporary designs. 96pp. 5⅜ x 8½. 0-486-25847-5

THE COMPLETE BOOK OF BIRDHOUSE CONSTRUCTION FOR WOOD-WORKERS, Scott D. Campbell. Detailed instructions, illustrations, tables. Also data on bird habitat and instinct patterns. Bibliography. 3 tables. 63 illustrations in 15 figures. 48pp. 5¼ x 8½. 0-486-24407-5

SCOTTISH WONDER TALES FROM MYTH AND LEGEND, Donald A. Mackenzie. 16 lively tales tell of giants rumbling down mountainsides, of a magic wand that turns stone pillars into warriors, of gods and goddesses, evil hags, powerful forces and more. 240pp. 5⅜ x 8½. 0-486-29677-6

THE HISTORY OF UNDERCLOTHES, C. Willett Cunnington and Phyllis Cunnington. Fascinating, well-documented survey covering six centuries of English undergarments, enhanced with over 100 illustrations: 12th-century laced-up bodice, footed long drawers (1795), 19th-century bustles, 19th-century corsets for men, Victorian "bust improvers," much more. 272pp. 5⅜ x 8¼. 0-486-27124-2

ARTS AND CRAFTS FURNITURE: The Complete Brooks Catalog of 1912, Brooks Manufacturing Co. Photos and detailed descriptions of more than 150 now very collectible furniture designs from the Arts and Crafts movement depict davenports, settees, buffets, desks, tables, chairs, bedsteads, dressers and more, all built of solid, quarter-sawed oak. Invaluable for students and enthusiasts of antiques, Americana and the decorative arts. 80pp. 6½ x 9¼. 0-486-27471-3

WILBUR AND ORVILLE: A Biography of the Wright Brothers, Fred Howard. Definitive, crisply written study tells the full story of the brothers' lives and work. A vividly written biography, unparalleled in scope and color, that also captures the spirit of an extraordinary era. 560pp. 6⅛ x 9¼. 0-486-40297-5

THE ARTS OF THE SAILOR: Knotting, Splicing and Ropework, Hervey Garrett Smith. Indispensable shipboard reference covers tools, basic knots and useful hitches; handsewing and canvas work, more. Over 100 illustrations. Delightful reading for sea lovers. 256pp. 5⅜ x 8½. 0-486-26440-8

FRANK LLOYD WRIGHT'S FALLINGWATER: The House and Its History, Second, Revised Edition, Donald Hoffmann. A total revision—both in text and illustrations—of the standard document on Fallingwater, the boldest, most personal architectural statement of Wright's mature years, updated with valuable new material from the recently opened Frank Lloyd Wright Archives. "Fascinating"–*The New York Times*. 116 illustrations. 128pp. 9¼ x 10¾. 0-486-27430-6

PHOTOGRAPHIC SKETCHBOOK OF THE CIVIL WAR, Alexander Gardner. 100 photos taken on field during the Civil War. Famous shots of Manassas Harper's Ferry, Lincoln, Richmond, slave pens, etc. 244pp. 10⅝ x 8¼. 0-486-22731-6

FIVE ACRES AND INDEPENDENCE, Maurice G. Kains. Great back-to-the-land classic explains basics of self-sufficient farming. The one book to get. 95 illustrations. 397pp. 5⅜ x 8½. 0-486-20974-1

A MODERN HERBAL, Margaret Grieve. Much the fullest, most exact, most useful compilation of herbal material. Gigantic alphabetical encyclopedia, from aconite to zedoary, gives botanical information, medical properties, folklore, economic uses, much else. Indispensable to serious reader. 161 illustrations. 888pp. 6½ x 9¼. 2-vol. set. (Available in U.S. only.)   Vol. I: 0-486-22798-7   Vol. II: 0-486-22799-5

HIDDEN TREASURE MAZE BOOK, Dave Phillips. Solve 34 challenging mazes accompanied by heroic tales of adventure. Evil dragons, people-eating plants, blood-thirsty giants, many more dangerous adversaries lurk at every twist and turn. 34 mazes, stories, solutions. 48pp. 8¼ x 11.   0-486-24566-7

LETTERS OF W. A. MOZART, Wolfgang A. Mozart. Remarkable letters show bawdy wit, humor, imagination, musical insights, contemporary musical world; includes some letters from Leopold Mozart. 276pp. 5⅜ x 8½.   0-486-22859-2

BASIC PRINCIPLES OF CLASSICAL BALLET, Agrippina Vaganova. Great Russian theoretician, teacher explains methods for teaching classical ballet. 118 illustrations. 175pp. 5⅜ x 8½.   0-486-22036-2

THE JUMPING FROG, Mark Twain. Revenge edition. The original story of The Celebrated Jumping Frog of Calaveras County, a hapless French translation, and Twain's hilarious "retranslation" from the French. 12 illustrations. 66pp. 5⅜ x 8½.
0-486-22686-7

BEST REMEMBERED POEMS, Martin Gardner (ed.). The 126 poems in this superb collection of 19th- and 20th-century British and American verse range from Shelley's "To a Skylark" to the impassioned "Renascence" of Edna St. Vincent Millay and to Edward Lear's whimsical "The Owl and the Pussycat." 224pp. 5⅜ x 8½.
0-486-27165-X

COMPLETE SONNETS, William Shakespeare. Over 150 exquisite poems deal with love, friendship, the tyranny of time, beauty's evanescence, death and other themes in language of remarkable power, precision and beauty. Glossary of archaic terms. 80pp. 5³⁄₁₆ x 8¼.   0-486-26686-9

HISTORIC HOMES OF THE AMERICAN PRESIDENTS, Second, Revised Edition, Irvin Haas. A traveler's guide to American Presidential homes, most open to the public, depicting and describing homes occupied by every American President from George Washington to George Bush. With visiting hours, admission charges, travel routes. 175 photographs. Index. 160pp. 8¼ x 11.   0-486-26751-2

THE WIT AND HUMOR OF OSCAR WILDE, Alvin Redman (ed.). More than 1,000 ripostes, paradoxes, wisecracks: Work is the curse of the drinking classes; I can resist everything except temptation; etc. 258pp. 5⅜ x 8½.   0-486-20602-5

SHAKESPEARE LEXICON AND QUOTATION DICTIONARY, Alexander Schmidt. Full definitions, locations, shades of meaning in every word in plays and poems. More than 50,000 exact quotations. 1,485pp. 6½ x 9¼. 2-vol. set.
Vol. 1: 0-486-22726-X   Vol. 2: 0-486-22727-8

SELECTED POEMS, Emily Dickinson. Over 100 best-known, best-loved poems by one of America's foremost poets, reprinted from authoritative early editions. No comparable edition at this price. Index of first lines. 64pp. 5³⁄₁₆ x 8¼. 0-486-26466-1

THE INSIDIOUS DR. FU-MANCHU, Sax Rohmer. The first of the popular mystery series introduces a pair of English detectives to their archnemesis, the diabolical Dr. Fu-Manchu. Flavorful atmosphere, fast-paced action, and colorful characters enliven this classic of the genre. 208pp. 5³⁄₁₆ x 8¼.   0-486-29898-1

THE MALLEUS MALEFICARUM OF KRAMER AND SPRENGER, translated by Montague Summers. Full text of most important witchhunter's "bible," used by both Catholics and Protestants. 278pp. 6⅝ x 10. 0-486-22802-9

SPANISH STORIES/CUENTOS ESPAÑOLES: A Dual-Language Book, Angel Flores (ed.). Unique format offers 13 great stories in Spanish by Cervantes, Borges, others. Faithful English translations on facing pages. 352pp. 5⅜ x 8½. 0-486-25399-6

GARDEN CITY, LONG ISLAND, IN EARLY PHOTOGRAPHS, 1869–1919, Mildred H. Smith. Handsome treasury of 118 vintage pictures, accompanied by carefully researched captions, document the Garden City Hotel fire (1899), the Vanderbilt Cup Race (1908), the first airmail flight departing from the Nassau Boulevard Aerodrome (1911), and much more. 96pp. 8⅞ x 11¾. 0-486-40669-5

OLD QUEENS, N.Y., IN EARLY PHOTOGRAPHS, Vincent F. Seyfried and William Asadorian. Over 160 rare photographs of Maspeth, Jamaica, Jackson Heights, and other areas. Vintage views of DeWitt Clinton mansion, 1939 World's Fair and more. Captions. 192pp. 8⅞ x 11. 0-486-26358-4

CAPTURED BY THE INDIANS: 15 Firsthand Accounts, 1750-1870, Frederick Drimmer. Astounding true historical accounts of grisly torture, bloody conflicts, relentless pursuits, miraculous escapes and more, by people who lived to tell the tale. 384pp. 5⅜ x 8½. 0-486-24901-8

THE WORLD'S GREAT SPEECHES (Fourth Enlarged Edition), Lewis Copeland, Lawrence W. Lamm, and Stephen J. McKenna. Nearly 300 speeches provide public speakers with a wealth of updated quotes and inspiration–from Pericles' funeral oration and William Jennings Bryan's "Cross of Gold Speech" to Malcolm X's powerful words on the Black Revolution and Earl of Spenser's tribute to his sister, Diana, Princess of Wales. 944pp. 5⅜ x 8⅜. 0-486-40903-1

THE BOOK OF THE SWORD, Sir Richard F. Burton. Great Victorian scholar/adventurer's eloquent, erudite history of the "queen of weapons"–from prehistory to early Roman Empire. Evolution and development of early swords, variations (sabre, broadsword, cutlass, scimitar, etc.), much more. 336pp. 6⅛ x 9¼. 0-486-25434-8

AUTOBIOGRAPHY: The Story of My Experiments with Truth, Mohandas K. Gandhi. Boyhood, legal studies, purification, the growth of the Satyagraha (nonviolent protest) movement. Critical, inspiring work of the man responsible for the freedom of India. 480pp. 5⅜ x 8½. (Available in U.S. only.) 0-486-24593-4

CELTIC MYTHS AND LEGENDS, T. W. Rolleston. Masterful retelling of Irish and Welsh stories and tales. Cuchulain, King Arthur, Deirdre, the Grail, many more. First paperback edition. 58 full-page illustrations. 512pp. 5⅜ x 8½. 0-486-26507-2

THE PRINCIPLES OF PSYCHOLOGY, William James. Famous long course complete, unabridged. Stream of thought, time perception, memory, experimental methods; great work decades ahead of its time. 94 figures. 1,391pp. 5⅜ x 8½. 2-vol. set.
Vol. I: 0-486-20381-6 Vol. II: 0-486-20382-4

THE WORLD AS WILL AND REPRESENTATION, Arthur Schopenhauer. Definitive English translation of Schopenhauer's life work, correcting more than 1,000 errors, omissions in earlier translations. Translated by E. F. J. Payne. Total of 1,269pp. 5⅜ x 8½. 2-vol. set. Vol. 1: 0-486-21761-2 Vol. 2: 0-486-21762-0

MAGIC AND MYSTERY IN TIBET, Madame Alexandra David-Neel. Experiences among lamas, magicians, sages, sorcerers, Bonpa wizards. A true psychic discovery. 32 illustrations. 321pp. 5⅜ x 8½. (Available in U.S. only.)　　0-486-22682-4

THE EGYPTIAN BOOK OF THE DEAD, E. A. Wallis Budge. Complete reproduction of Ani's papyrus, finest ever found. Full hieroglyphic text, interlinear transliteration, word-for-word translation, smooth translation. 533pp. 6½ x 9¼.
　　0-486-21866-X

HISTORIC COSTUME IN PICTURES, Braun & Schneider. Over 1,450 costumed figures in clearly detailed engravings–from dawn of civilization to end of 19th century. Captions. Many folk costumes. 256pp. 8⅜ x 11¾.　　0-486-23150-X

MATHEMATICS FOR THE NONMATHEMATICIAN, Morris Kline. Detailed, college-level treatment of mathematics in cultural and historical context, with numerous exercises. Recommended Reading Lists. Tables. Numerous figures. 641pp. 5⅜ x 8½.
　　0-486-24823-2

PROBABILISTIC METHODS IN THE THEORY OF STRUCTURES, Isaac Elishakoff. Well-written introduction covers the elements of the theory of probability from two or more random variables, the reliability of such multivariable structures, the theory of random function, Monte Carlo methods of treating problems incapable of exact solution, and more. Examples. 502pp. 5⅜ x 8½.　　0-486-40691-1

THE RIME OF THE ANCIENT MARINER, Gustave Doré, S. T. Coleridge. Doré's finest work; 34 plates capture moods, subtleties of poem. Flawless full-size reproductions printed on facing pages with authoritative text of poem. "Beautiful. Simply beautiful."–*Publisher's Weekly.* 77pp. 9¼ x 12.　　0-486-22305-1

SCULPTURE: Principles and Practice, Louis Slobodkin. Step-by-step approach to clay, plaster, metals, stone; classical and modern. 253 drawings, photos. 255pp. 8⅛ x 11.
　　0-486-22960-2

THE INFLUENCE OF SEA POWER UPON HISTORY, 1660–1783, A. T. Mahan. Influential classic of naval history and tactics still used as text in war colleges. First paperback edition. 4 maps. 24 battle plans. 640pp. 5⅜ x 8½.　　0-486-25509-3

THE STORY OF THE TITANIC AS TOLD BY ITS SURVIVORS, Jack Winocour (ed.). What it was really like. Panic, despair, shocking inefficiency, and a little heroism. More thrilling than any fictional account. 26 illustrations. 320pp. 5⅜ x 8½.
　　0-486-20610-6

ONE TWO THREE . . . INFINITY: Facts and Speculations of Science, George Gamow. Great physicist's fascinating, readable overview of contemporary science: number theory, relativity, fourth dimension, entropy, genes, atomic structure, much more. 128 illustrations. Index. 352pp. 5⅜ x 8½.　　0-486-25664-2

DALÍ ON MODERN ART: The Cuckolds of Antiquated Modern Art, Salvador Dalí. Influential painter skewers modern art and its practitioners. Outrageous evaluations of Picasso, Cézanne, Turner, more. 15 renderings of paintings discussed. 44 calligraphic decorations by Dalí. 96pp. 5⅜ x 8½. (Available in U.S. only.)　　0-486-29220-7

ANTIQUE PLAYING CARDS: A Pictorial History, Henry René D'Allemagne. Over 900 elaborate, decorative images from rare playing cards (14th–20th centuries): Bacchus, death, dancing dogs, hunting scenes, royal coats of arms, players cheating, much more. 96pp. 9¼ x 12¼.　　0-486-29265-7

MAKING FURNITURE MASTERPIECES: 30 Projects with Measured Drawings, Franklin H. Gottshall. Step-by-step instructions, illustrations for constructing handsome, useful pieces, among them a Sheraton desk, Chippendale chair, Spanish desk, Queen Anne table and a William and Mary dressing mirror. 224pp. 8⅛ x 11¼. 0-486-29338-6

NORTH AMERICAN INDIAN DESIGNS FOR ARTISTS AND CRAFTSPEOPLE, Eva Wilson. Over 360 authentic copyright-free designs adapted from Navajo blankets, Hopi pottery, Sioux buffalo hides, more. Geometrics, symbolic figures, plant and animal motifs, etc. 128pp. 8⅜ x 11. (Not for sale in the United Kingdom.) 0-486-25341-4

THE FOSSIL BOOK: A Record of Prehistoric Life, Patricia V. Rich et al. Profusely illustrated definitive guide covers everything from single-celled organisms and dinosaurs to birds and mammals and the interplay between climate and man. Over 1,500 illustrations. 760pp. 7½ x 10⅛. 0-486-29371-8

VICTORIAN ARCHITECTURAL DETAILS: Designs for Over 700 Stairs, Mantels, Doors, Windows, Cornices, Porches, and Other Decorative Elements, A. J. Bicknell & Company. Everything from dormer windows and piazzas to balconies and gable ornaments. Also includes elevations and floor plans for handsome, private residences and commercial structures. 80pp. 9⅜ x 12¼. 0-486-44015-X

WESTERN ISLAMIC ARCHITECTURE: A Concise Introduction, John D. Hoag. Profusely illustrated critical appraisal compares and contrasts Islamic mosques and palaces—from Spain and Egypt to other areas in the Middle East. 139 illustrations. 128pp. 6 x 9. 0-486-43760-4

CHINESE ARCHITECTURE: A Pictorial History, Liang Ssu-ch'eng. More than 240 rare photographs and drawings depict temples, pagodas, tombs, bridges, and imperial palaces comprising much of China's architectural heritage. 152 halftones, 94 diagrams. 232pp. 10¾ x 9⅞. 0-486-43999-2

THE RENAISSANCE: Studies in Art and Poetry, Walter Pater. One of the most talked-about books of the 19th century, *The Renaissance* combines scholarship and philosophy in an innovative work of cultural criticism that examines the achievements of Botticelli, Leonardo, Michelangelo, and other artists. "The holy writ of beauty."–Oscar Wilde. 160pp. 5⅜ x 8½. 0-486-44025-7

A TREATISE ON PAINTING, Leonardo da Vinci. The great Renaissance artist's practical advice on drawing and painting techniques covers anatomy, perspective, composition, light and shadow, and color. A classic of art instruction, it features 48 drawings by Nicholas Poussin and Leon Battista Alberti. 192pp. 5⅜ x 8½.

0-486-44155-5

THE MIND OF LEONARDO DA VINCI, Edward McCurdy. More than just a biography, this classic study by a distinguished historian draws upon Leonardo's extensive writings to offer numerous demonstrations of the Renaissance master's achievements, not only in sculpture and painting, but also in music, engineering, and even experimental aviation. 384pp. 5⅜ x 8½. 0-486-44142-3

WASHINGTON IRVING'S RIP VAN WINKLE, Illustrated by Arthur Rackham. Lovely prints that established artist as a leading illustrator of the time and forever etched into the popular imagination a classic of Catskill lore. 51 full-color plates. 80pp. 8⅜ x 11. 0-486-44242-X

HENSCHE ON PAINTING, John W. Robichaux. Basic painting philosophy and methodology of a great teacher, as expounded in his famous classes and workshops on Cape Cod. 7 illustrations in color on covers. 80pp. 5⅜ x 8½. 0-486-43728-0

LIGHT AND SHADE: A Classic Approach to Three-Dimensional Drawing, Mrs. Mary P. Merrifield. Handy reference clearly demonstrates principles of light and shade by revealing effects of common daylight, sunshine, and candle or artificial light on geometrical solids. 13 plates. 64pp. 5⅜ x 8½. 0-486-44143-1

ASTROLOGY AND ASTRONOMY: A Pictorial Archive of Signs and Symbols, Ernst and Johanna Lehner. Treasure trove of stories, lore, and myth, accompanied by more than 300 rare illustrations of planets, the Milky Way, signs of the zodiac, comets, meteors, and other astronomical phenomena. 192pp. 8⅜ x 11. 0-486-43981-X

JEWELRY MAKING: Techniques for Metal, Tim McCreight. Easy-to-follow instructions and carefully executed illustrations describe tools and techniques, use of gems and enamels, wire inlay, casting, and other topics. 72 line illustrations and diagrams. 176pp. 8¼ x 10⅞. 0-486-44043-5

MAKING BIRDHOUSES: Easy and Advanced Projects, Gladstone Califf. Easy-to-follow instructions include diagrams for everything from a one-room house for bluebirds to a forty-two-room structure for purple martins. 56 plates; 4 figures. 80pp. 8¾ x 6⅜. 0-486-44183-0

LITTLE BOOK OF LOG CABINS: How to Build and Furnish Them, William S. Wicks. Handy how-to manual, with instructions and illustrations for building cabins in the Adirondack style, fireplaces, stairways, furniture, beamed ceilings, and more. 102 line drawings. 96pp. 8¾ x 6⅜. 0-486-44259-4

THE SEASONS OF AMERICA PAST, Eric Sloane. From "sugaring time" and strawberry picking to Indian summer and fall harvest, a whole year's activities described in charming prose and enhanced with 79 of the author's own illustrations. 160pp. 8¼ x 11. 0-486-44220-9

THE METROPOLIS OF TOMORROW, Hugh Ferriss. Generous, prophetic vision of the metropolis of the future, as perceived in 1929. Powerful illustrations of towering structures, wide avenues, and rooftop parks–all features in many of today's modern cities. 59 illustrations. 144pp. 8¼ x 11. 0-486-43727-2

THE PATH TO ROME, Hilaire Belloc. This 1902 memoir abounds in lively vignettes from a vanished time, recounting a pilgrimage on foot across the Alps and Apennines in order to "see all Europe which the Christian Faith has saved." 77 of the author's original line drawings complement his sparkling prose. 272pp. 5⅜ x 8½. 0-486-44001-X

THE HISTORY OF RASSELAS: Prince of Abissinia, Samuel Johnson. Distinguished English writer attacks eighteenth-century optimism and man's unrealistic estimates of what life has to offer. 112pp. 5⅜ x 8½. 0-486-44094-X

A VOYAGE TO ARCTURUS, David Lindsay. A brilliant flight of pure fancy, where wild creatures crowd the fantastic landscape and demented torturers dominate victims with their bizarre mental powers. 272pp. 5⅜ x 8½. 0-486-44198-9

Paperbound unless otherwise indicated. Available at your book dealer, online at **www.doverpublications.com**, or by writing to Dept. GI, Dover Publications, Inc., 31 East 2nd Street, Mineola, NY 11501. For current price information or for free catalogs (please indicate field of interest), write to Dover Publications or log on to **www.doverpublications.com** and see every Dover book in print. Dover publishes more than 500 books each year on science, elementary and advanced mathematics, biology, music, art, literary history, social sciences, and other areas.